To Harriet
Very best wishes
Enjoy BRANKO!
Fondly,
Stu Tower
4/15

Praise for Stuart Tower's, *Branko*

In today's fast-paced, electronic society, plain old-fashioned, captivating story-telling is rare. In *The Wayfarers* Stuart Tower has done just that.

— **Filmmaker Steven Spielberg**
  On Stuart Tower's previous novel (and Branko's debut)
  Los Angeles, CA

The Wayfarers had me mesmerized. Now, Tower is again at his best. As an old army veteran, I particularly appreciated his descriptions of Branko's leadership for veteran's rights and his bold actions during the infamous 1932 Bonus March on Washington. To the very end I felt a certain kinship to this unforgettable character.

— **Donald "Boston" Simonds**
  WWII and Korean War veteran
  24th Division, 19th Infantry regiment
  Maui, HI

One hesitates to call Branko Horvitch a mere "literary creation" by Stuart Tower. Branko is "real" in every sense of the word. He is a vibrant, pulsating and complex human being. We first encountered him in 2003, as a central character in Tower's acclaimed epic, *The Wayfarers*. He has now reentered our lives a decade later and we have become immeasurably enriched. Twentieth century history has assumed a new reality by virtues of *Branko's* encounters with its pivotal events and personages. I promise you that the historical events of lifetimes will never appear as real, relevant and moving as they do now, thanks to the power and pathos of the author's writing. Indeed, this is a "must read."

— **Elijah Schochet, Ph.D.**
  Rabbi
  Sherman Oaks, CA

A taut, terrific novel! This tome is uniquely exciting, a cracking-grand story. Readers are grabbed on page one, hold on with vivid interest until the end and then wish there was more! Don't miss this one. It's an intensive, holds-your interest-read! Stuart Tower could have easily been a classmate of mine, in the eminent Iowa Writer's Workshop. As a career Officer/Pilot, I found Branko's military references to be spot-on!

— **Robert Stein**
 Colonel (Ret), USAF
 Iowa City, IW

Branko's life is the life every immigrant imagined in coming to America and more. Roguish, disciplined, fearless and principled, Branko has encounters with many who change America. The Author's admiration and affection for Branko will be yours as well, long before you finish the book.

— **Warren Alexander**
 Editor and award-winning book photographer
 New York City, NY

Branko Horvitch strides through much of 20th century American history like an award-winning documentarian. He doesn't miss a detail or moment of high drama. His brash but humane approach to life takes him from the depths of Europe's xenophobic *pogroms* to the staggering heights from which he gallantly serves his adopted, beloved America. As he interacts with those whose names we all recognize, we are given a glimpse of all that a citizen of this country might achieve. The uplifting themes of *Branko* shine brightly in Stuart Tower's newest novel.

— **Louise Margolis**
 Writer, editor, critic, reviewer
 Los Angeles, CA

Stuart Tower has unleashed his usual flair in this, his latest novel, to weave a tale like few people can tell in words. His books, essays and published work draw-in the reader like it's a fireside yarn with an easy-to-listen to style. This comes about because of the intimate knowledge the author has of the history and times involved. In his preferred genre of historical fiction, Stuart researches the subject matter of his books like few authors do, which makes for both fascinating and educational reading. Stuart's in-depth character depictions make the players in his books literally jump out from the pages. I actually felt that I was there on the trip into the country with President Coolidge and his buddies Firestone, Ford and Edison. Natural talent as a raconteur along with his "radio voice" gives Stuart the ability to make friends and acquaintances in his travels. With his eye for observation there is no doubt that more than a few of the people from his travels end-up as characters in his books. This latest work from Stuart Tower is a story not to be ignored.

— **Peter Brooke**
Freelance book critic and immigration law consultant
Kings Cliff
New South Wales, Australia

Also by Stuart Tower and available
from The Lighthouse Press, LLC

The Wayfarers

BRANKO

In Praise of a Good Man's Journey Through Life's Adventure

A NOVEL

STUART TOWER

The Lighthouse Press, LLC
Mobile, Alabama

The Lighthouse Press, LLC
Publishing books since 1998

The Lighthouse "L" icon is a registered trademark of The Lighthouse Press Limited Liability Corporation, formerly, The Lighthouse Press, Incorporated.

The Lighthouse Press, LLC is an independent, publisher previously out of Lighthouse Point Florida (after which the corporate name is derived) that has relocated to Alabama. We publish titles in fiction and nonfiction across all genres and represent established as well as debut authors. Our titles are available at or through local bookstores and on the World Wide Web. Please visit our web site for more information.

www.TheLighthousePress.com
P.O. Box 9612, Mobile, AL 36609

Copyright © 2013 by Stuart Tower. All rights reserved. No part of this material may be reproduced in any form or by any means without written permission from the publisher.

The Cataloging-in-Publication Data
is on file at the Library of Congress

ISBN: 978-1-932211-19-1

Printed in the United States of America
Book cover/dust jacket design by Camera One

This is a work of fiction. Names, characters, places and incidents are the product of the author's imagination or are used fictitiously and any resemblance to actual persons, living or dead, business establishments, companies, events or locales is entirely coincidental.

Dedicated to those who have served and are serving their country with honor and pride

CONTENTS

Author's Foreword..xiii

PROLOGUE..1

1. THE UKRAINE, 1941..3

2. THE WANDERER...9

3. IN THE SERVICE OF THE EMPEROR...41

4. SOJOURNING..64

5. THE GOLDEN LAND...93

6. AT WAR, 1917...107

7. AT WAR, 1918...126

8. THE WILSON WHITE HOUSE...148

9. THE HARDING WHITE HOUSE...175

10. THE COOLIDGE WHITE HOUSE...204

11. BLACK GOLD!...235

12. THE THREAT AND THE CRASH..265

13. THE COMMANDANT..290

14. CONFRONTATIONS...313

15. IN THE SERVICE OF HIS COUNTRY...356

16. THE FIRE AND THE FURY..374

17. HOLLYWOOD SCENES, TAKE ONE..389

18. EXEUNT: ACT ONE..424

19. EXEUNT: ACT TWO...439

20. EXEUNT: ACT THREE..444

21. EXEUNT: ACT FOUR..459

EPILOGUE...467

Acknowledgments..471

About The Author...473

Author's Foreword

Fashioning a credible and appealing character for a novel is no simple task. I know.

At least, I had some relevant practice, as Branko Horvitch was one of my most colorful characters in a prior book, *The Wayfarers* (The Lighthouse Press, Inc., 2003). But to sculpt him as the main protagonist in a novel about his "journey through life's adventure" was a challenging task. I wanted a perfect hero, while not sure if there was such a thing.

In the years that it took to research the historical complexities of his life and the many trials to fully develop Branko's character, I grew to like him more and more. Shaping him by imagination I gave him a sense of humor, perhaps warped at times, a sense of honor, sensitivity to those in need of love and support and a modesty that was not artificial.

Ah, the flexibility of fiction—where one can nurture creative license until eventually the clay model becomes an almost real, live person.

My intent, of course, was to share Branko and his fascinating life with my readership. But before reaching that apex, the fine tuning of a brilliant, tough and highly skilled editor begged to be applied. The effort of this demanded yet another year of my life in which I re-evaluated and polished every possible nuance of every sentence of which Branko's life was constructed.

But it was all worth it. Finally, I felt as close to Branko as I would be to a faithful brother: Actually, even closer than that, as I had breathed life into the man on paper. The result can be found as you turn the pages ahead.

So, ride along with Branko, on his trip of a lifetime—and keep on truckin'!

Enjoy!
Stuart F. Tower
Los Angeles, California
2013

It is not in the stars to hold our destiny, but in ourselves.
—William Shakespeare

BRANKO

In Praise of a Good Man's Journey Through Life's Adventure

PROLOGUE

Ignatovka, in the Pale of Settlement
October 15, 1881, 5:45 a.m. (0545 hours)

Alexander III, the embittered "Czar of all The Russias" had long-since proven he was every bit the fire-breathing monster feared by the downtrodden class of the 350,000 square mile Pale of Settlement. From the 14th day of March onward, the thundering of hooves, the incessant screaming of victims, the scorched earth, the smoldering embers of what had been hovels and shops and ramshackle farmsteads, was the *pogrom* program, day by day. It would gallop randomly, unstoppable, into weeks and months, far into a hopeless future. Insignificant Ignatovka, a townlet due west of the Ukraine's ancient metropolis, had escaped unnoticed until this morning's pre-dawn hours. And then it came without fanfare, without warning of any kind... a man-made earthquake. The churning bowels of hell burst open and spilled upon the fertile black earth of Mother Russia's ample bosom.

It ended quickly, mercifully, if one can summon up even the remotest meaning of the word. This was the truth and those who perished were indeed dispatched posthaste. The bullet to the nape of the neck, the razor-sharp cutlass ripping the gut from it's cavern, the throat sliced with the expertise of a *shochet,* and the palm-sized skulls of babes pulverized into a powder, soaked with a ghastly mixture of blood and brain matter, to be dried and blown away by a stiff autumn breeze. These were the dead. The maimed were another story—most of whom would soon wish for that misery-ending bullet or blade.

Secreted under the closet's floorboards, his scrawny, grimy hands cupped over his ears, too petrified to bawl or even whimper, gasping for every breath in this suffocating posture, an orphan-in-waiting dared not move a muscle. Father and mother had never been more adamant in their well-rehearsed instruction.

"Stay, Brachaleh," they had ordered, "stay put until we lift these floor boards. Do you hear? Don't utter a word. Don't cry. Not a sound! Stay, *mein zeesa.*"

And the six-year old did exactly as he was told. He remained face down in his musty cocoon while the haunting screams of his sisters, Raiseleh and Malkaleh, pierced the air in bizarre harmony. He stayed frozen in position when Mama shrieked a short blood-curdling note, cut off in midflight. He tried to press his hands even harder over his ears when Tateh shouted cries he had never used in the presence of his children.

"Mumzerim, Mumzerim! In der erd erein, ay, yi,yi, ge-e-e-e-valt, geeee…"

These were the last familial sounds the hidden one would ever hear and they were punctuated by the clop-clop-clop of running boots fading in the constant din, accompanied by a comrade's muffled, deep-throated command to move on: "Paidyom! Paidyom, malchikee! Paidyom!"

After what seemed like hours, the trembling little one arched his back ever so slowly. Once, twice, again, again, and the two boards began to creak open. One last time and he was able to achingly slip out into the open air, into the kingdom of hell. His full-body retching, intermittent cascades of vomit, Bracho's unceasing banshee wailing told the story.

And for the rest of his life, he would re-live the sight of this infernal imagery—the gory mass that just minutes ago had been a father, a mother and his siblings.

And so began his journey.

THE UKRAINE 1

September 11, 1941 (1130 hours)

Branko's mind was racing, as if his lifetime was in review, covering thousands of miles over war-torn Europe. From 1904 Birlad in Romania, to Sarajevo, to New York, to France, to Washington, to Texas and to California—spanning his sixty-six years of life on earth. His mind finally stopped racing and he settled his attention on the man in front of him—or rather, the man's jacket lapels.

Lightning bolts, he thought, *dammit. The insignias of the infamous SS lightning bolts on your lapels. What are you planning—scheming—you sonofabitch? Well, I can play this staring game. Take my glaring eyeballs for a while, you Nazi bastard.*

The two minutes of silence, seeming more like two hours, came to an abrupt halt.

"Sooo, my dear Brigadier General Branko Horvitch…"

"Retired, Captain. Retired. For Chrissakes, I'm sixty-six. Nobody salutes me anymore. No one calls me Brigadier General these days."

"Not even your Bolshevik comrades?"

"Especially not them. I've already told you they only know me as a civilian American. And that's all I am. Nothing more, nothing less, as they say!"

At this point in the interrogation, the two men were leaning toward each other, nearly chin to chin, like an irate baseball manager and the home-plate umpire. Suddenly, the blue-eyed Teuton bolted to his feet and began to pace, back and forth

Clearly, his ability to speak English had brought him this unwelcomed assignment. He was more comfortable commanding his all-SS Einsatzgruppe rifle platoon. Shooting Jews and Bolshevik commissars in the back of their heads was exactly what he was trained to do ever since he was selected for the prestigious SS in '38. And since the June invasion, he had more than ample opportunity to perform gallantly.

Climbing into the pits to finish the job when there was still visible life, the barrel of his Luger had little chance to cool down. This provided enormous satisfaction that defied any civil explanation.

If he were married, Captain Brichtoben would have dearly loved his wife to join him just as some of the senior officers had already quietly arranged: The unwritten rule being that they must be housed no less than 100 kilometers from the front. He thought that she, whoever *she* may be, would burst with pride to be there with him, her husband. He had several times thought to himself, *Hannelore? Annamarie? Helga? Ah, yes....Helga Richter!*

With this last thought, he cracked a toothy smile and returned his attention to the prisoner in front of him: "So, one more time, *Mister* Horvitch. What were you doing with these Communist animals? A staff car shows that you were important to them."

"And one more time, *Herr Kap-i-tan* Brichtoben, since I've repeated this information twice..." Branko paused, inhaled deeply, sipped from the water glass, and slowly issued each word of his tauntingly deliberate response, stretching out the syllables of a few of the words he deemed necessary. "I am a student of 20th century warfare. I fought in France in '17, '18, and before that served in the Austro-Hungarian army for twelve years. I immigrated to the United States in 1904. Actually, I do speak a fairly credible Deutsch, sir.

"Here in the Soviet Union since July, I only wished to observe the Red Army in their defensive positions—for a book I've been commissioned to write. My government has arranged it and in fact, I have also requested from my State Department the opportunity to similarly observe the Wehrmacht."

The response came curtly, the words coming forth in a spray of spittle and in a mixture of English and Deutsch: "Defensive positions?

"We are not holding, *defensive positions*—as if preparing to retreat. That is what you really mean, isn't it? Let me assure you we do not know the meaning of that word in German, English, Russian, Polish or French. I'm afraid you will never have the opportunity to observe our victorious army in any *defensive* position, ever, *Mister* Horvitch."

Branko knew enough to let it lay where it was. He was confident that sticking to his story would get him a release sooner or later. After all, his advanced age, the state of tacit neutrality that his country was in, lend-lease or not, his innocuous journalist papers in order, weak as they may appear—all added up to, at worst, a draw. At any given time there were literally thousands of journalists, advisors and observers on both sides—most from neutral countries. Branko figured he was a part of all that and it would work in his favor. As expected, his rank of Brigadier Generalship was probably the most intriguing item for these Nazis, but the Senate committee's deputy chair thought it important to include it in his ID papers, especially in light of the underlying reason he was here in the Soviet Union.

Everything had changed suddenly and dramatically just two long days ago when his Uzbek driver, under the influence of one too many swigs of vodka, took a wrong turn on a muddy rural road, hurtling toward certain oblivion. A tragic comedy of errors followed, one after the other. The originally scheduled four-hour drive from Bryansk to Moscow, all well within the rear of the front lines, ended in the opposite direction, in German-held territory.

Branko had been visiting the rear echelon headquarters of his old friend from his White House days, General Semyon Konstantinovich Timoshenko. He was then due back at Moscow's Metropole Hotel to make final arrangements to board a military flight to Murmansk. This was all part of his mission which was nearing completion. Until this unfortunate, quite avoidable fiasco, all had gone well.

After being challenged by a German reconnaissance unit, Branko's naïve driver foolishly jumped from the still-in-motion staff car only to be decapitated in a hail of machine-pistol fire. As the car came to rest against a mud bank, Branko gingerly emerged unscathed, hands raised high, steadily repeating the phrase, "Ich bin ein Amerikaner."

The disbelieving unit escorted him to their command post where the Corporal related the bizarre event to his Captain, who in turn, sent Branko on to the nearest SS unit west of Kiev.

Evidently, Kiev had not as yet been secured, with fierce last-ditch fighting going on in its easternmost sectors. However, with the same *blitzkrieg* campaign so vividly demonstrated during the first three months following the invasion along the 800-mile front, there was little doubt in anyone's mind that the forward advance would continue onward. Privately, even Stalin himself began to envision a massive pullback from Moscow into the Urals, if necessary. Already, many essential armament factories had been moved intact from White Russia and the Ukraine, settling as far east as Tashkent, Magnitogorsk, Kuibyshev and Sverdlovsk—workers, raw materials and all.

The Special Unit field headquarters temporarily based itself in what had once been the largest *yeshiva* in all of pre-revolutionary Russia. In the Stalinist '20s, it became a technical institute, with advanced classes in chemistry and physics for selected students from the secondary-level schools in and around the Kiev districts. Upon completion of the accelerated courses, each student, male and female alike, were at the time immediately assigned to chemical warfare units of the Red Army. Before the June invasion, there were still more than 200 students studying in the dankness of the 16th century behemoth of an edifice, along with a makeshift, skeleton faculty. However, most of the student body retreated eastward to Zhitomir when the overwhelmed Russian troops withered under a blistering assault by Panzer Divisions. A few weeks later there were still thirty-six future chemists who opted to stay behind to take their chances with the Germans, thinking their student status would provide some measure of immunity.

But three days before the Horvitch incident, all were summarily executed by Brichtoben's advance platoon of Einsatzgruppe "C" designated Army Group South. At this point, ten weeks after the invasion had begun, Army Groups North, Central and South had advanced to the east nearly equally as far. The Soviets, and much of the world, were stunned by the early successes of Hitler's divisions. Few, if any, strategists believed that they could be stopped.

The 259 remaining Jews in the nearby townlet of Ignatovka met the same fate two days earlier. A goodly number of these bodies remained unburied and were rapidly rotting in the oppressive latesummer heat. On the heels of the Russian retreat, there had been no time to have the victims dig their own usual pre-massacre burial pit. The resulting stench permeated every cubic inch of breathable air—indoors and out.

"What else can we possibly discuss?" Branko now ventured to say. "You know who I am. My papers clearly explain my purpose. What harm can I be to your aims and ambitions, my dear Captain. I merely ask for safe passage back to the Russky lines."

"Not so simple, Horvitch. I must keep you in my protective custody until my Commandant arrives. This whole story is too good to deny him."

"And when, may I ask, is he expected?"

"Momentarily. He has some unfinished business to attend to in Makarov."

That unfinished business was escorting Heinrich Himmler, Supreme Chief of the SS, and sponsor of the Einsatzgruppen. He wished to see for himself the organized process of elimination practiced so diligently by his four elite units; Einsatzgruppe "A" in the far north, covering the Baltic Republics of Estonia, Latvia and Lithuania, eventually scheduled to terminate with the occupation of besieged Leningrad; "B" ordered to follow the troops through White Russia, to Smolensk and Moscow itself; "C" thundering through the heart of the Ukraine; and "D" covering the Southern Ukraine, Odessa and the Crimea, with Stalingrad as its terminus. Each of the 900-man units had been given orders directly from Himmler, obviously with the usual tacit approval of Adolf Hitler, to roundup and execute Bolshevik party officials, particularly those of Commissar rank. Jewish men, women and children, were to be murdered at will. This was firm policy from the start of the invasion in June, and would only be relaxed temporarily when additional manpower from the ranks of the targeted victims was needed for one work project or another. In general, the Einsatzgruppen were to lag slightly behind the front, covering a wide swath of towns and villages to carry out this ethnic cleansing. To this date, there had not been one case of recorded refusal among the 3,600 willing perpetrators, nor would this likely occur.

Oddly enough, only Herr Himmler, the nondescript sadist who rose from a docile chicken-farmer's existence to the heights of the National Socialist Party, who personally devised the efficient killing-squad plan, was known to repugnantly vomit as blood and brain-matter splattered on the breeches and boots of his uniform. This historically notable event took place that morning while he was ghoulishly observing the surreal daily ritual in Makarov up close. Forever to his regret, much too close. Never again did the little poultryman in the pince-nez glasses venture forth to the Russian front, preferring the sanctity and safety of his Berlin offices, and the sumptuous lunches with his Fuhrer.

"I will save any further questioning for the Commandant, Mister Horvitch. I trust that you will be reasonably comfortable in our humble abode. You'll be happy to hear that a burial detail is looking after the bodies strewn about the futbol field. They were shot as spies, you realize."

"Spies? I saw the bodies laying there as I was being ushered into this office. Seems to this old man's vision that all had worn a brownish uniform, with red kerchiefs. *Soldaten*, wouldn't you say, Herr Kap-i-tan?"

"Not at all. We captured three of them at a town near here, and after a brief interrogation it turned out that they were science students at this school. I further surmised that they had been training to infiltrate our ranks with an assortment of toxic concoctions. It's commonly attempted under these rather desperate full-retreat conditions all the time as you must remember from the prolific use of deadly gasses in your great war—against us, I might add."

"Ahh, you are to be commended for your rather liberal use of rationalization and imagination. A potent pair, I'd say." Branko smiled, hoping to avoid an unnecessary argument where he would be the ultimate loser. He had heard stories of their butchery in Poland, in France and in each of the other countries they had conquered over the past two years, while the Geneva Convention seemed to have self-destructed.

As he was being led down the dark corridor to a pad-locked cell, Branko overheard an order given by Brichtoben. Only one word stood out. It was the name of a place—a townlet, a village.

Ignatovka, another massacre, Branko's mind wailed while the guard helped steady him.

Once inside his cell, a palsied, grotesque and twisted look came over Branko's unshaven face, rendering him unrecognizable. It was now the tortured expression of a little boy sixty years ago.

In this stupefying condition, slumping onto the woolen-blanketed cot, a convulsively gasping Branko Horvitch continued to sob over the indelible memories.

"Ignatovka…Ignatovka…good God almighty…Ignatovka…"

THE WANDERER

**Ignatovka, in Russia's Pale of Settlement
October 15, 1881 (0930 hours)**

Aside from little Bracho Horvitch, there wasn't a Jewish soul alive or mobile enough to give proper respect for the dead of Ignatovka's *pogrom*. A wagon-load of men and women from the *shtetl* a few kilometers to the west, which was spared bloodshed, hurriedly clattered into town to help with burials and rendering aid to the wounded. Of the latter, more than half would not live out the day. A Jewish doctor from Kiev had been summoned and was expected to arrive by carriage within the hour. Doctors from closer towns were already on the abysmal scene, with inadequate amounts of medicines, bandages and other emergency items.

Every structure in the townlet was either burnt to the ground or charred beyond recognition. The few shops had been looted and stripped clean before being put to the torch. The main gravel street and one of its perpendicular narrow dirt lanes were drenched with the blood of the victims. The lone pinewood *shtiebel* was no more, its beloved *rav* consumed in the conflagration. In the attempt to save him his wife and six children were each either brutally murdered by the *pogromchiks* or mortally felled by smoke inhalation.

The pitiful, plaintive wailing of the survivors reached out to the heavens, unanswered throughout the day and into the next morning.

The District Magistrate arrived, sitting on his chestnut horse, at a distance, on the muddy banks of the River Irpen, saying nothing, doing nothing. No one dared to approach the hated Jew-baiting blackguard, his role in the disaster suspicious at best.

A few of the local peasant-farmers trickled into town, saying nothing, doing nothing. No one cared to approach the silent bystanders.

And so it went. Just another of the hundreds of similar unspeakable incursions causing total destruction of life and limb, visited upon the impoverished Jews of the Pale during the months and years that followed the assassination of the Czar, Alexander II.

Attending to the trauma-stricken six-year-old Bracho, his only surviving relative, an injured Tante Shayndl, could only hold him to her bosom and gently rock him to and fro. She had wept so bitterly from the time she discovered a living Bracho and the bodies of his parents and two older sisters, her tear ducts could emit not another drop. Bracho's mother had been her oldest and favorite sister. Shayndl's husband, Berel, had been working at an uncle's brush-making shop in Odessa, since shortly after they were married that past April, and she was scheduled to join him by Chanukah time. She was desperate to get word to him via the telegraph office in Kiev. Though knowing that it would have to wait, she had already decided to ask the Kiev doctor's wife to send the message for her whenever she could find time to do so.

For all these mourning hours, Shayndl's head felt like it was about to explode due to the rifle-butt blow. Still, it had probably saved her life, as she was rendered semi-conscious and presumed dead by the murderers. Very obviously with child, Shayndl had not been a choice prospect for the rampant rape-fest that usually accompanied these dastardly, government-sponsored sporting events.

There were no other Horvitch kin, either dead or alive, in Ignatovka. Uncles, aunts, and cousins resided elsewhere in the Pale, most in Makarov and Berditchev. On the mother's side, the Rabinovs were scattered about the Ukrainian plains.

*****

Makarov, in the Pale of Settlement
January 12, 1882

Bracho came to dislike the Horvitch family. All of them. The uncle, his father's older brother, who constantly threatened to deposit him in an orphanage, the aunt who stood by with a frigid heart, the cousins who gloated that he had no mama, no papa, no sisters and no brothers. And they repeated this every day, from the time he arrived. He was the awkward, ugly duckling. The black sheep. They were treating him worse than a bastard son. Even the family's friends seemed to look upon Bracho as an urchin, someone from the nether world, a stranger never to be admitted into their circle. And the perceptive youngster deeply felt every negative emotion that this mean-spirited environment spawned. Oh, how he wished that Tante Shayndl's head injury wasn't as serious as it had turned out to be. Unfortunately, she had no alternative but to send for Moishe Horvitch in Makarov, to come fetch his *pogrom*-orphaned nephew.

A few months after he arrived in Makarov, he was told by the Horvitches that a fully-recovered Shayndl went on to Odessa to have the baby, and to be with Berel. He cried for joy, quickly overshadowed by a blanket of sadness.

Just before the Sabbath candles were lit the previous Friday, Bracho had quietly slipped into the back room, put on his heavy woolen sweater and overcoat, filled the pockets with chunks of *challah* and slipped out of the front door unnoticed. An hour later, on the main road leading out of Makarov, Shimon the drayman found him huddled against a deep snow bank, shivering, munching on a bit of the *challah*. He had to force Bracho into the wagon, loaded with hay which Shimon wanted to get back into the shed before sundown, and then deliver the child back to the Horvitch home.

"That does it, Malka. The boy doesn't want to be with our family. I'm taking him to my sister on Sunday. She wanted him in the first place. I told you it wouldn't work!"

Moishe Horvitch had spoken, and his word was the only one in this household. If the truth be known, mother Malka and her antagonistic brood were very happy with the unilateral decision ending Bracho's stay. Not a one of them hugged him, or kissed him, or wished him well.

*****

Vinnitsa, in the Pale of Settlement
June 25, 1885

From the Horvitch home in Makarov to the slightly more hospitable

Rabinov family, to distant cousins in Berditchev where he was treated as a child-servant, Bracho developed anger toward his parents. He felt abandoned by them. They died a horrible death, but left him behind. He believed their love for him had died with them. He was alone, even in a houseful of blood relatives.

Now, in his sixth "home" even the vilest of any Dickensian orphanage would seem bucolic by comparison. At the age of ten, Bracho accepted this draconian existence as his lot in life. He was sure it would never get any better. He was, by this time, certain that he would forever be punished by God—punished for surviving the pogrom and failing to save his family. This was his burden and he believed it more firmly as each long day passed into the next.

After being rejected by yet another branch of the Horvitch-Rabinov family in '84, he was moved to the overcrowded barn in Berditchev. Previously housing twenty head of livestock, the miniscule stalls were hastily converted to accommodate sixty orphans. The soggy hay remained, having been packed into filthy ticking that was a breeding ground for every known disease. Not one child escaped bouts of recurring infections. The food, what there was of it, left every stomach empty and churning. In short, the cows had it decidedly better.

In spite of all this Bracho miraculously blossomed physically, growing broader and a head taller than the others in his age range. Leveraging his size, he began focusing his anger on the only injustices he could control—the older orphans who terrorized the weaker children. But eventually, following a series of fights in which he roundly walloped three older bullies, Bracho was labeled an "incurably incorrigible." For this he was moved yet again—exiled to the *Rabbi Yaakov Tserkassy Safe-Haven for God's Little Children* in the drab southern town of Vinnitsa.

The Jewish Widows and Orphans Agency supporting the Tserkassy home provided a handsome stipend for each child in its care, which translated into healthy profits for the rabbi *cum* wily businessman. Corners were generously cut on every expense, including food, clothing, sanitary conditions and medical matters. As they were wont to say in the *shtieblach* of Vinnitsa, "Tserkassy grows fat and sassy while the *kinder* grow boils and rashes." Worse yet, the Rabbi and his staff of unsavory misfits—male and female—earned a well-deserved reputation as sadistic abusers of the most disgusting type imaginable. There wasn't an inmate without a "souvenir" of sorts. This, then, was the *safe* haven that the Rabbi Yaakov Tserkassy home provided to God's little children.

In 1883 Czar Alexander III had reluctantly appointed a special commission to oversee the orphanages within his realm, but Jewish orphanages were excluded from this oversight. Konstantin Pobedonostsev, Procurator of the Russian Orthodox Church, convinced his Czar that the Jews in the Pale would look after their own on all matters. In the case of the Tserkassy home, among many others, he was quite wrong. This followed the prelate's widely publicized statement early in the Czar's reign when Alexander III asked him how he would solve the ever-festering "Jewish problem."

"One third will convert," profoundly proclaimed the proud messenger of his Lord and Savior's good word. Of the other two-thirds, he said, "One third will die of starvation and disease, and one third will flee."

Tserkassy's enterprise was much like all others in Russia at the time—no better, perhaps worse. Although the children were officially available for adoption, this was rarely consummated. From time to time, local farmers or shopkeepers would take on one or more of the older and huskier children as temporary help, paying a daily rate to the rabbi. On occasion this would become permanent, and a lump sum payment was due. Although this was tantamount to adoption, it was not recognized as such by the authorities. That is, if the authorities had been at all interested in any activities concerning Jewish orphanages. In 19th century Russia, they were not. To say that Tserkassy and his ilk could do, or not do, anything they pleased was in every way, the terrible truth.

In the heat of July, the good Rabbi Tserkassy took his wife and six children to visit family in Odessa. Business had never been better and with seventeen new enrollees since June 1st profits were at their record highest since the home was established ten years earlier. Owing to the home's robust finances, the rabbi's perceived monetary acumen was equaled only by his stalwart image as a man of faith and family. After all, a man who prioritizes his family's vacation time before his business income was beyond reproach. Thus the rumors of mistreatment in the orphanage were easily squashed before gaining traction. The rabbi's sincere denials, coupled with his reputation and the solid support of the Agency's chief administrator placed him well beyond suspicion of wrong-doing.

The status enjoyed by the rabbi also translated to his staff, who perpetuated rampant brutality under the unconditional approval of their so-called disciplinary actions. This did not bode well for the children—especially during the rabbi's absence when he retired to his substantial home off the premises each evening and during the Sabbath.

Now, in his absence for the next month, both Vassily Korchakov and Luda Ludenkov would have a free hand. Both he and she possessed elephantine bodies and fists that had steadily wreaked havoc with the little waifs. They were ably aided and abetted by a cadre of kitchen help and a cleaning crew vying for the honor of "beast of the day." Interestingly enough, Tserkassy did not hire Jewish help. First of all, the Russian peasant would work for far less wages, and secondly, Tserkassy didn't care to have any local *yentehs* minding his very private, clandestine business.

There was yet a third and over-riding reason: Arrogance. The rabbi received a great deal of smug satisfaction in lording over his peasants. Here he was, a Jew—a rabbi—giving orders to his Russians, demanding loyalties, and all the while allowing them unfettered reign to knock the orphans about. All of these factors insured no respite for the hopelessly incarcerated at Tserkassy's satanic institution.

Bracho was determined to end this untenable association while the director was away. It happened much sooner than he planned. Sooner and spontaneously. Vassily, a raging alcoholic, had gone into town to buy whatever could be found in the way of cheap spirits. At the same time, the big blonde Luda was entertaining one of the male cleaning crew in her private room.

While it in no way was comparable to the preparations of a

normal kitchen, there was none-the-less the semblance of an effort to mix together a so-called meal for the orphanage. Partly responsible for this and working to that end, was the kitchen steward, Igor. And during this particular week Bracho was his "assistant."

"Bracho! Bracho, do you hear me, you little Jew-bastard?" Igor yelled from the dinning area. "Go fetch the pot of soup on the stove—Go! Go! Now!"

Though hopelessly illiterate like most of the staffers, Igor managed an understandable combination of Russky-Yiddish. The short, round hulking ignoramus and master of a vicious backhand slap, was seated at one of the six long tables with ten of the younger children. He had been especially hard on Bracho, who had developed a swaggering self-assuredness since his January arrival. This, of course, irritated Igor's village-idiot mentality. Of the other workers, only Masha the cook —and that's stretching the word a bit—remained in the kitchen at the time.

As the only adolescent who could handle the oversized cast-iron cauldron, Bracho arose to do as told. The soup, a watered-down, foul-smelling liquid of unrecognizable ingredients, was boiling hot. Using towels to protect his hands from the red-hot handles, he slowly carried it from the stove to the table. He stopped and then made a split-second decision without hesitation. With surging adrenalin the un-usually muscular ten-year-old marshaled the strength necessary to lift the cauldron and pour its scalding contents over the shaven head of the unsuspecting steward.

The immediate results were beyond excruciating. Igor's screams, as witnesses would later say, could have awakened the Czar's nap in far-away St. Petersburg.

But for Bracho there was no time to enjoy the aftermath. He ran at full speed, with Masha in a futile, short-lived pursuit. He didn't stop until he was down the lane and well along the Vinnitsa-Nemirov-Uman road on the way to Odessa. While that had been his goal all along, he had planned his break-out to coincide with working on a nearby farm to where he had been sent several previous times.

Now, with everything dramatically changed and the escape in progress, he had to find Tante Shayndl. He just had to. There wasn't anything or anybody else in his shattered life and there hadn't been since that calamitous dawn in Ignatovka.

Here was a ten-year old Jewish child. A fugitive from an orphanage. He could write Russian cyrillic characters. He was fairly conversant in the most basic Yiddish and still familiar with the Hebrew alphabet which he had learned as a six-year old in *cheder*—enough so that he could write Yiddish words, phrases and sentences haltingly, at best.

Alone and frightened of being apprehended he knew he would wind-up in a jail for the crime he had committed. Each hour of freedom meant not knowing what the next hour held in store.

Maybe Igor died from the burns, Bracho worried. *Maybe he's dying in the hospital. Is Vassily coming after me? Or Luda? I must keep away from the magistrates, the police, the soldiers. God, my God, I'm so hungry, I have nothing to eat. What will I do? Where will I go? Oh, Tante Shayndl, where are you? Odessa? I'll find you. How far is it from here? Where will I sleep tonight? I'd rather die than go back to Tserkassy. To Vassily? To Luda? To Igor?*

Never. Never again !

*****

**Odessa, in the Pale of Settlement
February 10, 1886**

Shayndl never tired of telling of Bracho's wild adventure. It seemed that every Jew in teeming Odessa knew of his bravura, his great escape from the terrors of Tserkassy, his incredible journey from Vinnitsa to Odessa, his detention by the police in Uman and his subsequent rescue by an ex-convict.

All this from a child, a *pishikeh*? There were the cynics who didn't believe a word of it. No matter how much Berel or Shayndl insisted that it was all true. The cynics would smile knowingly, wink an eye and offer the occasionally raised eyebrow. Unavoidably—even understandably—there would always be doubters of young Bracho's odyssey.

Admittedly, both Shayndl and Berel quizzed Bracho several times on the last part of his story, but he never wavered in the details. He said that he had landed in the custody of the Uman Police due to trying to steal a bread loaf from a bakery. At the time he didn't realize the bakery was situated next door to the Uman Police compound. The baker, catching Bracho red-handed, pulled him by his ear lobe into the Police commander's office. Even though Bracho was reticent with personal information—and had nothing in the way of identification—his hunger and desire to reach an aunt in Odessa engendered sympathy. Rather than press the matter, the baker instead gave the child a bag of rolls. With little else to go on, the police commander thought the boy was a local youth running away from home and decided to hold him.

Bracho was placed in the compound's only detention cell and in the company of another Jew—albeit a rather shifty sort. This other prisoner, a thief name of Mottke, had already spent a year as a cell inmate. He assured Bracho that their incarceration would end that night. Mottke confided they would be sprung by a previous cellmate, a now escaped second thief he called, Shlomo the Slick. According to Mottke, Shlomo's previous—and soon to be second—jailbreak was owed to the purloining of an obscure set of spare cell keys. And while Shlomo the Slick had been missed, the keys had not.

Bracho begged to go along, and threatened to expose the escape if they didn't take him along. It was an offer Mottke could hardly refuse.

At precisely 2:00 a.m., Shlomo slipped into the compound that he knew would be unguarded after midnight. A simple turn of a key and the prisoners were free. After telling Bracho to *get lost* the two thieves made for a two-horse wagon that had been quietly stashed for the jailbreak.

Bracho had the good sense to follow them. When he made himself known he also promised to scream his lungs out if he wasn't invited along for the get-away. This too, was an offer the thieves could hardly refuse.

After three solid hours a fast trot they halted to let the horses graze and drink. Now on the edge of a town named *Krivoya Ozero* the two thieves watched the sunrise. Bracho slumbered in the back of the wagon. Concerned that the embarrassed Uman police force may have telegraphed the escape to the local police, Mottke suggested skirting Krivoya Ozero by a few hundred meters of cross-country travel. After covering the suggested distance, the two thieves decided to further improve the odds of avoiding capture by splitting up.

It was a sound plan but both men were leery of the sleepy Bracho. Even though they were well-away from the ears of civilization they still wanted to avoid a third offer that could hardly be refused. Mottke took the initiative. While awakening the dazed Bracho, he shoved a handful of rubles into the boy's trouser pocket and lifted him off the wagon.

As the dumbfounded youngster stood by, Shlomo called down from the wagon seat, "The railroad tracks we've been following are for the Kiev-Odessa midnight train. It'll be coming into Krivoya Ozero any minute now. Go back to the station—we passed it at the edge of town a ways back. Give the rubles to the station master and board the train—he'll be the one in a uniform. Understand?"

Bracho numbly nodded.

"It's still early," Shlomo added, "and nobody is about. You should be all right. *Zayt gezunt, boychickel!*"

And with that Mottke and Shlomo changed direction, the two driving the wagon away on a deeply-rutted lane marked, *Kotovsk 50 km*.

Bracho Horvitch's innate fear of the "iron monster" which he had seen only a few times, was ultimately overridden by his anxiety to reach Odessa. By the end of the line he had begun to enjoy the exhilarating feeling of trees and houses rushing by the window. At 11:00 a.m., a weary and anxious Bracho de-trained at Odessa's massive new terminal. By noon, the resourceful lad had found one of the Jewish quarter's three brush-making shops and asked for Uncle Berel.

Shayndl's stunned husband couldn't believe his eyes. Within minutes and at their one-room apartment, neither could Tante Shayndl.

As for Bracho, he had not known the slightest happiness for nearly five years—half of his young life. He could not help but wonder what life would be from this day onward.

Odessa, in the Pale of Settlement
May 19, 1888

Thirteen-year old Bracho was called to the *bimah* where he read from the Torah portion of the day. He had crammed five years of *cheder* instruction into a little more than two years and thrived on it. Uncle Berel and Tante Shayndl were bursting with pride. Tante sat in the women's gallery of the small *shul*. With her sat six-year-old Channah who carried Bracho's mother's name, the curly-headed five-year-old Dovidl who was named for Bracho's father and the two-year-old Raisele, who was the namesake of one of Bracho's perished sisters.

The latter, perched on her mother's lap, periodically squeaked out, "*Brachaleh, Brachaleh.*" She was blessedly oblivious to the "shushing" of the surrounding womenfolk.

Walking back home, holding Channah and Dovidl by their hands, Bracho basked in the happiness of the Sabbath day. Yet, there was a bothersome longing in his heart that had established itself months before. It was intermittently intense, occurring at inopportune times.

Once, when he was learning the difficult and unfamiliar words in his *haftorah*, he stomped out of the *cheder* and had not returned for a week. Studying for hours with his teacher had become progressively more confining and confusing. He dearly wished to be a *bar mitzvah* and yet there was also a nagging desire—a need to strike out on his own. Even though the ghastly past had been disastrous, the few years with Tante and family had quelled his nightmarish memories. He had survived the past to learn that life was rich for the taking. He had only to reach out for the world.

Only upon the urging of Shayndl did he apologize to his *lehrer*. And in just the past week—when he was watching Dovidl and Channah at play in a nearby postage-stamp of a park—he abruptly left and walked two kilometers to the docks. He was certain that what he had encountered in that salty envronment, and the lure of the sea, could mean the start of the next page in his young life. He only had to pursue it. He had stayed until long after supper time.

Luckily, the children knew their way home, but Shayndl was greatly disturbed by the incident.

When she confronted Bracho about it, he refused to discuss it. To her credit, Shayndl had wisely chosen to not pursue the matter while in the heat of her anger. Today however, on the Sabbath afternoon, she felt it was a better time to talk with Bracho.

"Brachaleh, *zeesa*," she said, "I've noticed that you spend more and more time at the harbor—at the docks. It's a dangerous place. I always hear stories of kidnapping. Children never to be seen again. Placed on board one of those ships. Sold as slaves."

"I know, Tante. But I'm not there alone. I've been spending time with some of the old captains and seamen. They have great stories about the big world out there. It's so exciting! I want to go to those places. Do things. Learn about the world. I'm tired of Odessa. I don't belong here any longer. You have your days full with the three children. Soon there'll be another. You don't need another person to feed and to care for."

"But, *zeesa*, we all love you so much. The *kindeh* think of you as their big brother. For Berel and me, you are a son. We would all miss you terribly."

"I can never forget what you and Berel have done for me—taking me in when no one else would. Even now I sometimes remember when a life such as this was more than I imagined. All this love instead of hopelessness and hunger... I never imagined this kind of life. But now that I have all of this—I don't know, maybe I was meant to struggle."

"Meant to struggle?" Shayndl echoed with a bemused expression

He shrugged. "I don't know what to call it. But such strong feelings have come over me these last few months, I can sometimes hardly sit still. Even when I was preparing to be a *bar mitzvah*...I've just wanted to be out there, over the horizon.

Shayndl only nodded. If she was surprised, she didn't show it.

"I'll come back some day. I'll write. You'll write. The children will read my letters and some day they will write to me, wherever I may be. It's not forever, Tante. I'll be back. I promise."

"So when do you think you might make this decision?"

He looked at her for a second before realizing she was teasing.

"Oh, Bracho," she almost laughed, "You've obviously made up your mind. How can I possibly change it? *Oy, vay iz mir. Oy vay iz mir. Geh mit Gott, mein kind. Geh mit Gott.*

He smiled.

"You are so unlike other boys your age in Odessa, or even much older. Strange as it seems, I have faith that you know what you want and I know there's no stopping you. I'm sure Berel feels this way, too."

"That would make it a little easier," he admitted.

"So when have you planned to leave?"

Bracho had indeed made such plans but his concern was how to just outright say as much.

"And if you tell me you haven't made any plans," she interrupted his thoughts, "I will not believe it"

"I was thinking of leaving Odessa."

"Just thinking?"

"Well, Captain Rudoff said I could sail with him to Varna and Constantinople. He needs a hand in the galley. That's the kitchen on board a ship, you know. I can ship out on Monday.

"*Gevalt!* Monday, Bracho? The day after tomorrow?"

"I didn't know how to tell you."

"Well it's a good thing I asked!" she came back.

"I wanted to be called to the *bimah*—and I wanted you and Berel to be proud of me. So I was putting it off because there just didn't seem to be a right time to tell you. You know that I'm so thankful for what you've done for me..."

Everyone else was just as surprised when they learned the news of Bracho's impending departure. The tears and kisses as well as the hugs and goodbyes, went on through the evening.

And again on Monday morning. Then Bracho turned away, was out the door and down the street as if he had never been there.

There were things to do and places to see. Never looking back, he was once more a wayfarer—a jaunty one, walking to the docks with a buoyant stride.

Varna, Bulgaria
April 11, 1890

For two years aboard the cargo ship *Czarina,* Captain Rudoff mentored Bracho in all things worldly. The Captain's son and daughter-in-law, Mikhail and Natasha, treated Bracho like the son they hoped to have someday. Serving as his father's first mate Mikhail commanded a crew of ten while Natasha cooked their meals. Bracho primarily assisted Natasha in the Galley, but his duties ran the gamut as would have any other Ship-boy—an apprentice servant learning sea duties.

Bearing two masts and a yard arm amid-ship, the thirty-six ton *Czarina* was a sea-worthy but small cargo vessel. Among her runs were diverse ports of call that frequently included Constantinople and Odessa. The one or two-day Odessa layovers provided opportunities for Bracho to visit with Shayndl, Berel and the children.

The *Czarina* routinely sailed the famed Bosphorus Strait, visited Smyrna, Antalya, Haifa in Turkish Palestine, Alexandria in Egypt, Piraeus (Athens) and Salonika. Bracho drank heartily of this exotic variety in foreign cultures.

His next to last run on the *Czarina*—through the newly opened Suez Canal and into the Red Sea—took him to Aden. Through the long, humid days of cargo unloading and loading they were protected by the omnipresent British military, guarding against ever-present marauding gangs of thieves. The Sergeant-in-Charge, a jolly, hefty Scotsman, took a liking to the affable Bracho. By the time they set sail the lanky kitchen-boy was peppering conversation with English phrases—a few of them too salty for social use. Only Captain Rudoff, having served in the Czar's navy, understood some of the words and was able to tone down Bracho's enthusiasm for the strange-sounding language.

At the end of Bracho's last run aboard ship, the soundly constructed *Czarina* was showing the wear-and-tear of her years of service. Having long-postponed a growing list of extensive repairs, Captain Rudoff had increase his shipping business at the cost of the ship he had otherwise well-maintained. But with increased water seepage through her birch hull the Captain knew he had put off repairs long enough. They put in put into the port of Varna where the work was less expensive than the rates offered at Odessa or Constantinople. From a business point of view the bad news was that *Czarina* would have to be dry-docked for a minimum of three months.

The crew, of course, would have to find work elsewhere. Mikhail and Natasha opted to stay in Varna during the repairs and the Captain planned on taking the passenger ferry back to Odessa where he had family.

Bracho, however, had been bitten by the incurable wanderlust bug. He didn't want to work with another crew, but he could not be satisfied with a stationary life, either. He desperately wanted to see more of the world that his recent travels had ever-so-lightly touched upon. The crew members, Mikhail and the Captain, had spent two years intriguing the impressionable young man with stories that had fostered his active imagination and measurably shortened his adolescence. The tall, sun-darkened, broad-shouldered Bracho was every bit a man-child. He was ready to explore, seek out and burst forth into the unknown. He was beckoned by the exotic, the adventurous, the challenging and the exciting.

When Bracho spoke of his plans to go further west, Mikhail announced to the crew, "Watch out, world! Here comes Bracho Horvitch. Lock up your daughters, blow out the candles, hide your golden candlesticks, and shut the shutters so he won't know you're at home!"

Bracho joined in the laughter but privately pondered his decision. He confessed as much to Tante Shayndl in a letter he penned on the very morning of his choice to go west.

Saying his last farewells, with tearful hugs all around, Bracho walked off the gangplank and onto the pier. He turned for a last wave-salute to the Captain and the czar's flag and then took the dusty road into town. In his pocket was the handful of the Ottoman currency with which Rudoff paid off the crew. Bracho felt secure in thinking he had enough money to last for a year. He would soon be proven ninety-percent wrong.

Varna was, arguably, the most beautiful town on the shores of the Black Sea. Its profusion of spring flower gardens colored every street and home. Ubiquitous brightly painted window boxes, much like those in the villages of Southern Turkey, were neatly tended by the proud shop and home owners.

A great place to start the rest of my life, quipped the broad-smiling, self-satisfied sailor, talking to himself. It was the introspective art he had perfected since his never-to-be-forgotten orphanage days.

*****

**Turgovishte Pass, Central Bulgaria
September 4, 1890**

Continuously on the road since leaving Varna in midsummer, Bracho complained daily that the stifling heat was no match for the cool, breezy days and nights aboard the *Czarina*. His destination was Tarnovo, once the capital of ancient Bulgaria. It was a fairly large hillside town where he hoped to find work. This was vital to Bracho, after the last of his money, which he had secreted in his boots, went into the deep pockets of a band of highway brigands.

Under Ottoman rule, the interior of Bulgaria had been adequately patrolled by local police and the military. But since attaining relative independence by treaty in 1878, and still nominally a tributary to Turkey, Bulgaria was now dominated by Russian influence. This translated into severe economic woes for the troubled and newly established nation. As a direct result of large tribute payments to the Ottomans, major reductions in local policing gave way to an epidemic of highway robbery as common as dust in the wind.

The warnings for lone-traveling wayfarers to fall in with larger groups along the way to avoid these criminals went unheeded by a cocky Bracho—to his own detriment. He was now penniless. He resorted to begging for food, something that childhood had forced upon him far too often.

Since the Slavic language spoken in Bulgaria was similar to Odessa's Russian-Ukrainian dialect, Bracho was able to converse with only moderate difficulty. Approaching a carriage parked beside a public well at the crest of Turgovishte Pass, he politely asked the two occupants for some spare money or food. The younger man in the carriage was the grandson of a blacksmith in Tarnovo and took an almost immediate liking to the polite and sturdy beggar.

"Here," the young and gracious Bulgarian said while handing a slip of paper to Bracho. "Give this note to Grandpa. He needs help and I won't be back for a few weeks."

How lucky I am! thought Bracho.

Be it luck or fate, the Bulgarian grandson's trip was to help his ailing horse-doctor father-in-law in Romania. The young man's absence of a few weeks turned into a few months and a stable job for Bracho.

Boris Mandilev, the blacksmith, was a patient teacher and Bracho, a voracious learner. He was soon wielding the hammer and tongs like a veteran farrier, pounding red-hot iron into malleable forms. The customers liked him and Boris treated him as a man, paying a fair wage and allowed him to sleep in a corner of the barn. Nothing new to Bracho.

Before too long, the Serbian born-and-raised Boris took to calling Bracho by the popular Slavic name, *Branko*. As customers and neighbors around town began using the Slavic name, *Bracho* simply became *Branko*. And he rather liked the sound of it. Branko, as he now begin to think of himself, remembered that the Yiddish term *bashitsn* had the same meaning as the Slavic, *protector, defender*. Facetiously, Mandilev nicely summed it up by saying, "It goes with the swagger, my young Jew." Contributing to that swagger was not only the new name, but also the residual effects of the heavy hammer he used in his work at the forge. The shirtless Branko's muscles, noticeably sprouting from his tall frame, made him an even more imposing figure.

The ancient town was the site of Baldwin the Crusader's 12th Century castle and housed a miniscule Jewish community. They were primarily the Sephardic ancestors of those who had fled the Spanish Inquisition. The Ottoman's had always been relatively hospitable to the Jews within their enlarged borders, which at one time reached as far west as the environs of Budapest. Branko, who had never forgotten the yearly *yahrzeit* date to recite the memorial prayers for his parents and sisters, walked into the run-down wooden *sinagoga* during morning services on that very day, October 15th. Aside from his years in Odessa, he had never been able to determine the exact Hebrew date, so he ritually followed the common calendrical Gregorian. Although warmly greeted by the elders during the morning prayers, Branko felt little kinship. Expecting to find Yiddish-speakers, he instead listened to a Slavic tongue liberally-salted with a Sephardic Ladino of Spanish derivation. Only the universal ancient Hebrew prayers provided some semblance of commonality. Here was a Russian Jew who had spent far more time within the gentile world, being invited by the *minyan* attendees to join with the congregation two days later, on Yom Kippur, the day for atoning one's sins. He decided to do so. Kinship or not, there was a certain indescribable warmth therein that gave Branko a measure of rare comfort.

Branko borrowed some clothes from the much smaller blacksmith and marched into the crowded *sinagoga* in time for the *Kol Nidre* prayers that continued the ushering-in services for the Jewish New Year, 5650. Wearing Captain Rudoff's gift, one of his old Russian Navy caps, and the blacksmith's hand-me-downs, Branko still cut a handsome, though odd figure. Bursting out of the sleeves of Mandilev's shirt, he thoughtfully tucked the coarse woolen pant legs into the top of the shiny black military boots he was given by Mikhail and Natasha Rudoff.

Young girls my age? Branko wondered.

Yes, they were sitting in the stuffy women's gallery. The audible giggling and the finger-pointing, all aimed like Cupid's arrows at the peripatetic scare-crow below, caused one of the elders to shout, *"Silencio, por favor!"* It was the Ladino equivalent of the Yiddish *shah, shtill!*

This was quickly seconded by the embarrassed group of mothers, prompting the man seated behind Branko to whisper, in Yiddish, "Be careful, dear boy. These people frown upon any socializing between our kind and their daughters."

The man, in his early twenties, identified himself as a shoe salesman from Bucuresht. He was just passing through and attending services at the only *shul* in this part of the country.

The worldly beyond-his-years Branko sensed what was happening and correctly translated "frown upon" into, "prohibit." Immediately following sounding of the *shofar,* towering above all of the congregants, Branko darted for the one narrow exit door. Not wishing to cause trouble, he did not to return the next day. He instead fasted as he had always done on Yom Kippur and mumbled the *yizkor* prayers from memory.

Boris Mandilev seemed to understand and allowed Branko to stay away from the forge that day. At sundown, Borris politely asked his apprentice to do some of the back-logged farrier work. He sweetened the request by telling Branko to keep the undersized shirt and shin-length pants for his own while offering him some bread and fruit to break his fast.

The famished lad happily agreed and greedily feasted on the offered food.

But even as he ate, Branko Horvitch was beginning to feel permanence creep in—an uneasy state for him. Whether or not Mandilev's grandson returned, Branko knew he'd have to move on soon. His creedal litany, so often practiced, continued to drive him forward. Always forward. There were things to do, places to see, experiences to feel.

*****

Temesvar
Bordering Transylvania in the Austro-Hungarian Empire
June 3, 1891

The Romanian majority referred to its city as Timishoara. The Hungarians, Temesvar. Throughout the Empire's eastern regions this verbal and mental battle resulted in dual names for most towns, villages and cities. The names were interchangeable and, arguably, not very important in the scheme of things.

Branko enjoyed being in a city with a predominant Jewish population and felt more a part of it than he had in Tarnovo. For the three months since arriving in Temesvar, he had hired-out as a farm-hand. As it was the spring planting season he was earning substantial pay and easily affording room and board whenever it wasn't being provided in the work arrangements. In a letter to Tante Shayndl he wrote:

> *Dearest Tante,*
>
> *I have had a roof over my head nearly every day since arriving in this attractive city. The surrounding, rich farmland has kept me busy as an extra hand. I can plow more square meters faster than anyone else, man or boy, and the farmers notice this. They give me extra rations and are quick to offer me lodgings so that I won't drift over to any other farms the next day. One good man has employed me for over two weeks now. His wife is a wonderful cook, not quite as good as you. But the lard! My God, she bathes everything in it! I'm sure you realize that I long ago fell by the wayside. I was able to eat some kosher meals in Tarnovo, one in Pleven, a few in Craiova with the local shochet's family, but for the most part, it has not been possible. Please believe me, I try.*
>
> *I expect to be here for a few more weeks, and then I'll continue heading west. I've been told that the Austrians are gaining more and more Ottoman lands, and are tightening their control of Serbia and parts of Bosnia. I've been unable to find any blacksmith work since leaving Bulgaria, but I would hope to find some in Austrian territory.*
>
> *In your last letter, which I fetched from the Temesvar Postal Office yesterday, you asked what I was doing about schooling. Formally,*

nothing, Tante Shayndl. But I've learned more about life and about the world, about people, since leaving Odessa, than I could ever learn in a schoolroom, a cheder, a yeshiva, or an orphanage. Do you understand what I am saying? Captain Rudoff, Mikhail, Natasha and Boris Mandilev were wonderful teachers.

Now that I have lived more than sixteen years I will continue to look for opportunities to learn from whomever I meet. The world has become my cheder, my school, my teacher. Captain Rudoff taught me so many things. The geography of every country we entered, and its history, the bookkeeping and arithmetic involved with cargo shipping, how to use a sextant to navigate by measuring distances at sea using stars as focal points, and yes, of course, I can name and identify every constellation.

There were so many other things! From Natasha I learned to cook, bake, and fry. From Mikhail and other members of the crew I heard fascinating stories covering a world of information. Yes, a world! I learned a lot just by observing the blacksmith in his day to day dealings with customers, handling problems with horses, shoes, the forge, the angry and the happy dealings. There wasn't one question he wouldn't or couldn't answer and I asked, and asked, and asked. And I will continue to ask wherever I am and whatever I am doing. Uncle Berel taught me that when I spent some time in his brush-making shop, and asked question after question. When he answered each one he waggled his finger at me and told me to always ask for answers when you don't know. Please tell him I learned my lessons well. Maybe too well! I've been told I ask too many questions!

Now I have the opportunity to learn something about farming, about livestock, about planting and seeds, and harvesting, and who knows what else. Maybe I'll become a sailor-cook-baker-blacksmith-farmer! And in a few years I'll add a few things to that list. Don't worry, Tante Shayndl, I'll find my way in this mashiganah velt. Those wonderful three years I spent with you, Berel and the children, gave me the love, the confidence and the strength to go on, to become a man. I could never thank you all enough. But I'll keep trying!

By the way, the papers you arranged for me through Rabbi Dorshtein have worked very well. No one has ever questioned them. They have allowed me into Bulgaria, Romania and the Empire's Hungary so far. The Rabbi must have some secret influence over the antisemitten in Odessa's court house. Makes you wonder! Thank him for me, and tell him I'm using it for good purposes. I miss all of you. Give Dovidl, Raiseleh and Channah hugs and kisses.

My love to Uncle. Say hello to my cheder friends, Mottke, Sholem and Chaim.

You can write to me at the same postal office address, here in Temesvar. I will probably stay here until after the wheat harvest in September, unless the strong yearning comes before then. I never know when it will strike, as you must know by now.

Please go to Goldman, the photographer, and have some pictures taken of the family, so

you can send them to me. I'll do the same here. I promise. You'll then see that I'm growing a mustache! Slowly, but it's coming!
All my love,
Bracho
Temesvar/Timishoara,
Hungary

P.S. Use BRANKO on the envelope when you write. Everyone hereabouts knows me by that name now

Sarajevo, Bosnia
(Under Austro-Hungarian Administration)
December 12, 1891

Showing his papers at the military checkpoint near Sarajevo, Branko was ordered to dismount from the jet-black horse and to wait in the guardhouse. The horse—Branko's first—had been a gift from his last employer in Zombor.

When he stepped to the ground, he was no less a striking figure than when he had been atop the steed. From his boots to the skewed, broad-brimmed hat, the tall, rugged Branko was outfitted in black. He had earned his imposing physique and the handsome horse by working a month's worth of long days and nights while the blacksmith recovered from a bronchial illness. The work had included tending to the stable and exposed Branko's natural talent for handling horses. Of the four equines he groomed, one was a frisky, young black stallion. Out of sheer appreciation the generous smith insisted that Branko take the horse as his own, saying, "You have earned this, boy!"

The horse was named *Midnight* and in Hungarian, *Ejfel*—pronounced, *ee-ya-fel*—fit well.

Not exactly "born to the saddle" Branko first tried his horsemanship by riding Boris Mandilev's old nag. But even with daily rides each evening, the farmlands provided little opportunity to develop more than rudimentary riding skills. But after Branko reached the Hortobagy—the grassy plains of Hungary—the terrain was that on which fiery, swift horses had ranged wild for centuries. It was here, where the unfenced and hard-packed land of the plains stretched out in unfettered directions that Branko mastered horsemanship and became a true equestrian.

The Empire's soldiers on guardhouse duty immediately dubbed Branko, *Der Shvarzeh Cowboy*. The comparison was drawn from the immense popularity of the American west as it was colorfully described in German-language pulp booklets. There wasn't a military post in Germany or the Austro-Hungarian Empire without some of these strewn about. Even the illiterate could enjoy the dramatic pen-and-ink sketches of the western cowboy, six-gun drawn, galloping to a fair damsel's rescue. Buffalo Bill Cody and his exciting Wild West extravaganza, a favorite of Germany's Kaiser Wilhelm and England's Queen Victoria, had become more popular in the capitals of Europe than he ever was at home in America.

Once in the guardhouse, Branko was confronted by the Adjutant-Commandant. After looking over the papers the aide had handed him, he said, "So, Herr Horvitch, you are going to Sarajevo and you are already sixteen years old?"

"Yes, sire!" Branko said with a snappy salute, click of his boot heels and inwardly blanch at being called *Herr Horvitch*. His fluent Yiddish combined with daily use of the similar Germanic in Hungary, allowed him to comfortably converse, albeit it in a slow, wavering manner. To a lesser degree he managed the difficult pure Hungarian tongue and a smattering of the melodic Romanian prevalent in Hungarian Transylvania. While not his native language, his childhood Russian had been helpful throughout his sea voyages and years in Bulgaria. Unbeknownst to him these linguistic influences contributed to what the soldiers thought a slow-spoken *cowboy* would sound like.

The monocled Adjutant and his two aides broke out with smiles that were mirrored by Branko.

"I suppose you know," the Adjutant said, "that all males over the age of sixteen are automatically conscripted into our reserve units.

That is, we'll place your name on our books and expect you to report your Sarajevo address within thirty days. When you reach eighteen, you'll be assigned into a specific unit for three months of training. After that, you'll continue on our reserve list until needed. Do you understand that, Recruit Horvitch?"

"Yes, sire!" Again the salute and heel strikes.

"These Slavs still suffer from an Ottoman complex. They shirk their duties and run off to Greece or Italy to avoid it. I see that you are Russian by birth, but Jewish. No doubt, with a name like Horvitch—and that Yiddish-accented Deutsch. What are you planning to do in Sarajevo, if I may ask?"

"I will look for work and settle for a while."

"When called, you will serve, of course?"

"It will be my honor to do so, sire," answered Branko in a sincere tone. He had learned to be politically skillful.

"Good. Good, son. I like your spirit. Captain Hollenberger is the officer to whom you are to report in Sarajevo. Technically, you're a citizen of Russia. But while in Hapsburg territory you'll abide by our rules—including military service. He'll register you properly. Be sure to give him these papers with my seal and signature. Good luck, *mein junge Judische herr.*"

As thinly spread as a *crepe* throughout the vast segment of Central and Eastern Europe, Franz Josef's armed forces had long-ago made rules as to who was, and wasn't eligible for call-up. Desertions were at an all-time high, especially among the Bosnians, the Croatians, the Czechs and the Slovaks. Movements toward independence were rampant throughout the shaky Empire. Native Austrians and Hungarians tended to serve out their time so as to avoid self-imposed exile, imprisonment or worse, firing squads. Branko was unaware of any of this as he crossed the swift-running Milacka River.

In the distance he saw the minarets of Moslem Sarajevo, nestled under snow-topped mountains. This was to be his home—for now. Holding Midnight to an easy gait while late afternoon calls to prayer rang from the Moslem mosques on both river banks, Branko's mind was in a rapid processing mode.

Maybe I'll decide to serve in the military, he thought. *That means travel and adventure, doesn't it? The Emperor's cavalry troops seem to be everywhere within the wide borders. Saw so many of them in Transylvania, in Central Hungary, in Croatia, now in Bosnia. But that won't be for a few years.*

Meantime, I've got to get work. Plenty of it here, I was told. The Turks who initially remained when the Ottoman armies moved out, are now leaving in droves. No farm work now until spring planting time.

Should be many blacksmith shops in this town. I'll show them a few tricks in handling the hammer and maybe get a roof over our heads before we know it. Eh, Midnight?

I miss Magda. God, she was a pretty one. Wanted to come with me. Her father would have sent the militia after us, I'm sure. Why does that always happen? And Gittel in Arad. Most beautiful milkmaid in all of Transylvania. Jewish, too. But, two years older. I can't seem to forget those moonlit nights in the rye fields with Nadia, in Temesvar. I still taste her lips, as sweet as honey! Why do I still judge all kisses by hers? But, no, I'm not sorry I didn't stay—got to move on! No place for a girlfriend. Too dangerous for both of us. I've got plenty of time to get into that. Maybe after I'm called-up by the army. If I'm still in Bosnia.

Who knows?

*****

Sarajevo, Austro-Hugarian Occupied Bosnia
October 21 1892

In a letter to Tante Shayndl:

> *Dear Tante and family,*
> *Its happened. A messenger from Captain Hollenberger came to the shop this morning. Because enlistments have fallen off*

throughout the Empire, they are now calling up reserves at age seventeen. That's me. Next week I must report to the barracks for training. Of course I can leave the country and go to Greece or Italy, but I've decided to report.

Hollenberger told me that I would be a good candidate for the cavalry and I would be allowed to take Midnight as my horse, if I enlist in one of the regular units. This is good enough for me, even though it means a minimum of five years serving the Emperor. Yes, I'll do it.

Please stop writing me at the blacksmith shop. I think Abdul is planning to sell it as soon as I leave. He is getting too old and frail to continue the work alone and he wants to return to his family in Turkey, where he sent his wife last year. They have three grandchildren there. He's been very good to us and I've managed to save a good deal of money during these past ten months. Thank you for pestering me so much in this regard! As usual, you were right in doing so, Tante.

Haven't told my new girlfriend yet. She cries too easily. Her mother will be relieved. Her father, a teacher, and her sisters seem to like me, but they always refer to me as Branko the Russian. Never once have they said 'Jew' but they know. They know all too well. Just last week, when I was coming out of the sinagoga after stopping in for morning prayers, yahrzeit, you know, Professor Raznica saw me, tipped his hat, smiled and walked away. If there was ever a doubt in his mind, there is none now.

I bought a metal frame with glass at the

Harvest Fair, so now I can better preserve the family photograph. I love looking at all of you. The children look so happy. I promise to take a picture in my uniform, now that my mustache has finally reached full growth. I actually trim it with scissors once a month. The local photographers do not charge full rates for the military.

I expect to get an annual leave and you can be sure that I'll head for Odessa, but that won't be for another year. I'll send you the proper address as soon as I know where I'll be stationed after training. My German has much improved and I've managed to practice that difficult Magyar language to where I'm understood reasonably well. I've had no one to speak Yiddish with here, aside from a few Romanian peddlers from time to time. So, I hope you have no problems with my Yiddish penmanship.

My memories of Russian continue to help me with the local Slavic dialect. Turkish is impossible and I don't even try. So you see, Tante Shayndl, my education continues without a cheder or a school of any kind.

I read constantly. Mostly German versions of English-language or French stories. My favorites have been Charles Dickens, the poetry of William Wordsworh, two Americans, Mark Twain and Edgar Allan Poe, the Frenchman Victor Hugo and the Russians, Tolstoy and Chekhov, all translated to German. Captain Hollenberger allows me to take books from both his office and the barracks... and he helps with some of the translation. I like that man, and I think he will treat me well when I report for duty. The Training Officer, Captain Hermann, addresses me by name every time he sees me and returns my salute smartly, with a broad grin.

Abdul is calling me. Still have some horses to shoe. I love you all,
Branko

*****

Kiev
In the Ukraine
September 24, 1941

The headquarters for Captain Brichtoben's Einsatzgruppen unit was in preparation to advance to a western suburb of Kiev, now that the city was securely under German occupation. Their sole prisoner, still with them after nearly three weeks, was something of a phenomenon: Himmler's "death squad" did not take any prisoners—ever.

It was a question of neither diplomacy nor a humanitarian gesture. Brigadier General Branko Horvitch, USA, Retired, was a rare find and in all of the inner circles of the Wehrmacht his strange capture was treated accordingly. Opinions on just what to do with him varied widely, from execution to exploitation and every conceivable notion in between.

At the urging of Branko's old friend, General Timoshenko, Russian intelligence had made overtures of a prisoner exchange. The offer of a captured SS Major was turned down by no less than Otto Rasch, the General in command of Einsatzgruppe "C." This only angered the retreating Russians and, no doubt, the hapless Major in question.

Himmler, as was his usual modus-operandi, left all decisions to his Einsatzgruppen field commanders while Nazi Propaganda Minister Josef Goebbels was salivating at the prospects of announcing the situation to the world. Meanwhile, an embarrassed secret service office in Washington remained silent, praying that the Russkies would work everything out.

There had been twenty-three days and nights of interrogation. At least ten slightly differing confessions had been presented for Branko's signature—each of which drew a heavy stare along with a repeated refusal. For his obstinacy they had deepened the stress of interrogations with hourly badgering, round-the clock. Even though his resulting mental deterioration was obvious, they had resisted all but the most inconsequential physical contact. Branko thought this was because of his position—his status. But the truth of the matter was that the demoralizing was anticipated to lead to a confession worthy of film quality propaganda. And for that, Branko had to appear as an unharmed and willing participant.

There had been six SS-trained inquisitors, the most recent of which proudly revealed that he was born and raised in Cleveland. This particular officer introduced himself as a graduate of Western Reserve University who had returned to his parents' homeland in '33. He had worked as a chemist for Krupp and after falling in love with the Nazi ideology was recruited by the SS. This introductory avowal elicited only another blank stare from prisoner Branko.

Branko had long since tired of being accused of being a spy. A tool of the Russians. Or any of the other accusations in the litany constantly thrown at him. And now, punctuating two hours of fruitless questioning, the Ohio kid threatened to shoot him on the spot.

"You scum of a Jew-bastard," growled the Ohio kid, "your Franklin *Rosen-velt* has sent you here, personally. Why? What are you doing with the Bolsheviks? What diabolical moves are you planning? And if you don't have something better to offer than that pathetic catatonic stare, I may just put a bullet between your eyes!"

For Branko, the stare wasn't an act. It was the symptom of sleep deprivation and near-shock. With the prisoner just sitting there staring, the Ohio kid went to the pistol at his hip. This rare, American-born SS henchman, unholstered his black Luger and aimed at Branko's head.

Knowing the fanatical fool was capable of killing him right then and there—but not likely authorized to do so—Branko mustered the composure he could mange and slowly leaned over the table and toward the deadly pistol.

"You sorry-assed excuse for a human being," Branko growled back through clenched teeth. "Give me five minutes with you, no gun, and I'll forget I'm thirty years older."

Whatever the Ohio kid expected, this wasn't it. He could see Branko was at the precipice of a mental abyss, poised to snap like a twig at any moment. If that happened, the young American SS officer knew, only a bullet would be likely to stop the larger-sized Branko.

This tete-a-tete, teetering on the edge of certain disaster, ended abruptly. General Rasch stormed into the room and with the cursory wave of a hand, dismissed the over-zealous junior officer.

"You'll be returned to your room now, General Horvitch," Rasch said. "I'm afraid you'll remain in our custody until arrangements are made for your journey to Berlin."

With the near-madness of only moments ago now gone, Branko did not respond. He remained silent with pursed, badly chapped lips—the result of enforced dehydration and diabolically planned calorie restriction.

"Yes, sir, Berlin," Rasch went on smugly. "My superiors feel that returning you to your Bolshevik comrades will serve no purpose for the greater good, so to speak."

Branko found his voice again. He began, "If that's your plan, wait until I see our Charge d'affaire in Berlin when I—"

"I don't think you comprehend the gravity of your situation," Rasch interrupted. "No one is the least bit concerned about your demoted ambassador's reactions—to anything, for that matter. You and I know that it's merely a matter of time before American neutrality—sham that it is—comes to an abrupt end.

"Now, you'll please excuse me, my de-frocked Brigadier, I'm off to our victory celebration—in liberated Kiev."

Smugly grinning as he delivered that last condescending phrase, Rasch mockingly assumed a stiff Prussian attention, sharply clicked his jack-boot heels, and then signaled for the guard to return Branko to his room. The fog of persecution was still thickly clouding Branko's thoughts, but as he was being jostled away, the reality of his situation began taking shape.

The Nazi martinet had been more than just smug—he had been confident and Branko was now coming to realizations that had thus far eluded him.

Brigadier or not, he was was a pawn of sorts—a strategic pawn. He wasn't so important as to merit release, but he was tremendously important as a source of propaganda. The scenario literally made Branko sick to his stomach and his head began to incessantly throb.

The bastards could begin day-one of a war with the United States by laying claim to a captured ex-general, Branko thought and then the epiphany hit him. *Not just that, but a former White House staffer to three Presidents, U.S. War College commander, a heavily-bemedalled war veteran...and...a Jew at that. My God, no damned wonder they won't release me.*

"All because of a son-of-a-bitchin' vodka-guzzling Uzbek driver," Branko muttered out loud, startling his beer-bellied keeper. The enormity of it all left an indelible impact on him. He was about to become, he knew, an unprecedented international incident.

FDR will swallow his cigarette, holder and all and then he'll chew up Wild Bill and his whole damn O.S.S. for breakfast!

Later that evening, as he lay on his blanketed cot, the exhausted prisoner could barely make out any stars through the tiny barred window. He realized his mind was wandering—a sure sign of mental exhaustion. But he knew enough to also realize he hadn't been rousted for another round of integration. Whatever they had planned, he would at least get some long overdue sleep.

He could not know, of course, that less than 200 meters away, crouched in patient waiting, an improbable but daring solution to this twisted dilemma was about to swing the pendulum in his favor.

IN THE SERVICE OF THE EMPEROR

Mostar
Austro-Hungarian Occupied Bosnia
January 25, 1893 (0800 hours)

The crack cavalry regiment stationed in the district demonstrated their usual elitist snobbery in welcoming the newest recruits. The brunt of this treatment included enlistees Branko Horvitch and Azriel de Sevilla. The two recently acquainted friends didn't take the reception personally, for after all, they had been forewarned and advised to quickly assume the same mannerisms.

Being the only two enlistees of the fifty conscripted at the Sarajevo training camp, they had been treated as valuable goods by Captain Hermann. Their being Jews did not seem to make a difference to the Captain or cadre of trainers. The forty-eight disgruntled Bosnian call-ups, however, openly cursed the Captain's two favorites. Azriel, the son of Sarajevo's most influential Sephardic, was the most sensitive to this; Branko, though, thought lightly of most everything and accordingly coached his friend's frame of mind.

Of the two, Azriel de Sevilla was the superior horseman, pistol shot, rifleman and expert saber wielder. He excelled at everything, winning every training camp contest and serving as the standard for all to achieve. He easily aced the coveted "Top Recruit" Medal. Branko, a distant runner-up, was fervently proud of his co-religionist and comrade.

Neither recruit was surprised when they drew the Mostar Cavalry outpost assignment. Between their combined skills and the promises of garrison commander Captain Hollenberger, the assignment was part of the deal in their choice to enlist for a five-year term.

Mostar, the Slavic word for *old bridge*, was a strategic outpost since becoming a Muslim stronghold. Most of its population was as anti-Austrian and pro-independence as any other ethnic group in the vast empire. Its 15th century arched bridge, high over the River Neretva, was a focal point for frequent gatherings of highly-spirited and potentially explosive crowds of local youths. Thus, keeping the lid on rabble-rousing was one of the cavalry unit's two main responsibilities. The other main responsibility was its mission to squelch covert gun-smuggling—a rampant problem throughout the occupied regions of Bosnia, Dalmatia, Croatia and Slavonia.

From its Mostar base, the 19th Cavalry periodically joined with the Ragusa-headquartered 24th Infantry, forming a brigade that routinely swept the Dalmatian coast for gun-smuggling. Italian gun-runners were notorious for supplying Muslim guerillas with the latest in weaponry and the Cavalry was under Vienna directive to halt the organized smuggling and subsequent armed threat. It wasn't long after Branko arrived at the Mostar base that the platoon deployed and the soldiers found themselves trotting the last twenty kilometers into Ragusa—also known in Slavic as Dubrovnik. Just a few hundred meters from the city walls they were met by a messenger from one of the 24th's rifle companies. The messenger was from a contingent pinned down by gunfire on the shores of a small cove just 1,000 meters south of Ragusa's wide harbor. After briefly conversing with the messenger the Platoon Lieutenant barked-out orders for two squads of troops, including Branko and Azriel, to follow the messenger back to the skirmish—with carbines ready for action.

The trapped soldiers of the 24th rifle company had been pinned down as the result of events that had begun when an Italian schooner anchored on the Adriatic side of Lokrum Island the previous night. Launching three long boats full of smuggled guns the Italians had slipped into the nearby Ragusa Cove.

Meanwhile, a detachment of the 24th rifle company had remained in the area for rendezvousing with the 19th Cavalry while the bulk of its unit was responding to reported insurgent activity fifty kilometers north on the Spelato (Split) road. The remaining 24th detachment had then received, and acted upon, a local paid informer's tip about a gun-smuggling operation underway at the cove. The 24th contingent of infantrymen made a quick-time march to the cove and arrived at the crack of dawn. The rebels had already loaded three wagons and the Italians were about to shove-off in their three long-boats.

The arriving infantry squad saw only the escaping Italians. They stormed the path to the beach, not seeing the rebel wagons beyond the far end of the bluff. Of course, the gun-runners were startled when brightly-colored red uniformed soldiers came rushing down the path. But instead of fleeing, the well-armed smugglers open up with a blistering fusillade of weapon-fire, killing three infantrymen instantly. While the remaining twelve military men scurried for the virtually non-existent cover, the unnoticed rebels returned from the far end of bluff. The shocked troops were thus caught in a lethal crossfire.

This was this chaotic combat scene that Branko, Azriel and their cavalry comrades came upon. The corporal in charge of the two squads followed standard cavalry procedure: He deployed the men along the rim of the bluff and ordered Azriel to first secure the horses and then to take up a sniper position on the hill above the bluff. The horses meant transportation and speed—both meant life. With the animals secure and his offensive line on the high ground, the corporal knew that Azriel's marksmanship would speedily contribute to an already easy dispatching of the resistance.

The experienced rebel leaders recognized the rapid re-positioning of the military force. They realized that the fight was escalating beyond their ability to strike back victoriously. To overpower the troops would require not only brute force, but also the formidable strategic placement being held by those very troops. This they did not want to risk and began retreating to their wagons. In their haste they abandoned some of the valuable crates.

The Italians also saw their advantage deteriorating and gambled on a run for their boats. Losing only two men to the downward raining volleys, their gamble partially beat the odds as they rowed out of range.

With the engagement rapidly dissolving, the squad leader yelled orders for the troops to give chase to the fleeing rebels. As the soldiers ran for their horses they rounded a curve in the bluff side path. This is where they found Azriel de Sevilla. Now lying prostrate in the sand, he was a casualty of a rebel bullet to the nape of his neck.

The squad leader knew it was hopeless—the blood soaking into the sand was testimony to that. But it was also clear that the stunned Branko had yet to be hardened by battle. Because of his friend he would, for the short term, be more a liability than an asset. So the Corporal ordered Branko to remain and tend to the doomed Azriel.

As the horses and men thundered away, Branko was suddenly surrounded by a silence as sickening as the approaching death lying on the red-stained sand. Azriel's eyes were open and Branko was clutching him tightly, whispering words of hope. Wasted words of hope.

Azriel's last gasp of breath came. Even though Branko was no stranger to death, he wept. Through his tears he uttered the proper words to proclaim faith in God for both he and the deceased: "Shma Yisroel adonai elohenu, adonai ehod." *Hear O Israel, the Lord thy God, the Lord is One.*

Azriel de Sevilla was not the only casualty. In the ensuing chase three of the infantrymen and one horse-soldier were mortally wounded, each dying some hours later. Four rebels were found dead atop the bluff while fourteen were captured and returned to Ragusa. The others, having escaped into the hills, abandoned two of the three heavy wagon-loads in their haste. Inside the crates were an assortment of rifles, pistols and ammunition—all having been purchase with blood money and now recovered with blood.

Branko was granted permission to accompany Azriel's body back to Sarajevo for burial. Three days later he faced the grieving Moses and Rachel de Sevilla. In his seventeen years, it was the most difficult thing he had ever done.

*****

**Salzburg, Austria
November 16, 1897**

There was no question that Corporal Horvitch would re-enlist for another term, which had recently been increased to six years. The tallest in his regiment, young Corporal Horvitch was hailed as *Der Groisseh Soldat* or *Big Soldier* by all of his comrades. Although there was still an easy and cavalier nature about him, he also exhibited an almost determined contentment to be in the service of the Emperor. Excelling in everything he was ordered to do Branko had earned six citations—far more than any of the other young recruits. Consequently promoted twice during his first tour, and following his November re-enlistment, he was promised an early award of sergeant chevrons. Because of these changes, and in lieu of his time served from sign-up to first enlistment, Branko's records now showed that he was due an extra year's credit toward an eventual pension.

As he was now stationed in the beautiful city of Salzburg on the German border, even Tante Shayndl was convinced that another five years would be beneficial for him. On his last furlough—in '95—she, Uncle Berel and the children implored him to eventually settle in Odessa. But Shayndl also knew that their plea was an exercise in futility. She had long-ago realized that her orphaned nephew was a born adventurer. He had thus far proven this with every move he had made. Even given the periodic pogroms, the seeds of revolution and the unrest throughout the Czardom of Nicolai Romanov, Odessa was still far too tame for his liking.

Emperor Franz Josef had many reasons to fear a unified German nation that posed a real threat to his substantial empire. While they shared customs, language and phases of socio-political history, there were stark cultural differences as well as differing long-range goals. For these reasons the Emperor's Generals had unanimously decided to shore up the common borders with Germany by borrowing strength in the Balkans and Polish Galicia. Secret alerts and messages to all field commanders made this critical emphasis quite clear.

In some cases, shoring up the borders common with Germany meant pulling back from other areas. Such was the case for Barnko's regiment, which drew back from Slavic territories and now patrolled the 100 kilometers from Salzburg to Engelhartzell on the Danube. This was near the Bohemian border where heavy artillery units were firmly entrenched. Veteran infantry units were also dispersed at intervals along this same stretch. Not unexpectedly this upset a highly-insulted Kaiser Wilhelm who, in turn, feared the Russians, the

British and his perennial enemy in France. In the Central Europe of the 1890's, suspicions, intrigue and uneasiness reigned above all else. It was popularly said at the time "if you hate your enemies, wait a while and they're sure to become your friends." And vice-versa.

This political instability and especially the growing totalitarianism in the more eastern regions of Europe gave rise to steadily increasing emigration. Since coming north into Austria proper, Branko came face to face with these massive migrations. Along the dusty roads of Austria, Hungary, Bohemia and Moravia, thousands of Jews, Poles, Hungarians, Romanians, Slovaks, and gypsies were heading to the ports on the North Sea—Hamburg, Bremerhaven, Antwerp and Rotterdam. Branko wondered who they were, why they were on the move and to where they were going. A chance encounter and random conversation with a Jewish tailor in Salzburg provided the answer.

"The happy and powerful do not go into exile," the tailor explained, unknowingly echoing French journalist Alexis DeTocqueville's description of the early American immigrant mindset.

The veiled remark spoke volumes to Branko. Shayndl and Berel had readily acknowledged the stagnancy of life in the Pale of Settlement and the increasing frequency of deadly pogroms under Czar Nicolai's regime. What's more, Berel had described increasing trade boycotts in Odessa and throughout the Pale, all critically affecting his brush-making business.

Over the border—in Romania—there was talk of proposed legislation prohibiting any business trade between Jews and Romanian non-Jews. Poverty blanketed the Pale from the Baltic to the Black Sea, seeping into Poland, Slovakia and Romania.

These were the things moving the people, contributing to the emigration of men, women and children seeking to improve their lives. For most of them, America was their goal—a place in which they could not only survive but also thrive. America had been impressed upon them as a land of opportunity, compassion and eventual wealth. In all languages, it came to be known simply as *the golden land.*

Branko realized that Shayndl and Berel may have also given thought to America—or believed they had. Either that or they had chosen to protect him as best they could by no longer pressing for his return to Odessa. In their letters they had stopped mentioning his return while speaking of local families and friends who had recently emigrated.

And true enough, now for the first time since becoming a soldier in the Emperor's army, Branko thought of moving on—and why not America, he mused. As the idea grew on him, he began looking for information on America while voraciously soaking-up literature on world history, adventure, and famous personages. His interest in America led him further to Henry David Thoreau, Bret Harte and the works of Emerson, Longfellow, Hawthorne and Thomas Paine. He browsed and read every book with which he crossed paths, in particularly the beautifully illustrated foreign language translations offered at the army installations to which he was posted. He read nearly everything—some of it two or and three times. As his German language proficiency expanded he graduated from simplistically satisfying literature to tomes of greater heft. This opened a new world of possibilities fraught with more questions about his future—particularly concerning America. He pondered what might be in store for him should he emigrate. He wondered how the Jewish people were perceived by the Americans and whether there would be trade boycotts, pogroms or barriers of any kind. And he wondered if as an ex-soldier in America—a German-Yiddish-Hungarian-Russian speaking ex-soldier, he could find employment.

By the end of his second year in Salzburg Branko Horvitch was promoted to the rank of *Sergeant* in the 19th Cavalry. His current tour was due to end in November of 1903 and, as much as he loved being in the service of the Emperor, he decided he would not re-enlist when that time came.

*****

**Eastern Hungrary
Somewhere in the Hortobagy
July 22, 1902**

A long series of compromises failed to steer Austria and Hungary away from a collision course. In an effort to effectively govern the mosaic of nationalities, Franz Josef created a Dual Monarchy. He proclaimed himself the King of Hungary and the Emperor of Austria. But this proved far more tacit than realistic and brought the impending rift to a head, intensifying the proliferation of movements for independence throughout the empire. The ever-widening gulf between the two countries represented a chasm of internal crisis separating Budapest and Vienna. And thus, faced with shoring up German border security or quelling internal strife, the General Staff in Vienna foreswore political astuteness for vital expediency. In short, they now left the borders to fend for themselves while imposing three crack Cavalry regiments upon the unhappy Hungarians.

Branko's regiment—the 19th Cavalry—was sent to the Hortobagy. This was the vast, grassy plains of Eastern Hungary. It was a hot-bed of violent, anti-Austrian demonstrations fomented by heavily armed, hard-drinking, plainsmen. These were the reckless-riding *czikos*—the *wild cowboys of the plains*. This was the one place that a mounted cavalry, even when supplemented by a token all-Hungarian *Platoon Cavalier*—was certain to exacerbate animosities by several dangerous degrees.

Just outside a nondescript town on the banks of the Hortobagy River, the 19th Regiment bivouacked in field tents. Sergeant Horvitch had rejoined the regiment after a six-month detached duty tour with the Emperor's Honor Guard in Vienna.

The Nagycsarda—*the Great Inn*—was known all over Central Europe as a retreat of elegance for the upper class of society. Built in 1699, it was a "watering hole" frequented by not only the upper class, but also the nobility of the empire who came to hunt, feast and indulge. Now, however, the inn was receiving a different social stratum of patronage; the military. The fond memories for these inn visitors were of off-duty evenings sipping sweet *Tokaj* and swapping tall tales. Occasionally, the uniformed contingent squeezed their meager allowances to afford a sumptuous meal washed down with the rich, dark local brew.

After Branko's six months in sophisticated Vienna, constantly under a microscope as one of the Emperor's vaunted dragoons, this fashionable country duty was a welcomed respite. He even began thinking of the inn as his own private gentleman's club. And it was there that he met her—the baker's helper.

Slowly ambling through one of the several lounges, baker's helper Margit Vasary, barely eighteen, flirtatiously smiled at the tall and ruggedly handsome Sergeant Branko. Sizing him up, she thought he cut a most romantic figure in the colorful red-and-blue horse-soldier's uniform of the elite 19th Cavalry. As her work was finished for the day, she stopped beside his table.

"Where did you come from, Sergeant?" she purred. "I haven't seen you here before."

"Oh, I've been polishing the Emperor's jackboots back in Vienna," Branko drily answered. "So he sent me here for a well-earned rest."

Both laughed in harmony as Branko offered her a seat on the nearby sofa.

"Oh, dear, I cannot do that, soldier boy," she fired back, shifting her well-defined hips in the process. "They'd hang me tomorrow!"

Upon such simple things are the flames of passion wrought. Regardless of whether it was what she said or the way she said it, Branko was immediately captivated in a way new to him. He wasn't, after all, inexperienced. He had known both adolescent infatuations and short-lived romances. There had been short flings with camp-following, uniform-worshippers in Salzburg, in Melk and Vienna. There had even been a dangerous tryst with an artillery colonel's wife in Braunau that had made for some anxious moments. But this seemed different.

He was, of course, infatuated and Margit's returned flirtations did not diminish as his visits became rendezvous in her tiny room at the back of the inn. She was provided the room so as to be available to assist the pastry chef's daily, 4:00 a.m. breakfast roll baking. This arrangement alleviated an impractical 6-kilometer round trip from her parent's home in the nearby village of Hortobagy. The room was also, obviously, a discreet convenience for the couple's erupting passions.

As those passions ran their course, the neither naive nor virginal dark-eyed beauty became suspicious of the anatomical "defect" of Branko's circumcision. His covenant with God had been honored as prescribed, in the Tanakh, on the eighth day of his birth in Ignatovka.

While Margit veiled her concern in playfulness, his responses—off-hand and humorous—were typically punctuated with a quick return to lovemaking. He just didn't think his religion was germane to their delicious physical relationship in bed. He was, of course, quite wrong. She persisted and one day discreetly asked one of his regimental comrades, an Austrian half-Jew, if Branko was indeed a Jew, *zhee'do*, or one of the rare gentiles who had undergone circumcision. The comrade blurted out the truth.

The answer was, at once, devastating, although not entirely unexpected. Margit was petrified that her parents and older brothers in Hortobagy would also learn Branko was Jewish. They were all good Hungarians, loyal to their king and not the Emperor. In hypnotic awe of the papacy they were all *intensely* Catholic in addition to being hard-line nationalists and fiercely supportive of any independence movement. This equated to their being equivocally opposed to any foreign elements and uniformly despising those who reportedly caused the crucifixion of their Lord and Savior.

Their parting, tearfully insisted upon by Margit—excruciatingly and reluctantly understood by Branko—came swiftly and painfully for both. The soldier rarely returned to the inn. He knew that it just wasn't to be.

A year later, Margit married an alcohol-crazed, abusive *csiko* twice her age.

*****

Near Jaszapati, Hungary
May 25, 1903

Vienna placed the 19th Cavalry on full alert after one of its platoons was attacked by stone-throwers just outside the nondescript town of

Heves. Three of the targeted troopers required local medical attention while another, bleeding profusely from the head, was rushed by a four-horse wagon to the nearest hospital in Jaszapati. Of the estimated twenty perpetrators, mostly teenagers and young men, 11 were quickly taken into custody by troopers. But, adhering to strict Dual Monarchy policy, the eleven were handed over to the local magistrate. This was tantamount to setting them scot-free. There wasn't a police officer or magistrate in all of Hungary proper who would risk the wrath of his fellow citizens by incarcerating anyone for this "mild" anti-Emperor affront.

This attack had been most a protest against the presence of the Emperor's cavalry in Hungary. It was nothing new and not the first time stones were thrown at Austrian troops—especially when unaccompanied by Hungarian dragoons. And while it was true that weapons had never been fired at uniformed troops, historically speaking, stones and billy clubs preceded lethal gunfire.

In the midst of this perpetual unrest, the increasing hordes of immigrants from the east, the south and north continued to trickle onto the Hungarian plain. Some stayed while others were merely passing through, migrating to the west. The pseudo-benevolence of Franz Josef extended to the Southern Slavs, the Galician-Ruthenians and the Transylvanians, inviting them to settle in the Great Plains, the Hortobagy. The truth be known, Franz Josef's political advisors insisted on this policy with a seemingly rational objective in mind. By thinning the heavy concentrations of ethnic groups by providing hectares of uncultivated grassland to all comers, the revolutionary threats in three regions would be diluted—that was the theory. Minimized in this grand plan, however, was the increased wrath of the natives, most notably the chronically xenophobic *czikos*.

As a result of the settlement policy and the migratory activities, the 19th Cavalry was dangerously thinned-out. They had stretched their watch-dog patrols far beyond the point of sound military strategy. During one such sweep, Sergeant Horvitch and his eighteen-man patrol encountered a rare, large and single transitory group coming from the east. This was on the banks of the Tisza, across from the regional market town of Szolnok. Beginning in 1899 the log books of the cavalry regiment stationed in these parts, would eventually cite seven of these well-organized Romanian-Jewish groups. Averaging eighty people to a group these people were walking from their homes in Eastern Romania to the sea ports in Germany and Holland.

Sitting astride a black steed reminiscent of the long-ago pastured *Midnight*, Branko observed the ragtag group. He was both stunned and pleased by the sight of the *Mogen Dovid* with its star-of-blue on a white field, fluttering from a tree limb over the encampment. As Sergeant Branko sat tall and steely-eyed, one of his point-men approached with one of the Jews in tow.

"Sergeant Horvitch," the point-man called up, "this man seems to be the leader. And he speaks one of your languages—Yiddish, I think."

Branko never even so much as attempted to hide his Jewishness from his comrades. To them, even those who were outwardly anti-Jewish by virtue of their glorious hereditary culture, Branko was forever "the good Jew." He was well-familiar with the phrase "but, you're so different than the others." It was meant complimentarily but vaguely hid an obvious implication. But if any of them were cognitive of the subtle prejudice, not a man in the 19th would dare risk a broken jaw or smashed nose by making more of the matter. He may have been "the good Jew" but he was a formidable, Samson-muscled cavalryman. They knew it and he knew they knew it.

Branko politely addressed the young man: "Sergeant Horvitch, here, sir. Your name, please?"

"So you speak Yiddish, Sergeant?" The bearded, spectacled migrant rhetorically responded. "I take it you are either one of us or you've learned the language from the Germanic strain."

Still waiting for an answer, Branko made no effort to reply.

That hardened soldier atop the black steed was just a little unnerving and the migrant quickly rushed to answer the question that had been put to him: "I am Shimon Katz, head of this contingent of Romanian *Fusgeyers*. I have seventy-six people and all the proper papers, trans-Atlantic steamship vouchers, supporting documents—"

"Slow down, Reb Katz," Branko interrupted, now broadly smiling. "I'm sure you've been checked somewhere since crossing the border into the Empire. You could never have gotten this deep into

Hungary otherwise. *Fusgeyers,* hmmm? To me that says that you're going by foot all the way—to where?"

"From our *shtetl* near the Russian border, to Bremerhaven in Germany. Matter of fact, we left Birlad on April 18th, just two weeks after the Kishinev pogrom."

Dismounting, Branko was surprised at the ease of conversing, inasmuch as he had few opportunities to use his Yiddish these past years. In Vienna, he had found pure Yiddish-speakers only in the Polish neighborhoods. Sitting on the riverbank while his men moved menacingly about inspecting the campsite for contraband, weapons, anti-Hapsburg literature and such, he motioned for Shimon to sit beside him.

"Yes," Branko went on, "I read the newspaper account of the Kishinev pogrom. It appeared all over these parts. First time I recall any such coverage."

"You are right, Sergeant. Even the Yash pogrom in '99, where thousands were murdered, stayed out of the headlines. Can you imagine how many and how often these travesties occur while just 100 kilometers away no one is even aware?"

"In Vienna I was serving in the Emperor's Honor Guard when a man from Warsaw showed me an account in a renowned Berlin Jewish newspaper. The report, claiming to be substantiated, listed every village, town and city in the Pale, Congress Poland and Romania where the phenomenon had taken place from 1881 to 1903. It included approximate numbers of deaths and injuries. The numbers are permanently etched on my brain—I will always find it hard to comprehend. My parents and two older sisters are among them—may they rest in peace."

"*Omayn! Omayn!* Then you are a *landsman*, Sergeant!"

"Yes, born in the Ukraine, near Kiev," Branko responded in a low, deliberate monotone while his eyes followed the slow-flowing river. "I was hidden under the floorboards. It was 1881—Czar Alexander III's revenge for his father's assassination."

"My good God! How did you end up in the Emperor's army?"

"I'll tell all, but there's a price to pay. I want to know all you know —about what awaits you in America and the story of your *Fusgeyers*."

Branko dismissed his troopers, sending them back to regimental headquarters. Under these circumstances, he decided to spend the evening with Katz and the Birladers before returning to the regiment.

In the hours that followed, Shimon invited a few of his cadre to join in the discussions with the rare, Jewish cavalryman. Right from the start they began referring to Branko by the same name as did his fellow soldiers—*der goisseh soldat*. And just as with his military comrades, Branko towering stature singled him out as *the big soldier* to these men, too. After mesmerizing the Birladers with his incredible adventures, Branko peppered the cold night air with question after question, ably and succinctly answered by Shimon and his cadre.

Hearing of Branko's restlessness, Shimon and the others had little difficulty in convincing him that someone of his caliber would be a welcomed addition to the *Fusgeyers*. They gave him the name of one Mordecai Anieloff as the probable leader of the next emigrant group of *Fusgeyers* from the Birlad district, tentatively due to leave in the spring of 1904. Branko promised to get in touch with Shimon and the others when he reached New York that next year. In return, Shimon would immediately write a letter to Mordecai telling him to expect the "big soldier" after his separation from the Emperor's service in November. Thus the "contract" was made: From honorable discharge in one army, to an enlistment in another.

Branko spurred his horse into the starless, pitch black night. He rode into the biting wind, faster and faster, with cape unfurled and the loud send-off cheers from the Birlad *Fusgeyers* still ringing in his ears. He was intoxicated with his series of firm decisions to emigrate, to march with the wayfaring Jews of Romania to America. Looking toward the western horizon as he rode over the plains of the Hortobagy, his agile mind was brimming with the stuff of which dreams are made.

November could not come soon enough for him.

*****

The Ukraine
September 24 - 25, 1941

Rescue came quickly and quietly.

Rasch, Brichtoben and the other officers had gone to a "victory" celebration. Hosted by the Einsatzgruppe "C" Himmler-Liaison, Adjutant Manfred von Sturmer, the celebration was held as Kiev's finest—and still relatively intact—hostelry

It was just after midnight. Only two guards were on duty. Everyone else was asleep in the barn-barracks—exhausted after a day of annihilating 311 hapless Jewish women, children and old men at a village to the south. It had been one of the regional mop-up *cleansing aktsions*. The complacent guards went down first: Silently dispatched to a Deutsche Valhalla with slit throats. The soundly sleeping Branko was awakened by a rough-skinned hand muffling his mouth. Instantly wide-eyed, he heard a throaty Yiddish whisper at his ear: "General Horvitch, get dressed quickly and put on this jacket. It's very cold tonight."

"Who the hell are you?" Branko whispered back in knee-jerk English. He then repeated himself in Yiddish while slipping into pants, socks and a sweater. The man to whom he was whispering was a bearded, pint-sized man wearing drab camouflaged colors that made his outline difficult to distinguish.

"Simcha Greenberg, comrade," came the answer. "We are a partisan unit. Commissioned by General Timoshenko. We're to drag your *Amerikanisheh tuchus* out of here. Now, let's go Yankee. *Shnell, shnell!*"

Branko watched as the heavily bearded messiah broke into a winning, gap-toothed grin that lit up the pitch-black, makeshift cell.

Once out into the brisk autumn night, Greenberg gently shoved the still-stunned Branko along. They joined two others, running to a grove of stately elms. Hidden in the tress were yet six more men holding the reins of their mounts. Aside from foot-power the horse had become the "vehicle" of choice for most of the ever-growing partisan units. Replacement mounts and ample feed were made available by selected cooperative farmers throughout the occupied territories.

By the way Simcha Greenberg issued instructions, Branko realized he was the commander of the small unit. What Branko couldn't know was that the group actually numbered thirty men-strong. The absent men were temporarily based in the deep forest off the Kiev-Borodyanka secondary road twenty kilometers away. From there they had raised weeks of holy hell with rear-guard Nazi elements. They had dynamited supply trains, attacked truck convoys and lynched the enemy from trees. Dead enemy patrols were strewn across miles of country back roads. At each smoldering cite they left derisively taunting placards. The German language signs proclaimed various taunting messages such as, *Welcome to Hell*, *Mail to Adolf*, *Retreat or Die*, *Your Soviet Summer is Over* and *General 'Winter' Will Freeze Your Balls Off*. The latter was in reference to Napoleon's disastrous winter retreat westward from the gates of Moscow.

Historically, similar partisan warfare was nothing new. But in this ravaged occupied territory of the Soviet Union it had taken on a new meaning since the June invasion. The scope and viciousness of atrocities had spawned Germany's most motivated enemies in the form of thousands of soldiers, sailors, airmen, and underage youngsters denied military service. This included men cut-off from their units, escapees from capture during the over-running Nazi blitzkrieg, deserters opting for a less-restrictive military life and even older veterans of the First World War. Whether military or civilian, each and every one of them was firmly dedicated to defending their revered Motherland in any way they could. If harassing the enemy behind the lines was their lot, so be it—just as long as they could kill Germans.

There were partisan units made up of sailors without ships, airmen without aircraft, tank drivers and gunners without tanks, and courageous women from all branches of the military. Then there were the thousands of civilian volunteers: Jews, Gypsies, Tatars, Uzbeks and other ethnic groups which are a part of any guerrilla unit's secretive and unwritten rosters.

Among these kinds of resistance groups were the numerous and widely-scattered all-Jewish units such as commanded by Simcha Greenberg. Knowing all-too-well of the Einsatzgruppen dastardly excesses and successes, they possessed a particular sense of revenge to exact. Many had lost wives, husbands, children, parents and friends throughout the occupied zones: From Vilna to Odessa, from the former western borders to the constantly changing salients of the Nazi advance. They were defiant and desperate. Full of hate and vengeance, they were not to be denied their quarry.

The partisans throughout the Soviet Union were fighting an all-out, no-holds-barred guerrilla war. A white flag of surrender meant absolutely nothing to them; they took no prisoners except for occasional interrogations. The Geneva Convention? *Don't be absurd*, they would tell you. There simply were no rules, excepting one: Kill or be killed!

The seasoned Wehrmacht and Einsatzgruppen commanders undoubtedly felt that they would rather face a division of Red Army regulars than any these rag-tag splinter-groups of undisciplined *partisaner* savages. There would be no argument to this from any German underling on Russian soil.

Not knowing that Branko was an expert horseman and former cavalry sergeant, Simcha hadn't brought an extra horse along. Instead, he signaled Branko to ride with a sailor named, Alyosha. However, Branko took the initiative and hopped on first. The former Dnieper River patrol-boat veteran was forced to ride on the hump, grasping onto Branko for balance.

Within a kilometer, a burly giant of a man taking up the rear whistled to Simcha—a signal to halt.

"Simcha, everyone," the man gleefully said, pointing to the horizon where Kiev lay. "Look behind us."

The sky over the Ukrainian capital was lit up as far and as wide as the eye could see—a bright yellow with tinges of orange and red.

"Seems to have grown immensely in the last hour," Simcha observed. "The whole damn city must be burning by now."

"What's going on?" a puzzled Branko asked.

"I would say that our retreating comrades neatly planted their 'welcome' gifts to the Hun, General."

"Meaning?"

"The Red Army retreat plan calls for planting TNT in strategic buildings as they make their exit. I've never seen anything quite this encompassing, but that's what we're seeing. The Zhitomir fires were controlled pretty quickly, but it looks like they've done exceedingly well in old Kiev. They always leave behind civilian-clad volunteers to do the detonating and it's then up to them to catch up to their units."

With this, Simcha spurred his mount and lurched ahead. The others followed.

When the rescue detail reached the edge of the forest, a low-lying fog had settled in and they were challenged by two unseen sentries. The password, *Yehudah Maccabee* was called out and the Yiddish return phrase *mit groisseh glick—with a lot of luck*—came back.

As they dismounted in the deep pine forest, Branko saw something new to his military experience. Laying about, in threes and fours, the partisan unit appeared world-weary. They were ill-clothed in the widest assortment of incomplete uniforms, scarves, jackets, pants and hats. An accordionist and a balalaika strummer were softly playing some spirited Russian folk tunes beside a very low-lit fire. A group of three, with a pig-tailed woman in britches and boots, were wildly spinning into a *kosatzke*. Empty beer and vodka bottles cluttered the clearing. Much like a mob scene from a Bruegel painting, even Dali's surrealism would have been upstaged here under the pines.

They all stopped what they were doing and gathered round Simcha and the rescue team. Greeting Branko as a long-lost uncle, they gave hime bear hugs and slobbering, liquor-reeking kisses on both cheeks. There was a cacophonous and convoluted assortment of Yiddish, Russian and hilariously-fractured English phrases. One besotted woman grabbed Branko by the jacket sleeve and tried to get him to dance, calling for the musicians to "strike op di bend *dlya* Meeky Roontey *ee* Zhudy Golint." Simcha quickly stepped in to once again rescue the exhausted and bewildered General.

Later, after everyone retired to their corners of the clearing, Simcha spoke in hushed tones with his famous guest.

"I know this type of paramilitary scene is rather shocking for you, my General," he said, while handing him a bed roll and a stale piece of bread with jam. "But guerrilla fighting is unconventional in every sense."

"I realize that now, Simcha. And please call me *Branko*. And while I'm with you, I want to learn all I can. It will be a bonus to report this to my superiors."

Simcha nodded his head.

"You know, all those jealous American reporters in Moscow will hate my guts for this—but here I am, what can I do?" Branko added with a husky laugh.

Simcha nodded with an agreeable grin, even though he didn't understood the reference to American reporters. He then said, "My orders are to return you to the Red Army lines posthaste. The only problem is they retreat faster and faster to the east every hour, it seems."

Simcha paused for a moment, thinking of those comrades from whom he was separated when the enemy broke through and literally overran Rovno in July. Those of his infantry platoon who escaped the suffocating encirclement, scattered in small numbers and dispersed in every direction. The three who elected to stay with Simcha were fellow Jews. Before the week was over the word was out that a *Zhid* partisan unit was in formation. By the end of the first month they had attracted more than thirty "enlistees." To a man and to a woman, they agreed to fight on as a partisan unit. They made contact with several other splintered groups between Rovno and Zhitomir. In fact, they were encouraged by a Red Army radio broadcast to allow the blitzkrieg to pass beyond them in order to operate behind enemy lines. Their last official orders, via that broadcast, instructed them to use a code name, to label their highest ranking individual as *commander* and to be prepared to follow orders from the High Command. The penalty for disobeying was hot-iron branding that would identify each man as a deserter.

"They're hurting us bad across an extremely wide front, Gen—uh—Branko, Simcha continued. "I fear for Moscow and Leningrad now. The beasts will slaughter everything that moves in those cities. *Unsereh Yidden?* The Einsatzgruppen will erase them, with relish. Do you know of those bastards? Of what they've done thus far? Of their mission?"

"Yes, of course. Timoshenko briefed me thoroughly. Simcha, I know too well of this kind of terror. My entire family was murdered during a pogrom—sixty years ago—in a village near Kiev... Ignatovka."

"Ignatovka? Yes, of course, the Einsatzgruppen did their dirty duty there a few weeks ago. We were helpless to even attempt a confrontation. We had no re-enforcements available and they came in under cover of three *Tiger* tanks. They do this every time there is a chance that partisans are lurking about. Was it the same Ignatovka, do you know?"

"Yes," sighed Branko, "the very same. The first time was in 1881. I was six-years-old and hidden under the floorboards. Things don't seem to change for *unsereh.* Crusades, inquisitions, pogroms, and now the SS. What next?"

"That makes you, what, sixty-six?" Simcha responded with a raised eyebrow of incredulity. "I don't believe you, Branko!"

The General was accustomed to this reaction. His military ramrod stiff posture, relatively unlined facial features and only partial graying hair all projected someone a good deal younger.

Getting no discernible reaction, Simcha continued: "Well, anyway, you ask what's next? The Nazis aren't alone. Let us not ignore the eager little helpers. I've been informed that there are four Einsatzgruppen roaming the rear—ranging from the Baltic Sea to the Black. They're complemented by volunteer units from Estonia, Latvia, and Lithuania. The Hungarian, Italian and Romanian divisions accompanying the invasion have been ordered to help round up Jews, Gypsies and any known commissars. While the Hungarians and Romanians happily join in the executions, the macaroni boys have been known to refuse. That's directly countering orders from Mussolini. We believe that the *'talyeners* just don't have the stomach for this. On the other hand, here in the Ukraine, most of the actual shooting is done by local *Zhid*-hating anti-Soviets, police battalions. Never a shortage of willing Jew-killers, eh, Branko?"

"Simcha, in all my years, I've never known such gutless and murderous actions against civilians. Oh, yeah, in the old Empire we were tough on Jews, Gypsies, immigrants, prisoners-of-war... But this—never. I'm still ashamed of the way I've treated my *landsmen* so indifferently at times. No excuse: Just caught-up in the military posturing, I suppose—following orders. I tried to make up for it by joining in with a group of emigrants from Romania, walking to the ports to sail west. That's how I finally emigrated and became an American—1904. God, seems like another lifetime. What about you, Simcha?"

"Big gap between 1904 and today, eh?" Simcha responded. "With me, nothing unusual. Worked as a scheduler for a truck plant in Gorky. My father is a production supervisor. My mother teaches literature in a school for the elite—the party officials' little spoiled shits. I married the daughter of a Jewish petty commissar right before call up in '39. No kids, thank God. She's no doubt worried sick about me, but after a month I was finally able to get word to her after she was told that I was either dead or missing in Rovno."

"Does she know that you're commanding this partisan gang?" Branko asked.

"No, she doesn't. Better that way. I couldn't say much in my message, of course. My parents, my grandparents and two younger brothers were relieved to hear that I'm alive—and for the time being everyone is quite safe, so far east in Gorky."

"Can the krauts be stopped before they reach Moscow? They're rolling pretty fast right now."

"If Moscow falls, who knows what will be," Simcha answered. "When and if that happen. There were rumors that the plant would be removed to Magnitogorsk, deeper into the Urals, or further yet to Tashkent in Uzbekistan."

"Where did you pick-up English," Branko asked, noticing Simcha punctuated his Yiddish with stray English phrases.

"My Yiddish I got from my *zaydeh* and *bubbeh*, my mother's parents who have lived with us since I was a baby. The little English that I use comes from my mother who had been a very proficient student of foreign languages, including French and English. In fact, she taught English at the university in Leningrad before marrying my father. All of this was undoubtedly considered when my unit was given the order to snatch you from the Nazis. Most of my comrades here speak reasonable Yiddish—some more than others. Raisel Ehrenburg, your dance partner, speaks a little English, too. "

Broadly smiling, Branko interjected, "Yeah, I sure as hell noticed that tonight!"

"Well, she's a party member and was a professor of psychology in Siberian Irkutsk before becoming a political officer in the Red Air Force. Her fighter base in Staro Konstantinov was captured early in the fight. She was one of a few who escaped and was directed to join us in August. Probably to keep a wary spy-eye on her fellow Yidden. Eh?"

"Is that the way it is in your Red Army, Simcha?" questioned a puzzled Branko. "Spying on one's comrades?"

"Comrade Stalin's policy," came the answer, "his *Politburo* has always operated that way. There's someone planted in every unit, whether regular army, navy or air force—or partisans. Being a party official she was reluctant to join us. But she's since softened up. Even took to using her Yiddish name, Raisel, for the first time since she was little. She outranks everyone here, a captain to my new lieutenancy. But it was unanimously decided that the men would not look too kindly to taking orders from a female."

Branko was quick to add, "I suppose certainly not in a partisan outfit, eh?"

"Right! Never in a partisan outfit. Command agreed. Raisel undertsood, too. Smart girl."

Hearing Raisel's name, for some reason brought his Rivka to mind. *Rivka. Rivka.* The mere thought of her ricocheted Branko's thoughts from America to Birlad in Romania and the historic march across a hostile Europe. And finally to Rivka, the beautiful *fusgeyer* on that long ago trek.

The exotic one, Branko mused, *the dark eyes, the full lips. Haven't seen her in, what,—fifteen years? Not since she and Sendehr visited in Washington. Heard they moved up to Boston—editor of some ivy-covered literary mag. That suits Sendehr very well. Wonder if she's still writing plays? God, I was in love with that wonder of a woman. Just couldn't tell her—couldn't have done anything to even remotely hurt Sendehr der Shreiber, the writer. Beisdes, what would Rivka have wanted with a vagabond like me, anyway? Just watching those two—there was so much love there. Her beautiful eyes were for Sendehr only. When she introduced me to Miriam in New York, I felt like that was part of her. Maybe that's why I married her and stayed too damn long.*

Branko suddenly realized he had fallen silent during his reverie. To Simcha he now said, "Sorry. This old man is ready to drop off, I'd say. Haven't had this much excitement since my drunken driver crashed the staff car. But that's another story."

"Tomorrow begins in just a few hours," Simcha said. "Some of us are moving out before daybreak.

Simcha was caught up in his own thoughts: Now that the front had moved beyond the Dnieper he needed to use the radio to confirm any new plans. With Kiev up in flames, he knew retaliation was sure to come.

But from whom? he wondered. *Vehr vaist? Who the hell knows?*

Simcha snapped out of his own momentary lapse and smiled at Branko.

"Goodnight, Branko Horvitch."

"Goodnight, Simchaleh Greenberg, my knight in shining armor. Thanks for saving this old boy's *tuchus.*"

Two goodnights, two grins, two chuckles, two men soon to witness two of history's bloodiest days unfold before their very eyes.

Agonizingly frustrating. Helpless. Completely so.

SOJOURNING 4

Birlad, Romania
January 3, 1904 (2100 hours)

Retired Sergeant-Major Branko Horvitch, formerly of the 19th Austrian Cavalry, enjoyed wielding the hammer and tongs once again. His reputation as the district's most efficient farrier had caught on as quickly as when he worked in Bulgaria and Sarajevo.

Avrum Leventer couldn't have been more pleased at having the strapping ex-soldier working in his blacksmith shop. However, his joy was drastically tempered by knowing that the arrangement was temporary. Mordecai Anieloff, who had arranged for the job, made it clear that when *Fusgeyer* Contingent #4 left for America in the spring, Branko would be in their ranks.

When Branko had first walked into the Birlad *shul*, seeking out Mordecai on a *Shabbos* near *Chanukah*, he learned that more was known about him than expected. Shimon Katz's letter had been glowing in terms of the now famous meeting on the Tisza. Many of the *Fusgeyers* thought for sure that the *groisseh soldat* embodied the historical feats of Samson molded into one super-human being. Not even Bar Kochba or the Duke of Wellington rated such acclaim.

For them, the towering Branko was a mysterious stranger appearing out of the west. His mustachioed stature, greater than the tallest among them, was enhanced by his jet-black clothing: a broad-brimmed *csikos* hat, ankle-length great-coat and shiny cavalry boots. Carrying a large canvas bag while meandering through the quiet provincial outpost, he was a singularly imposing figure. Among many of the less sophisticated—and gullible—locals, it was whispered that Branko was some sort of pagan or spectral alien. This began, simply enough, because of a habitual drunkard.

It was a cold, snowy winter's eve one week after Branko's arrival. Riding one of Leventer's horses through town, his route took him by a drunkard exiting Corniescu's Tavern. The drunk looked up and saw a massive figure in black astride a black horse.

Branko

Falling to his knees in the snow, the drunk began to vociferously pray. He was certain the dark apparition was Father Death on horseback, waiting to take him to the devil.

"Yi, yi, yi," he shamelessly beseeched the Almighty, "forgive me—forgive me, sweet Jesus! I'll not ever take another drink! Have pity on me, dear Lord…"

Branko just rode on, not understanding what the poor wretch had been blubbering. The only witness, young Stefan Corniescu—the tavern owner's illegitimate son—merely passed along what he had seen. From there the story grew into rumors darkened ten-fold by superstitions run amok.

"The Jews have hired a fugitive killer to escort them to America," went one of the beginning rumors. From that there evolved a narrative that Branko was a soldier of fortune and private watchdog for which the Jews were paying big money. Others whispered that he was fashioning weapons in Leventer's shop.

"I saw him," one man breathlessly claimed, "he was forging gun barrels, by Jesus—long gun barrels!"

All of this culminated with an exclusionary official statement issued by St. Sophia's stoic Father Mihai from the Sunday pulpit in the district's largest Romanian Orthodox congregation. While the local magistrate, Captain Petra Polinou, stood alongside nodding approval, the diabolical fool claiming service to Christ spewed forth, spittle flying: "We are now certain that the man called Branko is masquerading as their messiah! The Jews will believe anything as long as it means their salvation without having to accept Our Lord Jesus! For all we know, the man could very well be the AntiChrist! We forbid any of you to talk with him—just stay away from his evil realm, do you hear me? Stay away or God will surely punish you to rot in hell!"

Branko hardly qualified as even a poor substitute for the Messiah. Nevertheless, his mere presence caused more excitement and controversy on that one day than the Yidden of Birlad had experienced since the false pogrom scare of 1899. At that time, while the treacherous Yash pogrom was in its third day, an escaping stripling of thirteen rode a stolen horse through every community between the beleaguered city and Birlad. Like a Jewish Paul Revere, he bellowed out the warning that the *pogromchiks* were coming, out to slaughter every living Jew in the border provinces. The lad announced that the genocide would be aided and abetted by the military.

While the slaughter never came to pass, the overhanging threat was an impetus to increased emigration. Shortly thereafter the initial *Fusgeyers* left from Yash and the first contingent, formed in the Birlad district, departed the next spring. The *Fusgeyer* phenomenon was like wildfire and over the next decade hundreds of groups emanated from the impoverished, boycotted and repressed Jewish communities throughout Eastern Romania, Russia's Bessarabia and Austro-Hungarian Bucovina.

Mordecai Anieloff was a sensitive and worldly young gentleman. Still mourning the tragic child-birth deaths of his young wife and son, he threw himself into the hard work and responsibilities of leading the contingent. He also quickly identified some of the potential problems represented by the mere presence of Branko. In order to keep in line with the tacit *Fusgeyer* creed, the 1904 Birladers unanimously agreed on two major points.

First, to garner recognition by powerful Western nations, their march would be a peaceful demonstration to protest the treatment of Jews by the Romanian government. This would be punctuated by flying the Theodor Herzl-designed Mogen Dovid Zionist flag. Heretofore, every group that had the audacity to fly "that rag of a Jew flag" had met with a wide range of hostile and ugly confrontations. While neither deaths nor serious injuries were ever recorded, the temporary imprisonments and other anxious moments were examples of what these young Jews could expect en route to ports. As a matter of political expediency, they would also fly the flags of countries through which they passed—Romania, Hungary, Austria and Germany. As had past contingents, they would also fly the Austro-Hungarian Empire Hapsburg emblem while transiting its prominent domain.

The second major point on which the 1904 Birlader *Fusgeyers* agreed was the most contentious: That they would carry no weapons —none visible, at any rate. And here lay the conflict: An ex-soldier might pay lip service to these points, but would he not try to circumvent them somehow? Mordecai did not have to convince any of his committee chairs that this would be an ongoing concern during the journey. Nonetheless, he advised them to be even more vigilant. Privately Mordecai knew that the more mature members of his cadre were eminently thankful that the "evil man in black" was to accompany them.

In early February, Branko took a short leave from his job, rode a passenger wagon to Galatz, boarded the Odessa Express train and spent a few days with Shayndl, Berel and the children. This was his first visit in several years.

When Berel announced that the family was seriously thinking of joining a colony of Russian Jews in Palestine, Branko did his best to convince them to emigrate to America. On *Shabbos*, in *shul*, the local Jewish Agency representative roundly chastised Branko for blatantly trying to counter-influence his recruits.

"You can go straight to Hell," Branko responded impolitely, "which is next door to Palestine anyway!"

Embarrassed, Shayndl grabbed Branko by the arm and they left before the *torah* reading even started.

"I apologize, Tante Shayndl," Branko said, once they were out in the steet. "But that self-serving, pompous *mumzeh* is simply not telling the realities you face in that God-forsaken place. He looks at me as a traitor to the Zionist cause for going to America, but he's inexcusably deceiving his potential recruits He's all pomegranates and honey—no mention of mosquitoes, malaria or Arabs and Turks

"Bracheleh, you're still a little boy," his aunt said. "*Oy, vay iz mir!* Aryeh Levinsky is such a nice man. He and his wife went with the first organized groups more than twenty-five years ago. Now he recruits new colonists throughout the Ukraine twice every year. Berel is enamored with the idea. I still am not sold, but we have to go—well, somewhere."

"Yes, Tante, but somewhere where a decent existence awaits," Branko responded.

Tante Shayndl's growing dilemma had been exacerbated when the aftermath of the Kishinev pogrom struck too close to home the previous week, following months of disturbing little flare-ups in and around Odessa. This especially unsettling incident was an attack on her street. Two of her friend's husbands and her grocery man were severely beaten and robbed by a gang of thugs, shouting, "Here's a taste of Kishinev for you!" At the time, a constable standing less than fifty-meters away turned his back and walked into a saloon.

This spike in the escalating violence only underscored the need to move. Shayndl was concerned that perhaps they were being hasty in their choice of destinations—due to Berel's affinity for Aryeh Levinsky and his Palestine movement. At this point in her life she certainly didn't want to jump into a more difficult daily struggle such as Branko had described in Palestine, but they were running out of time and hadn't considered other options.

At just over forty years of age, Shayndl had aged softly. Even after five children she still had a youthful figure and a regal face. She bore an uncanny resemblance to the handsome Czarina Alexandra, whose husband was a household word in the cosmopolitan, polyglot Odessa—*mumzeh*. Life had been kind to her, she knew, and she feared the future was not nearly as promising as had been the past.

She realized Branko was justified in his concern and that he wanted only the best for her, Berel and the children. They were, after all, his only family since that calamitous morning in 1881. Branko was understandably anxious that the family make the right move now. She too, was anxious.

The remainder of the brief visit was a pleasant one. Dovid, now twenty, had been unable to find adequate work in the severely de-pressed Odessa economy. Nonetheless, the handsome youth was courting one of his former classmates and a wedding was in the offing. Under these circumstances, even Palestine was looking good to him. The girl's concerned parents, however, were opposed to such *narishkeit*.

Dovid and Branko were able to fit in some private chats, but the young cousin's plans continued to lean eastward regardless of whether his parents were also going to *"mach aliyah"* to "go up to the Holy Land." He blanched at Branko's mild suggestions regarding emigration to America. Dovid was visibly frightened at such a prospect.

"I've been told that hundreds of immigrant Jews are murdered in New York every day," Dovid said. "There are police-sponsored hooligan gangs and the younger ones like me are kidnapped. They're sent to work in the coal mines and wheat fields in the west."

No matter what Branko thought of the wily Levinsky's underhanded salesmanship, if nothing else the agent had been convincing—especially to the young.

At twenty-one Channah looked exactly like her pretty mother, Shayndl. Channah's betrothed was comfortably entrenched in his father's imported spice and tea business. Despite worsening conditions the two planned to stay in Odessa. Seventeen-year-old Raisel and the two younger girls would remain with Shayndl and Berel wherever they finally decided to settle.

And so it went for most of the families throughout the hopeless Pale of 1904. Each of the downtrodden millions faced the agonizing dilemmas of separation through emigration or the critical decision to endure continuing acts of terror. The inevitable parting was the saddest of all, no one knowing when and where, if ever, they would meet again.

This was personalized for Branko as he prepared to board the train for the return trip to Birlad. Shayndl wept in his arms at the Odessa train depot. Managing a tear-filled wink, Branko smiled at a fidgeting Berel, saying, "See you in America, my dear uncle!"

"Not likely, nephew Bracheleh. *L'shana haba'ah b'Yerushalayim!* Perhaps we'll see you next year—with the help of God, in Jerusalem. *Omayn!*"

Leaving Birlad, Romania
March 31, 1904 (2330 hours)

Branko was unable to sleep. Tomorrow was the day of departure and his responsibilities never felt heavier. At one time or another nearly every parent had cornered Branko to solicit his personal assurance. They came, whether he was sweating at the blacksmith forge, at the *shul*, in the marketplace or wherever else in town he could be found. They came to him for their sons, daughters, nieces, nephews and grandchildren. They sought the promises in the mellow tones of his comforting words: *Of course I'll keep a special eye on your son…your daughter…your nephew…your niece…your grandchild—you can count on that…*

Comparing notes, Branko and Mordecai had found that the same parents, uncles, aunts and grandparents had sought assurance from them both. With Branko being the stalwart *soldat* and Mordecai the trusted leader, who else would they have come to? Even Rabbi Nachman—in a more sweeping sense—asked Branko to show his cavalryman's posture and strength in dealing with expected adversities during the forthcoming trek.

All of these concerned Jews of Birlad looked upon Branko Horvitch as *The Grand Protector*. The mantle sat excruciatingly heavy on his broad shoulders that night. Just before midnight he wearily took up his pen and began a letter to Shayndl. There was barely enough ink left in the well for anything more than a brief epistle.

Dear Tante Shayndl,

In a few hours we'll be marching out of Birlad and westward to a new life in America. It pains me to think that if Berel insists you will be going the other way before this year is out. Please tell Berel to reconsider. If America does not appeal to him then even Germany or France or England would be a better choice. You must leave Odessa and the Pale as soon as possible and I know you're trying to convince Dovidl and Channah to do the same.

The talk of revolution and another student uprising does not bode well. The Yash papers concede that the Czar's days are numbered and who knows what will be if chaotic anarchy arrives. One way or the other, the Zhid will be the loser. The whole uprising will be blamed on unsereh Yidden, successful or not.

You must leave, Tante. You must, and if it's to be Palestine, I wish you my very best. May God watch over all of you. Give everyone my love and hugs,

Your devoted plimenik,
Branko

Note: To remind you, letters can be sent to me at various postal offices during our journey. On the list and dates I gave you, please copy the following as an example of how to address the letters.. Do not use the Russian or the Yiddish-Hebrew letters. Print exactly as I've done:

Branko Horvitch	*Branko Horvitch*
Prejeszd, 11 June 1904	*Ehrkezes, 7 May 1904*
A Posta Centrum Praha	*A Posta Centrum*
Bohmen Osterreich	*Budapest, Hungray*
Branko Horvitch	*Branko Horvitch*
Onkommen, 2 July 1904	*Onkommen, 28 May 1904*
Postahmpt Central Berlin	*Postahmpt Central*
Prussa Duetschland	*Wien, Osterreich*

The inkwell ran dry just as Branko finished writing the postal instructions. Instead of pointlessly attempting sleep, he put on his long great-coat and walked out of the small cubicle attached to the blacksmith shop. The night air was more than just brisk, with a north wind whipping up a stinging swath. Thinking the night air would clear his overflowing mind, he decided to stroll into the thick wooded groves that closely bordered the Jewish quarter of Birlad.

By the time he had crossed over the footbridge behind the glass-blowing shop where Mordecai worked, he had mulled over everything that had been festering there, but the thinking apparatus moved on relentlessly.

What do they expect from me? That I should wrap everyone up in a cocoon and spirit them away to America? Mordecai is the leader and I shall only do my duty as Chairman of Security and Defense—nothing more, nothing less. I'll be there. I'll be watching everything. I'll make suggestions. I'll deal with the enemy using my German and Hungarian language skills. I'll play my Army release papers to full advantage in dealing with the military. I'll help Mordecai safely shepherd the Fusgeyers all the way to America. I'll do my job well—just as I served the Emperor with honor and distinction. It is not within me to anything less…

He felt relieved with this purge of his gray matter. But by the time he reached his return path, a cascade of old thoughts came back.

Why do these crazy boychicks insist on flying the Mogen Dovid? Damn! That's asking for trouble. I can't talk them out of it and they have a point, I suppose. If you're going to protest and demonstrate, then, by God in heaven, protest and demonstrate! At least they'll be flying the other flags. Maybe that will help soften things up a bit.

Gevalt! I know how badly my comrades reacted when the Muslim protesters flew the Turkish crescent in Mostar. Me, too! I can just imagine the repercussions when some highly-bigoted Austrian, Prussian, Hungarian or Romanian patrol encounters sixty Jews marching with the Mogen Dovid flying in the breeze.

Out of deference to me, my men were a shade less than their usual brusque selves when we came across Shimon Katz's Fusgeyers. Perhaps that's why there were no incidents. The mumzerim wouldn't dare! I wonder how they would have acted under different circumstances—under a different sergeant. I can just imagine. I heard plenty of barracks talk about the treatment of nomadic, emigrating refugees, Gypsies, Jews, Slavs and the like. I wasn't the picture of kindness myself at times—too many times.

Oh, God! Maybe I should have gone on to America without trying to be a hero! Too late now. At least I talked them out of using a horse or a jackass to pull the wagon. Stupid idea! Obviously none of them are horse lovers. After looking over the flea-bitten nag that old man Mandelbaum was going to donate I knew they'd have a dead animal on their hands before they saw Hungary. Would have been cruel. Of course, A little schlepping won't hurt these yinglach one bit.

    The Golubs. My new troopers. Oy gevalt! Rough as raw lumber. Yankel is trying so hard to be accepted. "You need a good blanket, Branko?" he says and within the hour there he stands with a heavy woolen blanket. "You need a pillow, Branko?" he says and here he comes with a pillow. Where he gets everything, I'm afraid to ask. I just wish he would stop standing at attention and saluting. I've got to stop saluting back. The three brothers could be a problem in a tight spot.

    There is not a sign of self-discipline in any of them. Little did I know that I would still be in the business of training troops. The Golubs will be a challenge until the moment we dump them onto the streets of America! Where are they going? Oh, yeah, sounds like "Skrentin, Pantsilwania" or such. Yankel told me they have an uncle there. But, Yankeleh is such a good-natured person. A shtarkeh, aber a guteh. Yoni and Yossi are cut from the same rough cloth, too, in many ways. So naïve, so innocent. At times, so infuriating. But what can I do? They're my defense squad, for better or for worse. I, for one, will follow the rules. For them, I cannot swear. Their father says that they were each known as trouble-makers in cheder. I can believe it. Mordecai assigned the Golub boys to me for that reason, I'm sure. Better he gave me some people less brawny, more brainy!

    Six maidelach. Good God, what are we doing? Imagine if they had ever given me six woman troopers. Mashugah, they would have driven all of us. I can't say that I'm not happy with Rivka. There's a woman for you! She'll be no problem. With her, her eyes alone can drive someone mad. They're like two shiny, black pools in the Gan Eden. But, woe is me, she's already partial to der shreiber. That Sendehr probably doesn't know it, but those dark eyes seem to be flashing in his direction all the time. He with his maps, his poetry, his writing from morning till night. Let me tell you, that will be some *complete journal he keeps. There's a bright lad, all right. He won't get lost in America... and I'm sure Rivkeleh will be right alongside him. A zay geht dos, vos vill zein, vill zein. And so it goes. What will be, will be!*

When the bell in the church steeple-clock struck one. Branko was shaken out of his reverie and retraced his steps to the stable and hut. He was resigned to what was left of a frigid and sleepless night—his last in Birlad.

As morning came, an entirely new set of circumstances awaited the Emperor's former horse soldier: fifty-nine eager young Birladers, each with absolutely no idea of the difficult road ahead or at their destination.

Or as Yankel Golub had innocently and frequently asked, and would continue to ask a thousand times, "America? Will it be good or bad for the Jews?"

*****

Overlooking the Ravine at Babi Yar
September 29, 1941 (0600 hours)

Simcha was well-prepared for sunrise. Before leaving the campsite he ordered that all gun barrels should be wrapped in rags. This prevented their being revealed by glinting in the sunlight. For that same reason he reminded the three-member task force to leave behind anything metal.

Branko smiled knowingly at the efficiency shown by the young and relatively inexperienced Greenberg. Although Branko was a tactical expert and practical veteran who didn't need reminding, he had insisted on being included: He wanted, he said, "to experience a partisan unit at work."

The leader had reluctantly agreed, politely observing that, "the old man was exceptionally fit to participate."

"I have no idea what this mission is all about," complained the young leader. "Appears to be nothing more than an observation exercise. But in these past two months, since our unit was accepted by the High Command, I've guessed wrong more often than not. If it turns into a fire-fight, a dangerous engagement, or I—"

"There, there, *boychick*," the American interrupted, "I've been at a few of those little tea parties in my time. Anyway, how many units can boast that they have a Brigadier General on their staff?"

"Retired, *tatehla,* retired," mockingly replied the commander.

The 0430 radio transmission giving rise to the mission had been matter-of-fact in every sense. As was usual no one knew from where it originated. The protocol required transmitting teams to move several times a day in order to avoid detection by Nazi range-finders. Nevertheless, even with such precautions the longevity for a radioman was not to be envied. Executions were swift and ignoble.

"Maccabee leader, Maccabee leader, stand by: You are to take a small force, no more than five, to the forested hills overlooking coordinates 112 and 239. Be there by 0630. It is imperative that you remain undiscovered. Do not engage. Repeat, do not engage. Report on everything you see throughout today. Do not leave your position until sunset. Before leaving, eliminate all traces of your presence and then move to coordinates 113 and 260. Dah sveedanaya, tovarisch. Out."

As with all Partisan units, the orders were transmitted one-way. There was rarely an opportunity to ask questions, seek instructions or receive clarification. Coordinates were coded so as to avoid jeopardizing the action missions. The few ethnically-homogeneous partisan groups were usually given the most dangerous—often suicidal—assignments. The two units in the Tetratev River marshes were practically decimated by mid-September while Simcha's Maccabees remained at full complement. They were strong, mobile and relatively unscathed while adding armed volunteers to their ranks daily.

Lev Soloveitchik, the unit's premier sniper, was Simcha's choice for the mission. Perhaps it was a premonition that marksmanship would be invaluable. The long-bearded Lev, a scarecrow of a man, had been the bookkeeper for a predominantly Jewish collective farm near Rovno. His visibly-shortened club foot had rendered him unfit for Red Army duty. But when the armored Nazi Panzers swept through Rovno, overwhelming Russian defenses, he took to the forests with his family and comrades.

By the time Lev fled to the forests, the reports of massacres were rampant throughout the Western Ukraine. This was the birth of the "scorched earth" policy which preceded the march of the invading hordes through the Motherland. Crops, farmhouses, barns, manufacturing plants—were all put to the torch and rendered valueless to the victor.

There was the usual tearful departure when Lev placed his wife and three youngsters onto the last retreating supply truck. By a stroke of fate the driver was the former manager of a neighboring collective farm. Even though now a soldier, the former manager couldn't refuse another friendly farmer from the past. With his own family stashed among the burlap bags of grains and rice, the harried soldier/trucker motioned for Lev to quickly put his brood onboard.

That had been in the middle of August and at the edge of an expansive tract of thick woodlands near Klementov. It was also the last Lev had heard of his family. His wife's parents were in far-off Rostov, and of course, the goal was for her to reach them. The sad and troubled Lev prayed twice a day that they would find safety where they were going.

After joining up with the Maccabees, Lev quickly developed into an uncanny marksman. With or without a scope, he demonstrated an unmatchable accuracy when squeezing the hair-trigger of his captured German Mauser. The week before Branko's rescue, Lev stunned the unit by dropping two SS pistoleers from 150 meters. The unit had come across the soldiers at the bank of the Dnieper river, ten kilometers north of besieged Kiev. Lev's successive shots came just as the pistoleers were to execute two Soviet agents they had captured behind-the-lines. For sheer coordination alone, the operation was something at which to marvel. As a speed-launch rounded the river bend, Lev's shots found their marks. The disbelieving agents leapt into the river, and swam to the wildly-waving rescuers approaching off-shore. Simultaneously, the slain twosome's stunned driver gunned his auto and sped to the riverside highway.

Simcha, Alyosha the sailor, and Kostya the Konotop heavyweight boxer, proudly patted Lev's back in congratulations for the most spectacular shots they had ever witnessed—or even heard of. But the sure-shot, serious Lev was only thinking of the driver who got away. This was the cool, unflappable, eagle-eyed sharpshooter every partisan commander fantasized for his ranks.

This particular spot along the Dnieper had been used daily by SS executioners who then cast the bodies into the river. The invader was certain to change venues after this remarkable and frightening display of partisan marksmanship. Vengeful *Zhid* partisans, at that.

Alyosha Alterman, the fleet-of-foot sailor, was a better than fair marksman himself. He was a veteran of several assignments alongside Lev and Simcha had selected him to join the mission. A native son of Kiev, Alyosha's general knowledge of the terrain was welcome on any assignment in the region.

While he could barely swim a decent stroke, he had been impressed into naval duty six months before the war began. His military service was a part of the effort to shore up a dangerous shortage of manpower in the fleet of gunboats patrolling the Dnieper River.

As it turned out, the Nazi airborne blitz during the early June softening-up processes obliterated more than half the Russian Navy tonnage. When his forty year-old vessel was sent to the bottom near the widened reservoir portion of Chernobyl's Dnieper River, Alyosha was one of the few to survive. Suffering shrapnel wounds and covered in oil, he struggled with an awkward dog-paddle for over two kilometers. Upon reaching the river's north forested shore, he collapse from near exhaustion.

With his strength nearly gone, he managed to rip the shreds of his striped, naval-issued undershirt and use it for tourniquet-tight bandages. This, coupled with the mud and oil mixture, served well as a wound covering poultices and stemmed his loss of blood. The spunky nineteen-year-old spent the next two days in and out of consciousness while immersed in a never-never reverie. When he finally came to his senses, he began laboriously making his way along one of the Dnieper tributaries. Gnawing on raw sugar beets afforded him enough energy to keep moving and helped offset the dehydration caused by vomiting the very brackish water on which he was forced to rely.

There wasn't that much left of him by the time he approached the unharmed city of Chernobyl. The one thing that had survived—even strengthened—was his determination to avoid going back into the ill-equipped, step child, the Red Navy. This dilemma was solved when he was approached by an older, broad-shouldered, paunchy man near the Chernobyl prefecture building.

His name was Kostya Polinoff and he was on a supply-seeking mission—*shnorring*. A moderately successful heavyweight boxer, Polinoff was unable to pull off the nondescript appearance he tried to project. But what he lacked in ability he made up for with mercy. After listening to Alyosha's feebly concocted story, he invited him to accompany him to an all *Zhid* partisan unit.

It had still been the surviving sailor's lucky day.

At 0600 they were a full kilometer from their destination of the thick birch and maple groves. Checking his watch, Simcha ordered the men to dismount and secure their horses. The rest of the way, he told them, would be on foot.

Ahead of them, high atop the northern edge of the steep ravine were the unkempt grounds of the evacuated Pavlov Psychiatric Hospital. The hospital had been evacuated weeks before. The deserted facility comprised the only buildings within the idyllic Kirilov Wood. Having grown up in this sparsely inhabited, westernmost sector of Kiev, Alyosha recommended the nearby ruins of a 12th century chapel as an ideal observation post: Not a soul or vehicle would be in sight. The chapel ruins offered the added benefit of being a hundred meters closer to the ravine's edge while heavily-camouflaged by the trees and early autumn foliage.

"This is called Babi Yar, Simcha," Alyosha explained. "We played hereabouts when I was a child. Now, what in hell are we doing here today? There is nothing of military importance anywhere near here

"Apparently not so, dear Alyosha. Here, take my binoculars. Scan the area below and tell me what you see."

Alysoha scanned the area with the binoculars. "Hmmm... Four Nazi trucks. A squad of rifleman. No gun emplacements. Nothing rimming the ravine's edges—nothing else within 300 meters."

"Not yet, sailor boy, not yet," answered the leader. Simhca had finally come to grips with the frustrations of never being given the big picture, never being told all of the details—such as those he didn't know even now. He added, "Presumably we're here for a very good strategic purpose. By 0730 we should know, I'd imagine."

Branko took in all of this conversation and thought, *obviously intelligence has word of something vitally important about to take place here. I'd say they're trusting us to be their eyes and ears.* He then said, "Simcha, I've got a terrible feeling that the Einsatzgruppen will have a hand in this. If that turns out to be true, then more than likely *unsereh Yidden* will be part of the equation—and that formula spells a bloodbath."

"I agree, Branko. Let's take up our positions in the ruins before the sun is on a fuller rise."

Lev had preceded the others into the relic of a chapel and laid claim to the best vantage point for sniping. Even though Simcha had said that it wasn't that kind of mission, Lev had already estimated distances and wind factors. He could, after all, always hope against hope. Having not pulled the trigger since the Dnieper hits, he had an uneasy feeling that he was getting stale. A message from his missing wife, Tanya and the *kindelach* would set everything right again, he thought. The frustration gnawed at his soul every waking moment.

With canteens full of water or *kvass*—fermented grains—some dried meats, fresh tomatoes and slabs of pungent dark rye to sustain them, the four interloping *provocateurs* settled in for the day. Not knowing any more than they had before setting out from the encampment, they expected activity soon. So, for the next two hours they divided their time between surveys of the area, jokes, war stories and Branko's never-ending adventures.

At precisely 0915 hours Simcha sat upright with a start, binoculars in hand. "*Boychicks*, we have movement. Lots of movement!"

All eyes focused on the sandy ravine below.

Simcha handed the glasses to Branko, with Alyosha and Lev standing by.

"They're civilians, by God, civilians. Yidden, I'll say! Marching by two's, like walking through a gauntlet and—"

Branko's report was abruptly broken by gunfire. The most infamous of all war-time massacres had begun. Branko saw the four pistoleers at the head of the line force the first four bedraggled people to a plank on the edge of the gigantic pit. The shots were point blank executions to the backs of the victims' heads. Each body toppled into oblivion, followed by four more, and then four more yet again.

Branko handed the binoculars to Alyosha for a quick look and he in turned passed them through a quick succession of Lev and Simcha. Suddenly the morning represented a well-worn grimness reminding them of their current lot as hunted renegades with prices on their heads in Nazi-occupied Russia. The immediate anger compounded by their queasy stomachs quickly erased even a hint of disbelief

"Gevalt! Vay iz mir! Now the squad of riflemen are letting twenty through at a time," Simcha reported, from the binoculars. "Lining them up and firing. Shit! A machine gun is being brought in! There! Three more! This is hell on earth. We've got to do *something!* We can't just sit here and watch it happen, for God's sake! God! God! Where the hell are you, God?"

Simcha's blood vessels were all but bursting from his high forehead. He grabbed his weapon. Lev and Alyosha followed suit

All three were suddenly blocked. An equally shaken but self-controlled Branko stood his ground

"Stop it," Branko barked. "Stop it right there! There's not a godamm thing you can do—and you know it. This is pure *narishkeit.* Put the damned rifles down. Do you want to commit suicide? Get hold of yourselves!"

All four men seemed to square off.

Simcha was the first to recover—his reason overcoming the bloodlust of anger. "He's right."

The other two look at their leader.

"He's right," Simcha repeated, lowering his weapon. "I see it now."

The others calmed down.

"There must have been a round-up notice," Simcha went on, leading the others back from blind passion.

"That's right," Branko agreed, seeing that they needed firm assurance.

"We, uh, we've expected this... since the planted bombs on the Kreshchatik went off last week."

Lev and Alyosha were now nodding.

"We know damn well who the Germans blame for that. Our few remaining intelligence blokes found out about it—and we're here to watch. Record. Puke our guts out, if we have to..."

Branko put a steady hand on Simcha's shoulder.

Simcha took a deep breath. "Lets get on with it. If anyone feels they can't do it, I'll understand. Go back to the camp—I'll stay alone if necessary."

No one said a word. Each man went quietly to his observation position. The binoculars were passed from one to the other with little or no conversation. Tears flowed freely. Lev, full to the brim with anxiety, sobbed and everyone knew why. If for any reason his family was caught in the web and brought to Kiev, they might well be in the long lineup of death below them. Alyosha was thinking the same for people he knew thereabouts

Branko had already been through this unspeakable terror, sixty years before and not more than a few kilometers from here. The traumatic memory was still very much alive in the inviolate hollow of his psyche.

Indeed there had been the widely-posted notice that was becoming a dreaded ritual throughout Europe since the outbreak of Hitler's war. It read directly, simply, as they all had. In Warsaw, Amsterdam, Rovno, Lodz, Krakow, L'vov, Minsk, Zhitomir, Berditchev and now, Kiev: Printed on gray paper without heading or signature, the most recent notices were posted throughout the devastated city.

All Zhids living in the city of Kiev and its vicinity are to report by 8 o'clock on the morning of Monday, September 29th, 1941, at the corner of Melnikov and Degtyarev Streets, near the cemetery. You are to take with you, documents, money, valuables, as well as warm clothes and sturdy shoes. Any Zhid not carrying out this instruction and is found elsewhere, will be shot. Any Russian civilian entering flats evacuated by the Zhids, or stealing property, will be shot.

    The text was in bold, Cyrillic-lettered Russian. Just below it, there was the similar Ukrainian dialect translation. This was followed in smaller print by the German version, interspersed with Hebrew-lettered Yiddish phrases.

    The streets were close to both Russian and Jewish cemeteries in the Lukyanovka district, within which was located Babi Yar and the Lukyanovka rail yards. That some of the notices were in proximity to railroad stations led many to believe they were being relocated west, into German-occupied Poland or Germany itself. But there were always those fatalists who, with a shrug of the shoulders, would murmur, "Only God knows where!" Reality came with the foreboding march past the cemeteries and into a narrow corridor between the two sandstone hillocks leading to the ravine. Here they were hemmed-in by a gauntlet of soldiers with vicious German Shepherd dogs and the cooperative, truncheon-armed Ukrainian police units appropriately called *hilfwiligers—willing helpers*. Such men were in eager abundance throughout the conquered territories.

    In short, crisp order, each victim was stripped of possessions—including clothing. They then were shoved to the front of the line, shot in the back of the head and thrown into the deep sand quarry. In the span of a minute or less a life was snuffed out, leaving only clothes and trinkets to be carted-off for sorting in a tent a short distance away.

It was so fast and methodical that few screams were heard. The well-worn phrase, *they never knew what hit them* was never more viscerally demonstrated.

Lest panicked rioting should prevail, the genocide was controlled by limiting the executions to groups of fifty and sixty people. While these manageable groups were slaughtered, thousands of others were held-back at the rail yards, out of earshot and assured of "processing" for relocation. The majority of victims were the elderly, the walking-infirmed and mothers and their children. The fit and hearty Jewish males had either been conscripted into the Red Army, Navy or the civilian defense labor teams before the June invasion.

This, then, was the day-long massacre—the lowest ebb to which humankind sank—that Branko, Simcha, Lev and Alyosha were soul-wrenchingly powerless to prevent. Early on, Simcha asked Branko to keep a count of victims. By noon Branko's ghoulish count was up to 6,000. Six hours later additional machine-gunners had killed 16,000 people. The nightmare continued beyond sunset with 24,000 Kiev Jews cold-bloodedly slain: They later learned that nearly 10,000 more died in the same way the following day.

When the heart-broken Simcha called for withdrawal of his emotionally exhausted men, none of them noticed Lev Soloveitchik lingering behind. He had positioned himself within the intact chapel dome—mocked, as it were, by the centuries-old faded frescoes depicting God's love. With darkness falling fast, he shouldered his weapon and painstakingly took aim. He briefly waited and then calmly, amid the covering sounds of machine-pistols, squeezed the Mauser's trigger. A Ukrainian policeman catapulted backward into the very sand pit piled high with the innocent dead.

The other three men froze. Branko was the first to recover and swung up the binoculars to scan for reprisals. As Lev came down the path moments later, Branko was still squinting into the darkening ravine below.

"Damned-fool stunt," Branko growled and lowered the binoculars. He glanced at the others. "But timed damned-well. Now we can go."

Simcha breathed a sigh of relief and warmly embraced Lev.

The sharpshooter gave an understanding nod of accomplishment.

He looked over and nodded an acknowledgment to Branko and Alyosha—both of whom were giving him a thumbs-up of approval.

The return ride was under the silence of darkness and over barren fields of recently scorched earth. Within a few hours they were challenged by the vigilant camouflaged sentinel of the muddy lane skirting their new base of operations.

The men were hard-pressed to tell their story and even the most battle-hardened of the unit wept—many beating their breasts while swearing bitter words of revenge.

That night, none of the shaken witnesses could sleep much—if at all. They instead lay awake amid the sweet smell of the pines engulfing the campsite and the death that seized their memories. They also thought of the the Nazi front— now thirty kilometers beyond Kiev—and the rear echelon troops that would be on heightened alert for the growing number of partisan units roaming the Western Ukraine.

Many of the assembled partisans had kin in Kiev who had been unable or unwilling to escape to the east when it had still been possible. Some of those kin, no doubt, were among the incredible number of Soviet Jews who naively thought the Germans were the lesser of two evils. The similar phenomenon had been even more prevalent among the three million Jews in neighboring Poland. The Jews of Poland had cultivated relatively fond memories of their more passive German occupiers during the previous war. The least literate among them had not since seriously considered the highly indicative actions of Herr Hitler from 1923 onward. The most ominous harbinger had been the sweeping statements made in *Mein Kampf— My Struggle*. It had been but a mere precursor of Hitler's less than paternalistic treatment of Jews in the other occupied countries, including Czechoslovakia, France and Poland. Certainly word had to have reached Kiev concerning the Einsatzgruppen shooting sprees in Rovno, Vilna, Minsk, Zhitomir and other Ukrainian, Lithuanian and White Russian cities

It would now be all-out guerrilla warfare.

But it was only the intensity of the battles that was expected to change. The invaders were still better equipped and if anything, more brutal. And they were having such a shockingly easy time of it that most of them would gladly trade places with their front-line comrades in the front lines, where, if anything, they were having a shockingly easy time of it. With their bold armored divisions on the roll, they were penetrating the Soviet lines with an invigorated heady demeanor. Radio commentators and all the journalists throughout the anti-fascist world waited impatiently for the Red Army to re-invent itself as a force to be reckoned with. To this point, there was only widespread disbelief and head-shaking disappointment in London and Washington, where many had been led to believe that the mighty Soviet military was near-invincible.

*****

Washington, D.C.
United States of America
September 30, 1941

"Harry, I'm becoming mighty impatient waiting for that report from Donovan. Where the hell is it and what in blue blazes is taking so long?"

"Mr. President, I'll phone Bill again this morning, but I'm sure I'll get his usual side-stepping. As you know, the man's a master at these cloak and dagger games."

The cigarette smoke curled around the commander-in-chief, and the Oval Office was once again covered with a nicotine-filled cloud. Harry Hopkins' cigar, on which he usually vigorously chewed, contributed only a minor amount to the tobacco odor. As the diminutive aide stood to take his leave, he assured the "boss" that he would keep after Wild Bill Donovan until he coughed up the demanded report.

"Look here, Harry, you know that the sensitivity of this issue has the potential of blowing-up in our faces. The United States, and I might add, this bumbling President, will look like rank amateurs if that happens. Laughing stocks? You bet your bottom dollar!

Hopkins, his hand on the door knob, turned and offered a parting promise. "I'll put the fear of God up his keester, Mr. President."

"See that y'do, Harry. I'm beginning to have second thoughts on this whole damn spy business we're getting into. I know we've got the best in Bill, but the man is such an independent cuss. I'm sure he knows how much influence General Horvitch has in this town—if we lose him that could be problem for the party.

"I've made that abundantly clear, Mr. President."

"We'll be crucified if that maniacal Berlin crowd grabs him again. By God, we'll be dragged into that European mess sooner or later—and I'd rather it be later. Mark my words, though, it will happen."

Hopkins was bobbing his head that he understood, but the President wasn't finished making the point: He went on, "Meanwhile, I've got to deal with the pesky Japs. And now, with the new premier, Tojo, and his military henchmen in full control of that damned warmongering government, he's sending over an envoy next month. Probably full of outrageous demands. By the way, didn't you tell Eleanor that this third term would be 'a piece of cake' after those eight nightmare years?"

It was true—Hopkins had indeed said that very thing to the President's wife. But if he had learned anything as a trouble-shooting confidante and advisor to this man and his unusual love-hate relationship with the public, it was the gentle diplomacy of silence. And so he forced a smile, turned and quickly walked out of the smoke-filled command center.

Hopkins sported more hats than a busy restaurant hat rack. Not only was he still admirably performing as a lame-duck Secretary of Commerce, but his old mentor and friend had recently saddled him with guiding the newly-introduced *Lend Lease Act*. With the fierce opposition among the isolationists at prey in Congress, "America First" and its clones had become a force with which to reckon—a festering thorn in FDR's backside. Now the "boss" had sent him to do battle with an old war-horse like Major General Wild Bill Donovan. Not that Hopkins wasn't more than obliquely involved with the brewing Horvitch fiasco.

With the recent successful funding hearings over, General Donovan was deep in the throes of efficiently organizing his proposed Office of Strategic Services. A mere month after a Senate Committee appointed him to "coordinate defense information for intelligence gathering" Donovan was forming the O.S.S. But his "cart before the horse" actions of sending his trusted, old army friend to the USSR on a critical fact-finding mission had nearly wrecked him—and the entire administration. Timoshenko's cable of the 25th reported that Branko was rescued from the Nazis and in safe, partisan hands. Arrangements for his delivery to Moscow, would take time, given the logistics involving the Red Army's current and desperate attempts to shore up their defenses. Another fly in the ointment was that Stalin had placed the aggressive General Timoshenko as general in charge of Moscow's defensive stand.

None of this was at all comforting to Donovan, the revered hero of the Great War. It all sounded rather like a last ditch effort with Timoshenko taking on the all-consuming responsibility in defending Moscow, against all odds. That sort of thing didn't sit well with the President and a tongue-lashing in the Oval Office was something everyone wished to avoid.

Hopkins knew it was quite possible that *Wild Bill*—as he was endearingly called by Americans since his derring-do exploits in 1918 France—had been immensely enjoying all of this attention before the Horvitch incident became ugly. Had the entire fiasco went through the President for approval, Hopkins would not now be bearing the brunt of political repercussions. The problem had been one of timing: Hopkins had agreed to clear the plan with the "boss" when discussing his added responsibility of the Lend Lease political hot potato. But the Horvitch operation went sour before Hopkins was able to discuss it with the President. And then, when Roosevelt heard about everything —after the fact—he was a lot more than just miffed at being by-passed.

It didn't help matters that the President also had an inherent mistrust of Branko Horvitch: It was because of the General's partiality to Republicans during his service as White House Building and Grounds Superintendent under Harding and Coolidge. Considering that his previous position fast tracked Horvitch's generalship, it was understandable that FDR could not now consider Horvitch as having merited a rank originally appointed during the former Wilson administration. Roosevelt had scoffed at the idea, calling it, "one of Mrs. Wilson's female emotional moves while the President was totally incapacitated."

And Roosevelt was partly right. There was no doubt that the appointment was tinged with an element of favoritism on the part of Mrs. Wilson. But FDR considered it politically dubious at best—a reservation unsupported by Branko's performance.

After leaving the oval office, Hopkins stopped in to see Donovan. He didn't bother to call ahead as usual and dropped in his office unannounced.

The roller-coaster of the Horvitch affair was on at the forefront of both men's minds and without preamble Donovan said, "Harry, I expect to hear something positive from Timoshenko—if not from Branko himself—momentarily. I'd prefer to wait a day or two before sending my report to the Chief."

"General, that won't do, and you know it. The Boss'll hang me first, and then have you shot. Or worse, he'll have you take a team into the USSR and attempt to rescue Horvitch yourself."

"Hell," Donovan, came back, "he's already been rescued by the partisans! He wouldn't have us re-rescue him."

"I wouldn't be too sure. If I were Wild Bill Donovan 'hero to millions, legend in our time' and all that tripe, I'd buy heavy mackinaws, sweaters and galoshes. Damned cold and heavy snows in Russia come October and November."

"Who the hell ever said that Harry Lloyd Hopkins was devoid of humor."

Hopkins only smiled. He didn't bother to recount the list of people thinking he was humorless: The First Lady, Senators Wheeler, Nye, Holt, and Secretary of State "old man" Cordell Hull. In fact, Treasury Secretary Henry Morgenthau had once remarked that Hopkins was so stoically dull that he had actually died and everyone had forgotten to tell him.

"Seriously, though, Harry, no one has really understood the objectives and I think I should clarify them. After all, if *you* don't understand it, neither does the boss.

"Fair enough," Hopkins agreed, sitting on one of the office sofas.

"When I was approached by Secretary Henry Stimson, it was rather mundane: Set up a so-called defense information system. I understood that to mean a spying operation. Frankly, the thing needed to be called *something* more definitive and so I named it—that's how we got to *The Office of Strategic Services*. That's exactly what it is—a spying, cat-and-mouse, cloak-and-dagger, agent-and-double-agent, covert operation."

Hopkins knew Donovan had just greatly simplified the gestation of the OSS, and that was typical of his disdain for political posturing. But Donovan's enthusiasm for his new hatchling, the OSS, was blatantly obvious to the Secretary of Commerce as he sat watching the man's face. Hopkins even had a fleeting thought that Donovan was about to admit to being the proverbial kid in the candy shop: There was little doubt that the man loved his spy-craft.

"But this is all-out war, Harry," Donovan was now saying. We'll be up to our balls in it sooner than anyone in Congress thinks. I know that FDR shares this opinion, too. If the Germans don't force us into it, the Japs sure as hell will. We're like a sandwich; they're the two pieces of rye and we're the ham in the middle. It's a question of who will devour whom. Now, what about the Russkies? There's the dilemma, old boy!"

"I know. FDR thinks the same way."

"That's precisely why I wanted Branko in the Soviet Union. While we were serving in France, he impressed me more than any American officer I've ever even heard of—much less met. The man was a veritable one-man gang. He speaks Russian haltingly, but well enough to get by on. More importantly, he forged lasting friendships with several of their top echelon while they were attached to their embassy here during the '20s. In fact, for many of them, Branko was the only Washingtonian above their suspicions. Don't forget, back then we equated every Russian with a bomb-throwing Rasputin. 'Red Terrorists' and 'Mad Russians' we branded them. There were Soviet embassy parties where he was the *only* American present, and understandably so."

"Okay, okay," Hopkins cut in. "What are you driving at?"

"Indulge me. Maybe I want belated justification here, just in case we can't shake Branko loose from the Krauts."

"There'll be hell to pay if that happens—God forbid!"

Donovan nodded in agreement. He said, "General Timoshenko has his hands full right now, but he was receptive to Branko observing his troops in action. I merely wanted someone over there, sort of my first strategic act before I get the OSS into gear. Call it a training exercise—for me."

Hopkins was becoming impatient. "That's easy for you to say, godamm it! Even with his *temporary rescue* by the partisans, Horvitch—that poor bastard—is out there naked for the world to see. Surrounded by the whole damn Nazi army. What is he, sixty—sixty-five? What a way to check out of this circus!"

"Well, I was saving this for last, Mr. Lend-Lease. In his last coded report, couriered through the embassy on Friday, he quotes some shocking information from a reliable source concerning Vladivostok. you're shipping most of your lend-lease materials through there, right?"

Hopkins nodded he was.

"He said that 600 General Motors heavy trucks just happen to be sitting at the docks—or whatever the hell is left of them—and idle for the last two months. No windshield wipers or tires. Spares missing, doors, seats, canvas covers—poof, gone! Stripped by the locals for the region's black market."

Hopkins was dumbfounded.

"Oh, and the warehouse holding thousands of arms you sent? Ransacked repeatedly. Rifles, pistols, Tommy-guns. ammo . All gone. Nothing there but empty boxes."

"Oh, my God," Hopkins whispered, "Kee-rist! We have three shiploads on the way there right now!"

"According to his report, port security is no longer military," Donovan explained. "All the able-bodied in Vladivostok are off to war. With nothing but old men and women, your store is being watched by easily bribable civilian guards—eyes closed, of course. The Brits have the same debacle at the port in Murmansk, on the Arctic. Branko was going there next—just before he was captured. Timoshenko still thinks he's in Russia gathering material for a book he's writing on the Red Army. He was doing just that actually—but keeping an eye on new weapons and tactics at the same time. Just in case we ever find ourselves looking down the barrels of a Russkie attack. You never know—Stalin's as fickle as a coed freshman. Just ask Hitler! Friends today, arch enemies at the drop of a hat."

"Wasn't Branko to spend a few weeks in Spain, Portugal and, uh, Turkey before he entered Russia?"

"I was getting to that. I wanted to use him as sort of an advance emissary. Get the lay of the land, make contacts with old friends at the embassies and the military. His age and rank were perfect cover for this. Between the two of us, we have dozens of potentially solid conduits in just those three places alone. Portugal and Turkey are goldmines of information. Franco is still a hard egg to crack, what with his running the country with an iron fist. And of course Hitler has Gestapo goons slithering around Madrid and Barcelona. Hell! Leather trench coats in July are a dead giveaway, wouldn't y'say!"

This elicited a chuckle from Hopkins, who was mesmerized with Donovan's review. It was most illuminating.

"If anyone thinks that Branko's assignment was unnecessarily frivolous—detractors and isolationists certainly do—they'd have second thoughts if they heard what I'm getting. Not that any of those birds will take kindly to the Vladivostok situation—which will sure as hell come back to haunt me."

"Who cares what they think! Once we're in, they'll jump on board! Even Lindy with his, America First' prattle. At any rate, these are the vital steps toward an eventual intelligence network. Branko's laid the groundwork, if you will, and the agents I'm recruiting will feed off of that. It ain't easy work, Harry, but if your boss and Congress stay off my Irish ass, I'll get it done and in action sooner than anyone believes."

"I just wish to God Branko hadn't been grabbed by the SS," Hopkins complained.

"Well, true enough, our cover is probably all but blown—but, it's been well worth it. Everything he's been able to accomplish in such a short time frame—"

"Well worth it, *if* we get him out before they recapture him. Otherwise, we'll lose the public relations war with Hitler before we get into a real battle. And, I really hate to say this, but if they kill Horvitch—"

"I know the drill. His blood will be on my hands. I pray this won't happen. I love the guy. You know he's an immigrant Jew, of course.

Hopkins nodded.

"Everyone does. But he's given back more to this country of ours than any native-born I know."

Hopkins rose to leave. He watched Major General Wild Bill Donovan rub his hands over his face. For the first time Hopkins noticed he looked tired.

"Buy me a few more days," Donovan said. "I'll have an update for the boss, Harry... Please."

"A few days. I'll do it, Bill, but make it a good update. He's going to rip off one of his steel braces and throw it at me."

"Just duck."

"I can still out-run him."

"I doubt it."

THE GOLDEN LAND

On the Hungarian Great Plain (the Hortobagy)
April 26, 1904 (1515 hours)

He did not want to go anywhere near the inn, but here he now sat staring at the place. Branko sat on a gently-rising bald hillock not more than a half-kilometer away. The undulating grasslands surrounded him and he could just make out the line of *Fusgeyers* as they continued west to a campsite on the River Tisza. Coincidentally it was no more than a stone's throw away from where he had met Shimon Katz and his '03 *Fusgeyers* just over a year ago.

But here and now it was the hulking old *Nagycsarda—the Great Inn*—luring him back. It wasn't really the building, of course. It was his desire to see Margit once again. But no, he would not be drawn back. It was far too regretful. A broken romance must remain there, on the floor, in little pieces—like a shattered keepsake, dish, wine glass or wounded heart.

When the setting sun touched the horizon, he slowly got to his feet, unwrapped a piece of candy from his pocket and popped it in his mouth. The grape-flavored sweetness was satisfying. Not as an antidote to the bitter memory, but as a reminder that life had been pleasing and could very possibly continue to have a goodly amount of sweetness in it. As the flavor swirled around in his mouth, a new surge of energy engulfed him. He strolled—then strutted—head held high, along the mud-rutted road toward the rendezvous on the river. A striking, determined figure…in black.

Yes, it had been good thus far. He secretly and begrudgingly admired Mordecai's leadership. Along with the "kids" they were an interesting and congenial group. That made some of his more necessary security measures easier to execute. The confrontations with military, local police forces and scattered brigand bands, had been delicate moments but their preparations—Branko's security measures—had thwarted a number of potentially violent encounters. He rightly felt a sense of pride in their success thus far. Throughout his years of military service, Branko had never given thought to the opposing ideologies of violence and nonviolence. But now, in conforming to Mordecai's strict policy of non-violent reaction, Branko was keenly aware that their safety was a measurement of their perceived strength and strategic positioning. To the experienced eye of a military man, police officer or thief, the group was not conveniently clumped together for easy pickings: And while there were no obvious signs of weapons, the ground formation of the *Fusgeyers* was highly suggestive of a potent defensive stand. In fact, Branko had to constantly keep a wary eye on his over-eager troops—the three Golub boys in particularly. This proved to be his most formidable task, but with each passing kilometer, it was becoming easier.

As a widely experienced father figure and because of his army experience, Branko was constantly sought out for advice, opinions, and as arbitrator of arguments or trivial disputes. He filled a quasi-parental need beyond that of the diligent Mordecai and other cadre members. Each Fusgeyer had a well-defined job to do, and each had done it effectively to this juncture on the Hungarian plains. As leader, Mordecai was very proud of this, and he had every right to be—this was no place or time for power struggles.

The schedule provided enough of a cushion to reach the Bremerhaven port with time to spare before the August 15th sailing. As long as they were not delayed by confrontations more time-consuming than those already experienced, Branko believed the goal was a realistic one. But it was still a dangerous Europe, and if they marched into port on time he would praise God or anyone else responsible for good fortunes.

As he entered the campsite by the rushing River Tisza, Sendehr approached him, in private. The journal-keeper had been concerned about Branko's hilltop vigil overlooking the Great Inn, thinking that perhaps the former military man was being cautious over something the rest of them had not noticed. To Branko he asked, "Anything wrong, big soldier?"

"Nothing, Sendehr. Just contemplating. Needed some time alone after playing nursemaid to all of you *kindelach* for so long. Had a few old memories to deal with, that's all."

"Hope they were pleasant ones."

"Hmm," Branko grunted. "Yes, they were. For the most part. Thanks for asking, my friend."

*****

Budapest, Austro-Hungarian Empire
May 7, 1904 (1030 hours)

Aside from an unnerving incident with a gang of heavily-armed *vildeh csikosh* demanding excessive river-ferry fees, there were only a few anti-Jew slurs from the peasantry in towns and villages along the route into Budapest.

For most of the *Fusgeyers*, the great city on the Danube was the most illuminating experience of their young lives. While there was nothing charming about the life Jews led in Eastern Europe, Budapest stood out in sharp contrast. This was sophisticated, cosmopolitan Europe at its best and Jewish Europe at its most surprisingly elegant. Here, the Birlader found Jews in one of the most welcoming environments of the modern era, including the *goldeneh medina*—the *golden land* of far-off America.

One of the ways in which the *Fusgeyers* raised funds for their journey was in performing a variety of entertainment for Jewish audiences along the route and "passing the hat" for donations. Rivka Demkin was the expert chairperson for these events and the focal point was her tightly-written adaptation of *Dos Vinshfingerl—The Wishing Ring*. Her stirring adaptation of a poignant story by the popular writer, Mendele Mocher Seforim, preserved the widely-acclaimed depiction of life in a poor shtetl of the Pale: It evoked a full range of emotions in audiences. With the intention of perfection Rivka's troupe had rehearsed and performed throughout the trip and the big city debut was to be in Budapest. Up until this point, Rivka was a hard taskmaster who felt that her "actors" could always improve. Nuchim Krasnigor, the overly conscientious Finance Committee Chair, continually prodded her with pointed remarks, including their need for a big payout in Budapest.

"The Yidden in Budapest are the biggest givers in Europe," Krasnigor had said on more than one occasion.

"We're always improving," Rivka assured him with a frequency equaling his own pleas for more funds.

"We'll have to set a substantial admission fee here," he had said when they arrived in Budapest, followed by: "Leave it up to me to find a place for the performance and the bigger ticket price, Rivkaleh."

And he did. The Great Synagogue—the largest in Europe—had the advantage of an enormous assembly wing and the cordial generosity of the host Budapestians proved very profitable. More than three hundred attended, and the highly-energized cast came through like the troupers into which they had been molded by the direction of the dark-eyed Rivka. Although flashes of improvisation had been encouraged all along, not a line was forgotten. Language difficulties notwithstanding, the gist of the heart-rending story of scant hope amid impoverishment appealed to the humanity of an audience living galaxies apart from the story's subject matter. If anything, life in the Pale was graphically portrayed, perhaps for the first time, to the largely unaffected Jews of comfortable Budapest.

As a surprise bonus, one of the congregants, a wealthy shoe manufacturer, magnanimously invited the Birladers to his massive factory where each male and female was fitted to a new pair of sturdy half-boots. For many, this magnificent gesture came not a moment too soon. The nearly forty days of marching thirty to forty kilometers per day had worn down whatever was left of flimsy, wafer-thin soled footwear to begin with. And they were still less than half-way to the port of embarkation at Bremerhaven.

The odyssey upon which they set forth sorely tried them to the very frayed edges of endurance. There was the dogged harassment by the Emperor's military as well as the constant threat of heavily armed scoundrels, bullies, thieves and ruffian hordes. In fact, they received the very attention Branko had expected when he first learned they were to fly the "enemy flag." But being hampered by every transient xenophobe incensed at their Star of David was only part of the struggle. There was also the ongoing need for a steady supply of funds for food and necessities.

The drive to reach Bremerhaven and thence on to America, was as difficult a hardship as it was a crystal clear goal. The great unknown assailed them at every turn, but the contingent of nearly sixty Birladers yielded not to fate, but to the destiny they shaped.

*****

New York City, NY
United States of America
September 10, 1904 (8:30 a.m.)

When the few *Fusgeyers* disembarked from the *Cincinnatus* in Boston Harbor, a pall of sadness overcame those continuing to New York and elsewhere. The goodbyes, hugs and the kisses were repeated several times before they could tear away from each other. When the "Bostoners" as they were called by the contingent's "New Yorkers" walked down the gangplank, each person paused every few feet for final farewell gestures of departure: It was unlikely any of them would ever meet again.

The overnight run around Cape Cod and Long Island was a voyage of anxiety about the unknown. Having trekked thousands of miles from Birlad and braved the ocean crossing they were about to step into the great unknown of a new country about which they knew next to nothing. Muted and serious conversations emanated from every corner of the decks and steerage—all concerning unanswered questions, tentative plans, alliances formed or abandoned, and financial survival in the new land.

The night ended in what seemed like the wink of an eye. That morning's silent passage in view of *The Statue of Liberty* evoked a river of tears for some and for others, a march toward Eden. Or was it to be Dante's Inferno? None of them were certain one way or the other. But they would all surely find out before too many days.

The jitney boats awaiting incoming immigrant ships at the New York docks, quickly whisked the hordes across the Hudson River and to Ellis Island, the heralded golden gate of Emma Lazarus' fitting poetry.

The island's dormitories were cleaner and better lighted than was generally expected. Likewise, anticipated horror stories did not materialize. After a few days, the immigrants relaxed in the knowledge of being near their goal. The sons and daughters of Birlad were realizing that the minor indignities of a final medical examination and a few military-like procedures lay between them and a short jitney-ride to the land of their hopes.

From the vantage point of Ellis Island the New York skyline was nothing less than overwhelming for the increasing masses of mainly peasant Europeans. All of them—and the *Fusgeyers*—looked on in mesmerized awe.

However, the more worldly Branko Horvitch was not as much awestruck as he felt challenged

So this is the big city of New York, he mused to himself while gazing out over the harbor. *Well, I'm Sergeant-Major Branko Horvitch, and I've come to look you over. If I like you, I'll stay. If not, there are things to do, places to see, experiences to feel.*

A wry smile was on his heretofore frowning face.

*****

New York City, NY
November 14, 1904

Two months after their arrival in New York, the exotic and talented Rivka Demkin married Sendehr Efraim. She took a seamstress job in a stuffy costume design shop, working alongside another Jewish girl named, Miriam Hoffman.

The curly-haired Miriam was, at first, a natural fit for a friendship with Rivka. Both of them were experienced with stage productions and acting. But whereas Rivka's theatrical efforts had been integral to the *Fusgeyers'* European survival, Miriam's mostly insignificant stage work was for self-aggrandizement more than for money or love of theater. Her motivations weren't obvious, of course, and when she spoke of the theater listeners heard only the passion of an actress for her art. She was a native born New Yorker—where her parents had settled in the 1880s—and had performed only bit parts in local Yiddish-language stage extravaganzas.

But what Rivka heard in Miriam's voice was further colored by her own fondness of, and concern for, Branko. Rivka had not been ignorant of Branko unexpressed interest and in Miriam she thought she had found the perfect solution for the Big Soldier.

Rivka arranged for him to meet Miriam.

And from there, nature took its course—a startlingly fast course. Within months Miriam and Branko were seemingly inseparable. The marriage announcement came before the end of the year.

During their first year of marriage Miriam continued working. However, when her pregnancy became noticeable she was summarily fired—such was typical of the times. Branko held a series of insignificant jobs for most of that first year, but then Miriam learned that the police department was to recruit hundreds of officers to accommodate the hordes of immigrants still coming ashore. Most of the newcomers were Russian and Yiddish-speaking Jews from Russia, Poland, Germany or the Austro-Hungarian Empire.

Miriam rightly argued that Branko was tailor-made for a police job within the immigrant community. Along with his improving English, his proficiency in German, Yiddish and Russian would be a major advantage, she said. In late-1905, Branko applied to and was hired by the NYPD. For Branko it was the best paying job he had found since arriving in New York. With a baby on the way, both Branko and Miriam were pleased at the substantial increase in money.

On the surface all appeared well between the couple, but Rivka began seeing the seeds of discontent. Miriam confided that she missed the artistic atmosphere of theater friends with whom she no longer associated, that she regretting pursuing the stage, that Branko was a good husband but too old fashion. It was a litany of complaints that Rivka felt was an outgrowth of Miriam's rollercoaster of emotions during pregnancy.

But Rivka re-considered her deduction when Miriam had a miscarriage. Knowing such a thing to be a traumatic experience, Rivka had rushed to the girl's side to offer support and comfort.

Miriam, however, seemed just short of cavalier about the loss. In fact it was Branko who needed consoling, not Miriam.

It was after that when Rivka begin seeing a dramatic change in Miriam. What had been an otherwise pleasant young person became a moody woman of unbecoming ideas and actions. At one point during a rather morose discussion, Miriam even hinted at the idea of an "open marriage" a rather new social phenomenon of the times. It was an idea that, oddly enough, was prevalent in the immigrant neighborhoods. To many of those, making the leap from a repressively suffocating regime to a free society, loosening morals wedged into their lives. Both Catholic and Protestant churches took it very seriously and condemned anything moving outward from Orthodoxy. On the other hand, synagogues where orthodoxy was slowly being diluted by the more non-traditional bent, tended to look the other way.

Rivka confessed to Sendehr that she wished she hadn't introduced Miriam to Branko in the first place. Sendehr agreed that that it was becoming a mismatch for both parties. It was a marriage destined to fail despite—even in spite of—a second pregnancy.

When Miriam intimated to Rivka that she knew of a "doctor" who could abort the pregnancy for $25, Rivka did not reprimand her. The union was, after all, beyond the help of any intervention. Rivka and Sendehr, who had long agonized over the turn of events, both felt that after the birth of the baby the Horvitches would rarely be seen together in public.

*****

New York City, NY
November 11, 1906 (9:30 p.m.)

The hospital was unlike any Branko had seen—in Europe or America. In every respect it was bright, clean and modern. The bevy of nurses wore crisp, white blouses, light blue skirts and caps. The doctors were professional, effective, a bit stoic, genteel in their dealings with patients and their families. Expectant husbands, like Branko, received a regal-like treatment: "Yes, Mr. Horvitch, your wife is doing well... No, Mr. Horvitch, we expect she'll go into labor within the hour, but we don't know for sure... Please be seated, Mr. Horvitch... Rest assured we'll inform you the minute she delivers... Is it a boy or girl you favor, sir?"

There were four beds in Miriam's room: In the one nearest the gingham curtains-covered window a fidgeting, bony, older Portuguese woman lay. The next bed held a grinning youngster of sixteen, who was already the mother of two children waiting at home. The presumed father of the youngster's expected third child was a tall, lanky kid with a face full of freckles and red tousled hair, who stood by her. The girl's mother was outside the room, pacing the corridor and speaking to no one. The third bed had been vacated by a patient who was in surgery for a minor procedure.

Just before Miriam was wheeled into labor she comfortably smiled at Branko. He smiled back, decidedly uncomfortable.

The birth was trouble-free and eight days later, as prescribed in the Torah, the celebratory ceremonial *bris* was attended by many of the *Fusgeyers* living near the massive Romanian *shul* on Eldridge Street. Some of the guests had even traveled from as far away as the South Bronx, Yorkville, and Brooklyn. While wielding a scalpel, the Rabbi/*mohel* loudly issued forth the baby boy's name: in Yiddish, *Moshe Laib,* in English, *Emanuel.*

Holding the child on his lap, Mordecai Anieloff—legendary head of the 1904 Birlad *fusgeyer* contingent—smiled. As did everybody. It was indeed a happy day for all and a hundred faces brightly shone throughout the 5,000-year old ritual. The steady hand of the eighty-year-old rabbi was more than appreciated by Moshe's mother, who had surreptitiously peeked in from the doorway of the ante-room where she was temporarily confined as ancient tradition dictated. The proud, but visibly shaking father, held tightly onto Mordecai's broad shoulders during the entire procedure.

Crying at a high pitch, Moshe's lips were dabbed with a cotton batting soaked with wine—the only anesthesia he was permitted. With the deed done, shouts of *mazel tov* boomed throughout the sanctuary's lower hall, while the mother rushed in. She took little Moshe to her breast, pecked Branko on the cheek and reveled in the pouring forth of hugs and kisses.

Schnapps freely flowed in the midst of braided challahs and moist honey cake covering two tables. To the feast was also added a potent slivovitz and a sweet kosher red wine. Most appreciated by Branko was the *modus operandi* for such events—as was customary, it was all paid for by the *shul* brotherhood and sisterhood.

"Mazel tov, mazel tov, lang leben di shayna boychick, Moshe Laib! Good luck! long live the beautiful little boy!" rang out when the ancient rite was over.

The *klezmer* band, two high-pitched violins, a wailing clarinet and a soulful trumpet struck up and began a loud round of old-country dance music—*horas, kozatskes*, followed by slow waltzes and fast quadrilles. The intermittent cries of *"mazel tov"* continued unabated.

But even in the middle of all of this joy, Branko still brooded. Things weren't good between him and Miriam. They had been married only two years and were a long way from standing the test of time. In fact, the steady deterioration had begun just after Miriam's first pregnancy and death-defying miscarriage. This second pregnancy had gone quite well and Miriam *seemed* happy about it. But she was always guarded and kept her feelings inside. Branko could no longer reach her, and was dreading what he expected next: Separation or Divorce?

*****

New York City, NY
April 22, 1907

Whatever was left of the ill-fated coupling went forward just short of another six months and then irreconcilably disintegrated. Miriam took the child and went to her sister, Ruth, across the river in Newark. The house was exceptionally large for a single family home and Miriam had a room for the baby and herself. She also took a clerical job with her brother-in-law's successful insurance firm—even though she had never used a typewriter. Ruth, a homemaker with two of her own little tots cared for Emanuel during Miriam's workday.

Almost immediately Miriam began seeing another man—one of decidedly questionable caliber.

Meanwhile, in a state off depression, Branko did not fight any of these changes. He was not cold, unfeeling or even in a silent rage. The truth was, he was numb to the anger he had every right to feel. For the first time in his life he avoided a fight.

Rivka, Sendehr and several other close *Fusgeyer* friends constantly implored him to get a lawyer.

"Don't just stand there and mope," they all variously told him. The more frustrated among them invariably added, "Damn it, do something!"

It was as if the Greek Chorus had advised a stone wall. When it became apparent Branko was beyond reach, they finally stopped broaching the subject altogether. Miriam, however, felt no such reservations and went speedily ahead with the divorce proceedings.

Branko signed the final papers in late 1907: No alimony, custody battles or complications.

He truly thought it was the best way, but it nonetheless crushed him to the core.

*****

New York City, NY
June 15, 1914 (11 p.m.)

Jocko Lanigan's Pub was for neither the timid nor sane. It was not an exaggeration to say that the place was three steps beyond rambunctious.

On this particular night the pub was an even more rowdy place than usual. Some of New York's finest were in full swing, hosting the wildest beer feast imaginable to celebrate a promotion within their ranks. When an officer was being feted on his promotion to *Lieutenant of Detectives*, all hell had to break loose—and it was getting there fast.

At the center of this maelstrom was newly minted head detective, Branko Horvitch. While he detested this kind of raucousness over something as mundane as a promotion, he could hardly argue against tradition. Nonetheless, even while assailed with revelers from all sides, he was alone with his thoughts in the crowd.

Covering the upper eastside of the city, the 31st Precinct was located at Lexington Avenue and 67th Street. Although set in the more seedy segment of the large precinct, it operated out of a handsome limestone and brick Victorian building built back in 1877. A stable adjoined the building and the pungent manure of police horses permeated not only the five story headquarters, but also the entire block. While mounted-police would long-remain the practical way of patrolling the myriad alleys and various, yet-to-be-paved streets, residents yearned for the day when motorcars would displace the smell of horses.

Branko had proven to be the most efficient horseman in the precinct, and possibly in the entire 7,000-man force. His twelve years with the Hapsburg Emperor's crack cavalry had served him well in this regard. But no more: As Lieutenant of Detectives, Branko was to be assigned a Ford motorcar and a patrol driver. Privately, he wasn't sure that he liked the arrangement but the substantial increase in his pay would go a long way in overriding any such trepidation. Or so suggested his closest buddy, Maxie Fleischman—a burly cop who was his replacement as sergeant. Between the two of them, they represented the only Jews in the 31st. The other three sergeants and most of the patrolmen were Irish, with a smattering of Italians, Germans, Swedes, and two Poles.

From the day he advanced from patrolman to Sergeant back in '09, he had waited five years for this inevitable day. Yet, to Branko it seemed a lifetime, among the many distinctive lifetimes he had experienced. He had been more than just a policeman—more than just a sergeant. He had been a leader, a mentor, a voice of calm in the midst of a storm and a good soldier. By some accounts he was even a beacon of light in a community that literally despised these men in blue, with badges of gold.

But was he, he pondered, *really making that kind of difference? Was he that kind of man to these people?*

The answer, from the lowliest rookie up to the Police Commissioner, was a resounding *yes*. But, Branko a European immigrant like many others on the force, was too embarrassed to believe that he was so praiseworthy or different. The firm, nurturing instinct with which he had shepherded the *Fusgeyers* to America had also carried over into his relationship within his precinct. Incorrigibles, plebeians, petty criminals, abusers, drunks, bullies, street hustlers and ordinary men, women and children—they sincerely respected the Sergeant.

And if that wasn't enough, even Commissioner Sullivan had beamed with pride that Branko—at a mere thirty-nine years of age—was the youngest man to reach the rank of lieutenant in the entire history of the New York City police force.

The big bash went on until the wee hours of Sunday morning. The luckier ones were thankful for the day off while the rest—including a sober Lieutenant Horvitch—went on duty drinking lots of coffee.

*****

New York City, NY
June 15, 1916 (12:00 noon)

The two policemen were seated in a corner table at Giuseppe's Little Italy. The one in civilian clothes had ordered two of Giuseppe's "lighter and cheaper" lunches that included a glass of house wine. From whose house, no one ever knew.

"What are you thinking, Branko?" The quizzical look on Max's chubby face, topped by the deeply furrowed brow gave away the seriousness of his question.

Branko, pausing for a moment, answered, "I've got to do it, Max. Can you try to understand my dilemma."

"What dilemma, for Chrisakes? You're going to throw away a 3G-a-year career, just like that, you godamm putz? To join the friggin army! Keerist, I can't friggin believe it, old friend!"

"It's entirely settled in my mind. No regrets. I'm resigning on the first of next month. More than ten good years with some of the greatest chaps I've ever known—you excluded, because you're a pain in the ass!"

The broad grin on Branko's chiseled face told Max that it was certainly said in jest.

"I've got you figured out, Mr. Mystery Man. You just need a good woman in your miserable life. It's been, what, ten years since she and the boy slipped out of your life? You've been silently brooding all this time. Right, Lieutenant of Detectives—New York's Number One Crime Buster?"

"No. Dead wrong, Maxie! I stopped *brooding* about it, long ago. Last I heard she was in Cleveland with one of her 'free love' deviates. I only worry about a poor, innocent kid who doesn't even know he has a father; a real one."

"Oh Really?" Maxie came back. "And you just happen to know where she is now, huh?"

Branko looked at his friend, deciding whether to volunteer a defense. He said, "Miriam stopped writing to Rivka years ago, but one of their mutual friends keeps in touch with her. That's how, from time to time, I get fresh information."

"Always the cop, Branko. You're still treating this like some godamm line-up, where every face is a number, and every number a face. Geez, we're talking serious shit here. Do you ever want to see the boy again? He needs you badly—from what you've told me about her rotten life style. And now you're throwing everything into the toilet—to join the Yew-nited States Army. What a friggin fool you are!

"I love you, my Becky loves you, Sendehr and Rivka love you. All of your *fusgeyer* comrades love and respect you—as does the New York City Police Department. You're sitting on top of a world that's given you the whole kit and caboodle. And you're turning your back on it. *Gevalt!* Why, Branko, just tell me, why?"

Lieutenant Horvitch just sat in silence while he picked at the remainder of his spaghetti.

The puzzled Sergeant pushed his marinara-stained plate aside, waiting for some semblance of an answer that never came.

AT WAR 1917   6

Camp Upton
Yaphank Long Island, NY
March 11, 1917 (1:00 p.m.)

The train ride from Plattsburgh, near the Canadian border in upstate New York, to Grand Central Terminal went quickly. The connection to the Long Island Railroad's rinky-dink conveyance that took Branko to Yaphank—wherever the hell that was—seemed to stop at every cow barn in the rural stretches of Long Island. The Camp Upton bus deposited him outside a ramshackle headquarters building and the driver pointed to the Commander's office.

With olive drab replacing NYPD blue Branko was once again a Lieutenant. He found it hard to believe what had transpired since his July enlistment at the ancient age of forty-one. It seemed as if a whirlwind had carried him to the office of Lt. Colonel William Donovan at this hastily constructed camp, sixty miles east of the big city. Dozens of such camps peppered the country, all vital in preparing civilian recruits for conscription to the sagging Army troop count of less than 400,000.

"This war in Europe, into which we are to be inevitably drawn, is going to need a police-oriented enlistment base," asserted the Lieutenant Colonel, sitting behind his government issued desk with both feet upon it. The placid former lawyer was eight years younger than Branko. "Those units will be the built from law enforcement agencies around this nation. I intend to recruit mature cops like yourself, Horvitch. I'm particularly after those with officer experience and that's why I had you sent here today."

"Yes sir, I understand, sir."

Branko Horvitch may have understood, but he certainly did not realized the effort and logistics involved. Donovan had previous tried to requisition nine veteran military policemen to serve anywhere from two years to twenty years. He was summarily turned down by former commander of the skeleton, Yankee Division, General Putnam. As far as Donovan was concerned, Washington was staffed with damn fools that had riddled his old 26th while knowing full-well the country would end-up in the middle of war. And yet, even knowing that, they demobilized 200 non-coms in the past year. Everyone knew that it had been the only adequately trained element in the entire army. That decision was then followed by assigning Donovan to organize and train the so-called "Fighting 69th" New York Volunteers. As part of that, Donovan's top priority was to meet the need for the type of military police unit Branko had been tapped to lead. Thus in January, Donovan had arranged for the rudimentary officer's training program that Branko went through in Plattsurgh. And that was followed by Donovan approving Branko's promotion to a commissioned officer's rank.

"Several senior, handpicked people reporting to you will be wearing two hats," Donovan said. "Overt and covert. While performing the usual MP and infantry functions, you'll also be forming a secretive, clandestine operation. You'll need to prepare for the possibility of behind-the-lines duty when we reach Europe."

"May I ask, sir—"

"Cut out that 'sir' crap, Branko—get used to little less formality. To be sure, the 69th Regiment, will be a battalion-sized unit of the 42nd *Rainbow* Division and will run per military regulations. But formality in the chain of command will be different. At least among your covert crew and your relationship with me, as your Battalion Commander. You led your detectives informally, and that's one of the reasons we're having this conversation."

"May I ask, sir—uh—Lt. Colonel Donovan, how you know so much of my past?"

"Your 12 years in the Austro-Hungarian military; service in Franz Josef's Honor Guard; fitness reports from the NYPD as a mounted cop, Sergeant of Detectives and decorated crime-busting Lieutenant of Detectives. It all tells me what I need to know. I don't care why you enlisted, but your past and your designing, developing and implementing training procedures at Fort Dix, was exemplary—and I do care about all that. You're my man, like it or not. Get used to it, Branko.

"Besides, I'm sure you know that your old boss 'Fat Franz' just croaked last November and his Empire may end-up as our arch rival. You do know all of the Emperor's secrets, right?"

The grins were a mile wide. The ensuing bone-crushing handshake—sans salute—accompanied a simultaneous grasp of each other's shoulders, cementing the beginnings of a mutually rewarding and enduring comradeship. It was something that the two men instinctively sensed.

*****

Somewhere on the North Atlantic
July 22, 1917 (0530 hours)

It was critical that all convoys were blacked-out during the hours of darkness. Branko, for some reason, could not fall asleep in the cramped, reeking, overheated officer's quarters this particular night.

He crawled from of his bunk and without dressing went out onto the deck amidships, near the six-inch guns mounted on all troop vessels. Because of the *no smoking* ban gun crews were constantly complaining, even though crew chiefs repeatedly explained that the glow of a cigarette could be seen through the periscope of any lurking German submarine. All it would take is one drag and *boom*, the men would be swimming for their lives.

The U-boats had been raising havoc with shipping. American and other neutral nations had been losing merchant vessels and passenger liners for the past few years. One of the most tragic loses thus far had been 1915 sinking of the British luxury liner *RMS Lusitania*. Torpedoed by German U-boat, *U-20,* off the coast of Ireland, she went down taking 1,198 of the 1,959 lives aboard—including 124 Americans.

The *Lusitania* sinking added fuel to the fire of an already growing "war element." Led by former president Theodore Roosevelt, they vociferously clamored for President Wilson to declare war. But despite an incensed public, Wilson balked.

"The President is nothing less than a Byzantine logothete surrounded by flubdubs, mollycoddles and flapdoodle pacifists," Roosevelt harshly criticized Wilson's inaction. But the rough-rider hero of San Juan Hill, who was a master of political fencing and didn't mince words when name-calling, once again failed to budge the isolationist bent of the time.

In Branko's opinion, Roosevelt was universally recognized as a premier leader of the NYPD long before he himself had joined the force. The former Commissioner and former U.S. President was a heroic figure revered by the city and its police. As President he was hailed by a goodly percentage of the immigrant horde as being the quintessential American—explorer, soldier and politician. *Speak softly but carry a big stick*, indeed!

Now, with the first troop carrier convoys plying the North Atlantic, the wolves would be lurking around waiting for prime targets. Just the week before two ships were badly damaged by torpedoes but suffered only minor casualities. And, at least, one of the wolf pack subs was blown out of the water by the destroyer-escort gun crew.

The week-old sub encounter nagged at Branko every time he was on deck and this time was no different. He looked out over the ink-black water knowing he could not see what might be there. They were six days out of New York and on several occasions Branko had chatted with the Marines assigned to the deck guns. They were mostly southerners with "y'all" drawls. Branko, whose English had improved immensely over the past decade, still lapsed into a guttural Germanic accent. As a result, there was occasional joking among the crews, charging the Lieutenant with being a hand-picked spy for the Kaiser. In good-natured exchanges Branko played along and was by far the most popular United States Army officer on the *USS Thunder Cloud*.

Branko returned to his quarters, dressed, picked up a bottle of ink and a cablegram form and then went to the officer's mess. After pouring himself a hot cup of java he pulled out the last letter from his aunt and once again re-read it.

Tante Shayndl had finally emigrated from Odessa, arriving in Paris in 1908, at the age of 45 years. Berel had died two years later— during a major yellow fever epidemic in Palestine to where he had traveled to explore the possibilities of he and Shayndl making aliyah.

Dovidl, their eldest child, had married his Odessan intended and the two immediately went to live on a kibbutz in Galilee in 1905. They and their two children were there at Berel's hospital bedside when he passed on.

After Berel's death, Branko had unsuccessfully tried to convince his dear Tante to come west. She consistently demurred, citing the close friendships she had with Odessans living in the predominantly Jewish, Marais arrondisement. And then there were her two daughters, both of whom married Parisian Jews and produced four of her eight grandchildren—all living nearby in the city. Branko's plea had been futile of course and he fully understood the ties that bound his aunt. But the war was already three years old. Paris was constantly in imminent danger of being overrun by the Hun and Branko still worried—even though he had more or less stopped his insistence that his aunt come west.

Tante was overjoyed with the letters Branko had been sending about his exploits in the NYPD, especially so when he announced that he was promoted to Lieutenant of Detectives. During basic training at Fort Dix, he had written her a short note about his abrupt enlistment. Mail delivery in wartime Paris was sporadic and Shayndl didn't receive the news until after he reached Camp Upton.

In a state of frightful disbelief she immediately cabled him at Camp Upton. Branko didn't have the heart to respond that he would be shipping out to France in short order, as soon as completing two parallel eight-week training cycles for the four advanced companies of the 69th.

After mulling over the events he would convey to his aunt, he pulled out his pen and the cablegram form to write another letter.

> *Dear Tante:*
> *I received your cable a few weeks ago. With Paris supply lines under siege all this time, I pray that you and your family are coping well. The reports we get here indicate that the city and its environs still manage to replenish basic food supplies from the*

agricultural region to the west and south, out of range of the enemy. I hope this is true.

I'm not going to try to explain by letter my reasons for joining the army. In fact, I'm now on my way to a port in Western France. I cannot say just where, but with any luck perhaps I can arrange to see you in the near future. That's a day both of us can look forward to. These days, that ray of hope can be cherished. The reality, even more so.

As an officer, I'll be able to cable this to you from aboard ship. The military censorshp does not extend to ship-board cables, so I have been rather loose with my information. Please do not repeat any of this to anyone. We've been told that Paris has become a veritable den of spies and German sympathizers. Oy vay!

You had once written, there are many English-French translators in your part of the city. Whomever you have used for this purpose before certainly has done a thorough job of it in our past correspondence. As you noticed, I have lately more often written in Yiddish which is still a solid second language to my English. According to your letters, it appears as though you have learned French as well as I have learned English, and you've only been living there for less than ten years now.

I was so pleased to hear that Dovid and his family were able to get to Paris for a long visit before the war began. That must have seemed heaven-sent for you and the girls. It will be an unmatchable joy for me to see all of *you if and when that happens. You can be sure that I will make a clandestine raid of our quartermaster food stores and will probably need two duffel bags to accommodate it all!*

This is likely the longest cable ever sent to Paris from a U.S. vessel! I'll write again when I get an army post office address in France. With all my love to you and the children, Tante Shayndl!

Your favorite nephew,
Branko.

*****

St. Nazaire, Western France
August 4, 1917 (0800 hours)

The troop ship U.S. Thunder Cloud was first in line to dock at St. Nazaire's spacious harbor on France's Atlantic coast. The doughboy passengers, including elements of the 69th Infantry Regiment, walked down the gangplanks. In single file they crossed the wide docks and boarded a fleet of local trucks that carried them to the St. Nazaire railroad station. After three weeks of dodging Germany's sub fleet, it was a temporary pleasure to sit on the train taking them to Paris. The soot encircling the trains was the only unpleasant annoyance but it was enough to cause them to already missed the clean smell of ocean spray

The stopover in Paris was only long enough for transferring troops to a wide variety of transportation before pushing onward to their first bivouac area some twenty kilometers (twelve miles) north of Paris. At this stage of the war, *variety* meant everything and anything: Run-down trucks, taxi cabs, private Citroen and Renault autos and battered busses. The French had mastered the art of confiscating everything. By and large the involved companies and individuals volunteered the use of their *confiscated* property—winning the war was all that mattered. Since the German invasion, and its announced aim to engulf the beautiful and historic Paris, winning the war meant surviving the war. Another German victory parade into Paris, as had occurred in the 1870 Franco-Prussian conflict, could not and would not be tolerated. This was especially true for older Frenchman who held vivid, unpleasant memories of that insulting, long ago embarrassment.

Nearing Montparnasse Station, the 200 advance troops of the 69th shared the same thoughts: *This is France's party: why the hell are we here? What's this all about, for Chrissake? Am I going to make it through this friggin hell or be buried in Flanders fields? The luck of the Irish, bullshit! Dear God, I wanna go home! Dammit, I wanna go home in one piece, now!*

This is not to say that every last non-com and officer in the 69th harbored the exact same thoughts. But to be sure, they all had similar feelings in one form or another. If there was ever anything eventually screamed by all soliders sent into battle it was "war is hell." And as many times as not this was soon followed by "Goddamit, war sure as hell *is* Hell!"

After debarking from the steam-spewing train the ensuing chaos would have given Dante a new inferno about which to write. The reluctance of the French to use their rolling stock for transportation to the front was difficult for the American Expeditionary Force to comprehend; that is, until talking with dozens of the living, but severely maimed, engineers whose engines and coaches had been blown-out from beneath them. Swooping enemy biplanes carrying bombs—and potato masher grenades hand-dropped from rooftop altitudes—had wreaked crippling results on the French patriots.

This certainly didn't make it easier for the truckers and busses or the ubiquitous cabbies and volunteer private car drivers—all of whom served as troop conveyers to the front. When they kissed and hugged wives and families goodbye, it had a grim, silently understood meaning. Each time, the tears flowed like good French wine.

As the Ford trucks rolled eastward, Branko announced, "Boys, we're heading to our bivouac area. But my guess is we'll soon be called upon to continue on to Belgium."

He saw inquisitive looks in some of their faces.

"Yes, Belgium," Branko added. "The Brits are having a helluva tight go of it up there. Lt. Colonel Donovan has been informed by General Pershing that their decimated Canadian, Australian and New Zealander units need help fast and we've been elected. Baptism by fire, I would call it!"

By most accounts, Branko was conservative in his opinion. During the recent rejuvenation of the 69th in Upton, the glib Father Duffy more aptly expressed the general opinion by saying, "Saints preserve us, we've got an Oirish Colonel and a Yid Looey leading us into battle, boys. How can anyone beat us?! When the Huns hear it, they'll fer sure retreat post haste to the beer halls of Berlin—and speaking of Berlin, did ye know we're the only regiment in the United States Army that has its very own songwriting doughboy? Yeah, Private Irving Berlin, that skinny little Son of Abraham with a golden musical ear. When he was drafted, the newspaper headlines announced 'Army Takes Berlin' and for five minutes, thousands of the more gullible New Yorkers thought the war was over.

This little tent-pulpit speech during initial orientations was a morale booster and had put the feisty troops of the 69th into a jolly fit. Branko had broadly grinned, wrapped his lean and mean 6'2" frame around the diminutive chaplain's shoulders, and whispered, "Saints preserve us, my ass, Francis!"

Bill Donovan had left New York on an earlier convoy in order to meet with AEF Commander, General John Pershing. Along with his staff, Pershing had been studying the grim situation in France for months. After several briefings in Paris, Donovan was then to meet with Branko and all platoon leaders at Montparnasse Station to bring them up to date. All of this went as planned and now Branko could join them to continue on to the designated staging area where the troops would bivouac. Donovan had left his trusted adjutant in charge of the

Battalion still in the final weeks of training at Camp Upton before also shipping off to France.

Logistically, Donovan was to be at the full Battalion strength of 1,000 well-trained men by the end of the year. Having been a star football player at Columbia he had earned the nickname, *Wild Bill* and was forever applying the gridiron lingo of grueling football to the task before him. In this case, Donovan was fully preparing for what he considered "the heralded spring offensive play, by God!"

*****

Paris, in the Marais
September 23, 1917 (1900 hours)

On the Rue ds Rosiers, near the Rue de Roi de Sicile, and her large apartment, Tante's family attended *Kol Nidre* services at a small *shtiebel*.

On a three-day leave, Branko had surprised Tante the day before —after having hitchhiked in from the Forest of Chantilly. It was a highly emotional event for all. It had been more than thirteen years since they had seen each other but it seemed like a veritable eternity. Channah, Raiseleh, their husbands and children gave Branko the first taste of family in several years. He wore a smile for all three days.

Branko had not been in a *shul* since his son's bris in 1906. He had never completely lost his Jewish faith, but the purely religious connection had long ago ceased to exist. Tante Shayndl understood completely and confessed that she only lit the Shabbos candles when the grandchildren were at her apartment. Both Channah and Raiseleh had married religious men who insisted on a kosher home and so Tante honored traditions whenever the family visited.

"Nu, Branko, have you seen Emanuel?"

He shook his head to and fro. His frown told Tante to let it lay.

"I've often wondered what it would have been like if we had made aliyah at the time—when Berel had such a strong attachment to the Zionst idea," she said.

"Wondering about it is a fruitless exercise. It's past, Tante. It's past."

The forty-eight hours went swiftly and the conversations filled with nostalgia made for a satisfying visit. They even strolled the neighborhood and some of the city's historic sites. Being on a wartime footing did not seem to take anything away from the beauty and mystique of Paris.

Due to wartime-related food shortages, AEF Commander General John J. Pershing encouraged servicemen to be generous with surplus food when visiting French families. Thus Branko was happy to have brought the promised foodtstuffs, as Tante Shayndl's cupboards were lacking many of the basics. He had brought enough in the two stuffed duffel bags to offer Channah and Raiseleh healthy *pareve* shares to take home with them. Family is family, the Lieutenant reasoned.

The hitch-hike back to the forest encampment went smoothly when a supply truck on the way to the front stopped to give the big American a lift to his temporary "home." Once there, they smartly saluted each other after Branko hopped down to the ground. With his empty duffel bags slung over his shoulder, he walked the last muddy kilometer. He whistled a nondescript tune as he headed down the wooded pathway, savoring his memories of the pleasant visit.

*****

Passchendaele, West Flanders, Belgium
November 1, 1917 (2400 hours)

For three days the troops of the 69th were snugly dug in and overlooking a burnt out village about ten kilometers north of the bigger town, Ypres (Ieper). The regiment had been bolstered by another 400 newly trained troops, fresh off the ship. With six full-complement companies of 100 men each and coupled with two equally-sized regiments, Wild Bill Donovan and the 69th regiment of the 42nd Division was as ready as it could ever be to replace the Australian 33rd Regiment. The 33rd had lost nearly a quarter of its men in the October battles surrounding the Ypres salient. Battle-fatigued to the point of terminal exhaustion, the Aussies had been manned and led by grizzled veterans of the ill-fated 1915 Gallipoli Campaign on the shores of the Sea of Marmara in the strategic Dardanelles. With little or no respite, the 33rd—or what was left of it—had been in battles giving "attrition" a new and gory meaning. Even when having nothing left to give, they had been ordered to lift themselves up by their boot straps, return "down under" recoup and regroup. That was when they were to be shipped to Belgium in the summer of 1917—for what they hoped to be the end. But such was not to be. As part of the rejuvenated Anzac contingent they experienced a bloody summer of which most would never speak. But, on this day, the remnants were melded into the 69th's two battalions, and greeted warmly with hugs far outweighing salutes.

Wild Bill and three senior officers made their rounds shortly after midnight. Branko covered the trenches of the entire left flank, where the daybreak offensive would begin. Major Charlie McNabb took the right flank and Lieutenant Tim Monahan, the tough cop from Pittsburgh—one of Branko's MP stalwarts—made the rounds of the reserve forces in the middle. Above all, their task was to quietly whip-up a feeling of, *we can do it*. They each frequently repeated the *"Garryowen and Glory" motto* of the regiment and dropped in the delicious, "poke us and you'll provoke us," another sassy phrase attached to the outfit. Within a half hour the four men rendezvoused at Donovan's ten-foot-deep trench digs and compare notes. All was ready and most men were catching their last hours of sleep. A number of them had remained awake, smoking or nervously chatting in whispers. The Aussies had been passing around some of their cherished King James Scotch—a gesture for which many of their American comrades-in-arms reciprocated with heart-felt blessings. They even offered a swig to Branko when he visited their trenches.

The Battalion was pronounced ready, willing and able. A cocky Donovan shared his last minute feelings with his most trusted officers: "If we can take that ridge behind the farmhouse as planned, that will make 'em think we've showed our hand. When the Bosh from the other side of Passchendaele shift to drive us out, our reserves should pick 'em off at will. Sounds good, eh?"

The others nodded.

"It's a godamm long shot that things will break that way," Donovan went on to admit. "But if the Brits and Canucks do their thing—and do it well—the day will be ours."

"Wild Bill," Branko cut in, "we've gone over the plan with our Brit/Canadian counterparts several times in the last twenty-four hours. I surmise that they all 'get it.' They sure as hell have had the experience up here and last month's near-catastrophic losses prove it. Time for a friggin win, don't ya think?"

Donovan, Monahan and McNabb nodded in agreement, moved by the authority in Branko's hoarse whisper and not realizing he was voicing the truth as much as perhaps drowning-out his inner doubts.

At exactly 0600 hours it began. From the tree-covered hillside a kilometer to the rear, the South African and Canadian artillery units, launched a thunderous barrage while fanning out to the perceived German lines. When it stopped, the platoon leaders' shrill whistles blew and all hell, pandemonium and chaos ruled the dawn.

The leap out of the trenches was something to behold and the Hun battalions followed suit. Donovan wanted no firing until the ridge was secure and within a mere ten minutes it was just that.

At that moment the Germans swarmed through the village's burnt out buildings, firing wicked volleys from their Mauser rifles. "Potato masher" grenades were flung with accuracy and casualties mounted just as the reserve riflemen sent blistering rounds of bullets into the advancing Germans. This stopped the Hun's ridge attack in its bloody tracks.

The pre-set broad line of South African and Indian-manned mortars now rained down on the village itself, decimating the attacking Hun battalion at the location of their largest mass.

Cheers went up from the ridge and Branko ordered his troops to continue firing. Branko saw some dazed and staggering German troops within range of his .45 caliber side-arm and blasted away. Three of the enemy fell on their faces.

The boys from the 69th, especially Branko's MP's, loved what they were witnessing. A somber Branko, however, never gloated over enemy casualties, which had been *modus operandi, de rigeur* among his Austro-Hungarian Cavalrymen. As a Sergeant-Major, he had constantly reprimanded his troops in this regard—something his comrade non-coms and officers never understood.

"Why not, Branko?" they had always asked in all seriousness. "They're just fucking scum."

But here, now, Branko knew these men were cheering a morality being righted rather than the death of others for its own sake. And so he held back his criticism.

As hoped, the veteran British and Canadian forces acquitted themselves famously, backing both the right flank and reserves. By mid-morning the stunned Huns, still alive and mobile, were in full retreat. Their withdrawal signaled that the first round belonged to the Entente English speakers.

But the victory had not come without significant casualties. Squad and Platoon leaders gave their counts to their officers, who in turn worked up the totals for Wild Bill. In his mind, even one death—or casualty of any kind—left little reason to celebrate success. Branko, Monahan and McNabb subscribed to this posture wholeheartedly.

The Battle of Passchendaele ground on for nearly a week. By the end of that week, the Germans were weakened far more seriously than the allied divisions. Their newly introduced tanks had been completely immobilized by two heavy rainstorms resulting in impassable mud fields. Repeated Royal Air Force bombardments had severely hampered German supply trucks and trains.

Supported by the AEF's 42nd Division and Wild Bill Donovan's Battalions, the 1st and 2nd Canadian Divisions mounted a final attack on the town and the adjacent strategic hillside. It took only three hours to secure both.

The beaten-down Bosh streamed out of the forests, surrendering en masse and giving British High Command the logistical problem of what to do with so the prisoners.

The long, drawn-out battle had come to a victorious end. The German High Command conceded a "strategic" win to the allied nations, but a "tactical" victory for the Central Powers. The street-fighting kids of the 69th rejected this statement as a bunch of sour *Bosh* grapes. The word *Bosh* was the "official" derogatory word for the Germans, arising from its use exclusively by the French and spreading to all other Entente troops. For the French, who had a long history of clashes with the Bosh, it translated into "pig-headed, obstinate and stubborn."

"Fuck 'em," one American soldier summed it up succinctly. "We walloped them fair and square. They can go home and drown themselves in a barrel of sauerkraut, the shitheads!"

*****

The Pripet marshes
White Russian SSR
November 1, 1941

The last two hit-and-run missions, though successful, left the Zhid Partizaners exhausted and hungry. Removed from their forested Ukraine, they were ordered to coordinates deep within the bleak, wet, and largely uninhabited Pripet marshland, along-side the river of the same name.

"Not fit for human life," complained Comrade Ehrenburg, the busty former Air Force political officer. The longer she fought with her fellow partisans, the more removed from the party line she became. In addition to that, she continued to take a shine to Brigadier Branko. This resulted in constant childish pranks, such as the time Kostya took one of her hefty bras from her carpet bag and hung it on a small pine above Branko's bedroll, while both were asleep. Breakfast *that* morning was like a kindergarten class having milk and cookie treats. *Oy vay!*

"So, nu, Simcha, how long do we hide out here?" Lev asked.

Hoping for word from his wife and children he had bravely held up his chin throughout the frequent skirmishes and raids. "There's not a kraut patrol within fifty kilometers."

Two days previously, he had led a raid on a *sympathizer farm* supplying milk, bread and eggs to a nearby Nazi rear echelon ammunition distribution base. The house and barn were torched by the raiders, but Lev spared the lives of the family. In these Western regions of Russia, such sympathizers were everywhere—primarily people and organizations hoping for better treatment from the "good Germans" than they expected from the Communist party's "bad *apparatchiks.*"

Simcha was at a loss for a definitive answer to Lev's question. He had wondered what the hell High Command had in mind for this very effective and loyal Zhid troop. But as always, questions were one-way down the command chain, and required succinct, non-argumentative answers from him. He was sure that they treated all other groups this way, too. It was the only thing that held his anger in check.

He and Branko had become fast friends and counted on each other for intellectual stimulation and comradeship. It was as if they were co-commanders—but of course, this could not be. Still, as a sounding board, Simcha could not want for anything better than Branko.

No, Branko had not given up hope for rescue. He allowed that General Timoshenko had more important things on his mind, like saving Moscow. The city still held on against all odds, hoping for an early and bad winter. But Branko often wondered why Wild Bill Donovan and the powers in Washington had not mounted some sort of negotiating round with the Nazis.

Maybe I'm not as important as I think I am, the retired Brigadier General silently mused. On the other hand, he half sold himself on the idea that perhaps talks were, indeed, underway. Meanwhile, he had to admit this adventure with the partisans was right up his alley! If truth be told, he damn-well enjoyed it.

In much larger numbers than the sympathizers, were countless loyal Russians who did everything for the motherland's cause; food, clothing, horses, recruits, blacksmiths, doctors, dentists, medicines, extra guns and ammunition. All of this meant extreme danger for those abettors and all proceeded with caution. And then, on occasion, the High Command would supply some of the aforementioned materials and services. On one recent radio transmission, Simcha was honored to be told that his Zhid unit was by far the most self-sufficient in the field.

Between the larger cities of Brest, Minsk and Kiev, scattered *partizaner* units roamed at will. This was mainly because the Nazis could only mount insignificant rear echelon activity. Aside from their general policing duties they now rarely strayed far afield from wherever stationed. This was not to say that the usual Einsatzgruppen massacres had disappeared. On the contrary, they went on at a steady pace. There was no shortage of Jews, Gypsies and ex-Commissars to eliminate and the Nazis eagerly carried out their inhuman tasks. The insidious rape of Western Russia was still in full swing, while the German armies advanced eastward toward the Urals—at times unchallenged.

To Branko, this lack of a more ferocious defense was of earth-shaking consequence. He and Simcha talked about this frequently and neither could understand how the Big Red war machine could have been so overestimated. Or perhaps, the two men variously opined, the Nazi juggernaut had been vastly underestimated.

On Sunday, December 7th at 2130 hours, while still languishing in the Pripet marshes, Branko's insular world was suddenly and vigorously shaken. According to a transmission from the Kremlin's Command Headquarters, the Japanese had pulled a sneak attack on the United States Territory of Hawaii. Details were scarce, of course: All transmissions were necessarily minimal, coming at times in just a short sentence or two. In this case, Simcha heard only, "Sunday, December 7th...unexpected...US fleet destroyed...Hawaii...act of war."

Branko was speechless. Although he was certain that his country would be drawn into the war one way or another, the abrupt and cowardly manner of the attack was stunning.

In retrospect, Branko realized that the news shouldn't have been so unexpected. Nearly a year previously, Wild Bill had confided that one of his Asian hacks warned that the Japanese navy was then capable of mounting a surprise attack. Hawaii was never mentioned, but the agent had sent two coded cables suggesting Manila and its U.S. Naval Station as the likely target.

Intelligence was not a perfect science, but this little tidbit of information was only off by a mere 5,000 miles of ocean. Branko pictured his old friend going absolutely beserk at that moment. A reasonable guess, at that.

Within minutes after Simcha announced the tragic news, the entire troop gathered around Branko, in a sincere display of deep comradeship and every last one voiced their personal sympathetic condolences.

After hugging the somber Branko, Raisel was the first to voice a more universal concern. With America facing a Pacific war with an especially strong adversary, what consequence would this hold for Russia? They were deeply embattled with a powerful German onslaught, and the new American conflict could dash their chance for any imminent second front.

Branko quietly reminded her that, on the contrary, America would have to declare war on Germany too and critical supplies would undoubtedly flow at a greater pace into Russia via Murmansk. He assured her and the others that there would be no limits to increased help from America. This would be in their mutual aims to defeat Hitler's Germany at all costs. A second front in the west could be an even more immediate goal by the Americans. At this critical juncture, Branko could fathom no reason for America holding back any longer.

This prompted spontaneous cheers and a round or two or three of vodka and beer for everyone. Of course, it never took much for this type of celebration to kick off. Toasts were raucous, sad, happy, funny and teary—all at once. Then and there, Branko was finally made an "honorary and respected citizen" of the great Russian nation—which was commensurate with a rash of kissing and hugging from all. The four women who had joined the troop over the past two months suddenly "adopted" the tall, handsome American general as a surrogate husband to fill in for their own dead, missing or imprisoned mates.

Simcha and the men laughed uncontrollably. Lost on them was the mostly innocent and purely symbolic gesture by the other Maccabee women—including Capitan Raisel, who feigned a spitfire jealousy. Comrades who had drawn guard duty that morning, could hear the shouts from a kilometer away, where the four guard posts were positioned to the four points of the compass.

Moments later, Simcha received another coded transmission, ordering a strike on a fuel train that evening. The train was scheduled to leave the oil depot in occupied Minsk at midnight and would be passing the coordinates within twenty kilometers of their camp site between 0200 and 0230 hours. This was just outside the White Russian town of Mazyr, also on the shores of the River Pripet.

Aside from the Lev farm strike, it had been a week since any major action. Branko, in his morose state, wanted to be in on this one.

"Dammit, Branko, I don't want you volunteering for this mission because of perceived revenge. The Japanese don't even know you exist! I just don't want to put you in any more danger than necessary —just in case someone in Washington remembers that you're still waiting to be rescued. The transmissions haven't mentioned you in the last ten days, but if I let their hero get blown to bits—"

"Simchaleh, your concern is appreciated," Branko interrupted. "But I've got to do something in grievance for those poor bastards in Hawaii who weren't even ready for what hit them. Call it revenge. Call it self-indulgence. Call me *mashigah*, but I'll be ready to go tonight and help to blast that train to kingdom come! I have to!"

Simcha understood and shrugged his shoulders, palms outstretched.

The "demolition" team consisted of Alyosha and Lev, both of whom had been with Branko on the heart-breaking Babi Yar exercise. A third team member was Flight Lieutenant Sasha Cohen, a downed fighter pilot who had parachuted far behind the lines and narrowly escaped capture. They each took an animated delight in having the Soviet Union's newest "honorary citizen" on board.

AT WAR 1918

Paris, Rue de Rois de Sicile
November 25, 1917 (1100 hours)

With the luck of the Irish, as Father Francis Patrick Duffy said, Branko's regiment was on three-day leave. It had been a brutal combat month of scattered skirmishes in and around Ypres in Flanders. Deployed back to the Forest of Chantilly's bivouac area, they learned that the 42nd Division qualified for "rest leave" at the end of Thanksgiving week. Branko was happy to get it. For the first time, he was feeling his age—and it was full of aches and pains. He was fatigued and needed this relaxation.

As one of the very few American servicemen with family in nearby Paris, Branko offered to take Chaplain Milton Weiss with him to Tante Shayndl's. Weiss, the only Jewish Chaplain in the 42nd Division, was a good Brooklyn friend of Father Duffy. But Weiss apologetically declined, having already accepted an invitation from a Parisienne rabbi to share his pulpit for *Shabbat*.

"The *Yiddishe boychicks* of the 42nd sure don't need me around to conduct services," Weiss remarked when Branko had asked if he was staying back in Chantilly for the three days. "If they haven't found God in the mud-filled trenches of Passchendaele, then they're beyond any help I can ever be."

A practical man, this Milton Weiss, thought Branko and then turned his thoughts to Tante's. *There sure as hell won't be any turkey, nor the usual fixin's, here at Tante Shayndl's.*

Having arrived from Chantilly close to noon, the smiling Branko was now standing in the vestibule of Tante's spacious apartment. He had again brought along two duffels full of food.

Tante flung herself into her nephew's arms. After squealing with joy she immediately set about to telephone her two daughters. While doing so, she managed to introduce a suave, middle-aged gentleman who was sitting on the couch, holding a demitasse of coffee.

"Branko, meet Charles Ohrbach, and Charles this is my dear nephew, Branko Horvitch."

The two men shook hands, and gingerly kissed one another on both cheeks in true European fashion. After she finished talking with each of her daughters, Tante Shayndl came and sat next to Charles. She quickly mentioned that he was proficient in both Yiddish and English, as well as French, of course.

"Branko, dear, Charles and I met at a cafe on Rosiers three weeks ago."

"Yes, Lieutenant, I've been hearing of your recent frontline heroics. Listening to your Tante, one might think that you've commissioned yourself to single-handedly beat the Hun into submission. For that, we the humble French, salute you, sir!"

This tongue-in-cheek remark brought a chorus of chuckles from all three.

"Charles, with her infinite pride, Tante neglected to mention that I have help. A whole street gang of battling Irishmen from the Fighting 69th Regiment!"

Again, laughter. This could have gone around for a while longer had not Tante offered some informative interjections.

"Charles manages two banks here in Paris. His dear wife Elsa passed on two years ago, and his two married children live in Geneva. I'm way ahead of him in the grandchildren department!"

Branko noticed how she had been pronouncing the man's name in the French, *Sharl*, and he took a mental note to do the same. The pleasantries went on until Channah and Raiseleh came by with their children and their husbands followed later. They were, of course, familiar with Charles and greeted him warmly

Looks like this could be serious stuff, thought Branko. *But then, why not? She's as beautiful as ever and he appears to be a nice enough gent with a wry sense of humor. I like that—and obviously, Tante does. I couldn't be happier if this is the real thing. She's fifty-four now, and I'd guess he's just a few years older. Great! For both of them—and Mazel Tov!*

It turned out that Channah's husband Raul had done business with Charles at the bank and had known him for some time. It soon became clearly evident that it was the son-in-law who had arranged for their meeting at the cafe.

Raul was the one who had spent two years in the French infantry right before the war began. Now with the two children, he was reclassified and placed in the *over age thirty-five reserves*, ready to be called-up if things got any worse at the front. This was a common, tense day-to-day situation in France and it was affecting the struggling haberdashery that Raul owned. He had inherited the business from his late father. Luckily he had two older, trusted clerks working for him. If he was recalled, the store could go on—if only barely.

Raiseleh's husband, Bertrand, had just turned thirty-six and his situation was almost identical to Raul's. The major difference was that he had suffered significant leg and shoulder wounds at the Battle of Amiens in 1915.

"The Hun would have to be dancing down Champs Elysee in *lederhosen* before Bertie would be recalled," laughed Raul. It was pleasing for Branko to observe that the two boys were close, as were their wives. This boded well for Tante Shayndl and it warmed his heart.

The dinner that was pieced together on that late afternoon was a thing of magic rather than the smoke and mirrors one would expect of an unplanned dinner. With Branko's PX loot, along with the scrounging efforts of the others, Charles included, a comparative feast was on the dining room table. Bread, the ultimate staff of French life and living, which was now plentiful since the October wheat harvest, competed for the "main course." Banker Charles traded one of his two expensive fedoras to a customer in exchange for a generous hoarded slab of scarce butter. Needless to say, his table mates cheered and toasted to no end. The meal was rounded-out with potatoes, endives, tomatoes, asparagus, carrots, aubergine and a fetching display of cooked haricots. Of course, there was wine. Some of it had been saved since before the war, for just such an occasion.

The real prizes were two small, kosher chickens, which the busiest butcher on Rosiers had limited one to a customer: In this case the butcher obviously had failed in his restriction—or rather, had failed at the hands of an unmentionably extravagant and inflationary wartime price. But it had been more than just money: It was the presence of a uniformed Branko that moved the butcher to package two pullets: One for his old customer and friend, Shayndl, and the another for, "your General Pershing."

In Yiddish, the butcher explained how grateful he was to the gallant Americans and kissed the Lieutenant on each cheek. The other customers, waiting for their one chicken, cheered as he left with Tante, and a pullet under each arm.

As Branko was leaving they added to their cheers, *"Geh, mitt Gott, un geh gezunt and koom gezunt, Americaine!"* Go with God, and go in health and come back in health, American!

Following the delicious repast, Branko was urged to tell the story of Thanksgiving, which he reluctantly did, to the delight of the four children. The Pilgrims, Chief Massasoit and his Indians, Myles Standish and the original Plymouth celebratory feast had never been represented quite as colorfully as this.

Massasoit, a defrocked rabbi and a *schochet?* As a grinning Shayndl handled the translation into French she managed to *not* actually say, *Oh come now, Lieutenant!*

All such good things inevitably come to an end—to be remembered and cherished. And so too did this reunion. Knowing the latest reports from the front, it was difficult for everyone to say goodbye to the American when he left a few days later. There were hugs and kisses all around and enough tears to fill a river.

Charles and Shayndl walked hand-in-hand with Branko to the Bastille Monument, where he boarded the Sunday evening military bus returning to the Chantilly bivouac.

*****

Near Chateau Thierry
Aisne-Marne Sector
July 22, 1918 (0900 hours)

The mission was to sniff out relative strengths of the German artillery during a brief lull in action.

Donovan had assigned Branko the task within just a few hours of when they were to start out. In the available prep time, he had a lot to do, including choosing the team. He drafted a plan, scanned maps, arranged gear, put on dark coveralls without rank or insignia, patted the lamp black on his face and insured his team was ready.

They were to encircle the lines in order to approach undetected from the rear in a type of infiltration Branko had practiced during countless training exercises in Camp Upton. Similar, but less demanding assignments had been undertaken in the Ypres and Passchendaele battles—both with far better odds for success. Branko had led three such forays; anxious moments, not one casualty. The Brits and Aussies particularly, were in awe of this display of derring-do, muttering, "Crazy Yanks!"

For this mission, Branko had selected four of his most battle-tested MP non-coms as team members; Sergeant Harry Dawes, Corporals Ned Banks, Peter Winchendon and Karl Mayer. The latter, an Alsatian Jew born in Strasbourg before his parents immigrated to New York, spoke German and some French. He had more than ten years of highly-praised police experience in Passaic and Paterson, New Jersey.

Together, the five men scoured the sector maps and by midnight set-out on a quick-step, silent march. There was a good piece of ground to cover in order to be back before dawn. The route would take them through a part of Chateau-Thierry and along the River Marne. A close-in Division sentry post had been alerted to expect them at that point and from there they intended to swing sharply southeast to the village of Crezancy. If reports were accurate, Crezancy was to be free of enemy activity. There they were to seek out a Frenchman who had on occasions given credible information to the Americans and British.

The Frenchman, M'sieu Ferdinand Bellancourt, was a spry sixty-six-year-old former pharmacist and born Hun hater. Intelligence had indicated that the man thoroughly enjoyed his role. He would be home in bed and so the agreed upon signal was to be a scratching sound on the rear window. Donovan had warned Branko that the man was known to be a crotchety curmudgeon at times, and known to difficult whenever the mood stuck him. He knew his services were highly coveted by the Entente powers, and he consistently played the role to the hilt. Branko had the usual fifty francs to pay him once satisfied that he did his job.

By 0100 hours they reached Crezancy, which had suffered enormous damage in attacks and counterattacks. During the past six months it had been relatively unscathed and was slowly re-populating. Still, most former residents would never consider returning. It was not a ghost town as were villages, towns and cities along the front lines, but it looked like one to Branko and the boys.

One of the first bombed-out buildings they came across looked like a matchbox somebody stepped on. It still proudly bore a sign reading, *Bellancourt Pharmacie*. The house was six doors farther down the deserted street. Even though in need of a new roof, it was not in very bad shape.

Within minutes the team was inside the completely darkened abode and drinking cups of hot tea. Their generous host was in a cooperative mood and had served the tea after quickly shedding his nightclothes and dressing for the occasion.

"My *anglais*," said Bellancourt, "it should be better after working closely with you *Americain* and *Les Canadiens*. My late wife and I hid and fed an Indian soldier for a month last year, during one of the big Hun offensives. I learned a good bit more from him. Poor *Rajah* was shot and killed just 100 meters from here when he tried to make a run for his lines. The same night my Marie was killed in the shelling barrage. No Hun around here now, I assure you. They've taken-up positions on the higher ground directly to the southwest of here. A few kilometers from what is left of the town of Fossy. Now, just what is it you want from me?"

At least it sounds like he's willing to guide us, thought Branko.

"Well, let's get to it, M'sieu," Branko responded, and with Karl Mayer translating he continued: "We want you to take us to a point which is on a line with the biggest concentration of German artillery. Their new behemoths have been pounding the living shit out of our trenches. We also want to know where their reserve troops and tanks are holed-up."

If there had been any doubt that Bettancourt could keep up the pace, it quickly evaporated. The pencil-thin, old scarecrow practically sprinted ahead of the team. They were literally surrounded by total devastation on both sides and the reed of a man scurried along without pause.

It was odd seeing the barren trees and bushes in July—and they realized that it was only the dark of night preventing them from seeing the blackened reality of destruction. But they didn't miss seeing the gaping, fifty-meter wide shell holes peppering the landscape. It was one bombed-out village after another—a *No Man's Land* personified to imperfection, just as Branko had witnessed in Passchendaele and Ypres. Only now the gloom was just north and east of Chateau-Thierry.

"So far so friggin good, boys," Branko whispered reassurance to the others.

twenty minutes later, Bettancourt stopped in his tracks and pointed to a hillside that was perhaps a half-kilometer away. He said, "There—over there—that's the exact location of most of the German artillery. They just moved everything there a week ago. I scouted it out. Thought the Entente would want to know."

He spoke like a machine gun, in French and fractured English. It was propitious that Corporal Mayer counted a fair bit of French in his repertoire. Branko had urged him to keep this under his hat, so the other regiments wouldn't try to borrow him away.

Sheltering his flashlight, Branko marked the coordinates on the sector map. Bettancourt was of vital help, showing exactly where the village of Crezancy lay in relation to the hillside of German artillery. There was absolutely no reason why the intact Entente artillery couldn't zero in with a deadly amount of accuracy, especially to soften up the enemy before any offensive began.

"My good friend, Theo Marchand, reported major troop movements last week—just west of here," offered Bettancourt pointing to just below the artillery emplacements adjacent to the camouflaged tanks and trucks. "The way the Hun operates, I guess that is where the reserve troops are en trenched."

Branko nodded, making a mental note of this information He then pulled out a crumpled-up fifty-franc note and handed it to Bettancourt. He said, "Aside from getting back to our lines, we're all but done here. Thank you for helping, M'sieu Bettancourt.

At that, the heroic Frenchman actually smiled and grasped everyone's hand. He also suggested a faster route to return to Chateau-Thierry from the opposite side of the Marne.

Without further adieu, off he went into the darkness.

Once the Frenchman was out of earshot, Branko turned to his men: "Boys, I've been thinking bad thoughts! Wouldn't it be a shame if we wasted the opportunity to a little noise tonight?"

"What in the hell does that mean, Branko," asked a deadpan Pete Winchendon.

"Gather round, boys," Branko said, with a hand gesture. Look here, I packed two sticks of dynamite and we each have two grenades. Right?"

They nodded.

"Those big hunks of iron up on that hill seem to be crying for a big bang, don't you think?"

"Explain, O leader of this motley crew," Harry Dawes implored, while bowing to the ground.

"Okay, we have plenty of time before daybreak. We can head up that hill; This far behind their lines, I'm sure the Bosh won't bother with a full guard. Once we're up there, we can easily eliminate the sentry or two they'll have. With the long wicks of these dynamite sticks, we'll have a good minute to run downhill into the dark—and boom!"

Branko spread his arms to signify a giant explosion.

The others were smiling.

"Now, let's talk about it, at least," Branko went on. "I'm not going to order you to do something dangerous, above and beyond the call of duty, if you don't want to. I'm sure you realize that if any of us are captured we'd likely be shot on the spot. Dressed as we are, we're not exactly standard military—more like in *non-uniform, spy status—*"

"What the hell, Branko, I'm in," interrupted Sergeant Dawes.

"Sign me up, Lieutenant," Mayer chimed in. "Do we get a $100 bonus for this little exercise in madness?"

With Dawes and Mayer having signed on, Branko looked to

Winchendon and Banks for their *yea* or *nay*.

"I guess it would be something to tell my kids when they ask 'What did you do in France, dad?'" said Winchendon, the edgy, experienced plain-clothes cop from Boston.

All eyes went to the brawny Corporal Banks, the former cop from Chillicothe, Ohio. He milked the attention for a full ten-seconds and then humorously voted by saying, "Okay, let's do it—I'm not about to wait here. I'm afraid of the dark, you know."

Quiet chuckles went around, but their bravado did not hide the obvious nervous anxiety. The die was cast and Branko hastily drew up a rough plan on the map. After all understood, the climb began.

Banks and Mayer were on the right flank. Winchendon and Dawes were on the left. Branko took the the middle, carrying the matches and two sticks of dynamite. They didn't know how much damage—if any—they could do to inch-thick steel. But they damned-well intended to find out.

fifty yards further uphill, there he was: A single sentry, half-asleep. He was leaning against a denuded pine tree with a Mauser cradled in his lap. In the absence of crunchy leaves or gravel, the stealthy approach across grass was all but completely silent. Dawes signaled he would take the sentry from behind. A moment later there came the crack of the Hun's forehead from the death blow at the butt-end of Dawes' rifle. Banks and Mayer didn't even pause on their way to the to the top of the ridge.

They didn't find anyone around the first four artillery pieces. Within a minute, they came back down to Branko and announced *all clear*. Winchendon and Dawes were tasked with the first two pieces, Banks the next and Branko, with the dynamite, would take the biggest and last. Mayer, stationed behind a tree midway up the slope, covered them.

The silence of the night came to a noisy end.

The grenades tossed into the barrels of the first two guns exploded in unison. Branko had already lit the wicks of the dynamite and all four men came running down hill. Mayer stayed behind for a moment —in case cover was needed. It was not. Then all five stooped down behind some tree stumps by the River Marne as the dynamite went off in grandeur. Black smoke covered the half-moon sky, followed by whistles, shouts, and klieg lights flashing all around. The shocked, half-asleep Bosh troops, wondered what the hell was happening.

Mission over.

A mountain of work for one evening's sortie, but Branko and his MP non-coms pulled it off, returning to their lines before dawn. Branko wrote up a one paragraph report and as regulations required, the four cohorts attested, each signing the appropriate form. It was then sent up the Chain of Command in order to feed red tape minutia.

*****

**Seringes on the Ourcq River
Oise-Aisne Sector
July 30, 1918**

The blistering offensive set-off after the Branko night escapade, continued for nearly two weeks. American forces in concert with the main French units gained ten kilometers westward beyond the Marne River salient. British, French and Canadian artillery laid waste to the vast German position as reported by Branko's team. The Bosh reserves took a major beating and were of little or no help after the artillery attack. Entente Supreme Commander Marshal Foch himself publicly announced that this was the turning point in the war for which they had been waiting and praying.

The time was ripe for further bold encirclement raids to prod the German weaknesses as they swiftly eventuated. Wild Bill led one of these raids in the vicinity of the Ourcq River near Seringes. If the Bosh had the remaining strength to mount one more massive counter-attack, this was the most likely area from which they would catapult.

Branko took his platoon leaders to a briefing at the "dugout" of the 165th Regimental "headquarters" and Wild Bill asked him to follow as soon as possible—if not sooner. The 42nd Division Commander issued yet another reminder for the Fighting 69th troops. They were to recognize having been "federalized" into what was now named the 165th Regiment of the Division, serving as one of two regiments under Donovan's crack 85th Brigade. Wild Bill, as was typical, paid little attention to things of this sort—it was little more the minutia of red tape that he felt was beneath him.

At any rate, he rallied the two regiments in his command to join him in what could be a harrowing exercise. They surreptitiously reached the coordinates of a location purported to be at least two infantry divisions strong and accompanied by a major tank force with assorted attack elements. In the intelligence brief it had all the earmarks of a German push across a broad front.

But the brief had been a matter of poor intelligence reporting. Wild Bill's force found nothing of the sort. He sent *"C"* company to the top of a ridge overlooking the staging area and…

No military presence. No artillery. Nothing.

During this reconnaissance one man was shot and killed. Sergeant Alfred Joyce Kilmer was hit squarely in the forehead by a sniper who was never located. Oddly and sadly enough, Kilmer, an occasional aide to Donovan, had actually volunteered for this mission. Bill was devastated and ordered the body to be taken back to the temporary medical station.

Father Duffy broke down—he knew Kilmer better than anyone. Beside being a converted, devout Catholic, the man was a published, renowned poet, writer and lecturer before joining the 69th. He had been one of the regiment's most beloved members. Of all of his literary work, the most noted was one which had become popular world-wide in 1914.

Three days later, on August 2nd, Kilmer was laid to rest in a makeshift American Cemetery near Seringes, at Freres-de-Tardenois. The entire platoon under his sergeantcy, stood-by, at attention. There were those in the ranks who wept as the poet's body was lowered and Father Duffy bid farewell by reciting *Trees*:

I think that I shall never see
A poem lovely as a tree.

A tree whose hungry mouth is prest
Against the earth's sweet flowing breast;
A tree that looks at God all day,
And lifts her leafy arms to pray;

A tree that may in summer wear
A nest of robins in her hair;

Upon whose bosom snow has lain;
Who intimately lives with rain.

Poems are made by fools like me,
But only God can make a tree.

*****

August 7, 1918

In a minor skirmish Wild Bill Donovan was wounded in almost the exact same Ourcq River location where Kilmer was killed. The doctors said that he was lucky—this time. With a deep flesh wound in his left side, he wanted to return to duty the very next day. While it was a minor wound, one look at Wild Bill's pasty complexion and high temperature and the doctor overruled Wild Bill. Between a flu epidemic spreading through troops on both sides of the conflict and the persistent dangers of gangrene and blood poisoning, the doctor had just cause to book his dissent.

During the second week of Wild Bill's convalescence, Branko's company came off the line and he stopped by the field hospital for a visit. Father Duffy, who was making his rounds with the injured troops, led Branko to Wild Bill's bed. Propped-up by pillows, Wild Bill began grumbling about being kept off duty by an over-protective doctor.

"That's all he talks about," Father Duffy remarked with a dismissive wave of his hand and turned to minister to the wounded private in the next bed.

"What the hell, Wild Bill," remarked a relieved Branko. "Now you'll get that, hotsy, totsy *Citation for Meritorious Service*."

Smiling at the joke, Wild Bill parried with, "Sure, it'll make me out to be a bigger hero than the high falutin' *Badge of Military Merit* that they used to call it—kind of had a Boy Scout ring to it!" He was further buoyed by Branko's report that there had been no other casualties for the past week.

When Corporal Mayer dropped by for a visit, the conversation momentarily reverted to Branko ribbing Wild Bill for "Getting a little scratch in battle."

"He didn't tell you how he got that scratch, did he?" Mayer asked.

"As a matter of fact, he didn't" Branko replied.

"Mayer—" Wild Bill began in a tone of admonishment that Mayer ignored.

"He took the hit after *personally* wiping out a sniper who had been raising hell with a nearby French recon position. Hell, he'll get the frog's *Crux di Care*, or whatever it's called, for that!"

"And I hope the hell he was the same son-of-a-bitching Bosh who murdered Kilmer—may he rest in peace."

"*Omayn,*" echoed Captain Horvitch.

The Good Father Duffy looked over from the wounded private in the next bed and shot back, "A big Hebe *omayn* from me too, boys!"

A raucous chorus of laughter went all around.

Duffy had helped to carry the wounded Wild Bill from the line and it wasn't the first time he had done that sort of thing. In the 69th, it was frequently said, "If ye see two litter-bearers on the battlefield, ye can bet your fookin' Irish ass one of 'em's Father Duffy."

Although the wound had been healing well, word from Division later came that Wild Bill would be kept out of the field until further notice from the medical officers.

**Between Reims and Verdun
Meuse-Argonne Sector
September 8, 1918 (1700 hours)**

Along with other officers and non-coms, Captain Branko Horvitch was honored with a battlefield promotion. It was a summer day not at all far removed from the recent successes of the Entente offensives.

Branko and Wild Bill had successfully lobbied for the "fabulous four" MP's who had joined with Branko for the midnight caper that had been credited as a turning point for the battle. In recognition of their suicidal efforts the men received *Citation Stars*. Harry Dawes was promoted to *Master Sergeant* and the three corporals made it to *Sergeant*.

Branko just wanted to keep them alive.

The American officer/non-com corp had suffered far too many casualties; this included Branko's MP units and the 165th. Major McNabb, badly wounded, was back at base hospital fighting for his life. Not so fortunate, if even that, Lieutenant Tom Monahan—the Pittsburgh cop—had been killed in a German counterattack two weeks previously. Of course the most widely known death was that of Sergeant Joyce Kilmer, the regiment's Poet Laureate. Because of these losses, and many more men just like them, the available-for-duty count in the 69th was just below 50% of the full complement. Similar discouraging numbers held true for most of the American units on the front lines. As hardened as he was to loss, Branko took every death as a personal affront.

He had immediately written a letter of condolences to Tom's wife in Pittsburgh. It hurt, but he did it. Wild Bill did the same, writing a letter to the wife of the bed-ridden Charlie McNabb, as well. Father Duffy wrote to Joyce Kilmer's wife and family on the very day Kilmer fell. The unwritten rule was that the officer with the same or next highest rank, closest to the deceased be the one to communicate with the next of kin. It was done without fail, religiously and going back to the American Revolution.

A month after being wounded, Wild Bill was being promised by the 42nd Division Commander that replacement troops were on the way.

"*Herr Kapitan* Branko Horvitch, we've got to end this godamm war fast, or it will be thee, me, Father Duffy and ten fucking, God-fearing Irishmen holding the last line against the Bosh, or Hun, or whatever you want to call 'em."

With only Branko within ear shot, Bill quietly went on: "Now that the Commander himself is going to be rotated to Pershing's staff—end of October—promotion to Division Command is between Doug MacArthur of the 84th and me. With his Brigadier rank, he'll get it and I don't really care."

"Bullshit!," Branko came back. "You have to care. There's still a damn war to be finished here, ol' boy!"

"Yeah, but I personally can't stand that pecker-head—just not the kind of guy I would have a beer with. I just want to stick with my Brigade and the Fighting 69th. Help you get that war won, eh, Captain?"

"Keerist, Bill, we'll never get any more replacements with that martinet at the head. I think I've had two words with him since he came to Division. He's another one of those snotty, slick-shit West Pointers. The guys in the 84th tell me they can't stand his guts! They say it takes a ton of will power for someone not to strangle him with his own godamm riding crop."

This was too good to let go, and Wild Bill didn't. "Riding crop! Mother Mary, what the hell is that for...is he gonna personally whip the Bosh?"

They were hoping for 400 replacements—if and when they arrived. They wanted two entire companies and Donovan intended to allocate each so that his units could get back to near-normal troop numbers. As always, he shared such things with Branko and knew that he would receive an honest assessment from him. As for prevailing view of MacArthur, both men were obviously in aggrement.

Command's promise had indeed been for 400 men but Branko strongly felt it sounded too good to be true—and it probably was. He was convinced that the war would end before full-strength would ever be attained. Having served the military of two countries, one now his enemy in this war, he had become a die-hard realist and everyday pragmatist.

Meuse-Argonne Sector
September 17, 1918 (1200 hours)

The Bosh artillery was weaker than at any time in the last two months. Branko and Donovan agreed that the German salvos were falling short or way off target. There had not been a hit on the trench lines where the 42nd Division awaited orders to move forward. They and remnants of six other American Divisions had reached this new frontline position, a full eighty kilometers northeast of Chateau Thierry and 150 kilometers from Paris.

A few weeks before, General John J. "Black Jack" Pershing had finally received full and sole command of what he appropriately named *the First American Army*. Heretofore, all American units were considered supernumeraries to help the French and British wherever needed. This would eliminate some of the inherent confusion that at times crippled Entente communications in emergency situations. It would now be far easier to procure ammunition, medicine and mess supplies as well as coordinate offensive and defensive postures.

It certainly cut down on the ongoing troop complaint that joked, "Hey, who's my boss? The Brit, Frenchie the Frog, the Canuck, the Kiwi or the Kangaroo?"

The Division Commanders hailed it as a wise and long overdue move. Everyone down the line from officer to private knew it was for the best. *Hell, I'm for anything that will get me home,* was the prevailing thought of the day, every day. With little new to discuss, the change continued to be the main topic of conversation throughout the trenches, latrines and messes. And probably on both sides of the conflict, at that.

St. Mihiel Salient
Meuse-Argonne Sector
September 20, 1918

Two days after Pershing's First Army opened an attack on the salient held by the Bosh since the beginning of the war, the Germans backtracked to their own border.

The entire Entente was pleased as could be. Pershing and his officers were damn proud of it—light casualties and all. The 103rd Aero Squadron, led by Captain Eddie Rickenbacker, coordinated their relentless bombing of Bosh positions with the 42nd Division's ground attack. Donovan's Brigade competed with MacArthur's to be the first to step foot in Germany, but it was the 129th artillery regiment from Kansas City and environs that paved the way. With precision salvos the 129th ripped the German positions to smithereens. Such pin-point coordination would have been nigh impossible before the September formation of the first "all-American" Division. The result was a stunning victory in less than forty-eight hours.

On the eve before the offensive Pershing directed all Brigade Commanders to meet with commanding officers of the Aero and Artillery units. Purpose: to tighten coordinating efforts.

Colonel Donovan assigned Branko and all other company commanders to join him for the meeting. Also attending was Captain Eddie Rickenbacker, ace pilot of the 103rd Aero and the senior officers for each battery of the 129th Artillery, 35th Division.

Branko was particularly impressed with the way one of the artillery battery Captains handled MacArthur. After the productive meeting ended, Brigadier General MacArthur signaled for Captain Harry Truman to meet with him. Branko, who had been chatting with the bespectacled Kansas City artillery chief, casually stood off to the side listening to the conversation. MacArthur was upset because ill-positioned artillery guns landed salvos too short of a target in one of the July battles. Captain Truman politely asked MacArthur for specifics that the man did not have. The intense Brigade commander apparently had only second or third-hand information that Truman knew was completely off base.

"When you get me the details, General MacArthur," the battery Captain said, "then we can sensibly discuss it."

That's Logical, Branko thought.

MacArthur, the starch-shirt West Pointer, snapped back, "Watch out for your wise-ass attitude in talking to a superior officer."

The testy Truman going nose-to-nose, not retreating an inch, repeated his request for details, saluted the Brigadier smartly and then walked away. Branko walked along with him, listening to a red-hot barrage.

"My God, Horvitch," Truman all but roared, "that spit-and-polish son-of-a-bitch doesn't know his ass from a shell hole. I'll bet I never hear from him again. He wouldn't know how to gather the details on that charge if they bit him in his kay-det keester! I'd sure like to get him working for me in civilian life!"

The two Captains had a quick laugh, before wishing each other the luck-of-the-Irish in the coming offensive. It later turned out that neither Truman nor Branko heard another word about the incident. Wild Bill loved hearing the story and the 129th artillery support for the next two days was spot on target.

*****

Landres-St. George
In the Argonne Forest
October 14, 1918 (1000 hour)

This time Wild Bill Donovan played it too close, nearly ending-up just another dead man in a Yank uniform. In an attack upon a fortified German position the troops were taking heavy casualties in a rain of weapon fire. Leading by example, Donovan rallied the men and issued re-deployment orders to platoons reduced to ineffective manpower. During one of his turns in a forward position, he caught machine gun fire to his leg. Gritting though the pain of the wound, he remained with the unit until the survivors fell back to a less exposed position.

100 yards away, Captain Branko Horvitch was in the up-front position while leading his troops to spell Brigade Commander Donovan. After almost a year of continuous combat, he knew full-well that the odds were against him.

Of course, Branko never saw the "potato-masher" landing just twenty feet away. The same grenade/mortar Bosh attack left the regiment in a vulnerable situation and within an hour they suffered 50% casualties. Branko's helmet—a tin *yarmulke,* he called it—flew off of his head in the concussion. After shrapnel penetrated his body in several places he was still standing but unable to hear a thing

He glanced down to see myriad shrapnel wounds and blood.

Well, damn, flickered through his mind.

Still, he moved forward. After seeing that Wild Bill was alert enough to refuse evacuation, he, too, continued to rally his men until the medics arrived. It took a very long and painful five minutes that felt as if though it had stretched into hours.

General Pershing himself put Wild Bill Donovan in for the highly prestigious Medal of Honor. This was to be bestowed upon Donovan and the very few other chosen recipients, during the planned *Arc de Triomphe* victory parade, after war's end. The citation read:

Medal of Honor Citation
(for actions occurring on Oct 14-15, 1918)

Lt. Col. Donovan personally led the assaulting wave in an attack upon a very strongly organized position, and when our troops were suffering heavy casualties he encouraged all near him by his example, moving among his men in exposed positions, reorganizing decimated platoons, and accompanying them forward in attacks. When he was wounded in the leg by machine-gun bullets, he refused to be evacuated and continued with his unit until it withdrew to a less exposed position.

—A.E.F. Commanding General John J. Pershing

For the next two weeks, neither officer returned to duty. Branko was moved to the nearest secured field hospital a few kilometers from Landres-et St. Georges where the engagement had taken place.

As uncomfortable as Branko was when shrapnel fragments had to be removed on an ongoing basis, Wild Bill had it worse. He underwent two major operations to repair the bone the bullets had split in his right leg. His return to duty was not scheduled.

On the first day of November, with the entire German army retreating to their vaunted Hindenburg Line, Branko was pronounced sufficiently recovered for return to his outfit. The concussion had not been as bad as first thought; his hearing came back but shrapnel would stay with him for the rest of his life. Along with Donovan, he too, was awarded another Citation Star. A unit recognition for meritorious service was given to the 85th Brigade, 42nd Rainbow Division.

Meanwhile, as Branko had predicted, the promised replacements that trickled in were nowhere near the numbers required to carry on sustained offensive warfare. He and millions of others in uniform could only hope that the war would end soon. Momentarily would have been even better.

Near Metz, with the 42nd Rainbow Division
"Cease Fire," all along the front
November 11, 1918 (1100 hours.)

The "war to end all wars," came to an end.

The German High Command negotiated the terms for its full surrender at 1100 hours on the 11th month, in the Forest of Compiégne. The Entente countries and particularly the long suffering French, were satisfied that the German war machine—or what was left of it—would be dismantled, piece by piece, weapon by weapon. Germany would never again have the wherewithal to mount another act of aggression, anywhere in the world.

The killed-in-action and casualty numbers for Wild Bill's and Branko's 42nd Division soared above 2,000 dead, with more than 10,000 wounded. The 69th (165th) was saddled with approximately the same percentages. Total American casualties, 321,000; of those 53,000 were killed in action. 201,000 were wounded and 62,000 died of diseases and the raging flu epidemic. Another 4,500 had been taken as prisoners. This all amounted to 7% of the entire mobilized force.

The French and British Empire percentages were far higher, having been in the fight since 1914. Add to this the dead, wounded and missing of the enemy's Central Powers—stretching from Germany proper to Turkey, and the several Entente members—and a staggering figure of nearly forty million, raised the ultimate question —*who was the lucky winner of this mother of all nightmares?*

*****

**The Pripet Marshes
White Russian S.S.R., near Mazyr
December 8, 1941 (0330 hours)**

The spectacular explosion lit up the sky as far as the eye could see. Large parts of the train rained down with lethal metal. Simcha had insisted that the TNT explosive packs be laid on the tracks at least two kilometers from the sleeping town of Mozyr. Unlike many of the partisan commanders, he strongly felt that collateral damage to the town itself was to be avoided—and it was.

Cohen, the pilot, was more or less neutral. But Lev and Alyosha didn't give a fat damn about what happened to Mozyr and said as much. In this part of the Ukraine and White Russia, it was well known that towns of this size were rife with Nazi sympathizers.

It might not be my ballgame, Branko thought in silent agreement with Simcha, *but blowing up that munitions train was just my little payback to the Nazi-Jap partnership. If Mussolini sends a macaroni train, hell, we'll blow that sky high, too!*

Within seconds following the first of three blasts, the four saboteurs were on their way to the horses. It was about 100 yards westward toward the marshes and back to camp, post haste. They could not afford to wait any longer than that. If any of the Wehrmacht train guards survived, they would be scouring the perimeter with any hands and legs still intact. But reassuringly, there were no shouts or whistles, so chances were good that everyone on board perished. At least that offered some satisfaction for Lev and Alyosha.

However, Simcha kept a close eye on sharpshooter Lev Soloveitchik, remembering how he had stayed behind for a few minutes at Babi Yar to cleanly pick off one of the *hilfwiligers—Hitler's willing helpers*—either Ukranian or Lithuanian. Simcha practically had to drag Lev to his horse.

"If there's even one alive, my bullet wants him!"

"Not tonight, Lev, not tonight," whispered Branko. He understood the powerful animosity that was consuming the tall marksman.

When the four reached camp and passed through the sentry positions, all was quiet, except for Comrade Raisel smoking in the far corner next to one of the ubiquitous pines. With snow falling the night was brutally cold and damp,

"We could hear the godamm fireworks from here," Raisel said with a broad smile. "Good going, *malchiki*."

General Horvitch was completely exhausted and wanted only to crawl into his bed roll under the lean-to—alone.

He did.

Evening over.

THE WILSON WHITE HOUSE

Washington, D.C.
November 18, 1919

A week at Walter Reed Hospital was not what Branko envisioned whenever the shrapnel splinters caused periodic discomfort. Now, having been discharged from Reed after the most recent episode, his taxi was en route to the White House. He had been surprisingly summoned at the behest of no less than the First Lady, Edith Bolling Wilson. The message stated it would all be explained during his meeting with Mrs. Wilson.

Since deployed to the Army War College at Washington Barracks, on Greenleaf Point next to the Navy Yard, Major Horvitch had been an outspoken proponent for veteran's rights. The present limbo of so-called "peace time" was the excuse for reducing the officer corp. Granted, it was probably necessary to recoup the billions spent on the Great War, but Branko had been asking, *at what cost? The loss of a standing army sufficient to meet the unexpected?*

This was neither the first, nor the last unpopular government action to be taken in this matter. The reduction—*cashiering* it was called—became more personal to the Major when even he, a widely recognized hero, received the War Department notice. Along with several of the college's other non-West Point educated officers who had elected to stay in the armed forces, Branko was on schedule for cashiering in January. West Pointers were exempt and encouraged to stay in the ranks. Branko had no intention of leaving the United States Army without a fight.

But it was a different kind of fight he was now waging. It was one of eloquence necessary to engender public support. For that purpose, he had granted the Washington Post an interview in October. He had also carefully guarded both his words and demeanor. As an officer in the United States Regular Standing Army—albeit a highly decorated one—there were limits imposed on his criticism of the army, the government and the White House. Additionally, he did not want to compromise or jeopardize his faculty position at the College, a post that he truly cherished.

He first heard about the pending cuts from Wild Bill Donovan. Oddly enough, Donovan had related the news while in attendance of Branko's receiving the *Croix de Guerre* in April. This was France's highest military honor and it was bestowed with all the pomp and circumstance of a ceremony at the French Embassy. Donovan, Father Francis Duffy—another "Croix" recipient—and three other veterans of the Fighting 69th made the pilgrimage to Washington to honor their comrade-in-arms. Branko couldn't have been more pleased. As ten medals were awarded, Branko looked at the familiar faces among the embassy guests. He saw his favorite *fellow Romanian Fu*sgeyers, Mendel, Mordecai, Sendehr and their spouses. He thought Rivka looked especially beautiful. How proud they all were when he had called to invite them—especially for those who had not seen Branko since before he had joined the army. There wasn't a dry eye among any of them.

Donovan had also been thusly honored in France—following the Armistice—and after having already received the United States Medal of Honor.

Bill and Ruth Donovan later hosted dinner at one of the city's finer restaurants. It was in a private moment aside, that Donovan spilled the tasteless beans of spending cuts to Branko. Branko was shocked that his country and government could even be thinking about such an ill-conceived affront. Donovan, who had joined a New York law firm upon returning to the states, had retired. Even though constantly lauded as the most decorated American in the war, he had given up his association with all things military. In effect, not having any appreciable influence in Washington, by voluntarily retiring he had beaten "them" to the sucker punch.

"Bill, I trust you know what you're talking about, but I'm at a loss for nasty words concerning this injustice. And in this environment, how in hell did you swing the War College assignment for me, anyway?"

"Old friend, I knew damn well that you wanted to continue your army career. Your telling me that you gave a series of lectures up at West Point in February, gave me the opportunity to make a practiced comment to Franklin Roosevelt—our illustrious Assistant Secretary of

The Navy. He latched onto it immediately. He forcefully said 'Dammit, Bill, that guy should be lecturing at The War College. I'll see to it! We need that type of proven fighter since this insidious post-war complacency settled in.'"

"Thanks for that, Bill. The automatic promotion to major helped the old wallet, too. Now, what goes on between you and the silver-spooned *'Mr. Hahvidd, who pahked his Packidd at the Hahvidd Yahd?'*" Both old buddies laughed loudly at this remark, mocking Roosevelt's pronounced Yankee accent.

"Franklin and I go back to our days at Columbia Law School, I'll tell you what all this means someday, when he gives me permission."

"Oh, God, spare me the clandestine, covert, cloak-and-dagger, top secret, spy-under-every-bed bullshit!"

"It'll be soon. I'll phone you in a week or two."

Wild Bill Donovan volunteering nothing further, it was left at that and Branko never asked again. Now, living in a city awash with rumors, he figured he would hear the whole story from some taxi driver, waiter, bartender—or barmaid. Prohibition had, after all, loosened more lips than it had dried out.

Branko had spare time before his scheduled command performance and stopped at his Georgetown apartment to change into his dress uniform. Satisfied with his appearance in the mirror, he snapped a salute, put on a wide grin and went to meet his latest destiny. The waiting cabbie greeted him with his own flop-handed salute: "Mighty spiffy, sir, yessiree!"

He had absolutely no expectations for this meeting. In fact, Woodrow Wilson was no favorite of his for solid reasons of his own. As an immigrant, with pride in his country and for what it should stand for in the aftermath of the war, he abhorred the President's chauvinism during the recent peace talks; his so-called fourteen points; his frustrating inability to rally congressional support for the Versailles Treaty and his well-documented segregationist leanings that made Washington more Southern than ever. All of this had created a suspicion of where he stood on the Jews and other minorities of every stamp. Wilson's supporters on this question proudly pointed to Wilson's Supreme Court appointee of 1916, the curly haired liberal, Louis Dembitz Brandeis. But the majority of Jews decided it wasn't enough while America's black began seriously questioning their devotion to the Democratic Party. As Donovan and Father Duffy intimated, the Irish in Ireland and America felt strongly uneasy about Wilson's public snub of Eamon De Valera, President of the Revolutionary Irish Republic. DeV, as he was called, had come to the United States in early 1919 to help raise money for Ireland's drive to independence. He had appeared in every city with a substantial Irish population and yet Wilson failed to officially invite him to Washington.

Educators of all races and religions vociferously took issue over the overt anti-Negro policies the President instituted more than twenty years earlier and while the esteemed President of Princeton University. Now that Wilson was so seriously disabled, Branko doubted he would right any of his wrongs.

Suffering from what could prove to be a fatal stroke. the enigmatic President lay abed in the very house Branko was about to visit. As for The First Lady, Branko had heard and read wild speculations that she would take over Wilson's duties, as sort of a surrogate President. The woman was not universally admired, especially in this city, and this current physical dilemma did not make it any easier for her.

Maybe she wants me to be her knight in shining armor and take over for Woodie, thought a facetious Major Horvitch.

At the desk of Mrs. Wilson's appointment secretary he was told that the First Lady was called to an emergency conference but would be free within a half-hour. With this delay, Branko's thoughts turned to the *freilacher* letter he received from Tante Shayndl the previous week. He took it from his tunic pocket and re-read it:

> *Dearest Branko:*
> *It is with the greatest joy I tell you that Charles and I will be married in the very near future. Yes, we are both so happy, as are all*

of the children and grandchildren, and it is truly destined to be beshairt. *We are planning a very quiet, private civil ceremony in front of a magistrate. Charles' children from Geneva plan to be there, but we are so sad knowing that your attendance will likely be impossible. I realize that you would have to be away almost a month in order to celebrate with us. There will be a veritable hole in my heart.*

We are so happy that we were able to spend a good deal of time with you when you were quartered in Paris after the Armistice. The photographs we took are our favorite possessions and they're hanging all over the apartment.

I'm so very happy that you and Dovid correspond once in a while. He, too, will not be able to be with us, but he and his lovely family seem to be thriving in Eretz Yisroel. I shudder whenever I think of the surrounding dangers that they and all the Jewish settlers face every day, but at least the Balfour Declaration is a move in a peaceful direction. Gevalt!

In the meantime, February is just around the corner: A very Happy Birthday to you, nephew dear. I can't believe my little Bracheleh will be 45. God Bless You! You're catching up...I'll turn a ripe old 57 soon thereafter. You should only meet a nice woman someday soon, Branko. I know you had your "Madamoiselle from Armentieres" flings during the war but now the time has come to settle down. Do you hear?

With love from all,
Tante

Branko thought it remarkable that after all these years he was still able to read and understand the Yiddish with very little trouble. At the same time Tante Shayndl had picked up a substantial amount of English and French had become her second language of choice. The smile on his face was the only indication necessary to show the joy he felt with Tante's tidings. Veritably, she meant nothing less than life to him, from the age of six.

When the secretary escorted Branko into the Oval Office of the White House, his coolness began to fade a bit. That came to an end, when a very warm greeting came his way. Reaching out her hand caught Branko of guard, but he daintily held it.

"Ah, Major Horvitch, I presume. Do have a seat? It is my pleasure to be meeting you, sir."

"Thank you, Ma'am. Do I call you Mrs. President?"

Both broke into silly laughter at this question.

"Edith will do nicely," she then said. "Any formalities between us are not necessary, Branko."

He nodded an appreciative acquiescence to her wish

"I've been reading of your various fascinating exploits abroad and here in D.C. I feel that I've known you for a long time—and quite well. Or is there more? Do tell."

The prescribed usual niceties went on for a minute or two more, until they moved into the adjoining meeting room and the secretary brought a tray with coffee, tea and small sandwiches. The President's wife and the immigrant from Eastern Europe sat across the polished mahogany table—and the immigrant was just getting warmed up. Mrs. Wilson seemed well-practiced in the art of pulling information from him, and he loved it.

This is a handsome and interesting woman, thought Branko, as he looked Edith over and listened to her. *She seems "to the manor born" but yet very warm and caring, with an intellect that can challenge any manner of man.*

The next hour went quickly. Branko mesmerized her with stories of his childhood, the Austro-Hungarian army, the *fusgeyers* of Romania, police work in New York and the battlefield in France. Every now and then he was prompted to say something meaningful and emotional about veteran's rights, his favorite subject these days. In this regard he was also able to lobby against the issue of dangerous and imminent cutbacks in the military, particularly of the seasoned officer corp. Edith listened intently, parried none-too-delicately with views peppered by the prevailing party line.

He decided not to mention that he would be released in January and she wondered—but didn't ask—whether he favored the Treaty of Versailles and its proposed League of Nations. Perhaps she didn't want to know his answer. After all, this would be the President's legacy, and in a way, hers as well.

"I suppose you know," she said at one point, "that I have invited many war veterans to meet with me, even when Woodrow was in better health. I launched a personal mission to show America that the 'war to end all wars' was a necessity—a horrible one—but one to make the world safe for democracy. The press has covered this quite well and constituents are usually in praise of the attempts I've made on this issue."

Branko was, in fact, aware of what she had done, and figured this was her reason for asking him here.

"No, that's not particularly why you're here today, Branko," she said, correctly reading his expression and body language. "Part of the reason for this meeting is that I wanted to get a feel for who you are. I have a complete dossier on you, but that's not the same as getting it from the horse's mouth, so to speak. But for a better explanation, you'll have to wait a while—until we meet again. All will be revealed at that time."

"My God, Edith, that last remark sounded just like my old buddy Wild Bill Donovan: Full of melodramatic mystery and intrigue, leaving loose ends. You sure he hasn't trained you somewhere along the line?"

There was the hint of a smile on her face—like something from an inside joke to which he wasn't privy. She said, "I know all about Wild Bill. And I have to agree with all you've just said. But now, I'm sorry that we must part. Until we meet again, my dear Major Branko Horvitch, it has been my distinct pleasure chatting with you today. Please leave both your home and War College telephone numbers with my appointment secretary. Thank you for a delightful afternoon."

"I look forward to hearing from you, Edith. I, too, thoroughly enjoyed our chat. Please give my best wishes to the President for a speedy and complete recovery."

With this, she shared another gentle touch of her hands. It was three seconds too long to qualify as proper, Branko felt. But then again, he had always been an incurable romantic with an occasional bent toward fantasy.

The First Lady had arranged to have one of the White House vehicles take Branko to wherever he wished to go. He decided against going back to the College and instead went to his apartment. From there he strolled to the cozy little bar on the corner—it was a good place to sit with heavy thinking to do. He had sold himself on this at other times.

Now what the hell was that all about? Branko thought to himself as he settled into a seat at the bar. After ordering his drink he began silently chastising himself for having been so easily disarmed by the First Lady. *Once I get wound up I never shut up, but she kept asking and I kept talking. That's me and there's no denying it. Old Captain Rudoff had it right, calling me,* blabbermouth." *Still, I hope I got across the need to show our veterans that the country cares about them. The veteran's unemployment rates are embarrassing. This country owes the doughboys from the trenches. Hell, if I can use Edith to get better national press coverage, I'll do it—you can bet your ass on that. Gotta admit, she seemed honestly disturbed each time I raised the issue.*

Damn. She's not an especially attractive woman and I'll bet she's older than me. Still, I suppose she's no doubt warm and friendly to all of the vets she meets—she seems that way. Hmm! How many Americans can say that they were hosted by The First Lady of the United States of America?

His thoughts stopped just short of his old "farewell" litany, *there are places to go, things to do, experiences to feel.* He was just too content with life at the moment and the haunting credo failed to materialize.

"I'll buy you one, Major, how's that?" the bartender intruded on Branko's reverie.

"Thanks, Lou. Say, with this prohibition to be put in force in January what's going to happen to this place?"

Branko knew of a number of these so-called "speakeasy" joints already setting-up around town. They were simply places with no outward signs of available liquor. More often than not, a private home or a cellar dwelling served the purpose. Thus far the police had turned their heads on the matter. But once the amendment was officially adopted it would be increasingly difficult for all involved—from producers and distributors through providers and drinkers. Many "drys" prohibition proponents, feared that the scofflaws would be too numerous for local and state governments to effectively enforce the new law. The "wets" were hoping for just such a problem.

"I wish I knew, Major," Lou replied. "My brother-in-law is the sole owner. He's already been talking 'speakeasy,' but my woman's dead-set against it. I'd take a chance, though—ain't much work around the district."

And therein lies the ugly crux of the problem, Branko thought to himself. *Unemployment; that's where my vets take the biggest beating.*

Branko shook his head and shrugged his shoulders. He wished Lou good luck and went home to a night of sleeplessness.

*****

**The War College
Washington, D.C.
January 9, 1920**

Major Branko Horvitch, senior faculty, stood by the lectern in his classroom when the day-orderly from the administrator's office delivered an "urgent" message from the White House. The Sergeant took great pride in embellishing this, slightly embarrassing the Major, while smug smiles and winks of disbelief filled the room. He had been in the midst of introducing a seminar on the subject of *Covert Operations in Time of Battle*.

The message simply read:

> Please call Mrs. Wilson at The White House today before 5:00 p.m.

Now what the hell did she do that for? thought Branko. *Could just as well have called me at home. But there is no sign that the word "urgent" was at all involved. Probably just the Sarge having some fun with it at my expense. If he wasn't a Purple Heart recipient from the 42nd, I'd be all over him.*

The fact was the non-coms on the College staff had the utmost respect for Major Horvitch. They knew that with his sense of humor he could certainly take a mild joke.

Quickly recovering, he leaned menacingly forward, fixing a stare toward the sixteen officers in attendance saying, "Let that be a lesson to you, gentlemen. With my powerful stance at the Commander-in-Chief's abode, I can have any of you summarily demoted with a snap of my fingers, just like that!"

As he snapped his fingers the raucous laughter was enough to awaken any sleeping students—or lecturers—in adjacent classes.

He adjourned his seminar at four o'clock. While everyone was filing out, Lieutenant Chuck Bronson—one of his sharpest students—facetiously and loudly remind him to be sure to "make that important phone call." Of course, it evoked another round of laughter that followed him down the hall and out of the barracks.

Branko went back to his apartment to make the call.

The phone call went smoothly and Edith sounded as animated as during their first meeting. She invited Branko to dinner on Saturday night. A few Senators and Cabinet members, along with their wives, would also be in attendance. She said that she felt that a decorated veteran of the Great War would make a nice touch. Branko reacted as though he was taking the causal invitation at face value but he suspected something else was afoot. At the back of his mind was the First Lady's vague subterfuge during their first meeting.

The past few weeks and through the Christmas holidays, Branko had been on a winning streak, of sorts. The proposed January "cashiering" that was threatened during the summer sessions would never take place. And while Branko had no way of knowing this yet, he had begun to suspect that it might not occur. But his *Washington Post* interview seemed to serve as a rallying cry with the country's major newspapers and radio stations as they relentlessly put daily heat on Congress to act in good faith with the nation's veteran officer corps, West Pointers or not. This soon extended to regular army officers everywhere. By everyone who knew of his *Washington Post* interview, Branko was credited for jolting the pants off congressmen who had even slightly favored the proposed reductions. In these days of international uncertainty a strong standing army was vital for diplomatic and defensive reasons. They would have to find other places to cut. Accordingly, the not-yet mended Wilson, had urged the committee to consider other options. He had said that the army, navy, marines and their respective air squadrons should be exempted from proposed reductions as long as he was President of the United States. Branko appreciated that and he intended to say so at the Saturday dinner.

He smiled while thinking, *Dinner at the Presidential residence— not bad for a little orphan* boychick *from Ignatovka in the Ukraine.*

Opening his mail later that evening, Branko was pleased to come across a letter from Donovan, postmarked from New York City:

> *Hello BH.*
>
> *I've been remiss in not contacting you regarding our discussion at the dinner party last spring. But, Franklin sworn me to silence and I intended to hold fast to it. However, the venerable New York Times printed a page-3 article a few weeks ago, pretty much blowing part of my cover. Franklin had recruited me as a covert officer into the Office of Naval Intelligence, under the jurisdiction of the Assistant Secretary of the Navy, none other than our "Hahvidd" boy.*
>
> *I have continued working with my law firm on a part-time basis. This is the perfect screen.*

My partners did not question my working less time on fewer cases. Besides, this way I keep my annual piece of the partnership pie without having to fake being a fat ass Wall Streeter.

Next month, I'm being sent to Japan and, hold your fur hat, Siberia, on ONI business. In fact Ruth is going with me as part of our cover: Just two Americans on an overseas vacation.

I'll say more when I can. You may have heard that Franklin is up to his ass in alligators over the Newport sex scandal involving a bunch of young sailors. He's going to stick it out as Assistant Secretary of the Navy until possibly campaigning for Vice President this summer. At any rate, my business with the ONI goes on for now, although I predict that the assignments will dwindle once Roosevelt resigns. Meanwhile, Ruth and I are excited about the upcoming adventure.

Please do not discuss this with anyone else, especially Edith Wilson. Yeah, buddy boy, wily Franklin Delano has snitches everywhere in the District, and we know about your meeting with her a few months ago. Watch your ass, old comrade, I'm told the First Lady can be a real bitch-on-wheels! With Woodie in bad shape and Edith pretty much running the show, who knows what intrigues float around that behemoth of a house.

Fair warning: There may be some fascinating near-future plans for you. In the meantime, have fun at next week's dinner, but and keep your Yiddishe eyes wide open.

Your fellow fighting Irishman,
Bill

Branko collapsed onto his bed after reading the letter.

Doesn't even sound like old Wild Bill. He sure as hell is tucked under ONI's wing and well underway to the world of spooky intelligence. Keerist, he even knows about the dinner Saturday—and I just found out this evening.

Japan? Siberia? What's going on? I just want to continue teaching at the College. This cloak and dagger stuff is just some more schoolyard drivel—and if this letter is any indication, I'm blindly heading straight into it.

*****

The White House
Washington, D.C.
January 18, 1920 (7:30 p.m.)

The First Lady sent a car for Branko, which made him feel rather conspicuous upon arriving at the House. It was a reminder of his occasional wish to have bought a Ford before coming to the District. He didn't like the feeling of being beholden to someone just because they had provided him a lift somewhere.

Of course, at Fort Jay he hadn't considered the importance of his own transportation. He was only on temporary duty (TDY) until the postwar thinned-down army found a proper post for a decorated soldier of his stature. He was told of his assignment to The Army War College on the day before the gigantic Victory Parade in which he proudly marched alongside many members of the old 69th. Wild Bill Donovan was in the lead and Father Duffy blew kisses to the sidewalk onlookers. The week after that, Branko embarked for Washington at Penn Station.

Edith was receiving guests in the main foyer and smiled widely when the Major arrived, resplendent in full-dress uniform. One of the servants took his overcoat. The First Lady, elegantly but simply dressed, lead him by the arm and began introducing him to other guests and their wives.

Among those first introductions were the power elite of Washington: Justice Louis D. Brandeis; Attorney General Mitchell Palmer; Ned

McLean of the *Washington Post*; Massachusetts Democrat Congressman Samuel Main; Virginia Democrat Senator Walter Keene; Retired General Theodore Chambers; Candian Ambassador Archibald Smythe; Vice-President Thomas Marshall; Tennessee Democrat Congressman Edward Fuller and the only non-Washington insider, a gangly ex-Sergeant Alvin York, also from Tennessee.

York had been a remarkable Appalachian turkey-shooter whose kill rate during the war was practically unparalleled. Branko could only envision a pile of German corpses, each with a York bullet lodged in a vital organ. He warmly put his arm around the Sergeant's civilian shoulder and was quick to tell his missus, Gracie, how lovely she looked. Her blush could be seen across the room and back.

"Dadgumit, Major," the Tennessean enthused, "I'm so pleased to meet you. How's come we never crossed trenches in France, eh? Reckon we were much too busy to be socializing. I've heard a good load of hay about you, suh!"

Branko had been so uncharacteristically overwhelming that neither York nor his wife had hardly managed to get a word in edgewise. In the State Dining Room, the two men huddled in a corner, swapping army bull while others animatedly gabbed away until the First Lady asked for everyone to be seated. Although cocktails had not been served in the White House since Prohibition legislation passed, there was a variety of soft drinks, coffee and tea along with plentiful, tasty *hors d'oeuvres*. It was all set on sterling trays placed at the center of the large dining table arranged for twenty guests.

Mrs. Wilson apologized for the President's absence. He had wanted to attend, she said, but he was not yet feeling well enough.

In reality, at his post-stroke stage the President simply didn't want to be seen in public and she had planned the dinner party without his knowledge of it. Edith didn't feel he would have been too happy with the guest list, anyway.

The sumptuous prime rib dinner met with everyone's favor. Branko and the Yorks thought it was possibly the most wonderful meal of their lives. The cross-table talk was every bit as eclectic as the attendees. Justice Brandeis had an innate distrust of the boozy Ned McLean and had never granted the *Post* an interview in his four years on the Court.

McLean, a notorious drinker, seemed lost without one in his hands and avoided any discussion with the Justice. Mrs. Brandeis, sitting next to Mrs. McLean, discussed only trivial niceties. Other than these two exceptions, conversation ricocheted from every corner of the room.

The two people drawing the most attention were Branko and York. Both were *Croix de Guerre* honorees and their dinning repartee equaled their battlefield exploits. York had the added distinction of also being a Medal of Honor recipient for one of the most amazing feats during the entire conflict. He not only captured 132 enemy troops, but also picked-off twenty nine. As coincidence would have it, York's exploits occurred in the Meuse-Argonne sector just a few hundred yards from where Branko's 69th Fighting Irish were dug in and holding precious ground.

Across the table was Tom Marshall. He had previously—and publicly—voiced the sentiment that Mrs. Wilson was over-stepping her bounds as First Lady by usurping many of the Vice President's powers. Throughout the evening he seemed to avoid her—and perhaps for justifiable reason. But at one point, when all were still seated, Senator Keene's wife, Martha, innocently asked Edith what, in fact, her responsibilities were now that her husband was incapacitated.

Mrs. Wilson answered with a smile and in such a loud, clear voice that the proverbial pin drop could have been heard: "Mrs. Keene, I see to it that only the most pressing matters get to the President. I never make any decisions regarding the disposition of public affairs. That is the purview of Vice President Marshall."

"Well, Mrs. Wilson, I'm sure you're doing a fine job of it at any rate," chimed in Senator Keene.

To his credit Marshall changed the subject quickly and politely: "Mrs. Wilson, please give the President all our best wishes when you see him later this evening. We pray for his rapid recovery, just as all America is."

Ned McLean thought this was way too good an opportunity to let pass. He asked Mrs. Wilson if he could bring in the camera he had left in the cloak room. She could have said *no* but instead only warned him to honor anyone not wanting to appear in a photograph.

Brandeis groaned, thinking this was all unnecessary but to be expected from a boor like McLean.

"Newspaper publisher, indeed," Brandeis muttered to his wife.

At cigar, coffee and tea time, easy chairs were brought into the room. The conversation turned toward prohibition, the treaty, women's suffrage, the so-called "Red scare" and the economy. Branko saw a perfect opportunity to lobby for veteran's rights and the veteran bonus that had stalled in committee. His eloquence was admired and commented on by Justice Brandeis and others. Along these lines, attention shifted to Alvin York for a story that was heartbreaking and all too true.

"When I got back home to Tennessee," he said, "the Rotary Club of Nashville, and a few other clubs around the state, wanted to give me a home on a farm. We certainly appreciated that, but as luck would have it, they couldn't raise enough money. Things are really bad in Tennessee, and veteran unemployment is high. Instead, they gave us an unfinished house which would have cost a lot of money to complete. And my Gawd there was a heavy mortgage, to boot. As of today, the deed stays with the Rotary Clubs. Gracie and I are living with family near Jamestown."

After a moment of silence, Congressman Ed Fuller spoke up: "Alvin, I heard about that, and I'm ashamed about our home state—and so sorry for your plight. I can only assure you and Major Horvitch that the top priority in the House is the veteran who fought for this country only to come home and find no work, no future, no bonus."

"We're not just looking for a bonus," York replied. "Just a little appreciation and an even break. But for my part, thank you for your efforts in the House."

Meanwhile, Ned McLean's flash bulbs were going off at a merry pace. He concentrated on York and Horvitch, figuring this would be incentive for *AP* and *UP* to distribute nationwide, with credit to the *Post* and its publisher, of course. There were also a half dozen guests who wanted "in." Edith Wilson just sat there and glared along with Brandeis and a few of the others. Both Branko and York waved off McLean after satisfying the hangers-on and walked out into the corridor.

In the meantime, the *Post* publisher began to feel like a jilted schoolboy, thinking, *Why is everyone leaving me and my camera?* What he had always failed to realize was that his impressive camera did nothing to add depth to the man carrying it.

Just like that, the party was over and the usual drawn-out *goodbyes* were abbreviated under the watchful eye of Mrs. Wilson. Branko maneuvered himself into remaining a few minutes after the last departing guest. He was determined to personally thank Mrs. Wilson for having invited him and for the presence of Alvin York.

"It made my night, Edith," he told Mrs. Wilson. "Breaking bread with that highly unusual warrior was a highlight for me."

"I'm sure Sergeant York felt very much the same. You met as relative strangers and he left as a comrade for life. So how did you enjoy the evening, Major?"

"Absolutely fascinating, and I can't thank you enough for asking me to come."

"Something is beginning to take shape as we speak, Branko. I'll know more inside of a week. All I ask is that you keep an open mind and for once, think of yourself and your continuing career. And no, that's not a bit selfish. It's reality."

"My God, Edith, are you sure you're not being coached by Wild Bill? That is exactly how he talks—in riddles. I think I've said this to you before.

"I just ask you to be patient. Next week I should have a solid proposal for you to consider."

"Okay, charming First Lady of America. But could you at least give me a hint?"

"Well...yes. It has to do with an exciting turn of events that you just might enjoy. In fact, if you're thinking that you love your work at the College too much to leave it, then certain compromises may also be possible. I'm saying nothing more. I'll call."

"Damn, Edith, you've just done something that not many have ever done. You've got my *Yiddishe kopf* spinning!"

With her eyebrows raised at the common Jewish expression, which she may not have understood, she actually gave Branko a quick squeeze of a hug. She then pushed him out the front door of the White House. With one foot on the threshold, he turned and smartly saluted her; one of the nearby attendants tried to hide a grin a mile wide.

The White House
Washington, D.C.
February 10, 1920

For a calmly composed man who was to turn 45 years of age, Branko's last three weeks were had been earth-shaking. Mrs. Wilson had used all the applicable words in describing these events while trying not to blurt out everything at once. Branko made note of everything into a small-ringed black notebook—Government-issued from The War College, of course:

1. *Appointed Superintendent of Buildings and Grounds at The White House, with the rank of Lieutenant Colonel, effective immediately.*

2. *Permission from War College Commander to develop a Guest Lecturer program of not more than two days per week, from 2-5 p.m.*

3. *Office will be in the White House and am expected to be on the grounds, available six days per week—other than lecturing as described in #2, above.*

4. *January 25th: Orientation personalized and conducted by retiring Superintendent, Brigadier General Ronald Riches. This to be completed within one month, when Riches' retirement officially begins. Riches will remain in Washington for the remainder of the current administration and available to consult with when required.*

5. *The 6 Military Aides will report me and I am to review them weekly, on each Monday morning. No visitors allowed.*

6. *I am to be on call 24-hours a day in case of any emergency.*

7. *Future administrations are not bound by this appointment.*

Above signed off on by Thomas Marshall, Vice President of the United States, January 25, 1920

Mrs. Wilson later told Branko that she had to round up a variety of recommendations to sew-up the deal—all of which were easily obtained. Of course, Wild Bill Donovan knew this was brewing before he left for Japan He had written a glowing report recounting Branko's heroic efforts in the war, his ability to exceptionally command effectively, his loyalty to the army and his country, etc., etc.

Brigadier General Monte Ferris, Commandant of The Army War College, wrote a brief statement and agreed to the part-time guest lecturing. He didn't want to lose Branko and was happy to keep him at least part time. The Commander of West Point had written that he had strong intentions of asking Branko to join the faculty after hearing his powerful series of lectures a year previously. He lamented being too late to corral Branko when the Army War College beat him to it. Secretary of War Newton Baker was pleased to provide a recommendation. Newton had been on the final selection committee for the Army War College when Branko stood head-and-shoulders above all other candidates.

The last, but most certainly not the least recommendation, came from the New York City Police Commissioner John J. Sullivan. In a letter full of accolades for Branko's prowess as a Lieutenant of Detectives, Sullivan illuminated Branko's abilities and character from a somewhat different perspective. Wild Bill Donovan had suggested obtaining the Sullivan recommendation, explaining that Branko's civilian police service had been integral to his selection as head of the Fighting 69th Military Police unit.

All of this input served to impress the Vice President, as Mrs. Wilson kept him abreast of the investigation. This, she knew, alleviated some of his overt distrust. Finally, it was the President himself who suggested this and it worked toward the successful conclusion.

For the past few weeks a still very weak and pale Wilson was spending a few hours a day at his desk in the Oval Office, with Mrs. Wilson usually standing by to assist in any way she could.

On more than one occasion Branko warmly thanked the First Lady for gathering the powerful recommendations and her lobbying for his appointment.

"Now you understand why I couldn't say too much," Mrs. Wilson explained during a respite from their respective schedules. "I knew that Riches was about to retire. But not knowing when, I didn't want to step on the Vice President's sensitive toes. So I volunteered to work on gathering the recommendations. And rather than the third baseman of the Washington Nationals, I suggested you —the man-about-town—who had been breaking three hearts a week, or so I hear!"

"Oh, that's a funny one," Branko responded, nonetheless flattered by Mrs. Wilson attention. "But with the Nats in the league cellar, maybe he would have leapt at the offer. You know the old saying 'Washington, first in war, first in peace, but last in the American League!'"

The First Lady, a lukewarm baseball fan who had watched an occasional game or two, retorted, "The kid is a sucker for a curve ball, Branko, and where do you come to know anything about baseball? After all, you're nothing but an immigrant Jew."

The Lady's sly winking smile could have killed a fly on the wall.

"I should ignore that, my dear. I've been in our fair country since 1904 and believe me; we immigrants fell hard for the game of baseball. Italians, Poles, Germans, Scandinavians—even a small contingent of Jews are playing the game professionally today."

Mrs. Wilson had unknowingly tapped into Branko's enthusiasm for both the game and his fellow immigrants. She listened to him hold forth, quite proud that one of his young *Fusgeyers* had learned to play baseball on the sandlots of New York. The player, Avi Semelweiss, became so proficient that he was signed to a Brooklyn Dodger contract in 1909. Thus he began his career in Bluefield, West Virginia and was later picked up by Newark, the Yankees minor league team.

Branko practically beamed in recounting how he and *Fusgeyer* friends had watched Semelweiss play shortstop for the Newark Bears just before the war. By then Avi Semelweiss had changed his name and the press was calling him, *Albie White, the Battling Bear from Birlad.*

Branko began to wind down by saying, "I don't know where he is today, but as a line-drive spray hitter, his speed alone was evidently not enough to get him to the majors. The last I heard he was playing in some lower minor league in the south. A really fine player, but at thirty-five, I suspect his dream has probably faded."

During his narrative, Mrs. Wilson had only occasionally injected comment and now that Branko seemed to be coming back down to the ground, she smiled.

"I am indeed impressed, Branko," she said. "Thank you for that marvelous story. You know the lingo, too! Is that the same kid you told me about—the one who was part of the rescue team during that great escape?"

"Yes, that was the one and only Avigdor Semelweiss. I'm surprised you recall, Edith."

The pleasant *tete-a-tete* had lasted longer than either of them privately thought to be wise. They each knew that there already was a bit of unfounded gossip floating around town. They parted and Branko headed to his new White House office. He was quite comfortable with his handsome office in the West Wing, but suspected that Edith would have to cut down her daily visits.

There was much he had to learn and within the hour General Riches would be coming for the daily training sessions. In the meantime, Branko still had reams of paper, contracts, vendor histories, blue prints, photographs and correspondence with which he had to be familiar.

He had to admit that at times it had seemed insurmountable. Could he perform? About that he had no question. He had already promised himself that by putting his entire being into the task, he would most definitely become the very best Superintendent the White House had ever seen. Still, though, he worried about the vast volume of responsibility the position encompassed.

During his forty-five years he had strove to be the best at anything to which he had applied his mind and body; the best blacksmith, cavalry horseman, Austrian Emperor's Honor Guard, head of security during the European *Fusgeyer* trek, New York City policeman and detective cadre' officer, leader of men in battle and the best Army War College faculty lecturer.

He was now prepared for this newest challenge and to climb any prodigious mountains in the years ahead. Clearly, here was a man who had battled through life each step of the way, and consistently prevailed.

*****

The White House
Washington, D.C.
January 3, 1942

Complete chaos would clearly describe the state of the union less than a month after the attack on Pearl Harbor.

The Pacific Fleet rendered helpless, the British and the Russians clamoring for immediate help on all fronts, Congress in the search for ways of raising more money to pay for the war rapidly engulfing the entire world. The White House, its West Wing and its executive offices burning the midnight oil, was in a dangerous knee-jerk reaction mode, something that would have to cease very soon.

President Roosevelt had been in daily touch with both Winston Churchill and Josef Stalin while biting his tongue and clenching his teeth as the one-way demands flew over the wires and telephones.

"We need more of this, more of that, when are you going to do something, dammit?"

Roosevelt's demeanor grew more brusque with each day, while Hopkins and Donovan steered clear whenever possible.

Until, that is, a letter from the Russian Embassy was delivered by messenger. Harry Hopkins himself rushed it to the President in the Oval Office.

PERSONAL AND CONFIDENTIAL
January 3, 1942

From: The Embassy of the Union of Soviet Socialist Republics

To: The Office of the President of the United States

Subject: Brigadier General Branko Horvitch, U.S. Army, retired.

Dear Mr. President:

   We are saddened to report that the latest communique from Partisan Group "Maccabee," somewhere in the west of Russia, states that General Horvitch and the group's senior leaders have been dispersed to another encampment. This is part of the standing order for such groups, never to stay in one place when ordered to other coordinates by the Soviet Information Bureau (SIB).

   He and several others left last night and the remainder will follow in two days. Officers of our Intelligence Command are certain that rescue operations will be more difficult to achieve as the partisan units frequently relocate. Due to increased patrols by rear echelon German Einsatzgruppen, we must continue more of these relocation orders. Only when we are able to mount a major counter-attacking force will the pressure on the partisan units diminish. We are still under siege in Leningrad and Moscow has been targeted by ceaseless artillery barrages and Stuka dive bomber raids.

As winter storms increase we hope for some relief. Now that you have joined us in the war on Nazi terror, perhaps we have already seen our darkest hours.

You can be assured that when failure has been minimized and it is feasible to do so, we will attempt to collect the General and return him to your embassy in Moscow. At present we have agents of the SIB working closely with half the partisan units in Belorussia and The Ukraine. Thus far, none have been in contact with the "Maccabee" force which has historically proven to be self-sufficient.

In the meantime, may we offer a minimal plan that General Timoshenko's propaganda office is willing to try. This will attempt to throw off the Nazi's top priority efforts to capture General Horvitch. If successful, we believe their diabolical goal is to parade him in front of the world press as the highest ranking spy in captivity. None of us wants this to occur, for the repercussions will be enormous and disastrous.

If you concur, then the news will be released tomorrow to all major news sources, most particularly Reuters, AP and UPI, simply stating that Brigadier

General Horvitch has been safely escorted by agents of the Soviet Union and is now in Moscow from where he will be returned to the United States. Of course, the announcement will be further embellished as a factual release with photographs of the General, safe at your embassy in Moscow.

Fascism has no place in the Soviet Union or in the United States. Together we shall prevent that from happening. Our kindest regards and good wishes for his speedy return to the family and comrades of Brigadier General Horvitch. Several of our seasoned staffers fondly remember him as an occasional honored guest of our ignored mission, and they too send their best wishes.

Sincerely, with fervent hopes for a speedy Allied victory!

Viktor Senensieb Makarov,
USSR Ambassador to the United States

The President, with a veritable, growing mountain of priorities to face, scanned the letter and then returned it to Harry Hopkins.

"Looks like some progress," the President said. "I agree with Timoshenko's proposal. You and Donovan take care of it. That's called *delegation of responsibility*—or my way of bellowing to get it the hell out of my sight, NOW!"

With his new Office of Strategic Services (O.S.S.) getting into full swing now, Donovan, too, was working sixteen-hour days. His first reaction to the Timoshenko Plan was one of pure, unadulterated skepticism.

"That Embassy letter is the Big Red machine on the march, for krisssake," he said to Hopkins. "Whether it's an eventual answer for Branko's safety, we may never know. And I sure as hell don't want to lose him. We need more practical and immediate action out of that Red General. He's our only hope, and Branko's only chance."

"FDR likes it," Hopkins responded, "or says he does. But I have that same empty feeling, Bill."

"There is absolutely no one else in that snow-bound country who even cares about our dilemma. And with an insane enemy knocking at their front door, who can blame them? They're trying to save the Motherland gang from the Fatherland bunch, and that's a highly doubtful proposition according to numerous expert strategists today."

"You think it's that bad?"

"They do. My new guys in London reported today that MI-5 fears complete Nazi domination and occupation of the USSR within a few months.

That made Hopkins' eyebrows climb.

"They feel that a long white winter holds Russia's only slim chance at beating back the invaders. I tell you Harry, this topsy-turvy world is spinning too damn fast right now. Our Branko will be only one of millions of victims."

"Hey, where's the old Wild Bill in all of this? That empty feeling to which I just confessed doesn't mean I'm close to giving up on Branko, or even on Russia. Somehow, he and they will come through. The survivor's mentality shines on both."

Later in the day, Donovan had a staff car take him to meet with Ambassador Makarov in the "temporary" Russian Embassy on 16th Street. Continued construction of a new embassy had been put on hold until after the war. Markarov apologized for the musty, cramped quarters.

Donovan was able to glean from the Russian a measure of encouragement.

"Timoshenko still feels a certain strong kinship toward Branko," Makarov assured Donovan. "It goes back to their days in the hedonistic Washington of the '20s. That in itself translates into the current faux news release to take some air out of the tenacious Nazi quest to capture him. Once that becomes evident—once the enemy sees the futility of nabbing their prize—there will be a more concerted covert effort to bring Branko back to Moscow."

Of course, thought Donovan, *if the Germans take Moscow, all bets are off.*

To address Donovan's quizzical look of disbelief, the Ambassador quickly described the monstrous evacuation plan to move all of Moscow's strategic papers, materials and key personnel to the Urals if the currently stalled German advance renews its deadly momentum in the spring.

"I wish I could buy your confidence and enthusiasm, Viktor," Donovan responded. "You understand that we will keep our own drop teams at the ready—should your people fail."

"My dear William, I sincerely hope this will not be necessary. Dropping your untested agents into the German occupied regions would be suicidal at best. At worst, they could all be captured along with Branko, severely compromising the partisan units."

Wild Bill didn't want to hear that. But hear it he did. It was as if the air came out of a party balloon. He politely thanked Makarov and sent off the staff car driver, opting to trudge slowly back to the White House in a decidedly disturbed state of mind

Within a week, the harried President Roosevelt told Hopkins and Donovan that the Timoshenko plan had initially worked out well. A photograph of Branko at the American Embassy in Moscow, sitting on a sofa next to a smiling American Ambassador, accompanied the widely distributed news release. Of course, it was taken in May, 1941 —a month before the Nazi invasion.

THE HARDING WHITE HOUSE

Washington, D.C.
June 3, 1920

Since his appointment to the Buildings and Grounds Superintendency Branko had twice briefly met with Woodrow Wilson. The upcoming meeting was a more official one, he felt. Mrs Wilson had arranged it, since President Wilson was slightly stronger than at any time during his painfully slow recuperation. He now handled a fair number of the more quotidian presidential duties, but always with Mrs. Wilson at his side.

Her "position" was diminishing, but her husband continue to count on her diplomatic and organizational skills. This disturbed the Vice President, the Cabinet, the House and the Senate to the point where the facetious title "Assistant President" cropped-up in all corners of the town. Ned McLean's, *Washington Post* particularly took delight in printing the phrase "petticoat government" usually when captioning photos of Mrs. Wilson. Concurrently, the rash of Edith Wilson/Branko Horvitch innuendos continued to gestate.

Branko was sure it would eventually lead to the end of his White House plum. The insouciant First Lady laughed it off as "utter nonsense" and "school girls masquerading as newspaper reporters." It was still too early to gauge whether Branko or Edith Wilson would prove to be right in their assessment.

The Oval Office held a fascination for Branko. Here he was, an immigrant European Jew, sitting across from the President of The United States of America.

"Thank you for coming, Lieutenant Colonel Horvitch," President Wilson said. "I've been remiss in not telling you how much I appreciate the job you've been doing. Isn't easy, is it?"

"Thank you for your kind comment, Mr. President. And it is a challenge, but with the support of the staff, I believe we've made inroads in organizing the daily maintenance functions to be more effective."

"Good, good! I just want you to know that I'll be recommending that you continue at the position no matter who the next president is. Even if it's a rapscallion of a Republican, perish the thought. But then again, my influence, especially across the aisle, is weakening by the day."

"Thank you for your confidence, Mr. President."

Managing a smile, the President rose from his chair with difficulty, extended his shaky hand to the Superintendent, saying, "Now, I must get some rest before my next meeting. Perhaps we'll meet again before they send me packing! Thank you for your good service, Branko. It has *not* gone unnoticed."

I bet that broke the all-time record for Oval Office meetings, Banko thought on the way out the door. *Guess it wasn't such an important meeting, after all. Then again, maybe he just wasn't feeling well. He looks so gaunt and bent over. But I won't negate the recommendation. Although, I can't envision a Republican going for any Wilson appointee. Damn, the old man actually called me Branko! Whaddya think of that!*

With these thoughts, Branko shook his head, smiled broadly and went back to work.

He was in a steady demand for speaking; the American Legion Posts, the communal organizations such as the Elks, Moose and Rotary; B'nai Brith, Hadassah, various churches and synagogues and the YMCA; Georgetown and George Washington Universities, University of Maryland, *ad infinitum*. Branko could have remained at lecterns all week long, every week.

To his credit and good fortune, he developed complete trust in the Senior Military Aide, Captain Jack Steel, to cover for him whenever he was speaking during the days. In case of a rare emergency on his watch, he made sure that Jack knew how to reach him by phone at any of the speaking venues. In the evenings, he was on call as usual, and the Chief Steward was charged with reaching him whether he was at the Hotel Willard or elsewhere in town. Both Steel and Larry Lincoln were highly competent in this regard—and above all, Branko learned to say "no" to speaking requests, every now and then.

Branko's weekly schedule changed only insofar as speaking venues and times. He kept track of these commitments in his small, ringed War College notebook and, as backup, frequent reminders from one of the staff secretaries. Illustrative of his workload, was one week in June that was arranged thusly:

Monday   *Breakfast meeting*
10 a.m.   *Retired Railway Club Worker's*
2522 Massachusetts Avenue
Topic: The State of the Proposed Veteran's Bonus

Tuesday   *Hadassah luncheon*
Noon   *Washington Hebrew Congregation*
Topic: The Story of the Fusgeyers of Romania

Tuesday   *Georgetown University Students*
7 p.m.   *World Affairs Council*
Topic: Officer Careers in the United States military, and The Army War College Curriculum

Wednesday   *Lecture at the Army War College*
2-5 p.m.   *Topic: Gaining Respect From Your Enlisted Men.*

Thursday   *American Legion Post 112*
7:30 p.m.   *2333 Connecticut Avenue*
Topic: The Fighting 69th Regiment in Battle, and an update on the state of the Veteran's Bonus. (Some 69th vets attending)

Friday   *Rotary International luncheon,*
Noon   *Hotel Willard*
Topic: The Functions of the Superintendent of Buildings and Grounds at the White House.

Friday	*Lecture at the Army War College*
2-5 p.m.	*Topic: Coaching Non-Coms for Improved Performance.*

This particular week of Branko's speaking engagements was the not the first time the fledgling American Legion was included. Based upon previous speaking engagements, Branko knew he would have to tread carefully, as if on thin ice, on the subject of the black soldier. In his prior speeches, a few of the Legionnaires had asked, in so many words, if the Negro soldier was entitled to the expected bonuses and whether blacks were of any use in the war. The subject had come up with other fraternal organizations like the Elks, the Moose, Kiwanis, Rotary and various labor unions. However, nothing was as pointed and blatantly racist. For this meeting Branko was determined to put the issues at rest, at least as far as his personal perspective was concerned.

"In France, such men were invaluable," Branko had responded when the anticipated questions arose. "They displayed courage, ingenuity and tolerance I couldn't have shown under the same circumstances. Yet there was not a colored man I ever came across in France, whether he was a truck driver, a cook's helper, an ammunition packer or quartermaster, who I wouldn't share a trench with. Yes, by all means, he will have full entitlement. Anything short of that would be disgraceful and grossly un-American."

There was usually a smattering of red-neck boos, but the silence each time was far more imposing. He could have gone on with true stories of outright heroism displayed by the black soldier in the battlefield—and occasionally did. There had also been times when red-faced post Commanders shut him off out of concern for more outbursts. Fewer still had been the times that such Commanders had denied Branko the courtesy of a handshake in gratitude for his appearing to speak at the Post. But it had happened.

And these were veterans of a war that was to have made America safe for democracy. He tried to keep a perspective that it was only a small minority of these fighting men that felt this way. And maybe that perspective was the right one. But the silence at some of those meetings made it difficult to know for sure.

How utterly irrational and totally contradictory, thought the decorated Lieutenant Colonel. In the cases of some of those *American Legion* Posts he did not expect to be asked to speak again anytime soon. Having lived in Washington for nearly two years, Branko had been forced to gingerly walk the racism line.

"Jim Crowism" was alive and all too well in the nation's capital. But he couldn't fathom the differing treatment of men simply because of color. It took no extra effort to be warm and friendly to the black servants, stewards and chambermaids at both the White house and the Willard. But to treat these people as less than the workers that they were, did take a despicably bigoted effort and he couldn't understand it.

The upside to the sessions where these issues arose was that there were occasional 69th vets in attendance. These men of like mind always took the time to chat with one of their most honored comrades. Branko typically invited them and their families for tours of the White House and a walk around "his" grounds. His offers had never been refused.

In addition to his busy calendar, Branko accepted invitations to newsworthy events and various parties. It was not uncommon to see him in the company of a noted widowed socialite on one night, the divorced daughter of a Congressman on the next night and a Hadassah lady's unmarried, shy daughter on yet another night.

Or however such things were described in the society columns or under other headings in the newspapers.

A "Branko sighting" alert of any kind was sure to make the *Post*, the *Washington Star* or any one of the hundreds of speakeasy nightly gossip sessions. None of it turned out to be very serious, although that exceptionally attractive widow from one of Washington's oldest and wealthiest families made her way through four "dates" or whatever each rendezvous was called by those discussing it.

The widow at issue was thirty-something-year-old Priscilla Lloyd-Montgomery. The most important evening was a dinner at her parents sprawling estate in Silver Spring. Following her much older husband's tragic demise during the killer-flu pandemic of 1919, she had moved back to her parent's home. Evidently, she had never told her family much about the handsome Lieutenant Colonel. They knew only of his rank, his White House position and his medals.

Once seated at the dinner table and having heard his surname, a nervously apoplectic and sputtering Amanda Lloyd remarked, "It seems you have a slight foreign accent, Colonel. German immigrant, I take it."

Even though the hostess mistakenly promoted him to a full Colonel, the tone of her remark triggered Branko to go off on a quasi-sarcastic tangent.

"No, Ma'am," he said. "Purely Yiddish. At birth, *meine Yiddshe mama un tateh, alev-ha- shalom,* gave me the name Bracho, or Brachela as a term of endearment. I hail from the village of Ignatovka, near Kiev in the Ukraine."

Of course, they had no way of knowing that in his native language he had invoked the prayer of *may they rest in peace* for his parents or that he had ratcheted-up his accent to goad his hosts. He had, however, politely forced a smile the whole time.

Not nice, but hell, they've asked for it, he rationalized.

Partially recovered from the initial shock, T. Everett Lloyd managed to harumph a throaty, "And are your parents still living, sir?"

"No, I'm afraid not," Branko responded gravely. "They were both *murdered* during a *pogrom* when I was six. My two older sisters suffered the same *bloody* end."

The harsh, drawn-out emphasis he placed on the words, *murdered* and, *bloody*, drew heavy gasps in unison from the three Lloyds and the two hovering, wide-eyed black servants—who, by the way, inwardly reveled at the comeuppance delivered to their employers.

The rapidly cooling conversation quickly turned to socially acceptable pleasantries for the remainder of the evening: A painfully uncomfortable one for the hosts. Visibly mortified, Priscilla managed to nonetheless hold-up quite well.

It was a rather short evening and Branko tried to imagine the conversation after he left!

Branko had moved from the older, run-down hotel used by The War College officer staff to the elegant Willard Hotel. The Willard was frequented by Cabinet members, the press corp, visiting dignitaries and the like. Located on Pennsylvania Avenue, it was just steps from the White House. Since opening in 1818, it had become the virtual center of Washington politics and social life. Branko had a nicely appointed two-room suite, paid for by the White House operating budget, which also covered the Chief of Staff and the senior officer of the Military Aides, if they wished. In both cases, they were married men with young families and opted for government subsidized housing in the suburbs.

After having accepted the White House assignment Branko had finally bought a used Model "T" Ford and parked it in the nearby Willard garage for preferred guests—at no charge. He drove the car sparingly, using taxis and busses whenever convenient.

Although he didn't contact Priscilla again, she left numerous messages for him at the hotel and the White House. He guessed that she would have followed him to hell and back, and had she not been alabaster white, probably would have taken a chambermaid's job at the Willard.

Edith Wilson had a good time needling Washington's own Don Juan about this and other broken romances. He in turn forever played the cool one.

The remainder of the excessively hot summer went by laden with the usual political folderol. The two conventions nominated anemic tickets. The Democrats chose Ohio's Governor James Cox and running mate Franklin Roosevelt. The party hoped to capitalize on the magical name of the latter's late cousin, Teddy. The Republicans countered with Warren G. Harding, Senator from Ohio, and Massachusetts Governor Calvin Coolidge. The ticket was predicted to win by a landslide.

There was just too much baggage trailing President Wilson, and Edith Wilson had known for the better part of a year that the Democrats' days were over for the immediate future. The single-minded, concerted push for The League of Nations had faced an impossible hill to climb and that was certain to be reflected in the voting booth.

Branko realized these things, too. But while he was certain of having to move out of the Willard before the March inauguration, The First Lady thought otherwise. She had carefully and quietly lobbied for him wherever she thought it could be effective—but always stopping just short of providing more grist for the rumor mill. The eight years of Washington bedlam had taught her some ugly and illuminating lessons. Her navigational abilities were unsurpassed and included a whisper or two in the right places. One of those targets was the ear of G.O.P. Senator George Norris of Nebraska. One of the more moderate Republicans, he subsequently lobbied for Branko in and around circles that counted. Norris confided to Edith that the probable incoming Chief of Staff had unofficially agreed with Branko's continued incumbency. In reality, the post was never considered political in nature and this improved Branko's odds of retaining the position. Of course, it was too early for anything to be final. There was still an election to be conducted within the next few weeks.

The election winner came as no surprise to either side, but the unprecedented margin of victory was unexpected to those with a view narrowly focused on Washington. The democratic ticket could just as well have run for cover than for the White House. Wilson and his party suffered the humiliation with stiff upper lips and the people of the United States had spoken, more than ready for a new day. Although the defeat was taken as a very personal, heart-breaking loss for a President who nearly gave his life for his country. His tireless work to bring about lasting world peace had made him a combat casualty just as if it were a tour of duty on the battlefield.

In the waning December days of his second and last term, Wilson was finally awarded the prestigious Nobel Peace Prize for the previous year. It was no surprise to his loyal supporters that his personal doctor forbade his journeying to Oslo for the ceremony. That was just one more blow in the long series of disappointments he had endured in promoting the idea of a League of Nations to Congress and the electorate.

By the beginning of January the Chief of Staff to the incoming President, finally agreed to Branko's retention. Edith Wilson was very pleased, as was the Lieutenant Colonel. He had grown to love every minute of his varied duties and had smoothly managed to work in the twice-weekly lectures at The War College with widely applauded aplomb.

"One thing, my dear, sweet innocent Branko," Edith remarked to him. "In politics a favor begets a reciprocal favor. Senator Norris is, if nothing else, a shrewd Nebraska politician. And a Republican, at that! He'll call his chips in whenever and wherever he wants to."

Even with this caveat in mind, Branko began to look forward to another four years as Superintendent of Buildings and Grounds of America's grandest, white mansion.

In mid-April, Edith phoned to ask Branko how he was faring with the new administration. She heard what she thought was a strange answer from the straight-shooting Superintendent.

"The man is never here," Branko told her. "He's either out playing golf, at a poker game in town or making clandestine arrangements for a tryst with a boozing flapper. Right in the Oval Office, no less! Trying to keep up with him is driving the Secret Service cuckoo!

"Damndest boss I ever had. He doesn't give a flipping minute of his time to business. Even his Chief of Staff says that Harding handles the presidency as sort of a ceremonial function. I was inspecting the spring flower planting today, and he came out to the garden. I introduced him to our head landscaper, and all he could say was 'We had a much more beautiful garden back at our home in Marion, Ohio.' That was it and he just walked off. Well, what the hell!"

"I'm told that he carried that insolent reputation all the way from that lovely Ohio garden," Edith responded. "Do you see much of First Lady Florence—or should I say First Lady Flo?"

"Yes, a pleasant woman who has little or nothing to say, but is forever smiling. It seems painted on her face permanently. From what I can see of that marriage, what she has to be happy about is beyond me. She insists that The Lincoln Bedroom needs an immediate paint job. I told her it had been re-painted just last summer. First time I've seen a snarl through a smile. Don't think she likes old Branko here, very much."

Edith Wilson went on to tell of her more placid life "off the reservation." The former President was getting on a lot better now that he was finally free of the stress he had borne. Though very few people came to call, she allowed as how that was typical when someone retired from the foreboding task of Presidency. It didn't seem to make any difference that the Wilsons were the first of all First Families to stay on in Washington when the clamor died.

"Since you haven't seen our house yet," the former First lady went on, "we'd like you to join us for lunch on Saturday. Nothing special—we're having a sort of house-warming for a few choice guests."

"Geez, I'm a choice guest?"

"Of course you are, dear boy. Bring one of your boozy flappers, if you wish."

"Ouch, m'lady!"

The Saturday noon visitors to the red brick colonial on S Street was typical of the eclectic gatherings around the former First Couple. Even the guests themselves never knew who would attend the soirees —and this time was no different. To begin with, the ex-President was much improved over the last time Branko met with him. Even his handshake was noticeably firmer.

Again, he called Branko by his first name, while referring to the other guests as *Mr. This* and *Mrs. That*. Only the hostess used first names in a way that still didn't ignore protocol. The veranda at the rear of the house was set with three round tables, four chairs each and Edith proudly announced, "Open seating, everyone. This is just a thrown-together buffet weekend luncheon. Hope you like the goodies."

After attacking the sumptuous "thrown-together" buffet, the guests sat at three tables. They were, for the most part, unacquainted with one another and much of the conversation reflected this.

An odd assortment, thought Branko. *There's a young man with a good-looking young woman, college bred no doubt, Washington society probably, certainly not a veteran of any kind. This guy coming to sit at my table looks like a Wall Streeter. He ought to be a barrel of laughs.*

"Mind if I sit here?" asked the man, while precariously balancing two dishes.

Branko responded by motioning him to take the empty chair.

"Name's Joe Kennedy. Mrs. Wilson tells me that you're a pal and former comrade of Wild Bill Donovan, sir."

"Yes," Branko said. "Haven't seen or heard from him in far too long. Pleased to meet you, Mr. Kennedy."

Kennedy reached over and shook Branko's hand.

"Your charming Boston-ese and my fake European accent will make for a lingo hodge-podge no doubt," Branko observed.

Both laughed at this, mainly because it was so noticeable to each.

"I first met Donovan after the war," Kennedy said, "when he was with a Wall Street law firm. He was a close friend with Franklin Roosevelt, it seemed, though he swore he was a lifelong Republican. Roosevelt was very high on Bill."

"I take it you were also well-acquainted with Mr. Roosevelt, then?"

Kennedy nodded, but Branko did not feel it proper to mention the Office of Naval Intelligence and Bill's association with Roosevelt. Mr. Kennedy was charming, but unlike Edith he wasn't so compelling that Branko volunteered information.

Branko need not have worried about secrets being pried from him. Joseph Patrick Kennedy was filled to the brim with both himself and his doings. Branko was certain that name-dropping must have been a sport at which the Bostonian excelled, from an early age. Within the few hours, Branko learned more than he cared to about his table partner. Edith walked by and winked more than a few times, knowing of Kennedy's reputation for pure unadulterated braggadocio, excessive womanizing and occasional profitable bootlegging. Kennedy was considered an influential party donor in town and moved among Washington's main movers and shakers. His success had less to do with what he offered and a lot to do with how badly weakened the Democratic party had become. He was part of the first family of Massachusetts Democratic politics, the erstwhile John F. "Honey Fitz" Fitzgerald's clan of favor-givers and takers. As he prattled on, his interest in the new exciting world of Hollywood moviemaking, caromed off the walls of the handsome Georgian Revival home on S Street. As was also his habit, he added to his "family man" image by saying, "My Irish Rose stays behind in Massachusetts to take care of the kids." And finally, the mentioning of his dabbling in grandiose plans to build a massive waterfront complex could never pass without his also slipping in a probably sincere, "You must come visit us someday soon."

Before the luncheon was over, Kennedy invited Branko to join him for dinner at the Willard, his hotel of choice in Washington.

"Mighty nice of that gang of miserly Harding Republicans to continue housing you there, Branko," was his added comment. "Maybe I'll have two of my D.C. hostesses dine with us tonight. They sure as hell go nuts over a uniform.

After all the guests but Branko had left, Edith apologized, saying, "So sorry, dear man. Joe can be a real pain in the butt."

The former President, standing nearby, smiled and vigorously nodded his head.

Before the end of the first year in office, the ill-fated Harding administration was failing on a number of fronts. Branko saw it coming due to his few brief encounters with the pompous Commander-in-Chief.

Commander-in-Chief... Every time he thought about these three words, he couldn't help chuckling out-loud. Branko Horvitch rarely held back his opinion that Warren G. Harding was an unfortunate, side-splitting joke perpetrated upon the vulnerable American people. No other candidate could have more aptly fit the character of the so-called "Roaring Twenties."

And it was Harding's own buffoonery that made disparaging him so easy. Here was a boss who thought it unfitting to continually refer to Branko as *Lieutenant Colonel* Horvitch. For no other reason than that, his solution was Branko's promotion to full Colonel.

It was, Harding believed, less awkward and more appropriate for a President to return the occasional salute to a Colonel. That was how the White House Superintendent of Buildings and Grounds became a full "bird" Colonel. And that was the lion's share of why Branko thought the man a joke.

Branko wasn't the only one thinking this. Army Captain Jack

Steel, Senior Officer of the Military Aides, thought so as well. He witnessed the burlesque promotion as it took place during Branko's weekly inspection of the Aides contingent. Steel, a solid friend and confidante of the Superintendent, agreed that the bizarre scene was nothing of which to be proud, and swore his aides to silence on the matter.

"*Colonel* Horvitch," Steel remarked at the time, emphasizing the new rank, "in years to come we'll wickedly smile about what happened on this hallowed ground today."

Branko snapped around to look at Steel's affected seriousness and then both men burst into hearty laughter. The mutual respect between the two officers was, perhaps, the only real Harding accomplishment —unintended though it was.

Just after Christmas Wild Bill Donovan phoned and congratulated Branko on his promotion. How he even knew about it was something Donovan didn't explain and Branko didn't ask.

It was their first conversation in over a year. Donovan had been on constant intelligence assignments from the ONI, especially after Roosevelt's ousting following the democratic defeat. He had been pushing for a cabinet office but none was forthcoming. The Republican power structure didn't trust the old war dog because of his association with Roosevelt. To them it was nothing less than incurable contamination. *So be it*, was Donovan's reaction.

And then Donovan mentioned Joe Kennedy.

"The man was impressed with you, Branko," Donovan said. "He confided in me that he had some challenging things in mind for a man of your stature. His exact words, soldier. But I have just two words for you, old friend: Be careful. Make that three words—be damn careful!"

"I hear you loud and clear, Bill. I sensed it two minutes after we met. And then, after all of his puffery, I knew it."

"Now," Branko said, changing the subject, "what's new with the famous Wild Bill?"

Donovan brought Branko up to date on his flitting around the world on "company" business. For Branko, the impression was that

Donovan portrayed international deception and intrigue as not only personally gratifying but also strategically necessary.

Damned more necessary than gratifying, I suspect, Branko thought. *Thanks but no thanks to that.*

"Branko," Donovan said in closing, "next time I get up some gumption to tackle Washington again, we'll get together, you old friggin, fighting Irishman."

*****

The second year of the Harding administration brought notoriety to the politics of Washington Through it all, Branko kept his eyes forward and his spirit up. There were times when he longed to be back at The War College full time, but discussions with Edith would bring him back to remaining at the White House.

The post had been good to him. He was as popular a United States Army officer as there was in and around the district. No social event with an "A class" invitation list left off the Colonel Horvitch name. There wasn't an embassy from the least significant to the big boys—Great Britain, Canada, France, Italy, China and the like—that would think of having an affair without Branko present. Even Edith was constantly amazed at his popularity. With the former President's improving mobility as a popular guest speaker, the Wilsons were now more frequently crossing paths with Branko at Washington social functions.

Branko was always pleased to see Edith and the feeling was visibly mutual. The rumors had steadily faded since the Harding election and they were more at ease with chatting together or dining at the same table. And it was verified by Edith that her husband genuinely felt a certain patronal kinship toward the be-medaled Jewish warrior. Branko developed several sincere friendships within these high-powered circles of influence.

Even at the unrecognized Russian mission headquarters on 16th Street, Major Semyon Timoshenko felt far more at ease with Branko than with his fellow Red Army comrades. He would have swapped uniforms, if asked, giving Branko the proverbial "shirt off his back."

Having successfully spear-headed cavalry units during the Red-

White civil wars Timoshenko had been sent to Washington for a six-month tour of political duty. He and the like-minded Branko got along famously, despite the worsening ideological climate. The "Red scare" and "a Red under every bed" cartoons in the major Western newspapers were driving a very volatile atmosphere. The depictions of a hideous, wild-haired Rasputin-type tossing bombs at capitalistic symbols would have dampened the friendship of lesser men. But to his credit, the rugged Timoshenko—an officer with an impeccable record in Russian military circles—just shook his head in disbelief at the scare tactics.

Regardless of escalated suspicions and hatred, the newly invested Union of Soviet Socialist Republics was here to stay. And working with them was still necessary for both countries. Inside the Mission's walls and in Timoshenko's company, Branko avoided compromising political discussions. It wasn't easy, but both officers knew that restrained cooperation was vital.

For this reason the two men even had to monitor their private lives —or at least Branko had to. An exotic, dark-eyed and comely brunette —one of the few Russian female staff—appeared to be smitten with the handsome American Colonel. The much younger Timoshenko immediately discouraged the potential dalliance, urging Branko to politely spurn her approaches. She was an experienced Bolshevik propaganda specialist, whose assignment was to counteract the very thing that made difficult her attraction to Branko. Specifically, she was to mitigate the growing anti-Soviet efforts in the United States and Canada—within the bounds of diplomatic protocol.

"This won't work, Branko," the politically moderate Timoshenko warned his friend. Oddly enough, the woman was Jewish. Making the matter more difficult for Branko, she still remembered her mother's Yiddish and always exchanged a few words with the Colonel in the *mama loshen* when no other staff members were around. Branko had a hard time adhering to Semyon's admonitions, but knew that the consequences could be ugly.

None of this is to say that Branko wasn't equally admired and courted at several other, more moderate enclaves in Washington—the Canadian and British particularly. However, the French came closest to canonizing the Croix de Guerre hero; if they could have managed a Papal agreement they just might have carried it off.

When Jack Steel had playfully suggested that very thing, Branko responded with, "Fat chance."

Succumbing to the fast rising anti-immigrant stance, President Harding signed anything even remotely supportive of decreasing entrance quotas. In reality, it wasn't ideology driving him. The man merely did everything that he thought would endear him to the wave of nativism flooding the once-hospitable nation. Branko privately recognized that the "boss" did perform acceptably as host of the Washington Conference on Naval Powers in the fall of '21. At the time Harding demonstrated what was the most competent act of his entire presidency. The overall reduction of warship production appeased even those Americans who were reluctant to reduce the country's military strength in any way.

Branko, as well as the growing liberal bloc, gave Harding high marks for his bold stance on providing some semblance of equal rights for blacks. He opened-up certain limited government jobs for them, and signed into law an anti-lynching bill. And much to Branko's pleasure, the President publically urged his party toward a long overdue veteran's bonus. This was and would continue to be the *raison d'etre* for Branko's undying crusade for the millions of fellow World War veterans.

None of this negated news of the poisonous corruption that began to steadily creep into the limelight. From 1922 onward the administration was rife with scandals heretofore never seen. But with so many errors of commission and omission and the vigilant press exploiting it all, Branko tried mightily to keep such things at arm's length. This was not always possible. Cabinet members, Senators, Congressman, vendors, camp followers and reporters seemed to enjoy cornering the Colonel in his office, out in the garden, in the circular drive, whenever he was in the lobby of the Willard or dining at a restaurant. Perhaps they presumed that his position as Superintendent made him privy to insider information more relevant than they had.. If so, this was a misconception on the highest order of magnitude. And on a number of occasions, Branko said as much. But it didn't matter insofar as Branko's popularity. At the same time, he began to seriously welcome the reality of everyday problems. This defined his lengthy list of Buildings and Grounds responsibilities while cutting short the time spent with political pests.

His frequent discussions with Edith regarding this dilemma usually ended with her saying, "So deal with it."

She was right, of course, and Branko had already handled the matter by making himself less available outside of his day-to-day tasks.

The scandals, big and small, began to trickle in during the first quarter of the year and went on into 1923. Harding was finally understanding that being President of The United States of America, meant working at it every day and night. The man who so off-handedly promoted Branko probably would have happily traded positions with him now. As it was, he avoided speaking with Branko, knowing of the Colonel's stature among so many of his cohorts.

Harding was cognizant that he made a major mistake at the outset of his presidency. He brought with him to Washington an entourage of friends and party hacks, all of whom sought a payback for their loyalty. The so-called "Ohio gang" had served its part in his undoing.

"I have no trouble with my enemies," Harding remarked to the news outlets, "but my damn friends are the ones that keep me walking the floor at night."

Until these rampant improprieties surfaced, the President enjoyed a measure of popularity and support rarely experienced by a sitting President. While Wilson had raised an army, fought an unpopular war and lobbied for universal peace, Harding had cherry-picked his way through the job. The former President had worked hard every day and left office under an unpopular cloud while Harding had enjoyed popularity for performing well on the surface—that is until the lights dimmed on him, his administration and a once promising legacy.

Many of his "Ohio gang" had used their influence to exploit the spoils of office for personal gain. It was unclear how much Harding actually knew of these goings on, but he had joined the rest of the country in reading the results in the newspapers: Tom Miller of the Office of Alien Property was indicted and convicted of bribery; Jess Smith, top aide to Attorney General Harry Daugherty, had blatantly destroyed incriminating papers and committed suicide rather than face imprisonment; Charles Forbes, Director of The Veteran's Bureau skimmed profits and received huge kickbacks while directing underground alcohol and drugs distribution—mostly within a few blocks of the White House. Convicted of fraud and bribery he received a jail sentence of two years; Charles Cramer, an aide to Forbes, committed suicide. All friends of Harding, or friends of friends of his—to a man they were Ohioans. The people back in Marion had suffered through two years of disbelief, coining the oft-said plea, "Say it ain't so, Warren."

As if these travesties in the administration were not enough, the newspapers were now hinting at the opening salvos of a scandal that would soon dwarf all those coming before it. In the coming months the spectacular Tea Pot Dome debacle would claim as its victims many of the administration participants. The President, however, was to be spared a trial in the court of public opinion.

Warren G. Harding, a man full of flaws in his personal and presidential lives, unexpectedly died of a heart attack while on tour in San Francisco in the summer of 1923. For the next man to walk the halls of the White House he left a literal mess to sort out.

The passing of Harding also left Colonel Horvitch to the whim of fate. Once again his tenure depended upon a man being sworn into office: This time it was Vice President Calvin Coolidge. As Harding's successor, he would decide if The Superintendent of Buildings and Grounds would remain.

**Somewhere in White Russia (Belo Russia)
June 12, 1942**

Neither Simcha nor Branko knew of the three top-secret failed rescue attempts within the past six months. The SBC evidently thought it best to keep this under wraps. The American would just have to wait.

This was typical of compartmentalized military strategy that served the purpose of a greater good. But in the case of Branko, a little news would have made his plight more bearable—for lesser men might have cracked under the misconception that they had become expendable or worse still, forgotten.

The Russians are just too damn occupied, Branko thought. *Occupied with saving their own retreating asses to worry about an old American Brigadier in the midst of enemy territory. Certainly can't say that I blame them.*

That about summed it up in Branko's weary mind. If polled, the Maccabee Commander Simcha Greenberg and others would have agreed.

"Simcha, don't be concerned that I'll probably be here until your Red Army begins to roll this way," Branko said. "You have enough on your hands already. Besides, if I stick it out with you, I can at least contribute to some much needed Kraut ass-kicking. As if I have any choice in the matter."

"Not another word, *boychick*. You are my very own, personal American advisor. *Nu*, how many *partizaner* commanders can claim that, eh?"

The unit had been on constant movement from one encampment to another for the better part of the year. At least once every week High Command had shifted the Maccabees and other clandestine units like chess pieces. For the last two months the unit's weekly movement had been restricted to the safe Pripet Marshes. Ensconced within this difficult to penetrate region, they had begun to think of it as home.

Unquestionably, their restriction to the region it had served to prevent discovery by rear echelon Nazi contingents. Further still, as the front moved eastward toward Stalingrad, the presence of veteran *Wehrmacht* units in and around White Russia diminished dramatically. Of course Nazi Police Battalions began to fill the gap but these rear guard units were comprised of ill-trained, raw conscriptees. Most of these were men forty or older and were former bus drivers, railway workers, butchers, carpenters, teachers, clerks and the unemployed. Certainly they didn't have the same innate taste for blood as the notorious Einsatzgruppen before them. This is not to imply that the

Battalions avoided murdering Jews, ex-Commissars and other, "civilian undesirables." They had already repeatedly shown that they could be prodded into acts just as despicable. In addition, they had the availability of the *hilfviligers*—those thousands of "willing helpers" drawn from the ranks of anti-Soviets; Ukrainians, Lithuanians, Latvians and Romanians. This all spelled continued trouble to the behind-the-line partisans.

When word was received that elements of such a police patrol, small in number, was bivouacked near the city of Pinsk, Simcha Greenberg saw it as an opportunity. Once Command pinpointed the enemies' coordinates, plans were swiftly drawn-up. There was no shortage of volunteers for the dangerous undertaking and the first to step forward was no surprise.

Lev Soloveitchik was ready to go with his Mauser and a box of pilfered ammo. Within moments, the team numbered thirteen men, including Branko. Simcha didn't even bother to discourage the American from participating in the mission. He was convinced that rescue attempts of the general would not be likely. Waiting out the war with the Maccabees was by now Branko's reality check.

Simcha left Raisel in command, and went over the hastily drawn-up plan while his dozen volunteer warriors sat cross-legged under a leaf-laden birch tree. The plan was simple. Under cover of darkness, the thirteen men would ride to a point in the pine forest surrounding Pinsk, leave the horses tied and trudge approximately five kilometers to the target site. They were counting on the fact that Nazi patrols were rarely, if ever, seen at night. Figuring the enemy complement would be one or two 12-man squads, asleep in their two-man tents, Simcha would lead those with automatic weapons and rake the hell out of the tents. Lev would take-up the rear with Branko and four marksman to drill any sentries or survivors. The team would then withdraw to the forest and return. The nineteen-year-old Mikhail Blumberg, who could run like a colt, would lead the way, the others following as closely as they could and in loosely spaced, parallel groups. They were to avoid any structures and hamlets throughout the mission.

At exactly 0200, after securely tying the horses, the assassins began there fast-walk toward the target area. By 0300, the body count included each and every enemy combatant. Lev and his trusty Mauser accounted for two sentries and two others fleeing the slaughter—one of those with his hands raised in surrender. That made little difference to Lev, who grimly mowed the man down. On both sides of this private little war, the Geneva Convention simply did not apply. Even Branko nailed a half-naked policeman who was scurrying toward the nearby river.

Not one shot had been fired by the rudely awakened Germans.

The SBI usually broadcast a coded description of the day's events and they included news of the Pinsk raid almost right after Simcha had transmitted his report. Just a few hours later, a unit consisting of defrocked petty criminals and incognito ex-commissars from the Bobruisk region, went on a wild rampage that dwarfed the Pinsk engagement. They completely destroyed a Nazi field hospital, eliminating doctors, patients and all. An estimated seventy were killed. They could have taken a large number of prisoners but opted to do the more bloodthirsty while ransacking the hospital for critically needed medical supplies. The rationale: *What the hell do we need with prisoners?*

For the next week, the Maccabees stayed out of sight. After word about the attack and its repercussions had reached the nearest police battalions, increased patrols sought out revenge. SBI and Command ordered Simcha and his people to stay in their current, secure location. Until things cooled down a bit further orders were not issued.

For other partisan contingents in the vicinity, the news of the Pinsk "victory" raid served as a morale booster and motivator for one-ups-manship. The general sentiment was along the lines of, *If the stinking Zhids can do it, than we can do even better.*

*****

The matter of survival logistics never ceased to amaze Branko. Whenever the Maccabees discussed it, their attitude coupled with Branko's ten months of close observation always left him shaking his head and wondering, *How in hell do you people do it?*

As a former faculty member of The U.S. Army War College,

Branko framed their logistical nightmare in terms of a class exercise thusly: *Your squad is way off course behind enemy lines, no way out without running into enemy units. How do you stay hidden and alive until help arrives?* But not even an imaginative Branko would have thought of duplicating this situation as a survival scenario for a war college. There were no established support and supply lines and yet he rarely missed having a meal, ammunition, weapons and munitions or warm clothing in freezing weather. There were no field tents or buildings but he typically had a soft bed roll atop pine needles, leaves, hay, bark, or had a sort of a dugout called a, *zemlyanka*, in which to sleep. He readily admitted that there were always anxious moments but no one panicked and somehow manna from heaven continued to bless the Maccabees.

Of course the Maccabees lived with a much more diverse and difficult supply chain than that which was experienced by Branko's microscopic exposure. It was ten steps beyond difficult, fraught with peril and a constant problem. It was a logistical nightmare faced by all partisan elements, as well as starving civilians, throughout war-ravaged Europe.

Heading their list of priorities were food and potable water. Most edibles were stolen, bartered for with local farmers or dropped by aircraft venturing into enemy air space. For those airdrops by night, the Maccabees had to risk signal flares or fires—which invited Nazi troops in the region. Obviously air drops weren't that popular. The usual source of food was chickens, geese, cows, pigs and sheep found within a fifty- square kilometer area of wherever camp was set up. Kosher was definitely out of the picture for those requiring it. In fact, only two of the Maccabees had ever tried to hold out on this matter: They eventually broke.

Times were hard and farmers were reluctant to trade or sell foodstuffs out of their caches. The business end of a gun was often the argument persuasive to this end. And while the group with which Branko was quartered were firm in the protection of civilians—even those not particularly friendly to *Zhid* partisans—others weren't so reserved. Many underground units simply shot first and didn't bother with persuasion. With hunger as a prime motivator, openly consorting with Nazi invaders was a sure ticket to food raids and the setting aside of any relatively humane tactics.

As for water, every farm and village abode sported a well, basket, pump and all. During the heavy winter, every tin can and water bucket was filled to the brim with melted snow. Some were kept on reserve for the drier seasons and everyone seemed to always have some kind of canteen full of water.

Fishing the copious rivers, ponds and streams of the region provided a massive bounty of fish. The Pripet marshes were known for every variety of fresh water fish one could want. Improvised fishing equipment made it possible for many of the partisans to partake of fried or boiled fish as often as they wished. Indeed, the Soviet regular army soldier fared nowhere near as well.

After the necessity of food and water, the partisans' concern was the reason for being in the war and that equated to the vital resources of weapons and ammunition. Parachute drops, which increased as the Nazi advance began to slow down, were the main suppliers. Supplemental forays into enemy encampments like the Pinsk engagement, ambushes of Nazi patrols and police battalions, provided windfalls of weaponry. Local police stations manned by aging officers were a favorite target in search of these particular goods. But the Nazi occupying forces did not usually arm local police officers. As such, it was only when—and if—the police had the rare wherewithal to resort to protective gunfire, that Simcha's Maccabees return it ten-fold. The vengeful Lev licked his lips whenever this occurred.

Occasionally, whenever partisans units crossed paths, they might trade ammo and weapons—depending on their needs. In light of the various and sundry methods through which the units were armed, the Maccabees "armories" were naturally diverse. Common place weapons included 9mm Lugers, Walther Gewehr forty-one pistols, Mausers of every type—including the Karabiner 98k and Schmeissen sub-machine guns MP34 and MP40 that were favored by the Waffen SS. To these the air drops added Russian M1928 sub-machine weapons, a ranging complement of pistols and both single bolt and semi automatic pieces. And, of course, there were always, boxes of grenades and whopping loads of ammo to size.

Sometime later, when Branko was made an "honorary citizen of the USSR," Flight Lt. Sasha Cohen had presented him with a gift of his trusted Russian-made TT33 side-arm which was similar to the caliber .45 Branko had used so effectively in Belgium and France during the 1917-1918 engagements. He had heard Simcha talk of Branko's wartime experiences, and Sasha had generated a personal feeling of revenge. His father had been killed in 1915 while the Czar's army fell apart under the German advance into Russia. Conveniently enough, the pistol's bullets were interchangeable with some of the more popular Mauser models.

Whenever flyovers dropped in the hard to obtain weapons, the shipments usually included a smattering of supplies anticipated to boost morale in practical ways. Specifically, boots clothing and gloves where highly sought after and prized. In one the most recent delivers, bundled among the clothing was an equally pleasant surprise: American "K" and "C" rations and chocolate bars. Hersheys, Baby Ruths, Mars, Almond Joys, and assorted chewing gum! Branko was so overwhelmed at this gesture that some of the Maccabees jokingly swore he was on the verge of tears.

After encouraging his comrades to enjoy the delicacies, Rivka insisted that he take a bite of her Hershey bar. He succumbed to the temptation with a grin a mile wide, saying, *"A meichel fur di beichel, eh!"*

Only three targeted drops were successful since October.

Another important element of the partisans efforts was medical supplies. When requested, they were delivered whenever feasible, although most units pilfered what they needed from local doctors and aid stations. The powerful new American sulfa drug, particularly sulfanamide, used to treat wounds and bacterial infections, was in universal demand. But it was rarely found in the rural regions of the USSR. Any partisan needing more special medical help could usually find it in the nearest town where he or she, escorted by a comrade or two, would clandestinely slip into a doctor's home or small hospital for treatment. If a known Nazi sympathizer was the only choice, he was threatened to perform, while the escort held a pistol to his temple. The Hippocratic Oath was never before administered, or adhered to, with such dire enthusiasm.

Since Branko's rescue by the Maccabees in September, the unit had fluctuated between thirty and forty strong. Although Jewish strays of all stripes continued seeking to join them, Simcha did not want a larger contingent. With eight women and twenty-six men, he felt the unit could effectively deploy and rapidly move. This balance of troop strength and mobility is what Simcha believed necessary to success and minimal casualties in the missions assigned by the SBI.

Classified as *Top Secret* by SBI and High Command Simcha's Maccabee contingent was a list of eclectic:

Simcha Greenberg, age 29
Commander, Army Lieutenant
Gorky USSR

Branko Horvitch, 67
Advisor, United States Army Brigadier General (retired)
United States

Raisel Ehrenburg, 33
Vice Commander, Air Force Captain, Medical Wing
Odessa

Alexander Cohen, 28
Air Force Flight Lieutenant
Moscow

Lev Soloveitchik, 27
Civilian sharp-shooter
Rovno

Alyosha Alterman, 26
Naval torpedo machinist
Kiev

Mikhail Blumberg, age 19
Army recruit, infantry
Kharkov

Yaakov Pilatovsky, 20
Army recruit, infantry
Kiev

Olga Goldenkrantz, 26 (Cousin, Masha Mandelbaum)
Army head nurse
Zhitomir

Masha Mandelbaum, 20 (Cousin, Olga Goldenkrantz)
Army clerk-typist
Zhitomir

Hyman Malkovitch, 23
Naval gunner's mate
Odessa

Esther Kriegner, 19
Air Force mechanic trainee
Vitebsk

Asher Lubarsky, 24
Army signalman
Odessa

Kalman Markoff, 16 (Twin sister, Miriam Sara Markoff)
Civilian
Irpen

Miriam Sara Markoff, 16 (Twin brother, Kalman Markoff)
Civilian
Irpen

Vladimir Dimitch, 26
Army artillery officer-in-training
Rovno

Mendel Hirschmann, 25
Army engineering officer-in-training
Kiev

Kostya Polinoff, 44 (Brother, Josef Polinoff)
Army veteran, ex-Soviet military boxing champion
Konotop

Josef Polinoff, 36 (Brother, Kostya Polinoff)
Army artillery sergeant
Konotop

Sendehr Tuvehr, 24
Air Force bombardier
Kiev

Clara Baumbach, 17
Civilian, 1940 Olympics gymnast
Irpen

Eliahu Abramovich, 24
Army infantry corporal
Stary Konstantinov

Mendel Litvack, 27
Army supply sergeant
Odessa

Ilya Feigenbaum, 24
Army cook/baker
Kiev

Piotr Zacharia, 22
Naval submarine radio technician
Leningrad

Fyodor Kleinman, 28
Army armament specialist
Leningrad

Simon Hirsch, 27 (Sophia Hirsch, wife)
Army supply truck driver
Kiev

Sophia Hirsch, 25 (Simon Hirsch, husband),
Civilian
Kiev

Sergei Kohn, 27
Air Force ground crew parts chief
Zhitomir

Sonya Lieberman, 22
Army supply clerk
Kharkov

Solomon Reiner, 19
Naval torpedo boat seaman
Kiev

Leo Asimov, 22
Air Force bomb loader
Minsk

Dovid Kohn, 19
Army infantry recruit
Dnieprpetrovsk

Viktor Reznik, 39
Civilian, former police officer
Kiev

The Maccabees were by no means *The Irishmen of the Fighting 69th*, but Branko had grown to love and respect these courageous people. Simcha typically limited the dangerous forays to the men but he occasionally included one or two female mission members. Raisel was the more experienced in this regard, but lately all the women were vociferous in wanting to go out on missions.

It was a delicate balance for Simcha. Each of the thirty-four Maccabees could handle a variety of weapons, even the gymnast who looked more like one of those rail-thin twelve-year-old girls on the balancing bars. Of course, Simcha realized what was at work. Patriotism aside, the women wanted to share their lives with the men and there was even a goodly amount of flirtation going on. Human nature and sexual impulses do not wither away during war. Psychologically, the life and death existence of a soldier, partisan or civilian, if anything, intensified the libido. It was a truth as old as the Garden of Eden, serpent notwithstanding. In this respect the Maccabees had proven to be very human.

Following the Pinsk raid, a lingering moroseness set in on Branko. Even the deceleration after the exhilaration of a mission accomplished No doubt his mood was also affected by command's orders for the Maccabees to lay low after the attack and its domino effect with other units wreaking vengeance on Nazi sympathizers real and imagined. This imposed period of inactivity allowed Branko to simmer in the thoughts of his predicament. In his bed on those warm June pre-dawn mornings, he was as likely as not to become wide awake with his mind racing. Laying in his bed roll under the trees of the thick forest, everything seemed to intensify his isolation.

There was no rain in sight and so the crisp aromas and subdued sounds of an inactive camp reminded him of his seclusion. On those mornings he would lay there, listening to the indistinguishable whispers of the young troops whose vigor compelled them to stay up until dawn, drinking tea, shots of slivovitz or vodka and smoking.

Trying to catch a few winks, the Maccabee's esteemed *Advisor's* thoughts wouldn't let it happen.

What the hell are they thinking back in D.C.? It appears that Timoshenko's plan isn't working as he expected. Either that or with the war looking worse by the day, my rescue priority has slipped to less than last place! I'm sure Wild Bill and Hopkins are doing the best they can, without interferring with their own critical duties. One broken down old Brigadier will just have to wait it out. Simcha has cautiously avoided mentioning my existence to any other partisan unit. If the word gets out that I'm here alive, every Nazi sympathizer, glory hunter, hungry civilian and the like would just love to turn me in. The price on this old Jew's head must be astronomical by now. Berlin has probably raised the ante one hundred-fold since September. Re-capturing me would be one helluva coup. For that kind of gelt maybe I'll turn myself *in! C'mon Russkies, get that godamm counterattack going—and soon!*

THE COOLIDGE WHITE HOUSE

Washington, D.C.
January 28, 1924

When Branko met with Calvin Coolidge's Chief of Staff, all was sweetness and light.

"Yes, Colonel, we expect you to continue Supervising the Buildings and Grounds of The White House, just as you've done so admirably within the Wilson and Harding administrations. Nothing has changed. I understand that you lecture twice a week at the War College and that is certainly acceptable to President Coolidge. If there's anything we can do, please don't hesitate to come to me directly."

This took place the day after Coolidge had chosen just a few staff replacements and two weeks after Harding had passed away. Due to the increasing exposure of the nefarious Tea Pot Dome scandal, Branko expected to stay on for yet another President. Coolidge had a mountain of cleanup matters to take care of and bringing in another Superintendent hadn't struck him as a likelihood. About that he had been right.

On this late January day, the President of the United States was scheduled to meet with the press. There were many rumors flying around the country regarding firings, indictments, resignations, reprimands, and Congressional hearings—all due to the late administration. Coolidge was advised by the Chief of Staff that the press and radio were demanding that the President bring it out to the public. Additionally, several cabinet members concluded that the President must do this immediately—before the administration was splashed with tainted water.

This conference would be quite different from the usual briefings he had in the preceding months, some of which were conducted by the official Presidential Secretary. Coolidge strode to the podium in the East Hall. The wiry, nondescript man, looking more like a village storekeeper or a minor minister, started out with his sharply accented Vermont voice.

"I want to share with you my knowledge of the Teapot Dome affair. Much of which we've only recently uncovered. A Higher Authority had something to say about it and now we own the whole blessed mess, which by the way, doesn't begin or end with the boiling tea pot. But it is the start for today. I assure you we will get to your written questions after this briefer than brief briefing."

He grinned impishly and there were barely audible chuckles. Branko, standing in the rear with his military aides, where they were posted for all East Hall conferences, glanced toward them and then thought, *good God, the cadaver has a sense of humor.*

The teapot scandal to which Coolidge referred had its beginnings well before the Harding administration. Massive acres of oil-rich lands in south central California had been first set aside by President Taft. Wilson later added several thousand additional acres at a place called Teapot Dome, just north of Casper, Wyoming. Both of these acts were part of a general conservation program so that there would be sufficient oil reserves at any time in the future, should the Navy find other sources of oil difficult to access.

"I should also mention" Coolidge went on, "that I eagerly seek your ideas regarding anything we talk about during these briefings—now and in the future. Now, getting back to Wyoming: For those of you who have spent the last two years second-guessing Warren Harding's decisions, Tea Pot Dome in Wyoming is one of the locations of the oil reserves in question. I'm taking you back a dozen years, to the Taft administration. Certain major improprieties, about which have been speculated in print lead me to believe that most of you know more than this poor old son of Vermont—and you probably do. Especially you and your *Washington Star*, Tom."

This brought another wave of chuckles. Everybody knew that Tom Wolverton was on a major crusade to paint Coolidge with the same brush that coated Harding. After all, the fact that he had been the vice-president would have seemed to make Coolidge privy to exactly what went on in the Oval Office. This was, in fact, the paramount theme of Wolverton's columns. The senior reporter was one of the more ultra-liberal newsmen, and his support for the Democratic Party was equaled only by the dogged pursuit of connecting Republican Coolidge to the Tea Pot scandal.

Coolidge was politically savvy enough to call out a few other members of the fraternity, negating the appearance that Tom was a personal target. It was a strategically magnanimous maneuver on the part of Coolidge and he reaped an immediate benefit. Everyone seemed to take it in comfortable stride and the conference went exceptionally pleasant considering the gloom and doom of the dark clouds hanging over Washington.

"Mr. President, we appreciate your giving us a quick, candid glimpse into a history lesson, but when do you expect to see some hard and fast indictments coming down the pike," asked the *Post's* old timer, Sam Stutz. It had been Coolidge's *modus operandi* to ask for written questions to be passed to the podium just prior to the conference, but this had not been one of those questions. Coolidge chose to answer Stutz regardless.

"Sam, that's above and beyond my marching orders. All I can say is that we want to do the right thing and everyone involved, though innocent until proven that his hand was in the cookie jar, is being studied with a magnifying glass, as we speak. I assure each and every one here today that corruption in any way, shape or form, will be dealt with harshly—but fairly."

The President went on for just a few more minutes, addressing the crux of the Tea Pot matter. Many of the press had not heard the more outrageous part of the story, mainly because of the meticulous care that Harding's staff had taken in covering it up. Most of the informative leaks began about a month prior to Harding's death. There had not really been enough time for thorough investigative reporting, and even the obliquely involved had effectively clammed-up. Coolidge referred to the three major culprits; Secretary of the Interior Albert Fall of New Mexico and his oil mogul pals, Harry Sinclair and Ed Doheny. Bribery could be the eventual charge, to the tune of $100,000 if it could be proven to have found its way into the Secretary's pockets. The much-maligned Secretary from Las Cruces had not resigned his post until the past week. He was still hanging onto his Cabinet seat only because Coolidge hesitated to condemn anyone until after the Congressional Committee posted its initial fact-findings, precipitating the urgent necessity for Fall *to fall*. More than a few of America's newspapers came up with headlines heralding "Fall is the Fall Guy" and, "Fall has Fell" or more grammatically correct, "Fall has Fallen." Even the staid *Wall Street Journal* chimed in with, "'Prince' Albert to go back into the Can!"

"Gentlemen, we'll have to do this again, won't we," the President wrapped-up without even a hint of whether he was being humorous. "Mr. C. Bascom Slemp, my esteemed Presidential Secretary, will stay on to answer questions from the slips you handed in. He's far more articulate than I am. Besides, I have to go and make lunch for Mrs. Coolidge."

The President swiveled and exited the East Hall. Trailing behind him was more than just low-key laughter and polite applause. The attending m members of the Fourth Estate seemed to genuinely like the man. Total time of his appearance: sixteen minutes. He had, after all, said it would be a briefer than brief briefing.

Branko and Jack Steel looked at each other grinning in awe of the President. He had never before had shown the lighter side of his "silent Cal" image. Both men later agreed that it was more than likely the President's calculated way of diffusing the possible "inheritance" of the scandal. If the briefing had been any indicator, Coolidge and the Republican Party were beginning to look like they would come out relatively unscathed—even with a placid leader at the helm.

A few days later, all of this was tempered by the death of Woodrow Thomas Wilson. It came as no shock. He had deteriorated to the point where his physicians had talked in terms of "a matter of a few days."

On February 2nd, he lapsed into a coma and death lifted him to the other side on the next evening. He was buried at The Washington National Cathedral and it seemed as though the entire government came to a standstill. The funeral was attended by thousands from across the political spectrum.

The great American President was gone and the legacies he left in many ways surpassed those of leaders before him. Here was a man who had a dream of America joining with other nations to insure a semblance of world peace guaranteed through a League of Nations. It was not to be, as he was repeatedly repudiated by Congress. Those who wanted no part of worldwide obligations made their voices heard clearer than the minority who knew that isolationism in a rapidly shrinking world would not be in America's best interests.

Edith was holding up quite well and was as gracious as ever while hosting the gathering following the funeral. Branko exited the Wilson home earlier than most of the guests, knowing that he would not have any opportunity to properly convey his condolences to Edith and to Woodrow's adult children and their families.

Edith understood.

April 2, 1924

The President and Mrs. Coolidge did not return to the Wilson House after the funeral. With the presence of the Secret Service, police cars and members of the press, they thought it was too much of an imposition at a time of mourning. Instead, they invited the former First Lady to a private lunch at the White House and arranged it for the next month. On the appointed day, how Edith managed to sneak out of her home, giving the assigned Fed-boy the proverbial slip remained a mystery—something she had repeated often.

But a short time later, she drove up to the White House in her Rolls Royce. The handsome Rolls Silver Cloud masterpiece had been a birthday gift to President Wilson from four of his Princeton alum-mates, who had been his most vociferous supporters. They had been there during the dark days of the war, and the fight for the Treaty and the League of Nations proposals. Bernard Baruch, Cleveland Dodge, Jesse Jones and Thomas Jones planned the surprise gift of the car for nearly a year. Sadly, Wilson did not have much time left to enjoy it.

After lunch, and before driving home, Edith stopped by to see if Branko was in his office. He was not, but she thought she had spotted him on the grounds earlier when she had driven in. And out on the grounds is where she found him.

They decided to stroll to the furthest point of the southern boundary, so as not to be cornered by the myriad vendors scattered across the property. On any given day there were plumbers, carpenters, electricians, painters, gardeners and tourists. It was easy to fall into the habit of seeing tourists as "gawking intruders" but Branko took another view: These were citizens visiting the people's house and checking in on the guy they had hired for the next four years.

"Well, well," Edith had said on first seeing him, "the superintendent is actually superintending!"

That earned her a genuine laugh.

"I really appreciated your dropping by last month," she said, after they had begun their stroll across the grounds. "I'm happy you had a chance to meet Woodrow's children. They all enjoyed seeing you. They had been staying at the house since the funeral."

"My pleasure, Edith. They sure are involved in fascinating lives of their own. I particularly found, Margaret, to be—shall we say, different in her world view?"

Edith Wilson smiled at Branko's description of the eldest child, Margaret. "Right. She's so smitten with her life as a singer; a year with the Chicago Symphony, toured France during the war, giving performances and entertained at Liberty Bond rallies all over the country. Woodrow always worried about her future as an unmarried woman. The other two, Eleanor and Jessie, happily married with children, were also a source of joy to him."

She didn't go on and express what Branko already suspected: That Edith wished Woodrow's children from his first marriage were more cordial in their acceptance of her as the second wife. He knew it was common occurrence with the children of a widowed parent and she, no doubt, did too.

"The Coolidges mentioned you a few times," Edith said, changing to a light tone of voice. "What with knowing that we're friends. And I still laugh at your hilarious description of that Press Conference. Calvin's a delightful book behind a boring cover, so to speak. He has that streak of self-deprecation, too. At lunch today, he told a very laughable story about himself. You may not be aware of this, but Silent Cal is chummy with a few Americans well-known in the public eye. Three of them were visiting just a few weeks after Harding died, and they insisted on taking a drive with him out into the country."

"Do you mean Henry Ford, Tom Edison and Harvey Firestone, the tire mogul? I remember seeing them on the grounds at about that time, and I introduced myself."

"Yes, yes. Well, Cal wanted to do the driving and he arranged to have the Fed boys follow a good distance behind. They got out into rural Virginia and stopped for some gasoline at a run-down little filling station. The three passengers got out for a stretch as the attendant stood by and admired the custom-built Ford touring car. While the attendant was filling the tank, Tom Edison proudly told him that he invented and designed all of the electrical parts of the car including the headlights. Not to be outdone by the Wizard of Menlo Park, Ford proudly proclaimed that he, indeed, actually *built* the car, while Firestone quickly chimed in saying that he manufactured the tires. The smirking, disbelieving local didn't buy any of it and said: 'And now I suppose you're going to tell me that skinny little runt behind the wheel is the President of the United States.'"

Branko roared with laughter and they both agreed that the President would probably tell this piece of probable fiction a hundred times more. Later, upon reflection, Branko would questioned, *how in hell could the press and the public so badly misjudge this President.*

But it was true that he was widely known only as the epitome of New England reticence and rectitude.

On the way back to her Rolls Royce, which Branko had already admired at the Wilson home, Edith looked him in the eye and asked, "Now what's this story of a serious woman friend, Senor Don Juan?"

"Whoa there! When I said serious, I probably jumped the gun a bit. I think you will like her. I know I do!"

"Do tell me more."

"Okay, okay, nosy one, get your steno pad out. Her name is Eva Kanter and she's an English teacher at Sidwell Friend's School here in town. Divorced for the past two years, originally from Massachusetts, Columbia grad, lived and taught in New York before winning the Sidwell position. Oh, yes, I know it's a Quaker school and Eva is Jewish, though only occasionally practicing the religious aspects.

Evidently they realized they were getting the best recruit, which overrode anything else."

"Sounds like you two are made for each other," Edith said with a smile betraying her next joke. "Maybe she can teach you a thing or two about good grammar and speech."

Branko grinned back.

"By the way, Sidwell is known as the uppity school of choice in these parts."

"So she tells me. Eva has a fifteen-year-old boy who is attending there. Seems like a nice kid but torn between the divorced parents. I guess that's not too uncommon. Spends most of his time with daddy, who lavishes all things material on the young lad. Tough on Eva who can't match anything of the sort. Not that she would want to."

"Branko, I want to meet her. I'll have you two over for dinner some-time next week. I'll call to set a date. Meanwhile, a*dieu, moi Colonel!*"

"Well," he mumbled with a grin, "okay."

Later that evening, with no engagements to attend, Branko chose to sit in the regally furnished hotel lobby, reading the stack of mail delivered by the concierge. Most of his personal mail was addressed to the Willard, while his "business" mail was directed to his office at the White House.

Sifting through the cards and letters, he was very happy to see a French postmark, knowing that it would be from Tante. A literary magazine postmarked out of Cambridge, Massachusetts brought another warm feeling to his heart: That could only be Rivka, he hoped, or maybe Sendehr.

A thick manila envelope marked *To Be Opened By Addressee Only* was from "Cloak and Dagger" Donovan. It was pasted over with a variety of foreign stamps. There was another letter from Hollywood, California—no doubt from Joe Kennedy.

Truly, my U.S. Mail cup runneth over, Branko thought with a smile while opening the letter from Tante:

Paris, Rue de Rois de Sicile
March 1, 1924

Dearest favorite nephew Branko:

We were so sorry to hear of your President Wilson's death. To most of the French he was a genuine hero. You are experiencing working under several of these leaders in a very short time. Now I'll wait for you to tell me something about this man Coolidge. Your last letter to me sounded like you knew little about him. If he hadn't rehired my nephew, he would have heard a thing or two from me, I'll say!

Charles and I have been very happy with our married life and the children accept him unconditionally. Meeting his two children in Geneva last summer was a treat for me. We stayed with his son and family in a beautiful little chalet on the lake. Waking up in the morning with that view was as close to heaven as one could get.

Dovidl writes frequently from Jerusalem, and he is now one of the kibbutz managers. They always ask about your adventures and you can imagine the conversations they have with their friends about their cousin, the Colonel, who is <u>the</u> Superintendent of the White House. I think that sounds more powerful than your full title with "Buildings and Grounds" in it. They probably envision you as Assistant President. Gevalt! That's even better than, what you call, Vice President. Oy Branko, we are all so proud of our little Brachela from Ignatovka! Seems like a hundred years ago. We could fill our <u>own</u> history book. I know you and

Dovidl correspond occasionally. Please keep that up.

Still no *kleine maidel*, Branko? Washington must have so many nice, smart girls just looking for a man like you. Nu, what are you waiting for, a Clara Bow, a Theda Bara, a Gloria Swanson?

Charles and I have talked about possibly planning a trip to America. It's just so expensive to cross the ocean. But who knows, maybe a gold mine will open up across the street from us. I love the song "Pennies from Heaven" but they should only be dollars or francs. Omayn.

Take care of yourself, Branko, and please help your Mr. Coolidge. He must have so many things that keep him busy day and night. Maybe you should offer to help him even more. Wouldn't hurt.

With love from all,
Tante

Branko kept only the letters he received from Tante Shayndl and Rivka. And receiving a letter from them at the same time felt like hitting the jackpot. He had yet to receive a letter from Tante that didn't leave him grinning from ear to ear. As his guardian angel from the ages of six to fourteen, she had a special niche next to his heart.

These days he found himself wishing that Tante, Charles and the Paris family should seriously consider emigrating to the United States. As French citizens the newly imposed restrictive immigration quotas would not be a deterrent. If they chose Canada, it would even be less of a barrier. He had a very unsettling feeling about the near future of Europe and little or no faith that a League of Nations would be effective. He had always carefully avoided discussing the topic with Edith who had fought unceasingly, alongside Woodrow, for the League of Nations. To this day, she believed that the futility of it all was the final blow that precipitated the stroke, deterioration and death of her husband.

At the same time, Branko could not help but draw a parallel to Theodor Herzl whose dream of a Jewish State was ignored, ridiculed and repeatedly shattered until he succumbed to heart disease at age forty-four. Both Woodrow Wilson and Herzl had an all-consuming dream. And Each man was rebuffed. In Herzl's case, he just didn't survive long enough to see the dream through to at least partial fruition. With Wilson, he had felt so strongly that there could be no lasting peace without the infrastructure of a peace-keeping body. Like Branko, Wilson foresaw the reality of territory-grabbing again causing skirmishes throughout the European continent. The eventuality was doomed to escalate into another brutal, all-encompassing conflagration.

At any rate, after reading Tante's letter Branko vowed to adamantly push for the family to emigrate. And not to Palestine, either. That wasn't even an option. Dovid's correspondence spoke freely and honestly of growing animosities between fellow Semites, Arabs and Jews. It would be a long time before some semblance of stability would occur in that region of the world—if ever. Both concerned men did not want to subject Tante and the family to these ever-present uncertainties. Besides, Charles had readily admitted more than once that he had no Zionistic fervor. Tante, at best, perhaps a shade more. The two daughters and their husbands would undeniably fit into Charles' camp. Dovid, as the man-on-the-spot, harbored the sensible reality that the present Palestinian economy was not equipped to provide adequate jobs and income for immigrants. So, without question, it would have to be North America, if anywhere.

Just after laying Tante's letter aside the hotel desk paged Branko to a phone call from Eva. When the two of them had met the bells went off in a sort of *coup de foudre*—love at first sight. Since then they had spent weekends together and phoned each other a few times per week, Sidwell operated like a small Ivy League college, with heavy teaching loads, frequent exams and a no-nonsense milieu. Teaching there was a major challenge for any teacher. Eva called to tell Branko that she would be grading mid-term papers for most of the coming weekend. They chatted, for a short time and he told her of Edith's lunch with the Coolidges. He ended the call by relating the hilarious "skinny runt behind the wheel" story which Eva, too, thought was a knee-slapper. They made tentative arrangements to meet for lunch at the Willard on Saturday so she could take a break from her grading. When Branko hung up the phone, he smiled and thought, *Dang! This lady is different. She has a career and a purposeful life pursuing it. She's highly intelligent, quite worldly in her views, and hell, I love being with her—Maybe, Tante, just maybe, this is it! Then, at least, you won't nudzheh me anymore!*

During the last year, Sendehr had accepted a position with a Cambridge literary critic's magazine—thus the move to Boston. They were still happily living in a spacious old Harvard Square, two-family house. Being in Greater Boston, they enjoyed renewing connections with the several *Fusgeyers* in the area. Their oldest son, Alexander, was already accepted to start his studies at prestigious Tufts College in the fall. It was a happy letter, and that came through clearly. But the underlying purpose was news about Miriam and Branko's son Emanuel. Now living in Cleveland, Miriam had just married for the third time—to a traveling dry goods salesman. She was so proud that her son had won a full scholarship to local Western Reserve University. She had told Rivka not to say anything, knowing full-well that her old friend would continue to be the only conduit to Branko.

The letter was signed, *love, Rivka, and Sendehr says, "Hello Colonel!"* They hadn't seen Branko since the *Croix de Guerre* ceremony at the French Embassy in 1919. His very confidential feelings for Rivka still made his heart go pitter-patter. He often wondered if she knew.

Perhaps, Branko's admitted to himself. *Then again, maybe not and she never will. Is there a slight hint of fragrance coming from the pages?*

He dismissed the thought almost as soon as it had occurred. The news about Miriam, however, was met with mixed emotions. It was nice to hear something about the son he hadn't seen since 1906—good to know that he would be getting a good education. But there was still an abysmal emptiness at knowing he would probably never see his flesh and blood. His one and only issue.

Instead of dwelling on it further, he tore open the thin letter from Joseph P. Kennedy of Brookline, Massachusetts.

Greetings old sport:

Hope all is well in that cesspool we call our nation's capital. I just returned home after spending the last six months in whacky Hollywood. Coming back to New England was like a breath of fresh air, Branko. Now I'm deeply invested in two movie productions, which means I'll be getting back to California within the next two months. I much prefer spending the summer on the Cape with my little (not so little) family and my wild Irish Rose. Christ, she's pregnant again. This Catholic life does pose a conception burden! I'm renting a beautiful place down there this summer. In fact, I have plans to buy it someday soon, and expand the property. Smack dab down at the shoreline.

I must be honest Branko, there is a mad rush to the senses when making a movie. I can't explain the excitement, the glamor, the satisfaction of seeing something on the silver screen that has your personal stamp on it. My partners, all experienced filmmakers, don't want any part of the day-to-day minutia. They're leaving that to me and I truly love every bit of it.

One of the projects is starring the great Gloria Swanson. Some dame! Gorgeous, sexy and smart as a whip. She has a big mansion in the hills and has invited me to stay there on an occasional weekend. Her entourage therein is something to behold. Starlets, agents, writers, "wannabees," "gofers," lawyers, maids, a chauffeur, a chef and you name it. Now there's some talk about adding voice to the flicks. Some big wigs expect these 'talkies' to come along within three to five years. One of my pals, Jack Warner, has set up a company just for that purpose. I had to cajole the hell out of him so he'd let me invest in a piece of it. I just bought out one of his brothers to enlarge my share.

Well, I don't mean to blow my damn horn so much. How's life with Calvin? He was a tough little monkey when he was governor of my state. Sure, we had a few run-ins, so <u>DON'T</u> say hello to him for me! That would be your swan song at the White House, for sure! Write or call sometime. Maybe we can get you up here this summer, to meet the family, and go out sailing with Joe Junior (9), Jack (7) and me.

Keep on tee-totaling, Colonel. I admire your undying loyalty to the prohibition gods!

Joe K.
Brookline phone: 664-799
After June 12, summer phone in Hyannisport: 455-378
(Keep these confidential, please.)

That left the official-looking, dog-eared envelope from the one and only, Bill Donovan. The return address was New York City, so Branko assumed Donovan was back in the country now.

Branko Horvitch,
You old broken down dog face, how the hell are you? Once again, scuttlebutt indicates that you are thriving in the "Coolidge House" like you did in the other two. Hell if you haven't found a home in the friggin army, soldier! So,

are we going to get serious about you retiring once you grab the Brigadier General star? Eh? I can use you in some very critical missions and the money will dwarf your piss-poor army pay.

During the last five years I've made more moolah than I did in the 10 years of service I put in. And it's not just about the money, pal, it's about the life I lead. You're a natural for it. Just say the word and I'll start laying the plans. You've got a name, Branko. That pulls some big weight around Washington as well as in some other parts of the country and the world for that matter. Don't you realize this, or has your ego been worn down by those Colonel-birds you're wearing on your epaulets and lapels?

The letter, on yellow-lined paper, went on in the same fashion for a couple of pages and Branko laboriously worked his way through it without falling asleep in the soft leather chair. Donovan wanted to get down to Washington in the next month, to spend some time with Franklin regarding plans for a worldwide intelligence network. Per FDR could spring the deal by the time a Democrat once again sat in the Oval Office. Probably even sooner in Donovan's estimation. He even hinted to Branko just who that would be. Why, Frankln Delano Roosevelt himself, of course.

That could be at least two elections off, Branko thought, not buying the idea. *What the hell are you thinking, Donovan. Coolidge is a shoo-in to be reelected, and Hoover is already busily grooming himself for '28. Probably for two terms. The Republicans have built up a powerful machine. Herbie's Secretary of Commerce cushion is a catapult to the presidency in disguise, for Chrissakes, and the GOP has never been very cosy with any international intelligence talk! Oh, yes. I will be happy to see my old comrade, have dinner, shoot the breeze, but that's the long and short of it. I love the guy, but I don't* like what he's doing. As Tante Shayndl would say, *nisht fur dir*—*not for you!* She'd be right, bless her!

April 12, 1924

Branko never felt better about his own personal goal: a bonus agreement for veterans. In fact, he had been an occasional invited attendee at several of the House's fact-finding committees regarding the proposed bonuses. He had also appeared before a joint session of the House and the Senate in early March.

As one of twelve vets who were each asked to share their opinions he was the highest ranking and the only one still in uniform. He kept thinking throughout, *I, Branko Horvitch, am actually speaking before the leaders of America. What a country!* Most of America knew that he was the popular, untiring spearhead for the bonus. His uniform and high rank made him appear even more impressive in this position.

During the past few years both Wilson and Harding had pushed for a veteran bonus, but the latter actually vetoed one form of the bill while tacitly and strangely showing support for an eventual bonus.

When Coolidge stepped into the picture, the bonus problems were dumped in his lap. He quietly—very quietly—took pride in the fact that one of his own staff was a spokesman for the country-wide legion of veterans. It was not lost on Coolidge that the Superintendent of Buildings and Grounds, a notable lecturer at the Army War College and decorated active duty veteran was pushing for the passage of the bonus.

Coolidge knew well that the veterans were a particularly large voter bloc. Now that the bill was to be taken up in ten days it appeared that it would pass even though another veto override was expected to be necessary.

On this same day of April 12th, there was another important event being prepared for in the nation's capital—a decidedly nonpolitical event.

The *Washington Nationals* were getting ready for the season's opener in three days. They had enjoyed an outstanding spring training season, winning eighteen of twenty-six games, and many in the baseball world predicted they would win it all this year.

The Washington Post
SPORTS
James Q. Murray, reporting

SEASON OPENER, APRIL 15th, 1:00 p.m.

Can this be the year when our beloved Nats hang the World Championship banner? From what I could observe down in Florida for the past month, unequivocally YES.

That is, if we don't blow it once again. I liked what I saw of our new skipper, Stanley "call me Bucky" Harris. This is a no nonsense field-general from the old school, where even ten-year veterans have to do the most fundamental drills, like it or not.

Seeing the venerable Walter "Big Train" Johnson running laps in the outfield taught me that this team and its manager just might do it. The starting line-up is one of the better balanced in several years. Can Johnson have yet another great year in his 37-year-old arm? I definitely think so. He's starting in the opener and the visiting Yankees are already shaking in their spikes. Well, I don't know about Babe Ruth, the Big Bambino; he's probably cool as a cucumber, ready to take "Big Train" into the tenth row of the right field bleachers.

One thing I can assure you, come out to the ballpark and you will see for yourself why I, for one, see a championship in my winless crystal ball. Y'all come on out to re-painted Griffith Stadium. See you there, baseball fans!

Don't forget, come early: President Calvin Coolidge will be throwing out the first ball. I hear he has a wicked curve and a pretty fair fast ball.

Washington Nationals Starting Lineup Wednesday, April 15th 1924

Muddy Ruel	C
Nemo Leibold	CF
Joe Judge	1B
Goose Goslin	LF
Sam Rice	RF
Bucky Harris	(2B Manager)
Roger Peckinpaugh	SS
Ossie Bluege	3B
Walter Johnson	P

April 13, 1924

Will wonders ever cease? Branko pondered.

The peripatetic Presidential Secretary, C. Bascomb Slemp, who never had come to Branko's office nor had spoken to him on the grounds, stood in Branko's office doorway, with his substantial nose up in the air, harrumphed twice, and without a howdie-do crisply barked out a simple order of the day: "Mr. President wishes that you meet him here in your office at 6:00 p.m.. Do not be late."

Slemp quickly left before Branko's dropped jaw had settled back to where it belonged.

What the hell was that all about? I'll have to snoop around this afternoon to find out what I can.

Of course, that was easier said than done. None of the military aides knew anything about this request. Why would they? Both Jack Steel and Larry Lincoln, having coffee in the kitchen laughed in disbelief and admitted they had never heard of this kind of presidential request before. Branko would just have to wait it out, but there was a message to call Edith. Maybe she would know something.

But no, she knew nothing of the matter. And she readily admitted it was a strange request at that. Actually, she had called to firm up the invitation for Branko and Eva to join her for a Sunday lunch on the 19th. Branko knew very well that Eva would be quite happy with this cordial invitation.

At exactly 6:00 p.m., when the White House was nearly empty the President appeared in Branko's office—it was a sight the Colonel would long and fondly remember. A very serious Calvin Coolidge, dressed in a blue-trimmed, white tennis sweater, a pair of white slacks and white tennis sneakers. He was carrying a brand new official baseball and two mitts.

"Branko," Coolidge said, "I'm very sorry if I have spoiled any plans you've had for this evening, but a most crucial affair of state requires me to ask for you help."

The incredulous Superintendent of Buildings and Grounds waited a few seconds to digest the bizarre sight before him before responding. "I'll be pleased to help you any way I can, Mr. President."

"I'll be brief and succinct, sir. With baseball season opening the day after tomorrow, I'm to follow the hallowed tradition of throwing out the first ball."

"That's a superb honor, but what can I possibly do, Mr. President?"

"I don't relish the thought of being embarrassed. I want to throw it well and far enough to reach the catcher's mitt. Problem is, I haven't tossed very many baseballs in my lifetime, but I'm guessing that you have. You appear to be quite athletic, Branko, and I've seen you play a spirited game of tennis on our courts on occasion."

"Yes, I also played some baseball with my New York Police Department precinct team. I was quite new to the game, having recently immigrated to America from Eastern Europe. But I'm sure I can coach you to be more than competent by Wednesday. Shall we get started, Mr. President?"

"Okay. Coach, let's go out to the south boundary where there will be less chance of any onlookers."

"Don't worry a bit, sir. I'll have you looking like 'Big Train' Johnson in no time."

Branko left his uniform jacket and tie in the office and out they went—the 30th President of the United States of America and his personal training officer.

In exactly ten seconds Branko determined that, indeed, this fellow knew little or nothing about throwing a baseball. He also couldn't imagine the enormous President William Howard Taft, who started this tradition, throwing a baseball—or anything— more than twenty feet. Wilson could throw with the best of them and Harding made a gallant try to little avail. Now, facing the most difficult assignment of his illustrious Army career, the Colonel went to work.

He didn't dare throw the ball back to Coolidge for fear that it might hit him somewhere on the body, so he walked it back to him after each of the President's pitches. Branko thought it might be best to teach him to throw side-armed. Of course, as any good coach would, he shouted encouragement after each throw.

And it worked! Inside the hour, the President was throwing accurately at a distance of about thirty paces. Branko was being honest in his assessment when he pronounced Coolidge ready for the game. But the President was buying none of this brush-off. No, he wanted to meet again tomorrow.

"Now see here, Coach, this is an election year, and I assure you that some pooh-bah Democrat is lying-in-wait for any little morsel to use against me. I sure don't want to be tripped up because of my inability to throw that bloody baseball!"

"Sir, I would never prematurely let you go to your sacred ritual on Opening Day. Trust me. You are as ready as you'll ever be and I'll stand behind this honest and impartial diagnosis."

Could it be that the Coach was having a little harmless fun with this project? If he were, the student didn't seem to be at all suspicious of it.

"I don't wish for you to stand *behind* me, dadgummit, I want you sitting *beside* me—in the Presidential box. My Grace will be there, and there are eight other seats. I'll have two tickets for you so you can take anyone along that you wish to. In fact, forget the tickets and plan on riding to the Stadium in my car. We don't have any parking problems, y'know."

The President took his leave in the usual brusque manner, once more making sure that Branko understood there would be a final training session the next day at 6:00 p.m.. To punctuate that order, he left the two gloves and the ball in the Superintendent's office—along with a still stunned Branko.

When Branko spoke with Eva over the phone that evening, he told her that he would be sitting in the Presidential box for opening day.

"My goodness. I can't wait to tell Jesse. He's quite a little ballplayer at Sidwell, the only freshman on the baseball team. He's a big Nats fan and will love this story."

"Eva, I have yet to meet Jesse, but by jingo, he's going to be sitting next to me!"

"Whaaat?"

"Yes, yes! Where can I pick him up at around noon time on Wednesday?"

"At the school. I'll arrange it with the office—and with his dad."

"Then it's done, Eva my sweet! Don't tell him anything other than that I'm taking him to the game."

Both couldn't wait for Eva to break this to Jesse the next day. He spent most of his evenings at his dad's spacious colonial in Chevy Chase, and an occasional weekend with Eva.

For Branko and Eva, "The Big Day" couldn't come soon enough.

*****

Opening Day
Washington Nationals Baseball
Griffith Stadium
April 15, 1924

Jesse Kanter's bulging eyes did not retract into their sockets until time for the opening toss. The fifteen year-old was thoroughly engrossed with the events of the day; meeting Branko, the ride in the President's car with the Secret Service entourage hovering around the box behind home plate while the President referred to them as "the Fed boys." Young Jesse was completely enthralled with the excitement of opening day and the red, white and blue bunting and banners all over the stadium." The boy periodically uttered, "Wait 'til I tell my dad about this!"

The Presidential pitch went fairly well, although the distance to Muddy Ruel's mitt, or where he stood for the catch, was measurably longer than the thirty paces Branko had estimated during the two practice sessions. Muddy made a heroic lunge for the ball and actually caught it before it hit the ground. Coolidge seemed quite satisfied with his effort, the crowd roared with approval. The cameramen everywhere clicked away. The President, grinning from ear-to-ear, kissed his wife, put his arm around Branko and whispered, "Thank you, Coach!" He even extended his hand to Jesse who afterward sank into his seat basking in the glow. Also seated in the box were the Coolidge sons, the Vice President and the Senate Majority Leader and their wives. A gaggle of Congressmen who had taken time from their busy schedules and several other well-known politicos were seated here and there in the same section of the stands. They were giving thumbs-up every time the President glanced in their general direction. This, of course, invited the time-worn, rhetorical question, *Who's watching the store?*

The game was a rather slow and boring pitching duel as Johnson looked to be in mid-season form. In the end, the locals won their first game of 1924. With 153 more games to be played no one could yet know if they were on their way to a pennant. Certainly it was too early to even think of a world championship. Obviously the reigning New York Yankees and Babe Ruth, their "King of Swat" would pull out all the stops to make sure that it wouldn't happen.

After the last out "Big Train" Johnson dutifully came over to the box for additional photos with the President. Jesse shoved his scorecard at Johnson, with Branko's pencil and the accommodating future Hall of Famer obliged, along with a pat on the teenager's head.

A few months after Opening Day, with the season in full swing, Branko received an unexpected letter from Duluth, Minnesota. The return addressee was *Albie White c/o The Duluth Red Birds*. Indeed, it was from The Battling Bear of Birlad, also known as Avi Semelweiss. In the weeks following the Coolidge pitch, Branko had received letters from more than fifty *fusgeyers* from all over the USA and Canada. The power of the press has no peers!

> *June 12, 1924*
> *My dear old friend Branko:*
> *Colonel Horvitch! What? I saw your familiar smiling face standing next to President Coolidge on Opening Day. What the hell, Branko!? Sendehr wrote me a few years ago telling me you were still in the army and part of the White House staff but we had no idea just how far up that flagpole you were. The Sports Section of the Duluth Tribune fish-wrap covers my local ball club with a skimpy two or three lines every game, but for Opening Day in Washington, they proudly extended themselves and added the photo along with all the Major League scores. The caption read, "Next to the President is Colonel Branko Horvitch, Superintendent of Buildings and Grounds at The White House," blah, blah, blah.*
>
> *Well, I'm telling you, I knew that guy Horvitch when we nearly ended up dead or in an Austrian prison back in '04, by God! Seriously, old friend, I'm happy that you've done it all since then...New York cop, world war hero, and now hob-nobbing with Presidents.*

You've come a long way, and I'm damn proud of you. We all are!

I really appreciated your coming to see me play in Newark. I've been around the minor circuit since then. Now I'm the playing-manager for this Class C team, part of the growing Cardinal farm system. A lowly part, I should say! At least I still get my licks at the plate. Facts is, I'm leading the team in average (.319), most hits (133), doubles (42) and stolen bases (77). Ain't lost the old speed yet, pal! But I'm paid my paltry sum to help develop the youngsters so they can move up in the system and someday make the Cards. At 35 this is where I'll probably stay for a few years, and hopefully the General Manager, Branch Rickey down in St. Louis, won't renege on his promise to give me a plum scouting territory. I'd like that. He's setting up wholly-owned farm teams by the dozens, and paying his scouting force good money to keep the talent coming through the pipeline.

By the way, I married a big, good-hearted Swede up here a few years ago. Second for me, first for her. We have a little daughter, and Greta's family, staunch Lutherans, are getting used to having a Romanian Yid for a son-in-law. Oy vay!

Seeing your picture and writing this letter, has given me some incentive for tomorrow's doubleheader against those weak-hitting Mesabi Miners. My first hit will be for you, Branko. Please write. I'm not sure I had your proper address from Sendehr.

Your old Fusgeyer comrade,
Albie (Avi) White

The deep and delicious nostalgia that followed was a welcome tonic for Branko. Something like this always gave him an incredible morale boost. Memories going back to '04 circulated through his gray matter. Recalling scrappy little Avi at age fifteen and his part in the great escape from Theresienstadt Prison's road gangs in Bohemia, naturally brought the exotic, nineteen-year-old Rivka Demkin to mind. Here it was twenty years later and Branko still marveled at the precise execution of the hastily drawn-up escape plan and the way in which Rivka trained Avi for his key role within minutes. The graphic picture of these two flawless performers rendering the armed guards completely helpless, still remained etched in Branko's memory. The two guards were incapacitated retching in cascades, having ingested an extreme overdose of ipecac planted in a bottle of the popular "Moravian purple."

July 28, 1924

With Coolidge's re-election campaign steam-rolling along, all of this election year's hoo-rah had been sadly clouded over by the tragic, untimely death of the Coolidge's youngest son, Cal Jr., earlier in the month. Junior had been playing tennis with his brother John and developed a blister. The blister rapidly morphed into a quick-spreading infection. Everything possible was done—all without success. Calvin Coolidge, Jr. was dead at sixteen.

This devastated Jesse, who had enjoyed chatting with the Coollidge kids in the Presidential box on that Opening Day three months earlier. He immediately sent a brief letter of sympathy to President and Mrs. Coolidge. When school began again in September, he took it upon himself to have his English Lit class write letters of condolence to the Coolidges. His mom's creative writing class followed suit. Calvin and Grace Coolidge sent a beautiful "thank you" letter to Sidwell. Eva was rightfully proud of the sensitivity Jesse had shown.

October 18, 1924

Perhaps Opening Day had been the promise of things to come. Maybe Silent Cal's prodigious throw, Coach Branko or perhaps Jesse was the magic charm—but whatever reason, the Nats slogged through the season, play by play, finally winning the American League pennant for the first time. They then went on to barely edge-out the potent New York Giants to capture the Championship of the World. The district and its environs could not be expected to settle back down to normal for weeks thereafter. The speakeasies literally overflowed.

Coolidge did not throw out the first ball for the series. Branko gently talked him out of it and offered a very able substitute. Former pre-war Red Sox outfielder, Billy Bantry, a paraplegic veteran of the Fighting 69th, was at Walter Reed for some treatments. Father Duffy had telegrammed Branko, asking him to pay a visit to Billy. He did, of course and was struck by a noble thought. Why not Billy, sitting in his wheel chair, flinging the first ball of the 1924 World Series with his good arm? President Coolidge liked the idea, and with Branko's approval adopted it as his own.

So it came to pass.

There was nary a tearless eye at Griffith Stadium on that October day.

November 6, 1924

Certainly no upset, the "Keep Cool with Coolidge" party won the election handily. They overwhelmed their Democratic opponents by a 2-1 margin, with the belated Progressive third-party candidate, Wisconsin's Senator Bob LaFollette, only attracting half the number of votes the Democrats tallied. Coolidge now had his very own vote of confidence from a rather listless electorate. What he would do with this mandate was still a question in the minds of that very electorate and the ever-present opposition.

It was merely a formality for Branko to be told that his Superintendency would go forward with The White House incumbent.

Hell, if he wants me to coach him again next Opening Day, I better do it! the Colonel wryly laughed to himself.

*****

Somewhere in White Russia (Belo Russia)
Minskaya Sector
December 7, 1942
(First anniversary of the attack on Pearl Harbor)

Simcha did not like the latest transmission from SBI in the slightest. He was fuming, stammering and breathing hard. He did not want his *partisaners* to see him this way. He simply walked over to where Branko was still asleep in his bedroll, shook him and gave him the sign. After all how many unit commanders had an American Brigadier as their own personal consultant? Branko just wrapped a ragged towel around his lower body, a fleece jacket over his shoulders, put on his boots and quickly followed Simcha out into the frigid night. No fuss, no mess, no noise. It was a drill they practiced often for private conversations.

Standing by a snow-laden pine, Simcha already had his cigarette burning.

"Wait until you hear this truck-load of shit, Branko. There is *good* news about the Red counter-measures beginning to develop in and around Stalingrad. The Germans will soon be on the run, in reverse. Advance units of the People's Tank Brigades are expected to soon break out of Stalingrad and fight their way westward to Rostov, Kursk and Kharkov. A small gain west of Moscow puts Red troops advancing ten kilometers: West toward Bryansk. This should reduce any German pressure on partisan units this far west. This was the most war news I have ever received from SBI. Maybe it's a morale tactic to keep us fighting. All good news, eh, Branko?"

"So, Simcha, what are you pissed about?"

"Only this, comrade: In view of the expected success of the counter attacks, SBI and Command are planning to consolidate the partisan forces in Belo Russia."

"So what does that mean for us?"

"Trouble, Branko, trouble and more trouble. They hinted in the transmission that smaller partisan groups would be the first to have to join the larger, better equipped units. The first five units to be affected by this are Maccabees, Bar Kochba, Herzl, Jabotinsky and Trumpeldor, all heroic figures in Jewish history. Why they assigned these code names in the first place is a puzzle that is beginning to come to light. The wily Stalinist power bloc just wants to keep us very recognizable as "Jewish partisans." Understand, Branko? Not just Russian or Soviet partisans, or Polish or Lithuanian partisans. No, we must be identified as Jews. For thousands of years continuous attempts have been made to label Jews all over the world. From armbands, to cloth badges, to Mogen Dovids. Now the Nazis on one side and my Russians on the other are both doing it. The Russians are being subtle, perhaps, but nevertheless they're tagging us again. Dammit, tagging us, branding us—pointing at us. Again, nowhere to hide. Nowhere to blend in. Nowhere to simply *live!* I've wrestled with this age-old phenomenon from the time I saw a newsreel showing the Nazi advance into Poland, the Mogen Dovid painted on merchant's windows, the mandatory yellow badges and so on."

Simcha began to weep.

"Simcha, for Chrissakes, you're becoming paranoid. Slow down, old friend. Could it be that this consolidation process is strictly a military, strategic maneuver?"

"I can only think about my wife and parents in Gorky. I weep for Lev and so many of our Maccabees, not knowing where their families are. Dead, alive or in prison. In so many ways, this is worse than death itself. *Oy, oy. Oy vay iz mir! Vu bist du, Adonai?* Where are you, God?"

He sat in the snow, face in his hands. Branko put his arm around his shoulder.

"To answer your logical question," Simcha then said, "yes. This is a strategic maneuver. Purely political at that. Mark my words, General; it's a typical Stalin ploy against his minorities. Make no mistake, I love my country, I have fought for her, and still do here in the forests and God-forsaken marshes of Belo Russia. But this does not negate the fact that the Stalinist's purification plan is to eventually rid the glorified Motherland from all undesirable elements."

As dawn seeped in under the thick clouds, the two comrades walked back to the makeshift, kitchen and took cups of re-boiled coffee. American, no less: Maxwell House—*good to the last drop.* From the last air drop!

As the rest of the sleeping fighters began to arise, the Commander was much more like his relaxed, old self. Branko was relieved to see this.

No sense of disturbing anyone with these most likely ugly truisms, Branko thought to himself.

Branko had always taken meticulous notes of Maccabee actions. Simcha had warned him to never carry the notes with him during a mission and to destroy them if capture became imminent. Looking over the scrawl of writing on yellow-lined paper, Branko was impressed by the Maccabee's contribution to the overall allied war effort. Since his September 1941 rescue by Simcha and his party, Branko had recorded: No less than six munitions trains blown to smithereens; three troop trains derailed with uncounted Nazi cut down; seven Nazi supply con-voys raided and annihilated; four small warehouses raided and emptied, with all Ukrainian guards slain; at least 100 of the enemy killed by Maccabee fire in hit and run raids; ten Nazi patrols numbering an average of ten men each, ambushed and slain; fourteen Nazi sympathizers not cooperating with the Maccabees on food and medicine raids, shot while "trying to escape."

All this in fourteen months, when self-survival was a top priority. The most impressive figures were the big "0" in the Maccabee "deaths" column and the "7" in the "casualty" column—all of whom recovered and returned to duty.

Simcha was constantly worried about desertions, especially by Maccabees with missing families. However, his concern didn't extend to Lev Soloveitchik: No matter how deeply the man mourned his wife and children or agonized over whether they were alive, he was dedicated to serving the cause. He had even promised Simcha that he would observe their situation closely for any indications of desertions by others. Likewise, Raisel Ehrenburg was also always on the alert for such things.

Of course, this was for everyone's benefit. A deserter trying to make his or her way in this chaotic climate was against the odds in staying free or alive. Torture and slow death awaited at every crossroads. Raisel, with her psychiatric training, held some low-key discussions around the campfire, offering help for those whose morale dipped below a perceivable and acceptable level of risk More than just a few sought her help.

And she was always concerned about Branko. She could never understand how he, in his uniquely untenable position, kept such a calm and stable posture.

Because of the tug-of-war between her feelings and psychology training, she vacillated between suspicions that Branko was masking an explosive mental episode held barely at bay to admiring his mastery over his emotional fate. With each passing week she had come to realize that he was indeed in control rather than being controlled by the trauma in his life. This dawning realization reinforced Raisel's silent admiration of the man. It was an admiration that gave rise to an occasional lustful fervor. For her, it always came back to her recognition of his inner strength and a growing respect. A number of the females were not so reserved. It was the error of youth, Raisel knew—that and the unrelenting stress under which they all lived. But the other females and their occasional flirting plays were always dashed against the wall that Branko had built around his emotions. He consistently drew the age line. He was not about to get into anything untoward with someone in their 20s.

And coming from a completely different world, romance wasn't the formative concern for Branko. Being rescued was. Returning to America trumped nearly everything.

I'm as sure as ever that my old friend Timoshenko just ain't coming to old Branko's rescue, he thought. *I'm here for the duration of this godamm war. I've learned to make the best of it, and besides, Simcha and these kids need my help. Not being able to communicate with Tante Shayndl has been very disturbing. I can add many people to that thought, but for what purpose, eh?*

Not getting any word of my country's war efforts is also heartbreaking. How are they doing? Are we fighting a two-ocean war? Where the hell is Bill Donovan's O.S.S.? Why hasn't he sent messages to me through Timoshenko? Yeah, yeah, I know. War-time priorities!

How are all those young officers I helped to train at The War College doing in this inferno? Are we losing as badly as the Soviets or are we maintaining effective offensives, wherever we are fighting? God, it's so friggin frustrating. And today is the first damned anniversary of the cowardly attack on Hawaii. The one transmission that Simcha received last summer only announced continuing losses and an occasional win. In baseball, you'd be in the cellar with that kind of record.

With this litany, Branko Horvitch, the only American in the White Russian War Zone, began to drift into a restless sleep.

BLACK GOLD

**Washington, D.C.
November 6, 1927**

The colonial-period chapel at Washington Hebrew Congregation's cemetery was filled beyond capacity. The eulogies were somber, emotional and long. She was unconditionally appreciated and adored by the students at Sidwell School and by numerous friends from all walks of Washington life. She had touched the heartstrings of anyone and everyone she met. In an all too short a life she had consistently given of herself for the betterment of others.

He had wanted a simple, private farewell for his sweetheart, but it was not to be. The bereaving Branko Horvitch—who at times was stoic and introspective, was now silently distraught. The *goodbye* had been long and painful; eight months of daily lows, touch and go, hospitals, doctors, nurses, all manner of specialists and medical gurus —all to no avail. Eva Kanter's death at a young forty came as Branko had begun to truly enjoy their life together. After less than three years of wedded love and devotion, he had now lost something rarely attained.

They had been married before a Justice of the Peace on Branko's 50th birthday in February 1925. The ceremony was attended by Grace and Calvin Coolidge as well as a small group of friends and family. Jesse had adored the idea of his mom marrying Branko, as the man and the boy had become fast friends.

All of this was preceded by a sizzling courtship and followed by a brief honeymoon to Florida during the throes of a northern winter. The day after the ceremony—just before the honeymoon—Eva had temporarily moved into the suite at The Willard. She and Branko had been unsure whether to stay at the Willard or at her spacious apartment near Sidwell. The practicality of her apartment's kitchen facilities won over the regality of the Willard and thus the month-long temporary arrangement at the Willard was ended: After returning from their honeymoon they then moved into the Sidwell apartment.

Eva's illness was a rampantly worsening bout with pulmonary

tuberculosis. Johns Hopkins in Baltimore had a special ward assigned to TB patients and Eva spent her last three months there. The National Jewish Hospital in Denver, which had a long and enviable record of specialization in such respiratory diseases, was recommended by the TB Department Chief at Hopkins. A new sanitarium in Little Rock, Arkansas was suggested as the secondary choice. By the time arrangements had been finalized with available beds and the discouraging waiting list overcome, her condition had deteriorated to immobility. Any place outside the D.C. area was out of the question.

In her last days, Eva had pleaded with Branko to look after Jesse as much as he could. She insisted that her former husband would not stand in the way, but Branko knew better. And he was right. Of course, he did tearfully promise Eva to fulfill her request to the very best of his ability. To him, this would be tantamount to having a son—to replace his own son and the relationship he had been denied.

He loved Jesse and thoroughly enjoyed being with him whenever he could: Redskin football games, the Nats and the silent films the Coolidges occasionally hosted. Several times—if the film was a western—Calvin even wore his often-photographed ten-gallon Stetson. Whenever a Hollywood star or a sports figure was invited to The White House, the hosts would be sure that Branko was asked to bring Jesse along to meet them. In a way, it was quite likely that the President and Grace saw the spirit of their late son Calvin embodied in an enthusiastically animated Jesse.

At Jesse's Sidwell graduation in June of '28, Branko was there to hug the boy afterward. Of course his father quickly whisked him away—presumably for a family dinner to which Branko was not invited. If he had known this scene was going to take place, then rather than hurt the boy, Branko wouldn't have attended. Branko had wrestled with the inane speculation of fathering the boy, knowing all the while that Mr. Kanter would never accept more than a token involvement in Jesse's life.

In September, Jesse began his freshman year in Charlottesville, at the heralded University of Virginia. Branko planned to visit him a few times during the year. Jesse beamed broadly when assured of this.

Edith Wilson had been Branko's main source of solace during Eva's illness. She had visited Johns Hopkins often, as the two women had become close since first meeting. At their wedding Edith toasted the couple by saying, "To see my loyal friend Branko enjoined with my dear friend Eva, makes me realize that there is such a thing as a soul-match made in heaven."

It was a heartfelt commemoration that did nothing to weaken those egregious rumors still buzzing around the capital. In the months that followed the funeral, Edith had no qualms about having Branko over for a supper or just to talk in a quasi-therapeutic manner. Whatever it was, it fed the rumor mill while also being beneficial for Branko.

After Woodrow's death, Edith and Branko decided not to further test the murky water by being together in public. Barring a social gathering of some sort—such as a wedding or funeral—they continued this practice right up through the death of Eva. Edith had even stopped calling Branko at the White House—that is, until he received a private number that didn't go through the switchboard.

The two were public figures and had done everything possible to avoid unwanted publicity. Still, the busy Washington gossip mill was insatiable, feeding off the lack of evidence as voraciously as it did the smallest provocation.

Before the 1928 Republican convention, Calvin Coolidge made it clear that he would not seek another term. He had flatly told reporters this the previous summer. As he remarked thereafter, with a mischievous wink at Branko, "Let some other unlucky rascal ruin the country!"

Grace was quietly elated with her husband's decision.

At this point, Branko began to think of seriously "campaigning," for the Deanship of the Army War College. Not incidental to this was that Brigadier General Cecil Raines would be up for retirement the following year. Raines thought very highly of Colonel Horvitch and had already hinted that Branko would be his choice to take the reins. Branko's being on faculty since 1919 had earned him a sterling reputation among the Army's officer corp.

The nearly five years of twice-weekly lectures and the glittering reviews for his post-war appearances at West Point were most impressive. All of this, and being in the vanguard of a minority of regular army officers beating the drum for a vets' bonus, underscored the Colonel as someone special in uniform. In the hidden circles of elite government power, Branko was tacitly credited for making that long-awaited bonus a reality. And to veterans everywhere he was once again a full-fledged hero.

November 30, 1928

Herbert Hoover, Coolidge's erstwhile Secretary of Commerce, won the contest handily over Governor Al Smith of New York. This effectively answered the gnawing question of whether the country was ready to share the presidency with the Pope, so to speak. It was not—even though Democrats and some moderate Republicans openly decried such radical statements. Yet according to the press and unbiased post-election analyses, Smith's outspoken Catholicism was undoubtedly the major reason for his downfall.

Now Coolidge's period of prosperity and peace would be tested by the man from Iowa—and Branko would be leaving the White House. Hoover's emissaries, including the incoming Chief of Staff, tried to convince him to stay on. It was a pretty feather in the Colonel's hat, but he had decided that he was better suited for leadership of the Army War College.

In the meantime, an intriguing interim assignment was presented by none other than Senator George Norris—his one-time benefactor. In the vaguest of terms, the "assignment" concerned a Congressional Committee being convened to deal with veterans' affairs—right up Branko's proverbial alley. But all Norris would reveal at this date was that the task entailed heavy travel for a few months and would not interfere with his expected appointment as Commandant of the Army War College. Branko agreed to meet with the Nebraskan lawmaker after the first week of January to discuss the matter in detail.

During the Holiday Season Branko had built a busy calendar with

Jesse who was coming home on December 14th. Their plans, of course, would have to get the approval of Harry Kanter, who had warmed-up to Branko ever-so-slightly. In early November, Branko had driven down to Charlottesville for a gala football weekend that turned out to be great fun and camaraderie. Jesse planned to try out for the baseball team and had a good set of statistics to show the coach. The kid played a nearly flawless third base with only two errors in his senior Sidwell season, with a healthy .355 average.

January 16, 1929

The memo to Branko read, in relevant part:

> The assignment is to begin on March 1st. You are to visit hospitals with separate wards for all categories of veterans, disabled and otherwise, as either out-or-inpatient. Report on the quality of care and interview patients and medical staff at each location. A list of the targeted institutions and the basic questions to ask is being prepared and will be given to you within the week. (Note: Military hospitals and any others under The Veteran's Bureau are exempt in this first stage of the investigative procedure.)

So here it was. The Senate and the House had convened two lean committees to investigate veterans' affairs, especially the condition of the disabled and the treatments they were able to receive and afford. Colonel Horvitch was to make the initial foray into eight urban areas: Cincinnati, Indianapolis, St. Louis, Oklahoma City, Dallas-Fort Worth, New Orleans, Atlanta and Richmond. Heretofore, the Veterans Bureau had established forty small hospitals and soldier's homes. Where needed, ward space and associated medical facilities were leased from major hospitals around the country. All of this was to be the precursor to an umbrella Veterans Administration as soon as the next year—during the present Hoover administration. This would be designed to replace the much-maligned Veterans Bureau that had been set up in 1921 and was later caught-up in the Harding scandals.

About time, thought Branko, and then wrinkled his forehead at something Edith had said some years earlier. *I'm still waiting for that other shoe to drop according to Edith's initial warning about eventual "pay back" to Norris.*

February 10, 1929

Edith Wilson hosted a farewell party for Grace and Calvin Coolidge, attended by a few of the President's closest associates and some cabinet members. As a matter of protocol the Hoovers were also invited and the incoming President made a beeline for Branko. After registering his disappointment that the Colonel planned to "resign," from the Superintendency, he added tongue-in-cheek, "I hope it isn't because of me."

"No, not at all," Branko assured him with a smile and a firm handshake. "You will be more than satisfied with Captain Jack Steel. The man is not only highly competent, but more importantly, a pleasure with whom to be associated."

Steel, within earshot, chimed-in, "Secretary Hoover, he's only saying that because it'll take your entire incumbency to straighten out the mess he's leaving."

The three men let out a restrained chorus of laughter. Both Jack and Branko were surprised to see that Hoover had some threads of the Coolidge sense of humor. Branko was pleased to no end that the Hoover administration complied with his recommendation of Jack as Superintendent of Buildings and Grounds.

As fate would have it, Branko's birthday corresponded with the party and he had pleaded with Edith to not mention this. He did not wish to take anything away from the Coolidge farewell.

Toasts were many, even though in keeping with prohibition Edith still banned liquor from her house. A variety of soft drinks and juices sufficed.

"Mr. President," Branko began with his turn at toasting, "you'll be happy to know that you have a tryout scheduled in April for the Duluth Red Birds up in Minnesota. My old friend Albie White, the manager, says he may have a spot for you as a left-hander on his pitching staff."

When the laughter finally dissipated, the man who would be out of a job in a few weeks, stood up with a manufactured scowl and said: "Branko, see here—I'm not a southpaw."

"Well," Branko came right back, "you could have fooled me, lefty!"

Another uproar of laugher went around the room.

The coach and his best student embraced to the delight and applause of the guests. Branko then walked over to Grace, kissed her cheek and wished her the best for the future.

As the evening wound down, Branko stayed on while the guests left the Wilson home. Once they were alone he and Edith rehashed the evening and she profusely added her thanks for his adding so much zest to the party.

"I truly like that man from Vermont, Edith. I pray for an enjoyable retirement for the Coolidges."

February 14, 1929

In the weeks leading up to the departure date of Branko's assignment for the Veterans affairs matter, Branko met with both select committees to study the overall goals of the project. They meshed perfectly with Branko's universally recognized fight for veteran's rights. The hospital issues were always at the forefront and now he could be directly involved.

The Commander-in-Charge of the U.S. Army Engineer's Washington office was helpful in providing Branko with a complete set of maps covering the regions he would visit. As a number of travel options were available to him, he was briefed by the Engineers on the up-to-date road conditions, not withstanding an unexpected snow fall, flooding rains or natural disasters that might occur along the way.

The logistics in preparing for the assignment were complicated by

Washington's infamous red tape, but the Colonel was ready to head west before the prescribed date and this left him a short time to consider actual travel arrangements. He had a choice of driving or taking trains and buses wherever he went.

The drawbacks with trains and buses were the usual delays, long layovers, and general discomfort. Since he had never seen anything west of Washington he strongly considered driving and soon decided for it. To do so, he was told that he would be issued a brand new government vehicle—an Oldsmobile touring car. This exceedingly more favorable mode of transportation would also offer the flexibility to visit some home-bound vets. And when he would be free for the weekends, it also allowed for unencumbered sightseeing.

Under Jack Steel's orders, the motor-pool mechanics at the White House serviced the Olds from top to bottom, front to rear: Lubrication, oil, air and a full tank of gasoline.

For daily expenses the General Services Administration provided him with $3,000 worth of Government vouchers in denominations of $50, cashable at any Post Office or Bank. Both the eager Colonel Horvitch and his vehicle were pronounced ready to hit the road.

March 1, 1929

He closed-up the beautiful apartment that he and Eva had shared so blissfully and for which he had signed a new lease. He had promised Edith to stop by, *S* Street to say *goodbye*, and he did. He gallantly offered to trade the Olds for the Rolls. That earned him a laugh and she packed a tasty lunch of roast beef sandwiches for his first day out. She promised to write from time-to-time and he made a list of the various General Delivery addresses at which he could be reached. They agreed to periodic phone calls.

The only other people following the same communication instructions were Jack Steel and, of course, Jesse Kanter. He planned to write Wild Bill from the road, as he had already phoned him about the assignment. He expected the mission would take less than three months, with comfortable room to spare for any contingencies.

The weather was a cold fifty-six-degrees and clear, with no sight of rain or snow. The maps, which he had studied for the past week, showed a popular route from the outskirts of the district through Winchester, Virginia on a route the Corp of Engineers had designated *U.S. 50*. That particular route would take Branko all the way to Cincinnati. He would pass through Winchester, Clarksburg, Parkersburg, and across the Ohio River to Athens, Ohio. From there he could continue to Chillicothe and finally cover the last leg to Cincinnati.

At Parkersburg, daylight was fading and he found homey lodgings on Main Street in the middle of town. For less than $5 Branko ate a delicious homemade dinner, slept the night and had a good breakfast the next morning.

Having skirted the regulation for military personnel to wear the uniform at all times, his driving attire was any one of his old uniform khakis and shirts. A normal-sized old Stetson from his NYPD plainclothes days completed the Colonel's uniform-of-choice for his road trip. He had also brought along a pullover sweater and a jacket for the more brisk weather.

But for this morning of the trip he changed into his dress uniform. He was fresh for the ride into Cincinnati right on schedule.

Yes, suh!

For that second day, the Olds continued to purr along nicely, needing only two fill-ups—at .15¢ a gallon. Each time a garage attendant checked the water, oil and tires: All remained in perfect conditions.

The routine of driving melded into the crisp day and he realized he felt good—better than at any time since his tragic loss. The road assignment was just what any caring doctor would have ordered.

March 2, 1929

Seeing the old Ohio River port rise against the afternoon horizon, he set out through the city to find the Cincinnatian Hotel. The Cincinnatian was arranged by the Senate administrative staff and it was clean and comfortable. It was one of the city's oldest and best rated, much like the Willard in D.C. After a quick review of his lodgings he was back in the car and on his way to the hospital.

Doctor Kershaw Harrington acted like a deer in the headlights: He seemed ready to jump out of his skin and starchy white smock at the same time. He finally calmed down and admitted he had never been interviewed by anyone with government credentials. Branko's personality soon won him over and everything went smoothly for the rest of the day. At lunch in the hospital cafeteria, Harrington intro-duced Colonel Horvitch to several of the staff doctors and nurses. Only a few of the more senior members were told the objective of his visit.

Making the rounds with Doctor Harrington, Branko only wished to see patients who were service veterans, disabled or otherwise. He was taken to two large wards with fifty beds each, all occupied. As it was nearly time for dinner service—which would take about two hours—Harrington suggested that Branko put off the bedside interviews until the next day. Branko agreed, but lingered in order to taste some of the food served. This would find its way into the written report. For the next day, he was determined to stop and have an informal fact-finding chat with each of the 100 bed-bound vets.

After an illuminating week in Cincinnati, Branko asked Dr. Harrngton and two of his staffers to a meeting for a discussion of his visit. He had a notebook full of papers, notes, and standard questions to cover. In general, Colonel Horvitch found that the overall treatment of the veterans was acceptable, but he withheld these comments from the staff during the meeting. The reasoning for this was ground in his military training: They didn't need to know. He also was confident that had he missed something intentionally hidden, and his reticence to bestow praise might loosen the lips of anyone squirming with a guilty conscious. However, no such thing occurred. Harrington and his people were genuinely kind and helpful. Later in the day, Branko wrapped-up his visit with a final *farewell and thank you* session.

This was to be the procedure for the assignment. From all of the eventual input the committees would generate a set of goals and regulations for the proposed Veterans Administration once a bill was passed. Both committees were aiming for adoption sometime in late 1930 or early 1931.

There were further questions to which Branko wanted answers, but these were not included in the packet he had received from the committees. So, he decided to include his questions in the reports. He believed his concerns were relevant to the plans for a Veterans Administration and should the answers prove to be so a letter from the committee chairs to the hospitals in question would be sent.

March 24, 1929
St. Louis, Missouri

> *Hello Edith!*
>
> *Thank you for your letter sent to St. Louis. I retrieved it without a hitch. I waited until now to answer so I would have more to report.*
>
> *Everything is going exceptionally well, and I'm having a rewarding time of it. The feeling that I'm doing something so beneficial that it will result in our government doing something of lasting appreciation for veterans is all I need for incentive. What I have thus far observed in Cincinnati, Indianapolis and St. Louis tells me one thing: Help is desperately needed. Hopefully it is now on the way. If any segment of American society would benefit from such assistance, the veterans certainly will—and they deserve it.*
>
> *I'll be on my merry way to Oklahoma City tomorrow morning, bright and early.*

I'm so happy that I chose to drive. Of course, it would have been so much nicer in your rattling old Rolls! This does indeed give me the flexibility, especially over the weekends, to explore some Americana. Sparsely populated, tranquil and quite attractive. The people I've met on the road have been very friendly and helpful.

I actually dropped into Shabbat services at reform Temple Israel last night, here in St. Louis. Am I getting religious? Unlikely. But I did enjoy the familiar liturgy, and since I was wearing my uniform, practically the entire congregation swallowed me up. I was told that the rabbi had been an army chaplain in France, so we had some nostalgic words to exchange. He even knew Chaplain Weiss who I had met in France. Seems they were classmates at Cincinnati's reform seminary. When the service was over, I asked him to take me aside so I could recite the kaddish for Eva. This meant a great deal to me. I'm still choked up. The Oneg Shabbat was sinfully delicious. They "made me" take some luscious nosh along for my drive and I didn't hesitate a bit.

Please write so I can receive something in Dallas where I'll be heading after Oklahoma. I'm about to write to Jesse and Jack now. Thanks for having Jack and his family over for dinner. It must have been a thrill for them to be breaking bread with the former First Lady of America. Drum roll please. Rahda-ta-tah-ta-tah!

Do I miss Mrs. Wilson, my best-est friend? Hmmmmm—okay, okay, a little bit!

Your favorite broken-down soldier,
Branko

Oklahoma City, Oklahoma
March 27, 1929

Driving through Missouri to Oklahoma, the terrain began changing. The former was forested with leaves just coming back to the bare trees, lakes everywhere, and rushing rivers; the latter was a more barren landscape covered with oil wells. Countless oil wells.

Even before becoming a state in 1910, black gold fever had come to Oklahoma while still a territory. Branko had just learned of the term when he stopped for lunch at a small roadside diner in Miami—which was not to be confused with Florida's Miami. No, this was a small, dusty town ringed by ubiquitous oil structures, or *rigs* as they were referred to by the locals, one of whom asked Branko, "Are you one of those pie-in-the-sky wildcatters?"

Caught just a little outside of his element and confused, Branko only smiled. He was soon to find out that neither the term "black gold" nor "wildcatter" was necessarily something from which to disassociate oneself.

When the inquisitive Oklahoman watched Branko leaving the diner and climbing into a slick new Olds, he figured whoever the hell Branko was, he had bucks.

In the previous drives most asphalt highways were frequently intersected by dirt and gravel roads. Smaller trucks were everywhere, hauling machinery, tools, parts of rigs, and families. Branko learned to differentiate between the little ones, or "pickups" and the big commercial vehicles having eight to ten wheels. The Colonel was get-ting a hardscrabble education as a bonus to his congressional assignment. With the nationwide growing animosities toward "big government Washington" Branko was reticent to let on what he was doing in their territory with District of Columbia license plates. His usual answer, with a smile, was, "Just trying to see more of our beautiful country."

The engineer's map notes picked out the most direct and popular highways for him. Coming down out of St. Louis, U.S. Highway 66 passed through Oklahoma City and continued on to Los Angeles and Hollywood. It was newly repaved for the stretch on which Banko traveled. The smooth ride took him through Springfield and Joplin,

Missouri where he stayed the night, then on to Tulsa and his destination of Oklahoma City. The Army Engineers had assured him that the main roads like *50* and *66* would be in the best of condition. That had been right and he was impressed with the new highway system all the way from D.C. to Oklahoma City.

At two-years old, the modern, spic-and-span Oklahoma Baptist Hospital was like the others Branko had visited: Veteran treatment was largely paralleled in every hospital while procedures, record-keeping and at-home follow-up care rarely varied. To date, time constraints had limited his visits to veterans at home. He was determined to start visiting more of them here and continue doing so as he headed back east. As usual, the hospital bedside interviews were a big hit with the patients, lessening their boredom, while being meaningful to Branko.

With only forty-two in-patients, he scheduled several home visits in and around the city, including the outlying towns of Norman, home of Oklahoma University, and Guthrie, the first capital of the state. Logistically, it was important for Branko to schedule residences within the city limits but he didn't neglect the home-ridden in the suburbs and towns.

A few days after his arrival he drove past the State Capitol, where an oil well and pumping-jacks were at work on the front lawn. He knew then that he was deep in the heart of black gold country. The fact was Tom Slick—one of the most successful oil men in the state—had developed the vast Oklahoma City field. He was drilling forty five wells a day all around the city and producing 200,000 barrels of crude every twenty-four hours. In this state, black gold was king, and for the past two decades Mr. Slick had worn the crown handsomely.

To visit a house-bound veteran on the same day that he planned on seeing another in Guthrie, Branko stopped in the blink-of-an-eye townlet of Perkins—on the banks of the muddy Cimarron River. There was a scattering homes and ramshackle shops dwarfed by the surrounding ocean of rigs. The two-room shanty was on the dirt main street.

Former 33rd Division army corporal Stanley Hagenworth had been severely gassed during his military service. Even so, his disposition was hardly remorseful. He welcomed Branko as a long lost buddy while asking his wife Nora to heat up the morning's coffee. They took their mugs and sat on the stairs of what served as a porch overlooking a dozen oil wells across the river. Nora dutifully disappeared to do the washing chores—what with four children, a necessary daily event.

Within the hour, Branko learned everything he needed to know about how disabled, poverty stricken veterans were barely surviving in Oklahoma, waiting for more government help or assistance from The Southern Baptist Convention. The generous religious benefactor for the Oklahoma Baptist Hospital and several more throughout the country had regularly sponsored food drives and fund-raising events to benefit the vets. The polite, soft-spoken Stanley told about his monthly two-day sessions at Baptist, reached by hitching a ride to Guthrie, and catching the express bus into the big city. His treatments were more or less ineffective and his lung capacity dangerously diminishing every month.

Stanley began to quietly weep as the thirty-five-year-old man confided that, according to his doctor, he may have little more than a year to live. The only hope the doctors offered, was dependent on the effectiveness of one of the newer, more radical treatments.

"What the hell happens to Nora and the kids, eh, Colonel?"

Branko had no answer worth sharing. Knowing that the man wasn't looking for empathy, sympathy or platitudes, Branko wisely held his peace.

Sensing the awkwardness of his plight, Stanley quickly regained emotional control and changed topics. He suggested that Branko might want to see some of the larger wildcat operations up-close. He further suggested visits to the once-booming towns of Drumright, Cushing and Shamrock—all to the east.

Branko not only thought the idea a good one, but also enlisted Stanley as tour guide on the spot. The downtrodden, heavily wheezing veteran, living on borrowed time, clearly enjoyed riding in the government Olds as he waved to Nora while she held a loaded laundry basket in her hands.

What Branko saw on this excursion was nothing short of other-worldly. The concentration of rigs, pump jacks and pipes all over the landscape was something Branko couldn't have imagined, much less described. The crews—men covered in grease, black oil and just plain dirt—wandered about the fields as if shadowed specters. There were ubiquitous oil field vendors selling coffee, doughnuts, sandwiches, cigarettes and drinks, from the beds of rusty pick-up vehicles. It was a bizarre vista repeated at every stop. Then there was the occasional woman, driving up to collect her dog-tired man after a twelve-hour shift in a hellish wasteland. The surreal scenes were unlike anything Branko had thus far come across.

Stanley explained that at the pinnacle of the boom, Shamrock had a population of over 10,000 and pumped out 40,000 barrels of crude every day. Now it was a mass of abandoned buildings. Still, surrounding the town of less than 1,000 people, there were a half-dozen profitable wildcat operations. A testament to the fact that it Shamrock had not yet run dry.

"Colonel Horvitch," Stanley wheezed, "I wanted you to see this—mainly because these wildcatters are responsible for what little money the counties spare for their sick and poor."

Branko patiently waited for Stanley to draw his next breath and finish his thought.

"The tax income," Stanley finally managed to begin again, "received from these operations throughout the state is substantial. I imagine the same can be said of Texas."

Even though he had seen many gas victims, it was sad for Branko to witness. During the war—at Walter Reed—he had seen in passing a number of such victims. But this was different: It was up close, personal and a permanent reminder of the cost of liberty. And Stanley wasn't the only one, as the trip through Cincinnati, Indianapolis and St. Louis had exposed him to a sizable number of gas victims.

During the remainder of the day, Branko learned a lot about black gold, wildcatting and the effect they had on veteran's lives—at least in Oklahoma. He expected to see more of the same in Texas, and possibly in oil-rich Louisiana.

After Branko had returned Stanley to his home, his next stop was in Guthrie. Bobby Ray Summers, the man he visited at his well-kept Guthrie residence, further clarified just what the term "wildcatting" meant. Stanley had given examples, but one-armed Bobby Ray expounded on the topic while spreading out a drilling map for Logan County, of which Guthrie was the seat. As an aside, he mentioned that his town was once the capitol of both the Territory, and in 1907, the new State of Oklahoma. He was a bit annoyed that his beloved town lost this position in 1910. To him, it was still the capital of his world. As a beneficiary of his late father's moderate success as a local oilman, he had attended Oklahoma A&M in nearby Stillwater. It was before his entry into the war and he spoke fondly of the experience.

He explained something that Stanley had already touched upon: The true and acceptable meaning of a wildcat operation. The term referred to the exploratory bore holes drilled in so-called virgin territory that was at least one measured mile away from the nearest producing wells. On the map, Bobby Ray pointed out the plethora of wildcat wells in Logan County. The oil well iconography peppered the map, looking as if someone had dumped a tray of ants across it. They were everywhere. He assured Branko that every county in Oklahoma could show him similar congested wildcat maps.

Bobby Ray had lost his left arm when a German machine-gun nest sprayed rapid rounds into his advancing infantry platoon. He had required immediate amputation. Stanley, proudly showed Branko his Purple Heart. When hearing these stories, Branko considered himself a lucky bastard to only have an occasional shrapnel splinter poking through his own back. In light of what others had sacrificed, he was even a little embarrassed to be the recipient of the *Croix de Guerre*—an honor rarely bestowed upon the enlisted man.

Seriously disabled veterans like Stanley and Bobby Ray qualified for government assistance of $80 per month, plus $10 for each child at home. Financially, then, the wildcat tax money each man had referenced was a life-saving supplemental boon to their desperate lives.

Branko was sure he would never forget these two very courageous Oklahomans: It was a sentiment that applied for the many great American veterans he had met over the course of his fact-finding assignment.

April 11, 1929
Dallas, Texas

The eight days Branko spent at Dallas' Parkland Memorial Hospital followed the already established pattern. The hospital had a population of nearly 120 veterans who were disabled or suffering from service-related ailments. However, to a greater degree than the previous hospitals, cooperation between county government and the Veterans Bureau had deteriorated.

Rebuilt in 1913 at Oaklawn and Maple Streets, Parkland had served Dallas County well but administrators disdained the amount of space and bed count set allotted for disabled veterans since 1926. They considered the accommodations "excessive." The lion's share of their concern was motivated by financial concerns and they pointed to a growing loss of hospital income for the county. Hearing that a new Veterans Administration was on the drawing board had further agitated the situation in advance of Branko's visit. Since the political powers of the County were already restrictive and apprehensive the American Legion's appearance at board meetings made matters even worse. The American Legion had been protesting the county's austerity toward veterans, going so far as to describe administrators as exhibiting "Un-American attitudes."

It was into this untenable battlefield that Colonel Horvitch marched with the same temerity he had deployed in actual battle.

In his first meeting with the civilian administrator, Carl Mornington, Branko requested an audience with the County Board of Supervisors. In doing so, he promised to allay their fears of a growing Federal demand for more veteran space at Parkland. On the contrary, he assured Mornington, that space requirements would dramatically diminish once the presently inadequate Veteran's hospital in Cedar Falls expanded and modernized. This, in fact, was one of the first proposed orders of business for the new Veteran's Administration. Work on the Cedar Falls facility was anticipated to start as soon as the President signed the bill, which included a budget attachment addressing the expansion in Cedar Falls

"I just want the opportunity to assure the County of the positive aspects of the plan." Branko summed up in his pitch to Mornington.

After the special meeting was arranged for later in the week, Branko phoned the State Commander of the American Legion in Austin. To this man Branko promised to do everything he could at the council meeting to quell animosities between Dallas County and the AL. The Commander agreed to call off further protests until after Branko had his swing at the plate.

Damned, if it all didn't work as promised! Branko thought as he hung up the phone.

After Branko's sweet-talking and painless mollification of the Board, the three Dallas and Fort Worth AL Commanders invited him to a prime rib dinner at the Texas Petroleum Institute's famed, *Oil Rigger's Grille*. Obviously they had never heard of Branko's clash with the racist post commander in D.C. For Texans, Washington was a small illusion a million miles away.

All of this in no way interfered with Branko's usual schedule of bedside and home visits. And even in the midst of the combative atmosphere, the cooperation from Mornington and his staff was a thing to admire.

Now if the Hoover Administration will only cooperate in the same manner, Branko reflected at one point.

On the weekend before he was to drive toward New Orleans, Branko had a burning desire to see Burkburnett as had been described by Stanley and Bobby Ray. Accordingly, it was considered a typical oil boom town.

He drove northwest on a fairly good road and halfway between Dallas and Wichita Falls noticed more of what he saw in Oklahoma—rigs everywhere, as far as the eye could see. Just outside of Bowie, he stopped for a cup of coffee at a roadside café.

Two ten-gallon hatters on the porch noticed his government plates.

"What's old 'Hoobert Heever' doin' now?" one of the ten-gallon hatters asked. "Sendin' you tax men out here?"

Branko smiled broadly and offered to buy the two some coffee.

"It's poison in there, bud," the other man said. "But how about we drink a few bootleg beers with you? Then we can say the President sent a revenuer out here just to enforce the 'dry law' and buy some votes for his next term, if there'll be one!"

Obviously, this pitifully run-down establishment, like so many others, didn't give one fat damn for prohibition. In Texas, it seemed, scofflaws ruled the roost. Branko realized it was probably an unfair generalization but then, on the other hand, the state was populated by the children and grandchildren of a once independent nation: A little swagger was to be expected.

But sitting at a cozy table, the three-way conversation that followed was educational for the government man. The two men were part of a wildcat, noon-to-midnight shift crew, at what they called "old Number 93" in Archer City—about fifty miles to the west. They explained that shallower wells were drying up fast and in order to drill deeper, wildcatter profit margins were precipitously shrinking. They reported having worked only six days in the last three weeks: There just wasn't money to pay them.

"So what in hell has happened to the big oil boom we've been hearing so much about back east?" Branko asked, incredulous at the news he was hearing.

"Gone, brother, gone. It takes some very big companies with very big money bags to drill down to the Promised Land. They're sending out city-slickers with insulting sales contracts to all the wildcat operations we know of."

When they invited Branko to Archer City for a tour of their operation, he begged off—after promising to drive down there whenever he got back to North Texas. Presuming that their work hours would continue to drop, Branko had a desire to give them some "rainy day money" out of his voucher stack. But he thought the better of it. It could only spell chaos if the word ever got back to the wrong people. More importantly, though, he didn't know how the offer would sit with two grand-children of the fierce and former, Republic of Texas.

Once back in his car, he finally followed the highway signs to Burkburnett a few miles away. Burkburnett, or as they called it "BB" was much like any of the places he had seen in Oklahoma, only more so. There were so many varied vehicles in states of disrepair that there were actual traffic jams throughout the town. Or Maybe it was the absence of stop signs at any intersection. If Logan County, Oklahoma was a mass of wells, then BB in Texas was the mother of all black gold ventures.

A mid-day meal at a greasy-spoon provided another in the series of amazing people-watching venues. When Branko went to take a "look-see" at BB's only decent-looking hotel, all of the "suits" in the dining room clearly indicated that the "big boys" were taking over from the remaining independents.

Likewise, on the sides of most every truck there were the colorful logos of the better known giants, such as *Flying A*, *American Oil (Amoco)*, *Texas Oil Company (Texaco)*, *Continental Oil (Conoco)*, *Sun Oil (Sunoco)*, *Halliburton* and *Sinclair*. Branko even saw a truck belonging to the world-wide French outfit, *Schlumberger* and the *British Petroleum Company*.

The black gold playing field was changing faster than anyone could have imagined ten years ago.

It was Saturday. On Monday Branko was due back in Dallas for a final morning debriefing. As such, he decided to stay the night in Wichita Falls, 150 miles northwest of Dallas. The city was a sizeable supply center for the oil fields. At a surprisingly attractive rate, he checked into the first class lodgings of *The Sagebrush Inn*.

After dinner Branko noticed that across the street, the *Majestic Theater* was playing a year-old Gloria Swanson picture called, *Sadie Thompson*. He wandered over to look at the movie posters and decided to see the film. Since it was Saturday night it seemed like every oil-chaser, his wife and girlfriend—or both—had decided to catch the same film. At two-bits for the feature, a short William Boyd western and a "talkie newsreel" it was a fair enough deal. Sound films were just coming onto the scene and so even a talking newsreel was a first for the attendees, including Branko.

Sadie Thompson, including Swanson's most provocatively erotic scenes to date, would quite likely be one of the last silent films this audience would see. Branko sat there smiling as he thought of Joe Kennedy's experiences in Hollywood and his "friendship" with the gorgeous actress posing on the screen with a sexy "come hither" look.

April 18, 1929
New Orleans, Louisiana

He accomplished everything he set out to do in Dallas. Most satisfying was his success in assuaging the Dallas County Board of Supervisors with their innate fear of Washington.

Colonel Horvitch hoped the American Legion protests were permanently quieted and that the new Veterans Administration would be the catalyst for a new level of normal operations for all involved. What more could a government emissary want?

The New Orleans ill-equipped, inadequately funded Flint-Goodridge Hospital for the Colored posed an altogether different set of problems. It was the bonafide leading medical caregiver for black army veterans throughout the entire southern region. And it was one of the all too few such facilities, at that.

The nearest Veterans Bureau hospital in Baton Rouge didn't accept the colored ex-soldier due to the lack of a segregated ward, a staff shortage and limited bed space. Branko's goal here was simple: He sought assurance that the black veteran was getting the same care that the white veteran was receiving. Discrepancies, if any, would be given extra attention in his reports to the select committees. He had served with all manner of men throughout his wide-ranging military life and he couldn't comprehend how the color of a man's skin or his religious persuasion made him any less a deserving American Veteran.

Whether Branko could ultimately influence the equality of treatment for all veterans, regardless of skin color, was anyone's guess. But regardless of the outcome, between now and the time a bill was passed, Branko would be riding shotgun—of that he was certain

Meanwhile, he had put himself in a position of being the facetiously labeled "great white hope" for the hundreds of thousands of black veterans of the War Between the States, the 19th century

Indian Wars, the Spanish-American conflict and the recent World War. It was a widely known and embarrassing fact that all of these veterans did not receive the same level of care, oversight, homage and benefits as their white counterparts.

The only reason Branko was assigned to this particular hospital was largely through the untiring efforts of one black Congressman: Atticus Thurgood. His constituency in Ward 9 of this exotic city was 80% colored. His tough battle to get New Orleans Flint-Goodridge onto Branko's list of stops was won with the concession of sharing Branko's time with New Orleans Charity Hospital. To make it work, Branko scheduled a nine to ten-day stay.

The Administrator of Flint-Goodridge, Dr. Samuel E. B. Du Bois —who pronounced it as *Du Boys*—gave Branko the use of one of his stenography staff to assist in the documenting of both healthcare facilities. In addition, Du Bois graciously invited Branko to his home for dinner that following Saturday evening.

"I have some important things to discuss with you," he explained the invitation, "and would rather save it for a quiet dinner of my wife's best Creole cooking. N'yaw Lins finest, of course!"

"Sounds like an evening I could use after all this time on the road, Doctor."

"Great, Colonel Horvitch. And how about we make it, *Branko* and *Sam*?"

"Fine with me, Sam," replied Branko, happy to erase the unnecessary formalities so soon. It also meant he could probably wear civvies for the dinner.

This doctor seems like a most erudite gentleman, thought Branko.

Steno LuAnn Bretton begin typing his voluminous notes and that gave him a good start on compiling the final package for when he returned to D.C.

The obvious deference shown to Branko that week was a welcomed change—even from the inpatients and homebound vets, two of whom lived out in the fascinating bayou country.

One even slipped in, "We know all about you, Colonel."

Branko didn't think twice about the comment, figuring it was just some doughboy flippancy.

The list of shortcomings in patient care, follow-up, and reporting was evident from the first day. Where up to three doctors were on duty at the other hospitals Branko had visited, Dr. Du Bois had avail-able only one physician to assign per shift. The emergency and rehabilitation equipment was archaic and in dire need of repair or replacement—even a layman could plainly see that. For critical and minor care veterans the death rate was abominable across the board. Veterans living in the bayou and in need of nursing assistance could expect to wait up to a month or more. Likewise, their transportation into New Orleans—be it public or hospital funded—was practically non-existent and untrustworthy when attempted. Branko was appalled and was withholding his comments to Sam until for the upcoming Saturday dinner.

To be even adequate, the new Veterans Administration had its work cut out for it, Branko realized. The evidence here called for an integration of services and facilities or a policy of separate but completely equal terms.

Sure, I can accept segregated wards, he thought to himself. *That's probably non-negotiable these days. But the colored wards would need to have the exact same treatment as the lily white wards. That, too, must be non-negotiable. I will fight to hell and back for that much.*

There was fire in his eyes, just thinking about it, and the unsuspecting Congressional committees would have to be ready to cage a saber-toothed tiger.

Sam lived in a large brick house on the one short narrow street in the upscale colored district. Branko's government car, no doubt, was a topic of intriguing speculation for the neighbors—especially for those who spotted the tall, white Colonel in uniform. He had decided on the uniform mainly because his civvie outfit needed some freshening up.

Branko brought flowers for Lillian Du Bois. She was as charming as her husband and certainly much better looking.

The combination Creole/Cajun meal, elegantly served by the Du Bois maidservant, was quite unlike anything Branko had experienced elsewhere. Asking Branko to follow him into the drawing room, Sam offered him a fat cigar and a brandy-flavored after-dinner drink.

"Prohibition is all but dead and not yet buried, Branko," Sam said. "And in N'yaw Lins it was never even born. Of course, a little caution never hurts—and so Lillian and I make it a practice to only drink in our home or in those of our friends and family. Hopefully, our two youngsters will someday do the same if they wish to. Flaunting our objection to that troubling amendment just isn't our style, and as 'uppity nigras' why tempt fate on the matter."

Sam had added his last comment with a dry smile that straddled the borderline of humor and truth.

"Same for me," Branko responded. "When I was in the White House I was very careful about being seen in a speakeasy. Now, I simply break the law—quietly. I won't tell if you won't tell, friend."

"In case you're wondering what I have to say to you of any importance, Branko, let's not keep you in suspense any longer. Your reputation as an untamed maverick and friend to any man regardless of his race or creed, has preceded you, sir. Seems that you took on the rednecks of the American Legion a few years ago, in Washington."

"How did you hear about that?"

"Well," Sam started to answer, "we heard—"

"Hold on there," Branko suddenly interrupted. "*Waaaait* just a second! Your patient, PeeDee Junior Matthews—down in Plaquemines Parish—said this past week that all of you knew about me."

"PeeDee isn't called 'the Chief Potentate of Plaquemines Parish' for nothing, Branko. He could probably tell you what you had for breakfast last July 4th! Evidently, there were three fellows from your old regiment at that meeting who were roundly disgusted with the Legion and its racist bent. Afterward, you arranged for them and their families to privately tour the White House."

"That's right," Branko agreed. "In fact, I had the Chief Steward escort them."

"You mean Larry Lincoln, of course."

At the mention of that name, Branko grinned broadly. "Yes. A dear friend—a wonderful man. He retired when Coolidge didn't run."

"Well, Larry is also a treasured member of the NAACP, of which my uncle, W.E.B. Du Bois, is a very active founder and provocative columnist. Larry phoned him with an earful about you, your character and your integrity. W.E.B. is my father's brother.

"W.E.B. and E.B?" Branko echoed while realizing the doctor's first name was connected with something he had read.

"I was given the E.B. at birth, never really knowing what the hell it stood for until he came down here to visit back in '98, Du Bois said. "I've thought about eliminating the letters from my name, but as W.E.B. became universally known and admired, saint to some, Satan to others, I hung onto them. Now I don't give it a second thought. I just rarely reveal the E.B. Part."

"Of course, Branko interjected. "I know of your uncle. His fame has certainly grown. Again, as you say Sam, with loyal followers and many detractors."

"Well the fame has been beneficial, at least. W.E.B. generously afforded my family some financial help so I could continue my medical education at Howard University in D.C. He had a great deal of influence, there. Locally, there was a school I attended after graduating from Grambling University up north near Monroe. But Flint Medical College suffered financial and A.M.A difficulties in 1910, forcing it to close it's doors. That's where Uncle W.E.B. came in to my life."

"So you're a Howard grad, Branko quipped. "Coincidentally, I was invited to speak there this month, but had to turn it down so I could rescue you!"

Branko's comment drew a chuckle from the doctor. He then said: "I loved living in Washington and studying at Howard. After getting my M.D in 1917, I did my internship at the 444th Quartermaster Corp hospital for negro troops at Camp Polk during the war."

"That's in Leesville, right?"

The doctor nodded that it was.

"And after that?" Branko prompted.

"I went into private practice. 1919. I joined the staff at Flint-Goodridge and became its administrator three years ago. It's been a horse race, Branko, and I don't know who's winning."

Branko smiled with brandy in hand and joked, "Now I know more about you then I ever wanted to know. So it was Du Bois who spoke with you about my coming to Flint?"

"I suppose your friend Larry Lincoln knows which buttons to push to get any kind of information around that city."

At that, Branko had an, *ah-ha*, moment, remembering that Larry's delightful wife, Aretha—Edith's maidservant—would have known Branko's schedule. He thought the better of letting on anything about that to Sam.

So, that's it, Branko thought, seeing all the pieces come together and make sense. *The NAACP founder is cozying up to insure that I will give the negro vet more than a fair shake. He needn't worry. Of course I fully intend to do that. They've been getting the short end of the stick. I saw it in France and I've seen it here—and in all of the places I've been since coming to America.*

When Lillian entered the smoke-filled men's lair, she feigned ignorance of their conversation—but Branko was sure she knew full well the purpose of his invitation.

"Has the old doc told you we met at Howard," she asked innocently. "I was singularly responsible for barely pulling him through his studies."

They all laughed.

At the end of the evening, Branko expressed his thanks for a wonderful evening and bid goodbye. They embraced one another while promising to keep in touch during the following week—and thereafter. This was not just the usual polite nicety: They each sincerely meant it. Branko intuitively knew that he had just made a pair of lifelong friends and the feeling was mutual.

En route to Atlanta, Branko had now experienced the good fortune of seeing a large portion of the United States in the raw—warts and all. After more than twenty-five years in the country he long ago began calling, *home*, his pride in being an American was never more pronounced. He had served his adopted nation well, and it had returned the favor. Now he would see if this 150-year-old noble experiment could do even better—and he was sure it would

But there was still a good deal of work to be done.

May 16, 1943
Somewhere in Central White Russia (BeloRussia)

After the SBI's plan to consolidate partisan units was put off indefinitely, radio reports began reflecting the latest Russian advances with pride and vigor. Even in code, Simcha was able to imagine exclamation points, bold letters and underlining. All in his dreams perhaps, but nevertheless, an accurate portrayal of skyrocketing morale at the fronts.

Stalingrad was history and the several salients from Kursk to Kharkov were now pushing beyond their bulges, steadily and definitively. This translated into new hope for the hundreds of partisan units and their chronic feelings of abandonment The Russian army's newly replenished tanks, increased air attacks harassing the retreating Wehrmacht, and encouraging reports all added-up to "going home." Or to what was left of it.

"Not so fast," counseled a weary and wary Simcha Greenberg. "In my cynical opinion, there are still hundreds of miles of Russian soil to retake. This means how many more killed and crippled Soviet troops? How many more orphans, widows and widowers? How many more burnt out villages and towns? How many more hectares of scorched and re-scorched earth? How many ruined crops throughout Mother Russia? Eh? I ask you, eh?"

The gathered Maccabees. who had battled increasing helplessness and despair, had no answers to these penetrating questions.

Lev Soloveitchik spoke out: "Simchaleh, what you say has to be said. It's a long way from over, but at least we can see that there is a positive ending somewhere in the great beyond. True? For now, we just have to accept the better news, temper it with reality and go on with our duties."

From the Maccabean reactions it seemed that most of the troop agreed with Lev's sobering, but hopeful view. Even Simcha reluctantly agree. Branko was asked his opinion by the usually argumentative Alyosha, but felt it was his unwritten law to decline. As an advisor/consultant, his views on battle plans, tactics and strategies was a given. But on Russian politics he opted out.

On the other hand, they were still reeling from the series of casualties suffered during the last two offensive actions. Concerning the badly wounded Asher Lubarsky and Fyodor Kleinman there had been no word from the makeshift partisan "field hospital." ten kilometers to the north. The two wounded Maccabees had been on a reconnaissance mission when ambushed by a group of seven Ukrainians, part of a rogue ex-convict unit who happily killed anyone in sight—no questions asked.

Once the Maccabee patrol, headed by the rugged Kostya Polinoff, scrambled to cover behind a muddy embankment of the River Nyoman, automatic gunfire filled the air. Five Ukrainian miscreants sucked in their last breath on earth, while two others dropped their rifles and ran away helter-skelter.

Asher had been hit in the left side and Fyodor in the upper femur. Kostya knew the exact and latest coordinates for the "hospital" and decided not to waste precious time transporting the wounded back to camp. Rather, he headed straight for he field hospital. The remainder of the sparse recon team, Piotr Zacharia and Eliahu Abramovich, helped Kostya deliver their wounded comrades.

Koslov, the "doctor" on duty, diagnosed the wounds as serious but not life-threatening. He was impressively equipped with sulfa drugs and assorted palliatives. Three members of a nearby, especially large partisan group, assisted Koslov, who had been a medic with an infantry regiment overrun in Zhitomir. He was a calming figure and appeared to know what he was doing—as if that would be enough to save the boys. He told Kostya that he was perfectly capable of doing the stitching once he removed the slugs. Giving aid to the *Zhids* didn't seem to bother him when seeing their circumcised penises after stripping them of their filthy clothes.

Just two days later, Kostya escorted Nurse Olga Goldenkrantz to the "hospital" to stay with Fyodor and Asher and see them through some modicum of bodily repair. The doc again assured Kostya, that the two partisans would be in good hands. Luckily, they were the only two patients for the only two cots available. Olga wisely had taken her bedroll along and also a variety of medicines from the camp, including additional packets of sulfa. Kostya had carried some adequate food supplies for the three of them.

Ten days later, another Maccabee casualty occurred during a raid on a Nazi sympathizer's dental office in a town close to the Maccabee's camp. This time, Kostya was the victim when the Nazi-loving bastard yanked out a Luger from his instrument drawer and shot him in the shoulder. The fascist dentist was summarily sent to Valhalla by Kostya's automatic machine-pistol barrage, nearly cutting him in two during the process. As the boxer slumped down in pain, he refused to be taken anywhere but back to camp, where the clean-through wound was sulfa'ed down and bandaged up, arm fitted with a sling and the patient fed a half bottle of cheap vodka. All in a day's partisan lore.

Simcha was always pleased to avoid any casualties, and in the twenty months of the Maccabee's existence his record was near perfect, considering the long odds. Not one death, *gott tsedanken*, an even dozen casualties, ten of the non-disabling gunfire-wound type. The two more seriously wounded, Asher and Fyodor, were expected to recover well enough to rejoin the unit within the month. They had no choice! Of course, everyone would have to inspect their ghastly stitchings...*oy vay!*

On top of all this bedlam, not one desertion.

THE THREAT AND THE CRASH   12

May 29, 1929

Before returning to Washington from Richmond Branko stopped in Charlottesville to catch an end-of-season baseball game. Jesse, as a freshman, was not yet a starter but was used often in specific bench roles. With Branko in the stands watching, he pinched-hit out deep to left, played third base in the last inning and with Duke down by eight runs acquitted himself nicely with two hot-corner plays.

Branko was bursting with pride and wistfully thought of Eva. She would have loved to see this. Of course, Jesse was ending his first year with Dean's List Honors and an A-minus average, which would have also made Eva ecstatic. Branko said as much to Jesse. At least that would serve as a reminder that baseball had its place, but should not overshadow the classroom and the quest for a degree. Thus far it had not.

The following week, a quiet "welcome home" dinner at the Wilson House was a fitting end to the long and tedious trip. Over coffee, and home-made pecan pie, he regaled Edith with stories about hospitals, veteran treatment and his time on the road. Naturally his narrative's departure into the "black gold" fields of Oklahoma and Texas was a high point. His pleasant association with the Du Bois family of New Orleans drew a series of wide-eyed questions from Edith. She was the perfect sounding-board and he flawlessly fielded her interrogation.

On the way back to his apartment, Branko kept thinking about Edith. He couldn't fathom why no suitable suitors had lined up for her. *She's worldly,* he thought to himself, *highly intelligent, attractive, fun, a great hostess and conversationalist. How can it be? I've never come right out and asked, but she would certainly tell me if there was anyone she seriously cared about. I've seen no evidence that there was such a person.*

That's when the thought hit him: *Me?*
He laughed out-loud at the idea.
A woman married to a man of Woodrow's presidential stature and

bearing hooking-up with a weary soldier of fortune—or misfortune, as the case could be made?

Don't be foolish, old boy! You're feeling sorry for yourself. One disastrous marriage with Miriam who runs off with my son, one indescribably beautiful love affair and marriage with Eva, bless her memory, and a bevy of very forgettable liaisons in between. Get on with it, man. Get on with life. There are still adventures beckoning out there. No, don't get into the old restless mode—the ol' there are places to go, things to do, experiences too feel, thing! Not this time. Not this time.

He slumped behind the extra-sized steering wheel of his government-provided Olds and concentrated on the tactile experience of driving the car.

If I play it right I could keep this baby until after the hearings, maybe even long after I take over the reins at The College. I could sell my Ford. The extra cash would sure as hell be most welcome.

The week at Charity Hospital in New Orleans, followed by Atlanta and Richmond, had not turned-up anything different. If anything, those visits showed that none of the conditions were an anomaly.

Branko now had the enormous task of compiling, sorting, studying, shuffling and reshuffling a mountain of notes, forms and questionnaires while also preparing to appear before the scrutinizing mavens of the House and Senate Committees. He would be in this paper harness until the committee meetings.

Branko intended his report to be crisp, concise and meaningful in every respect. This was neither the time nor place to couch information in ambiguity or beautify descriptive content. Even if predisposed to obfuscate, he was well aware that it was nigh impossible to get anything through Congressional Committees without a hassle.

As it was, he knew the challenge was to clearly demonstrate the vital need for centralized managed veterans care. No easy task that—even with the three months of data he had gathered in Ohio, Indiana, Missouri, Oklahoma, Texas, Louisiana, Georgia and Virginia.

Conversely, there wouldn't be a better time to make such a change. Even though fraught with problems the idea had been toyed with for the ten years since the war. Of course there was a good deal of opposition to such a new and powerful entity, especially in the ranks of the *laissez faire* crowd. Nonetheless, Branko believed an all-encompassing Veterans Administration was long overdue and his report could very well be the game-winning homerun. In his estimation there was no room for anything less than success—no room for even partial failure.

With July 16th finally on the calendar for the hearings, Branko had little time to reflect further. He used Eva's old Remington to type, refusing Jack Steel's offer of his secretary. With constant rewriting, Branko felt that another typist would be a logistical burden.

The typing pools all over Congress could have been a possible help but he doggedly persisted in his clumsy, hunt-and-peck typing effort. It was almost overwhelming and like a safety valve venting a build-up of steam, Branko's mind occasionally wandered. At one point he found himself mulling over the time in which he intended to relax before assuming the War College position.

He was still officially on temporary duty (TDY) with both houses of Congress. But TDY status retained the privileges of permanent duty and he had accumulated a significant amount of leave. At this stage, he figured he could retain the TDY status until at least September and then take leave—a vacation, if you will—until he became the Commandant after General Raines retired.

His last conversation with the General determined that the official announcement would come in October and January 2, 1930 would be the induction date. There was also the real possibility that he would soon be promoted to Brigadier General, the rank with which the *Commandant* position was historically associated.

But first things first and he returned his attention to the report for the committees.

July 5, 1929

In his apartment mailbox, Branko found a message from Senator Norris offering for a dinner meeting at the Willard on the 9th. He surmised that the Nebraskan wanted a first-hand preliminary discussion regarding the inspection tour.

Senator Norris was the hardest working politician under the rotunda and if he wanted a dinner meeting, then the busy Branko would graciously accept the invitation. He felt it was the least he could do for the man who had done so much for him. Because of the self-imposed pressure under which Branko labored to prepare his report, his eating habits had fallen through the floor. Edith had repeatedly chastised him for this, frequently asking him over for lunch or dinner, since they still were cautious of being in public too often. The never idle gossip columnists gave them little respite in that regard.

July 9, 1929

"Colonel Horvitch," Norris greeted with a smile. "We've only chatted briefly, in passing, since you returned from touring America on my constituents' tax dollars—"

There was something a little uncomfortable about the senator's joke.

"—but I'm quite familiar with your rush to get ready for the meetings," Norris went on. "I'm at it all the time, it seems. That's what doing business in this great city is all about, Colonel."

While enjoying the usual fine Willard dinner, Branko spent a few minutes describing an overview of his trip. As was his lifelong habit, he held back nothing. His descriptions were clear and he didn't mince words when it came to the plight of America's war veterans—especially the disabled and long term in-patients. He spoke of the negro hospital in New Orleans, emphatically describing the patients as engulfed in conditions that were downright gruesome in comparison to the all-white wards of other hospitals.

After dinner, Norris suggested they retire to the sitting room off the lobby to enjoy Havana cigars. Wanting to get back to his report, Branko hedged a bit. But he didn't want to insult a man who could probably handle a dozen such assignments without breaking a sweat—and so he capitulated to the sitting room.

Branko was not a smoker, but the Senator insisted.

"These Havana Premiums are absolutely the best," Norris said. "Dang, if Colonel Teddy Roosevelt didn't puff and chew on one while fighting his way up San Juan Hill!"

"He did?" was all Branko could comment.

"I wish he would've occupied the whole damn country, kicked out the *Span-yardis* and made it our own private rum and cigar store!"

While talking, Norris removed a small flask from his jacket pocket and offered Branko a swig of "Quebec cognac."

Going "wet" here at the venerable Willard was not acceptable to Branko and certainly not while in uniform—which is precisely how he answered Norris.

"Nonsense!" the Senator responded, taking another drink. "Before Herbie is out of office, the USA will be 'wet' again. Mark my words, Colonel. You can bet that there is not one member of my institution who has not sipped bootleg booze. They're all 'wets' and not because they peed their pants!"

His patience wearing thin, Branko only nodded.

Following another few minutes of small talk and non-sequiturs, the Nebraskan leaned forward in his leather easy chair, squinting and talking in a crescendo of stentorian, filibustering tones.

"Colonel, I had a long talk with Congressman Atticus Thurgood last week," Norris said.

There was a pause during which Branko realized the entire evening hinged upon what the Senator was now saying.

"He told me," Norris finally continued, "that *he* set up that visit to the New Orleans Negro hospital as part of your schedule."

This was old news to Branko and he again only nodded.

"You've been frank and I appreciate that," Norris added. "But what I want to know, is your overriding observation of veteran treatment at Flint-Goodridge—how will it be reflected in your report to the committees?"

Branko had been perfectly clear but now realized that Senator Norris thought like a stereotypical politician: He could be clear as a bell about what he thought and as indecipherable as a code for what he would say—and he expected the same from others in Washington. It was high-time to jolt him out of that notion, Branko thought.

"Senator" Branko said, "I'll be answering these questions when I appear with my report. However, as a courtesy to you, I'll share my answers, briefly and succinctly. As I have already said, compared to the white wards, conditions at Flint are appalling—grossly undermanned staffs, outmoded equipment, embarrassing budgets, a death rate two-and-three times that of other hospitals. In defense of the administration at Flint, Dr. Du Bois was among the finest of all the professionals I interviewed at any hospital on my inspection tour. He was highly intelligent, affable and understanding. But he was sorely handcuffed by the lack of anything even remotely connected with providing better care. In another setting, the man would be a standout all-around.

"Everywhere on my itinerary, I made home visits to patients where necessary, including Flint-Goodridge. In two of the poorest parishes outside the city of New Orleans, the Negro veterans are living in abject poverty and on starvation rations with little or no state or local help.

"From what I observed, Louisiana doesn't give a tinker's damn about its disabled Negro veterans. By contrast the white vets at Mercy Hospital—just a few blocks away from Flint—are recipients of acceptable care from the well-staffed, well-equipped wards—"

"Stop right there, Colonel," Norris interrupted. "This simply cannot be included in your report—not in those words. Do you have any idea of how big a bombshell this will ignite?"

Branko was caught off guard for a moment, thinking that Norris was concerned about the negro veterans' plight.

"Thurgood tells me that Dr. Du Bois is a close relative of W.E.B. Du Bois, founder and chief rabble-rouser of the NAACP."

"And?"

"And he could be a real pain in the ass! No, Colonel, you cannot —must not—include any of those highly inflammable remarks in your presentation to the committees. I assure you the resulting firestorm will do more than just singe your eyebrows."

"It's the unvarnished truth, Senator," Branko responded.

"'The unvarnished truth?'" Norris echoed sarcastically. "Perhaps you ought to think about an early retirement *now*—before you're embarrassed when General Raines is forced to re-think your appointment as Commandant of the War College."

Raine's choice was known all over town and even considered a foregone conclusion. Branko was pondering how to say just that without also sounding like a pompous ass.

Norris might as well have been reading Branko's mind. After a well timed-pause, he starred into Branko's eyes and said, "It's not a decision necessarily carved in stone and I think we'll just have to see about that, won't we?"

Colonel Branko Horvitch had heard far more than enough. He stood upright, face drawn, towering over Norris who had also stood, cigar and flask in hand.

"Senator Norris," Branko said in a commanding but restrained voice, "once again, I appreciate your help. We have nothing further to discuss. *Ever.*"

With this parting blockbusting salvo, the Colonel smartly wheeled an about-face and marched out of the bowels of shame.

A short time later Branko was on the phone with Edith.

"He threatened me!" he growled. "The bastard threatened me!"

"I never say, *I told you so*, but—well—I told you so, soldier boy! Welcome to bloody Washington. When you deal with politicians, you never get anything for nothing. There's always a payback down the line. Remember that. Please."

Branko had expected a little sympathy but knew that Edith was right. Now that the other shoe had dropped, Branko was concerned with what a vengeful politician of Norris' stature and influence could do.

"You know, Edith," he said, "I want that posting at the War College, but I'll be damned before veterans of any color will suffer just so I can sit on my ass."

Branko couldn't see the smile on Edith's face or know that he had said the one thing she had hoped and expected he would say. It just reaffirmed the depth of quality she had always recognized in the man. To Branko she said, "Washington's a battlefield, my friend. The casualities are hopes, dreams and careers. But if you fear that the threat will be carried-out, don't worry another second. General Raines is one of our old friends. He and his wife spent a good deal of time with us when Woodrow was alive. Your favorite senate benefactor is on very thin ice. I also know of a few embarrassing skeletons rattling in his closet that would love to find their way to the Post."

"Thanks a million, Edith. You're still my favorite *Dixie shicksie.* Okay, I won't give it another thought. Besides I have to get back to my Remington. There is still a massive report waiting to be finished."

With that, Branko bid goodnight and hung up his phone, more determined than ever to blow any shrill whistles he had, and some more he hadn't thought much about.

Take that, you old Cornhusker! You want vindictive, you've got vindictive!

August 18, 1929

His appearance as the key witness lasted only long enough for all committee members to ask further questions. In three weeks, they adjourned. It was expected that President Hoover would sign the bill following budget hearings in October. Until then Branko was asked by The Ways and Means Committee chair to stand by for any follow-up clarifications.

Senator Norris was still a no-show at the Committee Meetings. His threat died of self-suffocation by hot air.

The rapidity with which Branko's report was accepted and attached to the bill for a Veterans Administration left the Colonel reeling. His name was written into the Congressional Record commending him for a mission carried out well. Additionally, two of the committee members confided that in their many years there had never been such bi-partisan cooperation in a Congressional Committee effort. That it was all part of a budget-busting annual expenditure made it all the more historic.

A small celebration was hosted by an unusually, smugly satisfied Edith. She invited only a few close friends, including the Steels and U.S.S.R. Commander Timoshenko and his wife, who were visiting Washington on official business.

The Russians were still pushing hard for full recognition by the United States, the first step of which would call for an official embassy in Washington. Several former key *apparatchiks,* now high level commissars and a few selected high-ranking military were asked to assist in their, "pitching" efforts to the State Department. The powerful presence of Timoshenko, a Stalin favorite, was no surprise to serious Washington Russophiles or to Branko.

The conversations were, as expected, illuminating. It had been five years since Branko had last seen his friend Semyon and they had much to talk about. The latter was shocked that any government would establish a special department for veteran's affairs. When Jack suggested that the high-ranking Soviet officer ask Stalin to establish one back home, he laughed heartily and replied, "Major, I don't have warm enough uniforms for Siberian winters!"

His stunning wife Katiusha was not amused.

August 20, 1929

Jesse was not at home all summer. He elected to stay in Charlottesville in his dorm and chose to play in a summer league made-up of undergraduate baseball players from six schools.

The Virginia Amateur Summer Baseball League consisted of UVa, Virginia Tech, James Madison, Richmond, Washington and Lee and Virginia Military Institute. In exchange for dorm residency and food vouchers the university required Jesse and several other team members to handle weekly chores around the campus. When traveling between campuses, the league arranged a daily stipend for players.

Each school had set-up a reasonable fund to pay for umpires, equipment and grounds keeping—most of which the kids did. Since some of those on the UVa roster had plans for summer, Jesse was left to hold down third base, which pleased the boy no end.

Near the end of summer, Jesse was to play in a season-ending, noon-time game on the James Madison University campus in Harrisonburg. With his recent duties now squared away, Branko took the time to drive the hundred miles down to see the Saturday game. The scenic drive to Harrisonburg, through the Shenandoah Valley, was beautiful and Edith made the trip with him—they took her Rolls, in fact.

Since Eva's death, Edith had slowly developed a comfortable relationship with Jesse. While there would not have been a reason for these two to otherwise meet the relationship was made less awkward by the platonic friendship between Edith and Branko. The feelings between young Jesse and Edith had warmed up by degrees over the past year and the young man genuinely enjoyed her company. Neither Edith nor Branko could have been more pleased by this.

The UVa. Cavaliers managed to edge out the league-leading Madison Dukes 5 to 4 and Jesse played an errorless 3rd going 1-for-3. At game's end, Jesse got permission from his coach to return to D.C. with Branko and Edith. He only had to promise to be back in Charlottesville for practice on Tuesday—the playoff games were scheduled to start on Thursday.

Since Jesse's dad was off on a beach vacation Jesse looked forward to the familiar Sidwell apartment. He especially appreciated the dinner they stopped for while on the way home. No doubt, the growing 3rd-baseman's summer calories were on the meager side.

The dinner was also enjoyed by the unshakeable Charlie Hannah, the, "Fed-boy" agent assigned to protect Edith and who managed to follow at a discreet distance for the round trip. Edith and Branko watched on in amusement as the pleasant man and young Jesse enjoyed the, "delicious and delectable dinner" at Sam's Delicious and Delectable Grille on the byway near Culpeper.

September 9, 1929

Branko was relieved to hear that he would not be needed as a witness for the Ways and Means Committee sessions. The Chairman assured him that the bill now only required President Hoover's signature to establish the Veterans Administration—with an appropriate budget.

On this warm Indian Summer evening, Branko postponed his usual brisk walk after finding three letters in his mailbox. One was from Tante Shayndl, another from Rivka and the third—a nameless letter—was postmarked, *Hyannisport, Mass*.

The third letter, which he knew would contain some gaseous, self-serving nonsense, could wait. He sat on a comfortable stuffed chair in a corner of the lobby, and opened Tante's letter first.

> *Rue de Roi de Sicile, Paris*
> *August 25, 1929*
>
> *My dearest nephew, Bracheleh (OK, Branko!):*
> *How do you like this? I'm writing this whole letter in English! Maybe I'm practicing to come to America! I enjoyed your letter about the wonderful automobile trip you took. It seems like you saw a good portion of that wonderful Goldeneh Medina.*
>
> *I was moved by your stories of the hospitals and the poor, sick and disabled former soldiers. I worried about you for every minute you were in the front lines. Thank God you came through it, even with the wounds. Tell me, dear, is the shrapnel still coming out from your back? I hope that's over with by now.*
>
> *The wonderful descriptions of black gold and the oil wells of Texas and Oklahoma were very interesting to all of us. Charles must have re-read it a dozen times. He is*

ready to make his fortune in oil. Gevalt! I feel as though I know the young man with a missing arm in Oklahoma, and the negro boy in the swamps of Louisiana. Also the fine Doctor Du Bois in New Orleans with the very difficult job. You paint it like a picture

Tell me, dear one, are you meeting any maidlach? It's time already, Branko. It's time already! I'm sure Mrs. Wilson must have many woman friends who would be a match for you. She herself sounds like a lovely lady, a shicksela, but so nice to you. Maybe something there for you two! A former First Lady, why not? OK, OK, by now, you're ready to tell me "Enough, already, enough!" There, I'll stop.

Charles is spending a few weeks with his children in Switzerland. I didn't go along this time, as I had yahrzeit for Berel and I wanted to get ready for Dovidl and his family. They are coming for the holidays and this time they plan to stay for a month.

I am so happy. I just wish you, too, could be here with us. We all love you so very much.

I'm reading in Le Monde that there are economic worldwide problems in the wind. Charles, always the banker, agrees. He feels that America will be in for the worst of it and your Hoover seems to expect it. We certainly hope not, although our darling government is as shaky as always. The franc is holding up today, but tomorrow, ver vaist, who knows? Meanwhile, we keep a wary eye toward Germany which many Frenchmen think is still the threat to us it has always been. My

> sons-in-laws think that if the present Berlin government falls, waiting to take over are fast-growing unsavory elements that will mean another war in time. What a world! And we thought the Cossacks were the bad ones!
>
> Saving the best for last, we were thrilled to hear that you will soon become the head of the college. I could have told them that you were the best! Why didn't they ask me?
>
> I'm so very happy that you are keeping close to Eva's son Jesse. That's what she wanted. Such a gorgeous girl she was. The wedding picture is on my bureau. Oy!Oy!
>
> Zay Gezint, Brachela. My love to you!
> Tante Shayndl

The troubling conditions in Europe and in particular the rabble-rousing words of the *Mein Kampf* author caused Branko to have concerns, too. He had assigned one of his seminar students to read, analyze and report on the very poor English translation of the book a year ago.

"With ideas of this sort, Herr Hitler will be dangerous beyond imagination should he ever come into power. He must be closely monitored in every speech and every move he makes" read the summation of Major Dwight Eisenhower, Class of 1927.

The letter from Rivka was short and concise. As in the past, Rivka was the recipient of an occasional letter from Miriam. This time, Rivka reported that Emanuel was attending Medical School at Western Reserve and had received top honors as *summa cum laude* in his undergraduate work. The accompanying scholarship award assured him of tuition coverage through the four years ahead. This, of course, pleased Branko but at the same time gave him pause. So many times in the past, he had wanted to burst into the classroom and throw his arms around his son. He knew full well that he just couldn't and wouldn't do this. Maybe they could meet someday, somewhere. Where? When? If ever?

Meanwhile, he thought, *Damn, there's that same perfume from Rivka's letter!*

While reading he was occasionally interrupted by a phone calls and a radio playing music at high volume in the hotel lobby. It was after 11:00 p.m. when he got to Joe Kennedy's letter.

Always good for a few laughs, he silently mused.

>Hyannisport, Massachusetts
>September 4, 1929
>
>How the hell is it going down there, Colonel? Donovan tells me that you're up to be the boss or dean or something at the college. Sounds like a great deal for you. But there are better ones, to be sure.
>
>We've been putting the finishing touches on this great piece of beach property here on the Cape. Seems like it will never be complete. At least that's what Rose keeps saying, bless her. The kids love it and we plan to be here year round. Snow on the beach is as pretty a sight as you'll ever see. Maybe finally we can get you up for a weekend. Promise not to charge you the regular weekend rates!
>
>I know I had sent you condolences on the loss of Eva back in '27, but it sure must have been a big blow to you. What a damn shame. I hope your grieving has subsided and you're getting on with your life. That auto tour you took earlier this year is mighty interesting to me. Checking out the oil fields of Texas and Oklahoma, the wildcat operations, the boom-towns and all that.
>
>Donovan bumped into me in NYC and we had lunch, so he spilled the whole trip from a

letter you had sent him. I'll bet that wildcat properties start declining steeply in the next month or two and then I can buy some of God's little acres for ten-cents on the dollar. No, not now, but soon. Maybe you can give me some introductions when the time is right.

I tell you, sport, this country of ours is in for massive changes and my brokerage partners and I are planning to be in the right places to pick up the more valuable pieces.

Get it, Colonel? This may not mean much to you; I know you're not one to gamble your officer's salary check, but we're bullishly invading the market, buying "short" and counting on turning that into enormous returns. We've already driven stocks, like Libbey-Owens-Ford, for example, to a point where our "short" buys will be paying off like a goose laying golden eggs. I don't want to bore you with details that you may not understand, but there's a major shift coming in our economy in a very short time. Mark my words.

I look forward to seeing you soon, Branko. As I said, we may need some of your help in our oil field forays. Loosen up, old buddy, and have some fun.

Going sailing this afternoon with two of my boys, Joe Junior and Jack. I want to take along Bobby, the four-year-old, but Rose nixed that! Hell, the kid can swim much better than I can!
Joe Kennedy

Kennedy appended the letter with a parenthetical phrase reading, *Don't take any wooden nickels*. It was exactly as Branko had come to expect—another Kennedy exercise in deal-making, shaking and breaking. His head was still swimming a bit after reading the letter. A cup of tea might help. An aspirin wouldn't hurt, either. A Kennedy letter had this effect on him.

October 1, 1929

When Herbert Hoover took office in March, there were already many signals, going back to Calvin Coolidge's "era of prosperity," which spawned a continuing frenzy of reckless spending and runaway excesses in the stock market. It was *buy, buy, buy, buy low and sell high*.

Regulations? Little or none. Speculation? Manipulation? Lots of it, such as the buying, "short" described in Joe Kennedy's letter and all legal. The stock market continued its rapid and significant ascent into hog heaven. Americans were buying stocks by borrowing money, or they were buying *on margin*—buying with only a portion of the money down, and the rest out of profits. This had been going on since the early 1920s, but Hoover recognized that this type of activity in the stock market could be potentially dangerous when he served as Secretary of Commerce under Coolidge. Banks were also speculating in the stock market with their depositors' money, and there were no laws to stop them.

Free-wheeling was the ala mode flavor of the day on Wall Street and everyone was a player—some deep into the game. The druggist on Main Street, the teacher at the local high school, the farmer in Iowa, the worker on the Ford assembly line, "the butcher, the baker and the candlestick maker." All wanted, "in."

Joe Kennedy, one of the legion of beneficiaries of this market had warned, "When my shoe shine boy began to give me stock tips, I knew it was time to get the hell out of the market."

A major problem was, no one knew when to or how to stop and reflect. Perhaps no one wanted to. President Hoover, a scant few members of his Cabinet and Congress realized that there was a mammoth problem brewing, but their warnings were mere whispers into a high head-wind. Privately, the President tried to convince influential bankers to end loans to brokers who greedily encouraged this predicament. His fervent appeals to The Federal Reserve, Congress and New York Governor Franklin Roosevelt to propose stiffer regulation of the New York Stock Exchange, went unheeded.

The month of September had seen a rather strange market. A slight drop and a bit of hesitation, but within days prices were at a peak, and on the 19th there were many new highs. But this condition was short-lived. By October prices were fluctuating and the overall trend was definitely downward; here is where the brokers of Joe Kennedy's ilk found their eggs of gold. Nevertheless, the decline did not scare off too many buyers. On the 23rd the situation began to deteriorate, stabilized for a few days and then plunged downward again. The mother of all depressionary storms was about to make landfall.

October 29, 1929

And it came to pass on this blackest of all Tuesdays.

While the optimists were waiting in vain for a quick recovery, the average prices of the fifty leading stocks dropped forty points. Brokers were deluged with sell orders from clients who wanted to unload before the drop deepened and traders who were operating on margin were unable to raise enough money to save their accounts.

Thousands of Americans saw their life savings disappear. Farmers and homeowners lost their mortgaged properties and unemployment numbers were on their way to new stratospheric totals. By the middle of November, stock prices deflated to even lower lows once again.

Every walk of life was negatively affected and the catastrophic reality of it all was that the crash would resound throughout the world. Perhaps one of most telling illustrations of a crippled economy was the attendance of less than 300 people at a Red Grange-led Chicago Bear-Green Bay Packer football game that next Sunday. Hoover valiantly tried to shore up a crumbling house—which may have unintentionally made rebuilding that much harder. But whatever the case, it was not to be for some time to come.

December 20, 1930

Jesse was home for the holidays, staying at his father's house. The phone call was something Branko should have expected, but didn't.

"Branko, can I come over to discuss something very important?"

"Sure thing, Jess. Do you need me to drive over and—"

"I've got dad's car," Jesse interrupted.

He loved driving every chance he could and arrived at Branko's in no time.

"Everything okay, kid?" Branko asked when he noticed Jesse's reserved expression.

"It's dad," Jesse answered. "He's in bad shape. Lost a big chunk of what he had in the crash. His shoe stores are in hock up to his eyeballs. The big house will be foreclosed any day now."

"Jesse, I'm so sorry. I had no idea. But it seems like everyone I've talked to in the last month has been affected."

"He can't afford for me to stay at UVa, either. My tuition is paid-up to the end of the semester, January 12th, and then I'm afraid it's goodbye Charlottesville."

"Whoa, there, Jess. Are you saying he has no money to pay—what is it—about $1,000 to get you through the year?"

"Yeah. The tuition is somewhat less than that. I can try to find work for peanuts but there are so many unemployed I wouldn't have much of a chance. I'm sure the same conditions are evident here in D.C."

"Don't worry about tuition, Mr. Baseball," Branko said. "You *will* be at least finishing the year—and if I can swing it, the next year, too—and the next. As you know, your mom had some savings in your name and I'll add to it. You're going to be swinging a bat this season, but I want you to choke-up a bit more on the handle, y'hear?"

He put his assuring arms around the boy.

The tears were bound to flow and they did. Branko had talked to Jesse before about the little savings account and they agreed to save it for emergencies. And an emergency had arrived with a big bang. Branko asked Jesse to tell his dad about this meeting and the boy promised that he would do so the next day. Branko wanted to avoid embarrassing Harry Kanter and he felt that would best be accomplished in this way.

Within two days time, all had been arranged: Jesse would finish the school year. Harry felt beholden and insisted he would repay, but Branko graciously pushed it aside. He was certain that even with the military's notoriously minimal pay scale, a promotion to Brigadier could easily provide the money necessary for Jesse to get through to graduation. Besides, as Commandant, his expenses would be manageable: Free Commandant housing on college grounds, a free car and driver, expense account, no utilities and most meals on the premises. He also hoped that by the next year Kanter would recoup somewhat.

This same sort of financial drama played out throughout America —and the world.

Don't fret, Eva, Branko thought to himself, *it's going to all work out well for Jesse. I promise.*

The long-awaited move associated with the War College appointment finally arrived: General and Mrs. Raines moved from the Commandant's residence and into their handsome new bungalow in Manassas. They insisted that Branko begin moving his possessions into the Commandant's residence immediately, which he did over the holidays. The four bedroom, beautifully landscaped and furnished manse on the War College grounds had served as the resident Commandant's home since 1915. The single widower, Colonel Branko Horvitch, would at last have room for his memorabilia collection which had cluttered up the apartment. His new apartment tenants were quite pleased to take over the sub-lease sooner than planned.

January 2, 1930

This was the day, a most meaningful one in Branko's life of many significant days.

President Hoover and The Secretary of War, Patrick Hurley, had asked General Raines to slightly tone down the induction ceremony due to the earth-shaking events of the past two months. Both Raines and Branko fully agreed. Aside from the College faculty, the guest list would be limited to certain selected Hoover administration personnel, including Cabinet members. At precisely 3:00 p.m., people began filing into the massive auditorium.

Among those in attendance were the President and Mrs. Hoover; former President Calvin Coolidge and wife Grace from Vermont; Vice President and Mrs. Charles Curtis: Secretary Hurley; Supreme Court Justice Louis D. Brandeis—chosen by Branko to conduct the investiture proceedings; the Speaker of the House; the founder of the Army War College, 84-year-old Elihu Root, a most distinguished statesman and a few Senators and Congressman.

Branko's personal guests were Edith Wilson, Jesse Kanter, Larry and Aretha Lincoln, Major Jack Steel and Mrs. Steel. Before the ceremony started, Branko made a beeline for the first row where *his* folks were seated and proceeded to lovingly hug each one. Along with the raised eyebrows, there was the muted sounds of gasps permeating the hall.

But it was just Branko being Branko, pomp and protocol be damned!

As his last official act, General Raines gave brief opening remarks and received a standing ovation. Branko led the applause and went on to salute and hug the outgoing Commandant. At this intimate move, if the General had a monocle it would have popped off into the audience —something akin to a baseball manager dealing with the antics of his star player; You just gotta put up with him.

Raines introduced a former student, Major Dwight David Eisenhower, Class Leader of 1927. The Major was stationed in the District and was delighted to be asked to say a few words honoring Colonel Horvitch, his favorite lecturer. He gave a brief talk on the theme, "Why a War College?" He ended by paying homage to the great Elihu Root and his endearing quote on what the War College stood for: "Not to promote war, but to preserve peace."

The ensuing standing applause elicited a gesture of acknowledgment from Mr. Root.

Justice Brandeis then briefly spoke and presented Colonel Branko Horvitch with the Hebrew Bible, the Tanach, on which to place his right hand. Seeing this—something other than the Christian Bible for the swearing-in of a public official—raised a few eyebrows. The Colonel gracefully accepted the broad range of his duties and swore to uphold the Constitution. He was now the seventh man to serve as Commandant of the United States Army War College.

In full dress uniform, he stepped to the podium for his first official words. Following the necessary salutations, only mentioning Hoover and Coolidge by name, he went on:

"You are all aware that I speak with a slight accent. I am a fairly recent immigrant to our beloved country. I arrived at Ellis Island in 1904, leading a group of persecuted young Jews out of a repressive and inhospitable Romania, trekking across the unfriendly xenophobic stretches of Europe and on to the promises of this Golden Land. I am proud to say that all of these people have since become exemplary, hard-working, patriotic citizens of the United States of America. Each of them—and I—look upon our respective citizenships as a privilege, not a birthright. As a Police Lieutenant in New York City, as an honorary Irishman with the Fighting 69th Regiment on the battlefields of Belgium and France, as a lecturer at West Point, as The Superintendent of Buildings and Grounds under three administrations at The White House, and as a faculty member of this esteemed institution, I am merely paying back for what I have freely taken from America. You can be assured that I will continue to do so.

"General Raines, it has been my pleasure entirely, to serve under your great leadership. You may expect that I will be calling you whenever I have a question or a problem—even in the middle of the night."

There were broad smiles and laughter.

"May the countenance of God shine upon America. God Bless this country and its people. Amen."

With this closing and his stepping away from the podium, Branko was besieged by an avalanche of well-wishers. He slowly made his way through the gathering well-wishers and to his invited guests for another round of emotional embraces.

A new chapter in his life was officially underway, and it would be, "Back to school tomorrow."

Somewhere in Western White (Belo) Russia
August 22, 1943

The revitalized Soviet juggernaut continued to break out of all the salients caused by the counterattacks of retreating Nazi armored elements. The Soviet Bureau of Information (SBI) was ordering all partisan units to join the attacking Soviet army as it entered their sectors.

The Broadcast: "Comrades and heroes of the Partisan Army of the Union of Soviet Socialist Republics. Finally, we are pleased to report the best of all news. Our armies are making progress far beyond what we have been hoping for. Crossing the Dnieper is within sight, Orel is in our hands, Smolensk, Bryansk and Kursk also. If the war proceeds as well as it has, the Motherland will be free of the Fascist swine by mid-1944. The all-powerful Red Army will be on its way to Berlin and unconditional victory. This has been a most difficult trial for all of us, but we shall prevail

"None of this good news could have been possible without your gallant deeds in the field. Now the time is fast arriving when there is one more major assignment for all of our partisan units throughout the western extremities of our beloved land.

"Without hesitation, it is vital for each unit in The Ukraine, Belo Russia and the Northwest to join up with the Soviet forces as they reach and continue to advance through your coordinates. They will welcome all of the help, manpower and guidance you can provide. Your duty to your country is widely appreciated but it is far from over.

"This communiqué shall be treated as a firm order direct from Comrade Stalin. Long Live the Union of Soviet Socialist Republics. *Das veedanya!"*

For the Maccabees and all within their circle, this posed a pressing potential problem. Many of the affected partisans wanted no part of the Russian armies; they just wanted to go home—wherever that may be. They harbored a premonition that it would be all-too-easy to be tagged as a deserter, depending on the whims of the individual Soviet commanders they would encounter. Battle-hardened survivors of Stalingrad, Kursk, Moscow and Smolensk would think, unfairly and bitterly, "How easy the hit-and-run partisans have had it all the while."

Simcha made his decision but put it to a vote. He owed this choice to those who had loyally long fought beside him under the harshest of conditions, meager rations and ever-constant reality of isolation. He thought it best to break-up the unit and then, "To each his own from there." Some of them felt that electing to separate and take chances on blending into the general population as the war wound down, was guilty of irrational naiveté. The belief was not an unfounded one: The Soviets were bearing down on central Belo Russian coordinates and driving the panicking backtracking Germans ahead of them.

The vote was heavily in favor of total dispersion, each going his own way, carrying his own rations and weapons while riding his own horse or walking.

As for Branko, he sat squarely on the proverbial horns of a dilemma. His way to home and safety was by an altogether different path. He figured his best chance lay with the Soviet Army. He felt that after he joined them and explained who he was and what had happened to him there was at least the probability of transportation to Russian high command. From there it would be only a step away from Timoshenko, or perhaps someone else familiar with the strange course of events going back to September of 1941. He strongly felt it would be close to common knowledge by now. Ensconced in Moscow until the war ended was the best thing that he could imagine happening to him. At least he could get back in touch with Donovan and Roosevelt. Maybe even Tante, Edith, Jesse and Sara. His eyes teared-up when he thought of those near and dear to him who had no word since the invasion, summer of 1941.

Commander Simcha Greenberg could not argue with his comrade's clear logic. He would have liked nothing better than to keep Branko at his side until the Red Army marched through Belo Russia on its way west. But he fully understood the merits of Branko seeking them out as soon as possible.

The reasoning went back and forth for the next two days. They were encamped about ten kilometers west of Baranovich, in a large and thick forest of pine and fir. There was also another unit nearby—twenty-two Jewish partisans and three Siberians from Yakutsk. Simcha had met with the leader, former Red Army Tank Corp

Captain, Eliahu Kuznetsov. They shared the very same life-threatening or life-saving options. Kuznetsov's people unanimously decided to disperse and set the date for the following three day period where seven fighters at a time would leave the forest, most moving eastward.

Lev Soloveitchik was the prime Maccabee mover for dispersal and he had only one goal; to reunite with his young family. He wanted to head east, since he last saw his wife and child boarding a Red Army truck retreating to the east. But the sensible choice was to head south solo and eventually end-up at the farm near Rovno. The owner, if still alive and in control of the farm, was a Zhid-friendly Ukrainian. He had, for five pre-war years, counted on Lev to manage the place, keep the books, buy and sell equipment and hire and supervise the farm-hands.

Lev had little doubt that if the man was still alive, he would provide food and shelter—and put him back to work. The marksman's thought of picking off retreating Germans made his decision to disperse more difficult. But perhaps while on the back roads to Rovno he might yet have a chance to add a few notches on his Mauser handle. The thought pleased him, but the greater puzzle still was how to find his family. He hoped that they, too, would try to get back to the farm following behind the advancing Soviets.

Everyone in the unit, including Simcha and Branko would sorely miss the tall, thin, limping figure and his trusty Mauser.

Raisel, the former political officer, Kostya the boxer and Alyosha the torpedoman, seemed to have no fear of rejoining the Reds. This was especially true of the busty, outspoken woman. One could only pray that all three were right. Alexander "Sasha" Cohen, the downed pilot, felt the same way. He was itching to get back into a fighter plane and strafe the living hell out of retreating German elements. He had been very careful to preserve the brown leather jacket, fur lined boots and white silken scarf from his air force uniform, just for the purpose of giving him an advantage when meeting up with Russian advanced patrols.

Every one of the Maccabee unit had a personal agenda and some sort of old identifying papers that might get them through. Three of the younger civilians, the twin sixteen year-olds–brother and sister–and the Olympian gymnast, would attempt to blend-in, especially in the larger towns and townlets between here and their destination. They felt secure in choosing as their elder and guide, former Kiev police officer, Viktor Reznick. He accepted the vote of confidence and they would be among the first to leave. All were from Kiev or its vast suburbs, which was expected to soon be in Soviet hands once again.

It was the Bard who wrote that, "parting is such sweet sorrow." But no one had experienced it this way nor had they planned on it coming with complications. There was nothing sweet about it, and little doubt that there were many insurmountable challenges ahead for all thirty-six Maccabees.

Safe journeys with happy endings?

There were no guarantees, and if there were, what fool would guarantee the guarantees?

THE COMMANDANT

U.S. Army War College Barracks
Washington D.C.
January 5, 1930

Appointing the ever-loyal Larry Lincoln to be his driver/civilian-aide was mutually agreed upon months earlier. Today, Larry reported to work for the first time. His salary was fairly close to his previous income as White House Chief Steward during three prior administrations.

Larry was elated, of course, and Aretha was pleased as can be. Edith had also discussed this with Branko and she actually came up with the suggestion first: Larry and Aretha would still live at the Wilson house. Larry would commute to the College five days a week, using his car or local bus.

Branko arranged with General Services to keep the 1928 Oldsmobile touring car in which he made his western trip. Much as he did back in his NYPD days, Branko felt awkward in having a driver—even more so because of being personally acquainted with Larry. In fact, Branko initially dispensed with the idea of having a driver. But former Commandant Raines explained that all prior Commandants had a driver/civilian-aide and asked Branko to do the same. Branko thought it a pretentious arrangement but Larry made it tolerable by saying, "Colonel, if you ever wish to drive, we'll just stop the car and I'll slide into the passenger seat."

They both laughed while envisioning this flagrant rupture of protocol, which Branko took one step further. He said, "No, Larry, when I drive you'll be in the back as *my* passenger. If we're going to shake up Washington let's do it all the way!"

The following week Branko was summoned by Secretary of War Patrick Hurley. Hurley informed him of the expected Brigadier General promotion that was to occur in February. They also had a productive, "meeting of the minds" session reviewing all of Branko's duties and the associated rules and regulations. It was nothing new to Branko who had several times discussed this with General Raines. Raines had, in turn, adopted some of Branko's recommendations.

Branko liked Hurley, who seemed to be a no-nonsense guy, but with a warm manner. Their relationship, Branko was certain, would be a mutually rewarding one. When the meeting was over, Hurley broadly smiled and said, "When we're in private I would like for us to be Pat and Branko. Okay with you?"

They shook on it, each placing his left hand on the other's shoulder.

Then there came the faculty review. It was a bi-annual event, the first scheduled for mid-April. With budget cuts anticipated, Branko feared it would not be pleasant. While two projected retirements and a transfer request would make the review less severe, there would still be a resulting heavier teaching load.

To lessen that load Branko had expressed his willingness to personally continue holding the seminars he had conducted for several years. Secretary Hurley saw that as a noble gesture but didn't think it would be necessary.

January 30, 1930

Jesse, happily back at Uva this semester, reported that his dad salvaged one of his shoe stores from a healthy Baltimore bank along with a nearly complete inventory. He planned to re-open it within a few months. Unfortunately, his heavily mortgaged Chevy Chase home was irretrievably lost, foreclosed by the mortgage-holding bank. Harry Kanter and family were now sharing a house with an old friend near the University of Maryland campus. The situation divided the rent. This sort of thing was happening all over the country and indeed, the world. Grandparents were re-filling the old homestead with adult children and grandchildren returning out of dire necessity. Obviously many of these arrangements were fraught with tensions and there was no end in sight.

Branko occasionally corresponded with his closest *fusgeyer* friends and heard several tales of woe. He was helpless to do anything significant and this hurt him immeasurably. Sendehr and Rivka were making ends meet in Cambridge, but Rivka also took on a resident directorship at the famed Brattle Street Theater. She loved it, and Branko was very happy to know that. Mordecai and Pessel were on high ground with his adequate income as a union arbiter, and he had years before become Samuel Gompers key representative in New York state. In their last letter, right after the crash, Mendel and Esther were comfortably solvent: His professorship at CCNY was tenured, but significant pay cuts were expected. Their three children were all married young adults with passable income situations, but as the depression deepened, the cold, hard fact was that overnight anyone's lot could drastically change for the worse.

President Hoover struggled to find a cure. Of course the newspapers, magazines and popular newsreels had a veritable field day blasting him for spending. And, in fact, the Hoover administration expenditures ultimately increased more in four years than what was yet to come during the *New Deal* years. In response to the 1929 stock market crash, Hoover undertook a massive 259 percent increase in nonmilitary federal spending.

Economists aside, there was no shortage of, "financial experts" spawned by the crash. But these were the few manipulators who sold, "short" during the September market peak. As Branko would say, "I know one, and his initials are JPK!"

Branko's senior clerk, Master Sergeant Bill Winslow, announced a Henry Luce on the phone.

"And just who is Henry Luce?" Branko asked.

It turned out that Mr. Luce, Editor and Publisher of the upstart *Time* magazine, had been trying to arrange an interview with the new Commandant since his induction. But Luce's interest wasn't the War College or that Branko was its, "first soldier." It was, Luce claimed, that he wanted more about the long-time notable activities of a renowned war hero who had lead the fight for improved veteran's rights. After this brief introductory phone conversation, Branko agreed to an interview for the following week.

With Hoover's signing this month's bill establishing a central Veterans Administration, Branko's name had appeared everywhere as the military's top advocate. The story of his inspection road trip was taken from the Congressional Record by publisher Ned McLean of the *Post,* and circulated widely. With several illustrations and photos it was actually seen as sort of a National Geographic, "travelog Americana" by some readers.

Dr. Du Bois called Branko from New Orleans to say that he was being inundated by both negro and white reporters, and was overjoyed to see any measure of publicity in his constant fight for better conditions. Privately, Colonel Horvitch was honored and proud to see the story get such wide circulation.

Branko was not the least bit reticent to ask Edith if she had been adversely affected by the events of the past few months. She assured him of her financial well-being. Woodrow had been wisely conservative in his handling of all things monetary and she, too, managed a timely withdrawal of minor holdings out of the grasp of Wall Street. There was talk of making the beautiful "S" Street home into a Woodrow Wilson Museum at some point, which didn't hurt the current market value. Her Rolls also retained its substantial asset value in spite of the downturn,

"Of course, I may have to ask you to start paying for meals here, Commandant," she joked. "Either that or I'll have Aretha learn to prepare hot dogs thirty different ways,"

"Well, how about I make a low bid on the Rolls for Jesse to drive around campus," shot back the unperturbed soldier.

February 11, 1930

The Luce interview was without doubt the most comprehensive Branko ever experienced. The interviewer knew what he wanted and went after it in a polite but persistent manner. Basically, he wanted an encapsulated version of America's treatment of its war veterans going back to the Revolution. Branko had done his homework diligently since returning from France and beginning his work at The War

College. Luce was visibly amazed and impressed with Branko's historical knowledge of this oft-forgotten subject. The more Branko shared, the more Luce came back with questions relevant to what he was learning.

It went on for three hours, after which they adjourned to the faculty dining room for yet additional give and take during dinner. It can be said that they met as strangers and parted as new mutually-impressed friends. As he got up to leave, the young publisher announced that the magazine was planning this editorial piece to also include Branko's views on the much-discussed veteran's bonus problems that were expected to flare up again in the near future.

The cover, Luce said, was to be a photograph of Brigadier General Branko Horvitch.

Branko shrugged.

Edith was awestruck.

Time magazine had grown very fast from a cheap pulp vehicle to a respected news outlet and its circulation was growing geometrically.

"That Luce has really come up with something to be reckoned with in the context of a popular news magazine," Edith remarked. "And, now, ta-da, with His Excellency King Branko on the cover, sales will catapult it to new heights. Copies will virtually become collectibles. I read where English-language issues will be printed in parts of Europe, to be especially sought after by ex-pats." The uncontested female world champion of "tongue-in-cheek" had spoken.

"Well, you sure know a lot more about Henry than I do, although he did confide in me some of his future business plans over dinner. I'm seriously thinking of posing with my dress uniform, sword held vertically in a rigid attention posture. Maybe I'll even grow a British campaign mustache. Or better yet, I'll sit in an easy chair, smoking a pipe, with a wolfhound at my feet and a brandy in hand."

"Now, now, don't get carried away, kiddo! You're still that scrawny refugee imp from the Russian Ukraine. Those nice people at the orphanage from which you escaped are still looking for you. Something about an attempted murder charge, eh?"

The Former First Lady was still the best balloon burster on the block.

The promotion to generalship was official and without fanfare on February 20th. Secretary Hurley dropped into Branko's office unannounced and delivered the official papers. He then smartly gave Branko his first ceremonial salute. Now the Brigadier had to trade in his handsome, shining silver eagles for one star. A bit in advance, he had sent Larry to purchase a handful of the stars at a military surplus shop in Foggy Bottom. He even gave Branko the change so he would know that the stars were worth exactly $1.00 each, but a bargain at twelve for $10.50. After all, he needed them for his shirt collars, epaulets for his three types of uniforms and his "painter's" hats. The newly honored soldier was as proud as a peacock.

General Raines had made it clear that the Commandant solely controlled the implementation of policies, programs and curriculum. With this tradition, which actually went back only to the turn of the century, a Commandant's ingenuity was not only encouraged but also expected. In a straight, unencumbered line of access, the Army War College Commandant had full reign in reporting to the Secretary of War. Fortunately, in his role as Commandant Branko could never have been accused of any reluctance to generate and exercise new ideas and innovations. Without uncalled for hand-holding or bureaucratic interference he could become a whirlwind of meaningful, result-oriented actions.

One of his major goals for the fiscal year was modernizing the curriculum. He had already assembled the senior faculty task force necessary for the changes. As an example, air warfare had vaulted light years beyond the "olden" days of world war aero squadrons. To underscore the importance of these changes to the college curriculum, Branko planned to engage men such as Captain Eddie Rickenbacker, Charles Lindbergh and Billy Michell to address the task force. Lindbergh was now only two years removed from his historical trans-

Atlantic feat, and the exceedingly controversial Billy Mitchell was a mere four years beyond his resignation of his commission in order to avoid the court-martial conviction for insubordination Branko knew there could be repercussions with the inclusion of Mitchell, but he gave a green light regardless. Mitchell's grandstanding for headlines may not have won favor with the military, but the man knew the value of strategic air raids over enemy lines and advocated a separate air force. He had proven that aircraft could sink battleships and had made some disturbing predictions concerning U.S. vulnerability in Hawaii by eventual Japanese air attacks.

In his instructions, a six-page confidential document, the Commandant also recommended that chemical and tank warfare be given ample time. Since the tank was no longer just a supportive warfare weapon, its role might well depend upon the next generation of military strategists now being educated. The latest strategic maneuvers of 1929—at Fort Bliss in West Texas and California's Mojave Desert—clearly showed the tank capable of leading integrated infantry attacks. The war had illustrated this but it had taken nearly ten years to change the archaic thinking of the military's old guard, especially the horse-cavalry blokes. Both air and tank warfare would hence be a permanent part of the College's regular curriculum, where heretofore, they were given short shrift. Of course, with the depression in full sway, faculty specialists in these arenas would be added only as the budget allowed. When Pat Hurley received his copy of the task force agenda, he sent Branko a message of full endorsement.

Chemical warfare posed an altogether different proposition. In 1925, sixteen major nations had signed The Geneva Protocol, pledging never again to use any form of gas in warfare. As of this date the United States had not signed and the matter had languished in the Senate for nearly five years. The impasse was not expected to end in the near future

This was the dilemma that the Commandant and his task force faced.

As Branko added, "Few combatant nations had expected the use of gas during the big war, and preparedness was either absent or totally inadequate. I, for one, would not want to see this same state of inertia occur should we be drawn into another major war. In France, anything chemical was our greatest fear, bar none. At the very least, our College can address the subject, call in experts and draw-up readiness procedures for dissemination to U.S. military units around the world."

Thus, one panel member was assigned to recruit an expert witness to help develop a training manual.

At any rate, the Commandant was well on the way to gradually remaking the War College to meet the changing demands of intensified modern combat.

During these fascinating, inchoate days, Branko could not help thinking, *"So they have entrusted me to oversee the graduate program for the well-proven Officer Corp of the United States Army. How did I get here? A miracle. A bonafide miracle. And I love every challenging minute of it! It's what I do!"*

Washington, D.C.
April 3, 1930

At mid-semester break no baseball games were scheduled. Earlier in the week phoned from Charlottesville with some interesting news and that he was coming to spend time with his father, Branko and Edith.

On Saturday, he drove-up in Branko's old Ford—presented to him at year's end, just when all had seemed lost. Branko, reading the Post, bolted down the circular driveway when he heard the old familiar clanking motor. Just as his phone call indicated, Jesse had a passenger in the car.

"Now who's this pretty lady?" Branko said, even before the boy had stepped to ground. "You need an assistant driver these days, Jesse, m'boy?"

The young folks giggled at the question and Jesse took the raven-haired lass by the elbow to introduce her to Branko. "I love seeing that Brigadier's star on your shirt collar. Mazel Tov, Branko! I want you to meet Sara Beth Bernstein, a local from Betheseda, no less!"

"I've heard Jesse's stories of your life, General Horvitch," she said. "I'm so pleased to meet you in person."

Ever the gallant European, the General kissed her extended hand, eliciting a blush not from Sara, but from Jesse. Branko then replied, "I'm particularly overjoyed to see that the good taste his mother and I cultivated in our Jesse has not gone to waste."

All of this repartee was in the best of spirits, with smiles and laughter all-around. Branko immediately liked the girl immensely.

Back in the house they chatting over iced tea and Branko invited them to the faculty dining room for a late dinner. Although many of the faculty had met Jesse at various times, they enjoyed seeing him as a strapping young adult. He introduced Sara Beth, who handled the attention like a well-bred heiress. It was more or less the scene of a typical debutante surrounded by dashing officers at a military ball.

During dinner, Jesse announced that they would visit his dad and family up in College Park that Sunday. Branko mentioned that Edith would certainly love to see them.

"You don't think I'd miss that, General," Jesse quickly replied,

Sara Beth and her parents had made arrangements for Jesse to share her little brother's room, so everything fell into place as they had planned.

Later that week, after a delicious, "Aretha dinner," at the Wilson House—the best food the kids had eaten since the second semester—Edith and Branko walked the couple to the old Ford. They promised they would all see each other before the vacation week ended.

As they parted, Jesse was sure to tell Branko and Edith that he was getting much more on-the-field time than the last season, at third base, second and in the outfield, while sporting an over .300 batting average. This was sweet music to Branko's ears!

Sara leaned out the window, adding, "And looks *soooo* adorable in his uniform."

As the car pull away, Branko noticed the expression on Edith's face.

"Don't say it," he said to her. "They're only sophomores. No marriage plans that I know of."

"I know, Branko. But it's still nice to see. The girl is ravishingly beautiful, a very intelligent conversationalist, well-mannered and fun to be with. And guess what? She's Jewish. Wouldn't Eva be happy knowing that? I think, deep down, you are, too."

He smiled broadly and nodded firmly.

May 6, 1930

Hoover finally signed the long-awaited V.A. Bill. The Veterans Administration was now a reality. But Branko could rejoice for only a short moment because the catastrophic economy was a perfectly acceptable excuse to vote down the veterans bonus.

In the existing climate no one knew how Congress would react to increasing the overall debt. Every congressman wanted his constituents to believe that they were being fiscally responsible and what more sensible way than to postpone paying the vets bonus until the country was on its way to recovery. Naturally Branko knew of a few million ex-doughboys who would disagree with that and their unquestionable patriotism a dozen years earlier was sufficient reason for their stance.

Along with other observers of the situation Branko expected there would be some dangerous confrontations. So many vets had counted on borrowing up to 50% on the 1924 endowment certificates they received in lieu of cash, that they had formed groups demanding their right to borrow immediately. And there was a large segment of the vet population that were even arguing for payment of the full amount now.

In September, General Horvitch appeared before a joint session of Congress to plead for immediate recognition of the veteran's demands, but he addressed only the 50% bonus—not payment in full. He brought along with him six destitute D.C. veterans, all of whom had lost their jobs in the months following the market crash. Congress politely listened to their plights. The popular Commandant received a standing ovation after a quiet, yet powerful plea.

Left-handed promises made by both the Speaker of The House and Vice President Curtis evidently fell on the President's deaf ears. Branko attempted to get a meeting with Hoover, to no avail. Now more than ever he truly feared the aftermath of continuing the inaction of terminal procrastination.

These last few months of 1930 saw the deepening spiral of the American depression as well as the continuing growth of overwhelming worldwide poverty. As administration critics contended, the next two years could bring major deepening and widening increases in the financial crisis.

Outside private and local relief headquarters breadlines lengthened by the day. Panhandlers lined the streets and the downtrodden unemployed sold apples, rummaged goods, what was left of their clothing, wedding rings, old books and personal effects *ad nauseam*.

The nation's press and radio joined the legions of naysayers. Their message was now saying that it was no longer a matter of when things would get better, but whether things would ever return to comfortably livable levels.

Although there were appreciable budget cuts, staying afloat at the War College was not a question—at least for now. General Horvitch and his staff were successful at introducing some distinctive curriculum changes and the number of students admitted for each session was never compromised. Asking faculty to take on a moderate additional load was met with full cooperation in every case.

The offerings at the faculty dining room also showed evidence of the cutback efforts. As the Commandant said in his memo, "Some of us desk-job jockeys could do with smaller portions and less dessert, or none at all at the very least." Such belt-tightening had truly become a national sport.

November 19, 1930

Henry—*call me Harry*—Luce phoned to announce that the *Time* edition featuring Branko would be out mid-January. The photo shoot had taken place the week Branko appeared before Congress and the article was expanded to three pages. It would also include some snapshots of Branko in France, as a NYPD detective, at the White House and as Commandant. The layout depicted Branko at his desk, in his home on campus while in uniform and with a serious expression.

While the sword, wolfhound and brandy glass were nowhere to be found, the cover title, "Advocate General," still held. The cover picture glossies were sent to him a few weeks earlier and Edith, with her good-natured deprecatory remarks, approved.

"Good thing they didn't include your phone number and directions to the College, old man, you'd need a fire hose and a bodyguard to keep all the ladies away, " quipped the quipster. "As it is, they'll be storming the gates the day after it hits the newsstands,"

January 5, 1931

Branko warmly welcomed a phone call from Wild Bill Donovan over the holiday season. They had not been in touch for a few months. Bill recounted the number of foreign Gardens of Eden he had visited since September—all on clandestine intelligence business.

For example, the disturbing story of what was happening in Germany: Between the scuttle-butt and personal observations, Wild Bill was certain that Adolf Hitler was a hair's breadth away from taking over the Chancellorship. Talk of illegal military and armament buildup was buzzing all over Europe. Bill's private discussions with military leadership in England revealed the same information from their continental agents.

After this inside peek of Europe, Bill once again made his, *come join me* pitch. Branko laughed it off, as usual.

"One of these days, you stubborn army mule, you'll be godamm sorry you didn't join up with me today. There's a pile of work to be done and I'm stuck with some milquetoast characters who were hired only because they have Wharton School, Harvard, or Yale degrees in business or anthro-friggin-pology, fer Chrissake. They have as much sense of man-on-the-street intelligence as a cheese-making dairy farmer from upstate Wisconsin. I need you, General!! I need you now, man!"

Not getting any reaction, positive or negative, Bill blatantly went on with some exceptionally indicting statements concerning the eminent Squire of *Hyannisport*: "Seems that Joe Kennedy is in frequent communication with Adolf, the would-be *fuehrer.*"

"No," interrupted the puzzled Commandant, "Not the Kennedy I know and love"

"Yes, Joseph Patrick Kennedy. I know from personal observation that he's an outspoken anti-Semite of the highest order. In fact he'd qualify as anti-everything non-papal or non-female! Any Jew I know on Wall Street—brokers, bankers, mortgage lenders—consider the little shit *persona-non-grata*. It's purely mutual. Joe doesn't like Jews, and they think he's a cartoon—but to be closely watched! Scotland Yard and Brit intelligence confided in me that Kennedy is high on their own, "watch lists." They also know that he covets the ambassadorship to The Court of St. James. How's that for first prize in irony, General?"

"Bill, if a democrat unseats Hoover, that could possibly come into play—according to yesterday's *Post*. We both know that Kennedy's a virtuoso when blowing his own horn."

"So I hear, from my guys in London. But here's even more unbelievable news. Are you sitting down? The ever-busy Wall Street rumor mill is convinced that he's also on a confidential Democratic list of candidates for the eventual post of securities czar, after Herbie is defrocked and goes back to Iowa."

"What? You wouldn't kid me, old comrade! Or should we say that will be a case of the fox guarding the hen-house, eh Bill?"

Branko always enjoyed contact with Wild Bill Donovan. They had been through hell and back together and Branko felt a great deal of respect for the man. Whatever else Bill's faults might be, he was neither a liar nor exaggerator and his comments about Joe Kennedy's unsavory bigotry left Branko, roughly shaken. It was especially disheartening because he expected Joe to be in touch with him in the near future—in consideration of the economic disaster that was crippling the oil business. In his letter just before the crash, he made credible comments about snatching up distressed wildcat oil properties in Oklahoma and Texas. He most certainly was aiming to pick Branko's brain about his long motor trip throughout the region. Based upon Kennedy's previous remarks, Branko assumed the man was closely monitoring where the country was heading. Kennedy certainly didn't need any more proof that the direction was straight into the sewer.

But even beyond that, Branko saw Joe as a source of succor for so many people left destitute in wildcat oil country. Some fresh eastern money from the coffers of Kennedy could spell re-employment, especially for some of the vet friends Branko had made. He didn't want to purge that from his mind.

For days following the Donovan phone conversation, Branko periodically reviewed the damning comments concerning Kennedy. At first, he almost hoped that Joe would just leave him alone and never cross his threshold again. On the other hand, if Kennedy was indeed going to ask for help, Branko's agile mind was spinning at a hundred miles an hour on how to deal with this formidable adversary. He had formulated a few ideas, none of them conventional, but one in particular included a diabolical game Branko just ached to play! Tomorrow, he planned to have a conversation with his friend, Major Hal Lerner, in the Adjutant General's Office, for some relevant legal advice. It was that sensitive.

To that end, and without tipping his hand in regard to the specifics, Branko was explicit in his inquiry: He wanted to be certain of his legal options insofar as investing and business transactions as they related to his role in government. It was still a fairly wide-open request and Lerner whittled away at Branko's reluctance to expose what he was planning. In the end Lerner leaned back in his chair and promised to look into the matter.

*****

Washington, D.C.
September 3, 1943

It was happy chaos in the Russian embassy. The tide had been steadily turning in the Motherland's favor for a good part of 1943. Walls were adorned with photographs of Soviet troops, tanks and aircraft in victory postures; Red troops broadly smiled in celebration of yet another victory on their long counter offensive. Of course, they all privately knew that the next few thousand kilometers to Berlin wouldn't be a picnic.

Nevertheless, the catastrophic days of Stalingrad were receding into a dark abyss. Ambassador Viktor Makarov had not been known to often smile since the *Nazi Operation Barbarossa* began in '41. Today he quickly stood, walked around his desk and greeted FDR's emissary, Harry Hopkins, with a massive bear hug. The wafer thin, slight Midwesterner gasped for breath.

"Aha, Mr. Hopkins, I am so honored that you are visiting our embassy. Your Bill Donovan usually meets with me. I understand he is at his other office in New York. I'm sorry he has to miss what may soon become very good news regarding your man in Russia."

"Your message indicated that very clearly and the President insisted that I be here in person to receive the latest information. As you know, it's been two frustrating years, so let's get right to it. I know we're both very busy working toward the same end and I won't take-up much of your busy day."

"*Kharasho, gaspodin* Hopkins. I received this message from Timoshenko this morning. I'll translate it for you."

```
Comrade Makarov:
A month ago, orders were issued to partisan
units in Belo Russia to join with our
advancing troops as soon as possible.
General Horvitch's "Maccabee" team has not
been heard from for two weeks, other than
their Commander's message that his 36
people were looking ahead to rejoining
Russian forces. He stated that the American,
my old friend Branko, emphatically announced
that he would go off independently to
locate Russian troops as quickly as he
could. I have alerted all vanguard brigades
to be on the watch for him on foot or
horseback. Addition-ally, I gave them a full
description. Hopefully that day of a
glorious reunion will come soon. I will be
in periodic communication with you until
then. Here is my salute to victory in this
Great Patriotic War!
```

Hopkins was wide-eyed and even a bit tearful at hearing this.

"Thank you, Mister Ambassador," Hopkins said. "That, indeed, is very good news. It seems that General Horvitch did not want to be slowed down with any other group, and thought he would have a better chance alone, to quickly find Soviet elements as they pushed into Belo Russia."

"Mr. Hopkins, as of this week, the troops have continued to roll forward with only weakening opposition. From what I've been told, I expect concerted advances over a broad front from the Baltic to the Black Sea. Once they cross the Dnieper, what's left of the German army should turn into a rout. Helter-skelter, all the way home to their sauerkraut and unconditional defeat. Now that your boys are getting a proper foothold in Sicily and will soon be attacking Italy proper, that will put on further pressure for a landing in France and the long-awaited Western Front."

"Italy has been bloody, Ambassador. Eastern Sicily has bogged us down. Siracusa is not yet in our hands and that's delaying the invasion of the Italian coast. In central Sicily the casualty reports are devastating, especially for the volunteer Poles and Free French who are getting the brunt of it."

"Hopkins, can you possibly imagine how I sat here day after day reading of our mounting losses in Stalingrad?"

Before it turned into a pissing contest as to who had suffered more, Harry knew the Russky would win hands down. A Pyrrhic win at best. At this, Hopkins got up to leave before submitting to another bear hug. Too late. Both men were obviously delighted to see this breakthrough in the compelling saga of the missing Branko Horvitch.

Harry was itching to give FDR the news, but if today had been another bad one in Sicily or the Pacific, he knew the boss would be in a bitch of a mood. Harry was also considering whether to send a note to Edith Wilson. If he did, he knew that she would forward the news on to Jesse Kanter and likely cable Shayndl in Europe. She would also probably write to three or four *fusgeyer* friends to apprise them of the news. *Premature?* He pondered. *Probably,*

But then these people—the closest to Branko—had not much in the way of hope to go on for the past two years. And Branko himself had arranged with Donovan to contact these same people should anything adverse happen on his trip to Russia.

Harry decided to check with Wild Bill over the phone before doing anything.

Donovan did everything but cartwheels when Harry phoned. It made his day, as for the past two years he and every other American were constantly grasping at any war news that spelled something even vaguely positive. As for Branko, Bill continued to feel personally responsible. He volunteered to phone everyone on Branko's list, and to cable auntie Shayndl, but would do so with the necessary cautionary *caveats*. Harry was visibly relieved to pass on the responsibility to Bill, leaving only FDR to be briefed.

Not much of a trade, thought the peripatetic Mr. Hopkins.

*****

Western Belo Russia, near Baranovich.
September 9, 1943

Riding mostly at dusk and at early eventide to avoid the retreating Wehrmacht, Branko followed the back roads through the enormous Belo Russian forests. His ultimate goal was to reach any road to Smolensk—mainly because the transmission before Simcha destroyed the radio indicated that the furious vanguard of Red Army attacks were emanating from just west of that city.

At the break of foggy dawn, his trusty chestnut mount stumbled hard and fell over a fallen tree. Its front legs, shin bones sickeningly protruding, were obviously broken. The pain had to be excruciating as the horse issued forth a wailing whinny. Branko, only slightly shaken, had no choice but to immediately put the animal out of his misery.

The former hard-riding cavalryman of the Austro-Hungarian army and avid rider had never shot a horse. Cringing as he aimed his revolver between the horse's soulful eyes, Branko squeezed off two rounds. He then wept.

It had been nearly two weeks since he parted with Simcha and other comrades who pledged to go along with their commander. To where, no one knew exactly. But after the order to join-up with the nearest military units, every partisan element throughout the German-occupied Ukraine or Belo Russia was heading east to meet-up with the advancing Red Army. Some, of course, were going back to whatever was left of home or chancing entry into a rare neutral country.

In reality, the nearest countries fitting this label were Switzerland to the west and Turkey to the south. All others were combatants with varying degrees of participation under Germany's far-reaching axis. The Romanians and the Hungarians were largely pro-Nazi whose troops had fought not-so-gallantly alongside the Wehrmacht since the invasion. In the Baltic SSR's, Belo Russia and the Ukraine, murderous Hitler helpers were everywhere. Running into any of their blood-thirsty roving bands meant sudden death.

Ironically, once the Russians rid their Motherland of the retreating Nazis, these ethnics would easily blend back into the population. But for now, lethal problems abounded for partisans of any stripe—*Zhids* in particular.

Branko was as well-armed as an individual could be and if need be intended to fight to his last breath. In almost as critical a scenario as facing the enemy, Branko was constantly considering about how to present himself to an allied Russian soldier. He prayed that any such encounter would be with a rational-thinking officer rather than a trigger-happy sharpshooter.

After having put down his horse, he dawdled in the forest, resting his aching body for a few days. He munched on the meager rations of food he had brought along and sipped sparingly from his canteen. His thoughts, once again, turned longingly to fantasies of reaching home. He had colorful visions of being in Timoshenko's Kremlin office, recounting his adventures while with the Maccabees and perhaps talking to Edith, Jesse or Shayndl on a patched-in radio-phone.

Coming out of his reverie he chastised himself that time was of the essence. He didn't want to allow this self-indulgent exercise any longer. He had to reach the advancing Russian army, soon, and day-dreaming about the effort just wouldn't do.

Reality, he knew, was his only ticket to Moscow and then home.

Several kilometers and two days earlier—when he had been comfortably mounted—he had passed a peasant farm with a faint light in the window. He hadn't noticed any signs of life in the early evening moonlight. Even though the little farm had not escaped the ravages of battle, the scene had been peaceful enough. In the off-chance that they would sell him a horse, he now contemplated backtracking to the farm. He had a fair amount of rubles and didn't imagine having to pay more than fifty for a horse. That was, of course, if they even had one they would sell.

Then again, he thought, *who would "they" turn out to be? Friend, foe or indifferent? Tomorrow I'll take another look.*

A disastrous decision of the highest magnitude.

In what was left of the summer heat, the odor of his now rotting horse was accompanied with swarms of black flies and buzzing mosquitoes. Branko had avoided the unpleasantness by moving at least a kilometer deeper into the pleasant-smelling pine groves. A good sleep, beginning at dusk of his second day afoot and arising before dawn of the third day, gave him the resolve needed for the hike back to the farm.

For nourishment, a piece of stale rye, a crumbling salty cracker and an apple that had seen better days had to suffice. From the last parachute drop some weeks before, he had a reasonable Russian version of an American *Milky Way* candy bar. It was the culinary piece-de-resistance, providing a sugar rush and newfound energy. He hid his bedroll, put his identifying papers under a pile of pine needles, and pressed on toward the targeted destination.

As the farmstead came into sight, Branko had been trekking for two hours according to his wind-up Bulova. He guessed that this was likely a small part of one of the many collectives that suffered the scorched earth policy of the invaders. The dilapidated house looked as though it could be blown over by a huffing and puffing human and there was still nothing in sight. He edged up to a windowless frame and what he saw gave him nervous pause.

A lit candle, three mugs presumably holding tea, and three bed rolls on the floor.

The grassy plot around the house was knee deep in weeds, and a small cultivated field was lying fallow. Conversely, dozens of corn stalks at the rear of the house looked healthy and over-ready for shucking. As a habitual precaution, Branko had taken his revolver from his waistband and cocked it.

That was the last aggressive move he would make for some time to come.

The inhabitants had seen him coming around the bend in the trail and secreted themselves in the back room. At a given moment one of them leaped out and grabbed Branko from the rear by his arms, forcing him to drop the revolver. His other weapon, the automatic machine pistol strapped over his shoulder, was yanked from him and quickly rendered useless. His sixty-eight-year-old firm, but aching body, was pinned to the ground by the brawniest of the three *mumzerim*.

Why don't they just kill me here and now, Branko wondered.

After searching his pockets and dragging Branko into the poor-excuse for a barn, they spoke an unaccented Russian/Ukrainian dialect, making it easier for Branko to decipher their remarks. His native childhood Russian and that which he had picked up in two years of daily conversation with his fellow *partisaners,* served him well in this rather untenable predicament.

"You are not Russian, pig? What the hell and who the hell are you, uncle?"

Struggling for the proper words, Branko threw caution to the winds and told some partial truths, as if it would make any difference.

"I'm a native of this region, but have lived in America for many years."

"*Amyereekanyets?* Ha! You expect we should believe that lie?

"Your communist comrades probably sent you to language school to learn," interrupted one of the other two. "But you still have a Russian tone to your speech. *Amyereekanyets!* So much the better!"

Branko had sized them up quickly. They were youngsters, Ukrainian Nationalists, anti-Soviets, collaborating with the Germans insofar as they could. Simcha had learned that these bands would occasionally turn-in Russian captives for a handsome fee from the occupying Nazis. As for *Zhids*, that might be a different story. On the other hand, an American General could be a prize with big money thrown-in. There was no way for them to know that, naturally—not unless reward notices had been posted by the Wehrmacht and S.S. hereabouts. Branko knew he had to be extra careful with the young thugs.

The three captors left the barn where they had tied Branko to a post amid stacks of hay. Looking just beyond the hay, he could now make out a grizzly scene. It looked like three bodies entwined, myriad blood splotches and no sign of life.

The poor bastards who lived here, no doubt, reasoned the disgusted Branko. *These mercenaries have as much compassion as a dead amoeba. Am I going to join that pile soon? Maybe the American bit has given them reason to think it over.*

In short order the three young brigands returned while sharing a bottle of vodka.

"We are not going to waste precious ammunition on you, *Amyereekanyet!*" one of them said to Branko. "But you'll bring a handsome bag of rubles for us. The Germans pay well for stray dogs, and you, *tovarisch,* are nothing more than that to us—or to them, we think."

Branko was relieved when he translated the, "good news," and struggled to his feet when they untied him. To his surprise, he was marched to the rear of the partially roofless barn where there sat an old 1928 Mercedes truck; It was popular throughout Europe. The German army had fleets of them, new and old, and a Wehrmacht or S.S. Officer had probably given it to these Ukes for hauling their prey —either that or they had stolen it, Branko figured.

"No reward for the peasants you dispatched so neatly back there?" asked Branko as he was being re-tied and roughly shoved into the back of the truck. The barred tail gate was then locked, and the heftiest member of the band answered with a smirk: "No, *Amyereekanyets, droog moi,* they don't pay for commissars, peasants or *Zhids!*"

Branko was evidently not yet thought of as any of the three inhuman species.

The truck, with springs and shocks long overdue for replacement, bounced over the country roads of Belo Russia, all still under weakening Nazi control. The captors had given a full canteen to

Branko, and some strips of dried meat. After two hours, Branko could see they were driving through a sizeable occupied town on the banks of a river. He caught the name on a sign—*Brest-Litovsk*. On Simcha's regional maps it had appeared to be a major railhead. Brest-Litovsk had been Russian, and then Polish, and then reverted to Russia after 1918. Branko figured it was now an important staging area for the occupiers—perhaps as a critical supply line between the Fatherland and its back-stepping troops.

Having been stopped only once during the journey, Branko assumed that the "boys" were well-known at the sentry posts they had passed.

What this meant to him and his well-being was an uneasy thought. He was in a frustrating dilemma, fraught with speculation—none of it good. He even began to feel that the best thing would be to reveal himself as *General Branko Horvitch*, stating exactly who he was. The only qualm was that he knew damn-well Berlin would make this a big and embarrassing item of propaganda news. To be sure, Goebbels and his Propaganda Ministry would squeeze this for all it was worth. With their backs against the wall the Germans could be expected to grasp for any straws on which they could lay their hands.

Hitler will piss his pants in sheer ecstasy at the prospect of announcing that they've captured an American General, Branko thought. In that one split second, he decided to remain anonymous insofar as he was able.

The vehicle crossed over a bridge spanning a river that Branko remembered as the *River Bug (Boog)* on Simcha's map. The poorly paved road, potholes at every turn, passed through a village with a faded sign reading, *Swavatyce* (Swa-vaticheh). They paralleled the Bug for another two hours and then came to a stop in a clearing with road signs pointing to *Lublin* and *Zamosc*.

Another truck had parked here and its cargo of twenty ghostly, ragged men were loaded onto Branko's heretofore private transportation. This time, two guards with machine pistols positioned themselves in the rear compartment with the twenty-one prisoners while the three captors stayed in the cab. Branko quickly surveyed the situation and ruled it pure suicide to try and overpower the guards.

Besides, he noticed both had their machine pistol safety levers off. A few bursts from each would cut everyone in half. All he could do is hope that no one would be foolhardy enough to try this.

Rattling down the byway they came to a stop at a sentry post. The sign on the guard shack was freshly painted in black on white...

SOBIBOR

CONFRONTATIONS   14

Washington D.C.
January 24, 1931

As Luce promised, the January 22nd issue of his popular, *Time,* hit the newsstands. Before Branko even saw a copy, there were telephone calls and telegrams. During lunchtime almost the entire War College staff filled-up his approachable, "open door" office. The cheers—and even a few jeers—were not exactly music to the Commandant's ears. But for the most part, he knew it was well-intentioned.

Sergeant Bill Winslow taped a rolled-up piece of paper on a broom stick, serving as a microphone—as if interviewing him for Movietone News. Others asked for autographs and whether they were sincere or mocking his embarrassed response was always along the lines of, "Aw, gee fellas." One old-time faculty member, who had always been stuffy and serious, impersonated Cecil B. DeMille while beckoning the General to drop everything for the next train to Hollywood film stardom alongside Joan Crawford.

Edith Wilson dropped-off a big bouquet. The card read, *From Tootsie Pfefferman, a long-time admirer.*

Even Larry Lincoln got into the act, bowing and saying, "Exalted Potentate, your Oldsmobile limousine awaits your presence!"

Branko indeed did have an appointment at the State Department, otherwise this craziness would have gone on *ad infinitum.*

Among the Telegrams and Cables:

```
ARE YOU THE SAME BRANKO HORVITCH I KNEW IN FRANCE?
YOU'RE A REGULAR GROWN-UP NOW, AREN'T YOU?
BILL DONOVAN


LAST TIME I SAW YOU, YOUR FACE WAS FULL OF MUD AND YOUR
UNIFORM WAS FILTHY AND RAGGED. CONGRATULATIONS. I EXPECT
TO BE IN WASHINGTON IN AUGUST NEXT YEAR, FOR A JUDGE'S
CONFERENCE. WILL SEE YOU THEN.
HARRY S. TRUMAN
```

BRANKO, CAN'T WAIT TO TELL PEOPLE THAT I KNOW THE TIME MAGAZINE COVER BOY. THOSE SELF-ADORING ACTORS I DIRECT AT BRATTLE STREET THEATER ARE ALL ABOUT THEMSELVES. NOW I CAN TRUMP THEM!
LOVE, RIVKA

BRACHELEH! OY, OY. YOUR FACE IS ALL OVER PARIS. YOU NEVER TOLD ME THIS WAS HAPPENING. A BARUCHEH AUF DEIN KEPPELEH, SWEETHEART.
YOUR LOVING TANTE SHAYNDL

HEARTIEST CONGRATULATIONS, BRANKO. WE ALL LOVE YOU!
THE FUSGEYER NYC CONTINGENT

HEY, BOSS, UP HERE IN SCRANTON PEOPLE ACTUALLY READ, EVEN TIME MAGAZINE. YOU LOOK GREAT. BEEN MEANING TO MAKE A JAUNT DOWN TO D.C. MAYBE SOMEDAY.
THE GOLUBS

I CAN NOW SAY WE HAD DINNER WITH A TIME COVER HERO. AGAIN, THANK YOU FOR WHAT YOU'VE DONE AND ARE DOING. OUR HOSPITAL IS BENEFITTING IMMEASURABLY FROM YOUR GALLANT EFFORTS.
DR. AND MRS. E.B. DU BOIS
NEW ORLEANS

WOW! SO NICE TO SEE YOU ON TIME MAGAZINE'S COVER AT OUR CORNER DRUGSTORE. WE AND THE COUNTRY'S VETS WILL NEVER FORGET YOU, SIR! GUTHRIE WESTERN UNION IS GIVING US FREE USE!
BOBBY RAY SUMMERS,
GUTHRIE, OKLAHOMA
STANLEY HAGENWORTH
PERKINS, OKLAHOMA

```
GREAT PICTURE, GENERAL. I ALWAYS KNEW YOU WOULD
MAKE SOMEBODY'S COVER. BY THE WAY, I'M NOW HEAD
ST. LOUIS CARDINAL SCOUT FOR THE UPPER MIDWEST.
COME VISIT DULUTH, MY BASE.
ALBIE WHITE (AVI SEMELWEISS)


BRANKO, GRACE AND I ENJOYED YOUR FRIENDSHIP AND
NOW YOU'RE FAMOUS AND WE'RE RETIRED COUNTRY
BUMPKINS. GOD BLESS YOU!
CALVIN AND GRACE COOLIDGE
PLYMOUTH, VERMONT
```

And there were many others, along with phone calls and letters by the dozens. Branko knew that the arrival of the new class of War College students in March would, no doubt, reinvigorate the hoopla. It was not something he sought or to which he looked forward. But he was, after all, human and privately enjoyed some of the attention. He was quite adaptable in coping that way.

January 24, 1931

His old friend Major Harold Lerner, in the Adjutant General's office, finally awarded Branko a green light in response to his mystery query.

He was now free to participate in any business transaction, just so long it didn't involve the United States Military. If it were to concern a foreign country, Lerner also indicated, more research might be necessary.

Just in case there were wrinkles that might remotely affect Branko, the Major asked to be kept abreast of developments every step of the way.

This clean bill of health was all Branko needed. He was now comfortably ready for the wheeling and dealing shenanigans of the Squire of Hyannisport.

As he had suspected, there wasn't much of a wait. Returning from a weekend of Jesse's baseball games in Charlottesville, Branko was informed by Sargent Winslow that a Mr. Kennedy made a tentative appointment for whenever he was free during the week of June 10th. The timing was acceptable, so Branko immediately wrote a letter to his boys in Oklahoma, Bobby Ray Summers and Stanley Hagenworth.

This can be one helluva boon to those fine young lads, thought a smiling Branko. *I'm really going to enjoy this!*

**From the desk of
The Commandant, U.S. Army War College
Washington, D.C.**

*Bobby Ray Summers
169 High Street
Guthrie, Oklahoma*

Hi ya Bobby Ray:
First of all, thank you so much for the telegram. So nice of you and Stanley to think of me. I have yet to live down all the commotion that went on with that silly jackass cover picture. I have to admit though, I had a barrel of fun!
Now, to get down to business, I need your invaluable help, An acquaintance of mine is in the market for some potential producing properties in your neck of the woods. The man is exceedingly wealthy, in fact damned rich. He is known in financial circles throughout our country and has been watching for distressed properties since the crash. He feels that by now he can gobble up all he can eat for fractions on a dollar. He may be right from what I've heard. You would know better than I do. He has read of my travels in Oklahoma and my interest in these sort of things. He's coming to see me next week and I plan on

referring him to you, and Stanley. I'll find out more exactly what he's planning after the visit.

I will present both of you as, "local experts" and I'm not too far off about that. I don't think that Stanley has the depth of knowledge you have demonstrated, but he's been in the oil business for a goodly part of his working years. He knows the territory and equipment operations. Obviously I was deeply impressed with your grasp of wildcating, in particular. Hang onto that detailed map you showed me, B.R.

You mentioned Tom Slick. I have since learned a good deal of his history and why he has been known by the affectionate title, "Mr. Suck-it-outa-the-ground." God knows he must drink oil for breakfast. I want you to call on him in Oklahoma City, introduce yourself and tell him a Mr. Kennedy will be coming to see him about buying some good fields. Following that, when Kennedy gets to meet you boys, he'll then want to meet Slick somewhere down the line.

I know you can handle this well, B.R. and I'm sure Stanley can be of help, too, especially now that you tell me he is responding well to that new pulmonary medication. I'm sending him a shorter letter and I suggest the two of you get together a few times before Kennedy arrives. I'm giving Kennedy your address. I'll also give him the phone number of the A & P in your neighborhood (334-527) where you can receive messages. Remember, that's the way we got together with no problems. Please alert the market that you'll be getting a call from a

Mr. Joseph Kennedy and for them to get you the message immediately. Damn, I wish you had a phone, and maybe when all of this is said and done you'll have that and a lot more.

By the way, the vet bonus is not making any real progress, so don't count on it. I strongly feel that vets like you around the country will march on Washington within a year. I dread that for many reasons I'm not free to discuss in detail, but if it had a code name, it would be, "Armageddon."

Any questions you have, please place a collect call to me at my home on the College grounds any time after 7:00 p.m. my time, which is one hour ahead of you, District 9-799-435.

Well, soldier, that's all I know now, but the moment Kennedy leaves my office on June 10, I will be back to you via the A & P. Be available and call collect to the above number right away. If it's early in the day, try my office number, District 9-768-339, and Sgt. Winslow, my clerk-aide, will accept the call and put you through.

Let's pray that all goes well, Bobby Ray!
Your comrade,
Branko Horvitch

June 1, 1931

Edith phoned and asked Branko to come over for lunch on Saturday.

"I have some great news for you, Cover Boy, c'mon over."

"Do I have to wait until tomorrow for this earth-shaking bombshell to drop?"

"Yes. It's something I care to divulge only in person. Besides, I love the fact that I can be entertaining *the* General Horvitch, without his newly-gained entourage of lovesick tootsies hanging about."

"You sure take the wind out of my starched sails, m'dear."

And so it went. He'd have to wait, and couldn't imagine for what —no idea.

The next day, Branko drove over to S Street about a half-hour before Edith had suggested. "Okay. Now tell me!"

"Absolutely not. You will sit down like the gentleman everyone mistakenly thinks you are, we'll have a light lunch lovingly prepared by the incomparable Aretha, and then I *may* possibly share the news with you."

And that was the way it was to be.

Dawdling over a cup of coffee in the drawing room, Branko awaited the word.

"I'm sailing for Europe in September," she said demurely.

"Whaaat? Europe? That is smashing news, alright. Now, tell me all!" It was more or less a mild surprise to Branko, and a pleasant one at that. Edith had been talking about taking an ocean voyage for some time now. He was truly excited for her to finally be doing it.

"I'm taking Margaret along with me. I think it's something we both need. As you know, we have a long, tense history of not getting along. I'm hoping this will somewhat repair things."

"Good idea, Edith. Now, what's the itinerary, dates leaving and returning, and so on."

"We'll be leaving for a week in New York on September 8th, take in some shows, shop a bit. Something I've wanted to do for years. On the 14th we board the Cunard liner *Mauretania* for Southampton, a week in London, off to Paree—*oo-la-la*—for two weeks. Guess what? I plan to visit Tante Shayndl."

"Bless your golden heart. That would be superb! What a wonderful gesture. I'd better not mention anything to her until late August. Otherwise, she won't sleep until you arrive. She'll start baking and cooking for a month prior. I've told you several times, Tante is the world-class model for *Yiddishe mamas* and all mothers everywhere!"

"We also plan to train down to the Riviera. Our ticket calls for return on the same ship, leaving Southampton on October 21st."

"That is some wonderful planning, Edith. I'm so happy for you and Margaret. However, I do hope you can avoid the press. When word gets out that you're in London, and especially Paris, they'll hound you. Remember, Woodrow is still a hero to the French, and his —uh—gorgeous widow will certainly be a magnetic attraction."

"I know. Maybe I can finally match you in a popularity contest, eh, kid?"

"We'll have to throw a bon voyage party in early September, Madame."

"*Oui, oui, M'sieu Commandant. Tres bien!* I'll invite Fifi Pfefferman for you!"

June 16, 1931

Kennedy Day had arrived. Bouncing into Branko's office, dapper Joe wore his usual broad and toothy smile.

Is this guy ever down? thought Branko.

This time, the New Englander shed his restraints and gave the General a hug. He said, "It's been too long a time, soldier boy. I'm still waiting for you to call on us up at the beach, but I know you are too busy earning your General's pay."

"I love the challenges of being Commandant of this fine institution, Joe. It gives me enormous satisfaction, and keeps me off the mean streets of the nation's capital."

"Well said. I'm happy for you. Not too many people I do business with can say the same thing, with money being their one and only god. I confess a tinge of guilt on that end, too. Many a day, I'd rather be at the beach. But, let's get down to business. I have a lunch date with my Massachusetts Senator—the damn bore that he is!"

"Why am I not surpised that you came here for business reasons. You're on the air, Joe, and I'm tuned-in on my RCA."

Joseph Patrick Kennedy wasted no further time and showered the General with his master plan. Not that he hadn't a long time ago given him an inkling of his aim to buy-up distressed oil properties at pennies on the dollar. Clearly a man who was among those making piles of hay out of the depression, he came to the point quickly.

"Branko, you once said that you have connections in Oklahoma who could give me the lowdown I'm looking for. Do you recall?"

Branko was well prepared to meet Kennedy point by point, quickly, with no beating around the proverbial bush. "Right Joe, two well-informed Oklahoma vets, one who lost his right arm for his country, the other who suffered severe lung problems as a result of a gas attack. They in turn, can give you some fast and solid schooling, followed by introducing you to some of the most renowned deal-makers in the business who are on the constant lookout for folks with the wherewithal to step up to the plate and act fast."

"Just what I want, old boy. Happy to see that the cover on *Time* hasn't dulled your business acumen at all! Where can we start? Both my New York and Boston partner groups have made some minor touch-and-go forays into black gold country, and now want me to close real deals in the field."

The trap was closing. This couldn't have gone better. No time for being the least bit timid, Branko asked for Joe to get his chief accountant in New York City on the phone.

Joe hesitated.

Branko insisted.

Within a few anxious moments, Branko had dictated basic terms to Kennedy, who relayed everything verbatim to the accountant with the final instructions to have the company legal beagle in the same office draw up the proper papers and send them to Branko's office post haste. Branko gave him a firm deadline, one week away.

Again hesitation.

Again insistence.

Kennedy knew very well that the oil land rush had been on since earlier in the year, and thus far few—if any—sizeable deals were consummated. He wanted to be the first, or at least get in heavy before the opportunities began to fade.

Undoubtedly, Kennedy had a giant-sized portfolio of cashable assets to spend and pompously pointed this out more than a few times during the meeting. Each time, Branko had to force a serious expression while enjoying a bit of the comic opera. In reality, Kennedy's anxiety was based on the promise by Democratic party bosses that he would be made the first head of a much needed securities department, to be established as soon as the 1932 election finally returned a democrat to the White House, as expected. In the meantime, it would be critical for him to avoid any lengthy, unfavorable escapades. He could easily disperse his oil income into voluminous family trusts during the full year before the election.

Branko saw this as a master chess game, with Kennedy vying and dying for a quick check-mate. He would root for him.

Before he left for lunch, Kennedy asked Branko to join him for a night on the town.

The Commandant politely declined while actually thinking, *Not about to*. The last thing he wanted was for some kind of compromising situation to ruin the deal that was speeding ahead.

Quite assured that Major Lerner's assessment of legality was foolproof, Branko sat back in his chair, hands behind his head and smugly smiling. He looked like the hero who had rescued a damsel from the clutches of the villain.

June 23, 1931

Joe Kennedy phoned to say he would meet with Branko on the 27th in order to finalize the contract. Meanwhile, Branko was expecting a visit from Major Lerner to go over it with him in advance. Within an hour of arrival, Lerner gave an enthusiastic thumbs-up and took the extra copies with him. In true lawyer fashion, the Major didn't trust leaving anything of the sort around the College. For safekeeping he also wanted the original contract after Branko and Kennedy signed it. Branko thanked him profusely for his valuable help in the matter.

Indicating how anxious Joe was, he hadn't permitted his New York attorney to make anything more than a cosmetic change to Branko's terms.

Those terms included 12% of gross income from any and all

properties that Kennedy acquired through the efforts of Bobby Ray Summers and Stanley Hagenworth Per Branko's specific instructions each time, said percentage would be disbursed monthly from Kennedy's New York office. These instructions would stay in place until such time as Branko issued a Change Notice to Kennedy's accountant.

Bobby Ray and Stanley would each receive off the top an exclusive agent fee totaling 2%. As Independent Trustee, Branko, would oversee the disbursement of funds totaling the balance of 8%. These funds would be deposited into specified entities whenever the monies were forwarded to Kennedy's New York office. Obviously, Branko didn't want Kennedy presently knowing about the recipients to whom payment would later be directed—hence Branko's contractual inclusion of the Change Notice. Greed, Branko knew, would temporarily guide Kennedy into thinking that Branko was taking for himself a major portion of the money.

The list of recipients was something that Branko intended Kennedy to learn with the filing of the Change Notice. And the General mightily wished to be within earshot when Kennedy would hear of the following Change Notice list:

> B'nai Brith International, Anti-Defamation League Fund, K Street, Washington (2%).
>
> The Washington Hebrew Congregation, directly to the Eva Horvitch Education Fund (2%).
>
> The Sidwell Friends School, Eva Horvitch Library and Scholarship fund (2%).
>
> Remaining 2% to be equally divided among Shayndl Ohrbach in Paris, Flint Negro Hospital Equipment and Nurses Training Fund in New Orleans, c/o Dr. Samuel E.B. Du Bois, and to General Branko Horvitch as Trustee's compensation.

The meeting four days later was merely a formality. Kennedy and Branko each signed two copies and Joe announced that he would be leaving for Oklahoma in two weeks.

Branko gave him all the contact information, they shook hands and that was that.

As soon as Kennedy walked out the door, Branko was on the phone. He placed a call to the Guthrie A & P, alerting Bobby Ray that everything was finalized and to expect to hear from Kennedy within a few weeks.

Having already met with Tom slick at his Oklahoma City offices, Bobby Ray happily reported that Slick was pleasantly anticipating the meeting with Mr. Kennedy—of whom he had never even heard. That was very welcome news to Branko. It was better that Slick knew little or nothing about the machinations of one Mr. Kennedy. Less was certainly more in this case.

Bobby Ray also proudly shared that there were at least 135 properties just in North Central Oklahoma that he could bring in for Kennedy. Bobby knew a goodly number of the wildcatters and knew that they had been marking time waiting for offers of modest salvation, not having any substantial money to spend on production. Very few wildcatters in Oklahoma had a cash flow that would permit anything but oil well maintenance at this time. Foreclosures were rampant and they believed that only a true messiah could save the day. Little did they know that one Joseph Patrick Kennedy would be winging his way to them in an American Airlines Ford Tri-Motor. In his possession he would be carrying that proverbial bagful of U.S. Dollars, which would be manna from heaven—even at cut-throat, cut-rate terms.

September 1, 1931

While Kennedy was cutting a wide swath through black gold country, he wrote Branko that he was more than satisfied with the assistance provided by the boys from Oklahoma. He was seriously thinking of hiring them as trouble-shooters even after he cornered the market—at substantial salaries. Branko dearly loved hearing this which was even beyond his highest hopes. He also wrote that heavy money would be rolling in right after the first cluster of wells began daily, steady pumping.

He had even given Stanley $100 to buy his wife Nora and the kids some clothes. The following weekend he took them all out for a rib dinner at The Cattlemen's Barbecue Heaven, along with Bobby Ray, his new girlfriend and his mother.

Branko was elated that the plan certainly couldn't be going any better.

Damn, he thought, *maybe everyone contractually involved, including myself, will be blessed with a little gelt.*

But all the time, devilishly, he had one picture in mind—the day that Joe would learn who some of the Trust beneficiaries actually were.

The next Saturday evening, the gala Bon Voyage party for Edith's European trip was held at the Wilson Home. It was a snazzy, dress-up affair befitting transatlantic voyages and so Branko trotted out his rarely-worn dress uniform.

Edith and daughter Margaret were positively radiant in their full-length gowns. Jack Steel wore his dress togs and Mrs. Steel, with a fourth child on the way, was in a maternity dress. Aretha and Larry Lincoln, dressed as party goers, helped with serving delicious *hors d'ouevres*, but everything else was buffet style—including dessert.

Guests who frequented Edith's home knew very well that Aretha and her husband were treated as family friends. Additionally, word had long-ago circulated that many times Larry rode in the backseat of the touring car while the General drove. After the initial shock and inevitable tongue wagging, no one seemed to any longer give it a second thought. Of course, Jim-Crowism in and around the nation's capital never quit but Branko's quietly defiant actions put an unusual damper on it in some circles.

About to enter their senior year at UVa, Jesse and Sara made the scene and were suitably gushed over. The entire Wilson family was present and along with Branko enjoyed one another's company after so long a time apart.

Even though Edith still eschewed the drinking of spirits in her home as long as prohibition was still in force, there were a few husbands who surreptitiously brought out their snort flasks—like little boys sneaking first cigarettes.

Jesse and Sara planned on returning to Charlottesville during the following week and departed ahead of the usual lingering pack. Branko wished them good-luck and hugged them.

"Once more I have to say I am proud of you," Branko said to Jess. "Foregoing summer baseball in order to help your dad with the shoe store was mature and commendable. Now you two go knock-off some great senior grades! I want some *cum laude* graduates in my family!"

The evening was one of fun and good cheer, providing a memorable send-off for Edith and Margaret, complete with a noisy, off-season chorus of, *Auld Lang Syne* and shouts of, "Bon Voyage! Bon Voyage!"

Cynthia Sharman, Society Editor of the *Post*, had crashed the gathering as she was wont to do and looked aghast when the prankish Branko asked her to take a photo of Edith, Aretha and Larry, standing by the punch bowl.

"Now be sure to print that, Cyntha," whispered Branko. He smiled charmingly, putting an arm around her bare shoulders. "And tell Ned I said so."

She did, in the Morning Edition column, with the caption: *Mrs. Wilson with Mr. and Mrs. Lincoln.*

The *Post* readership raised some eyebrows and giggles over that one.

Rue de Roi de Sicile
Paris, France
October 8, 1931

> *My dearest Branko:*
> *Having Edith Wilson visiting is so special. Yesterday she took me to lunch. This evening she and Margaret will be here soon to collect*

me for the ballet. Ay, yi yi! I feel like a Queen.

She is a darling! No airs, no formalities, just honest love and friendship. My friends are so envious, having a famous American First Lady call on me. My nephew's dear friend, yet! She even brought Charles a Woodrow Wilson Presidential Commemoration Coin. He's so proud, I think he'll sleep with it under his pillow. Oy vay!

Dovid writes from Palestine that there have been a continuing series of violent Arab attacks on the smaller villages in the Galilee. They seem to leave the Kibbutzim alone as they are so well fortified. I worry about Dovid and his darling family every day. Can I help it? I'm a Yiddishe mama! There is the door knocker, they're here .

Edith wants to write a few words. I'll finish tonight when we get back from the ballet.

Hey, there, soldier, how's it going? Are you eating properly? I told Aretha to expect you every now and then. We are having a grand trip, Paris is heavenly and these visits to Shayndl have been magical. She's as lovely as I imagined her, and it's easy to see your softer side in her demeanor. I can imagine how she'll ooh and aahh at the theater tonight. She says she has never been. We'll go out for an after theater supper, also. I did send you a few notes from London and I'll write more later. Send me a letter to the Ritz Hotel here in Paris and I'll probably get it when we return from the Riviera for two days before going on to Southampton for the voyage home. I still have an element of guilt being here in the midst of our lingering depression. But the pep talk you gave me before I left helped to dissuade it noticeably. Do I miss you? Here in Paris? Nah!
Edith Wilson

Dear Branko, I'm back from a most memorable evening. The performance was a breathtaking Swan Lake. The costumes, the scenery, the beautiful dancers and the orchestra were altogether outstanding. (Nu, my English writing is getting better and better. No?) Tonight was the monthly dinner meeting for Charles' retired banker's club, so at least I know he ate. Actually, he does a pretty fair job in the kitchen when I'm not here. Now he wants to know all about the ballet before we go to bed. Edith and Margaret each gave him a kiss "hello" tonight, so he's a smug and happy yidl! They both looked so very special in their formal dresses. I tried not to look like a schlepp so I wore my best High Holiday outfit.

The car was from the American embassy with a handsome uniformed driver. Oy, could I get used to this! When she arrived in Paris, Edith merely walked into the embassy to say hello to Ambassador Cannon, an old friend from your State Department during her husband's time as President. He insisted on arranging a car and driver for her personal use while here.

Again I say, Branko, why not Edith? Okay, I can tell you'll be frowning when you read this from your meddling yente auntie. Not another word. My lips are zipped shut, and I'm lying!

With all my love for my favorite American,
Tante

November 11, 1931

The District always had a special parade on Armistice Day and today was no exception—cold and blustery though it was. The War College faculty and staff and many of its current students, led by the Commandant, Brigadier General Branko Horvitch, joined veterans from a dozen or so American Legion and VFW posts. Troops from Fort McNair, Fort Belvoir, Virginia, "middies" from The Naval Academy and the 322nd Maryland National Guard. Of course, the popular U.S. Marine Marching Band from Quantico was on hand. Also present were several high school and college bands, complete with high-stepping baton twirlers. It all made for a colorful display marching down Pennsylvania Avenue.

President Hoover, his cabinet and a bi-partisan Congressional contingent all stood on the reviewing stand opposite the White House. Branko caught the eye of his dear buddy Colonel Jack Steel who was leading White House aides in step with The Daughters of the American Revolution (DAR). They were followed by open touring cars carrying Civil War nonagenarians and Spanish-American vets.

The Boy Scouts, Girl Scouts and George Washington University's R.O.T.C were in full force, while the spirit of American patriotism filled the air—even in the midst of the greatest economic disaster in history. This was a display of resiliency that still made the American Republic the envy of struggling democracies throughout the world.

The parade continued over the bridge leading into Arlington National Cemetery where homage was paid at the Tomb of the Unknown Soldier, with the Marine band led by John Philip Sousa. After playing a soulful rendition of taps they launched into a stirring and upbeat, *Star and Stripes Forever.*

At seventy-seven, Sousa as a guest conductor, had lost none of the renowned panache he exhibited when leading the band in the 1890's. He had since been conducting his own band, from which he had recently retired. As he was no longer accepting the conducting requests that still came from all over the country, his appearance was all he more special. President Hoover and General Horvitch thrilled the onlookers when they smartly saluted, "The March King" in a fond farewell.

Larry Lincoln drove Branko back to the Wilson House to warm-up with hot tea and some of Aretha's best cookie recipes. He had only seen Edith once since her return from Europe and now she finally had her film developed. Branko thoroughly enjoyed seeing Tante Shayndl and Charles. They looked well and happy in the photos.

Branko commended Edith on her photographic talent as shown in some professional-looking shots of London, Paris and the Riviera. Branko privately admitted to Edith that some of his long-past wanderlust was at least temporarily fueled by these seductive photos.

In the late afternoon, Branko returned to his home just as the phone was ringing

It was Kennedy calling. After months in the oil fields—where he had been in almost daily contact with Branko—he was now in New York City. He was putting together final documents that would sew up his Joseph Kennedy/Tom Slick Partnership with sole ownership of 83 producing wells. An oil-thirsty America, depression and all, insured substantial income would already begin rolling in this month.

A week earlier Kennedy's Chief Accountant, Sid Millman, had let slip that aside from the percentages accumulating for the accounts of Bobby Ray Summers and Stanley Hagenworth, the four "Horvitch entities" had already been credited with $14,000. This had been the news that assured Branko of Kennedy's certain success in his black gold ventures. Kennedy's accounting staff would issue regurlar disbursements to the Horvitch group right after the first of the year.

As a result of the previous week's news, Branko had stopped by the B'nai Brith offices to alert the International President, Albert Cohen, that there would be a steady income flow specifically designated for the Anti-Defamation League fund. Cohen was stunned to hear this and when he asked Branko for further clarification, the Commandant merely shrugged it off by saying: "Sir, just think of it as something from an anonymous gift horse who so believes that the ADL is doing gallant work in a sense of good will that he wanted to help support it."

Cohen appreciated a good build-up as well as the next man, and waited a beat for the Commandant to come clean.

"The checks will come from the Kennedy-Slick Foundation—signed by a Sidney R. Millman in New York. As you know, Mr. Cohen, there are hundreds of benefactors, even in an economically depressed America, who wish to remain behind the scenes while doing God's good work." Cohen could do nothing but shake his head in disbelief. Branko thought he might again contact Cohen—when the checks began to roll in. If only to hear the anticipated incredulousness in Cohen's tone.

As for the immediate phone call from Kennedy, his conversation sounded pre-occupied. Evidently there was something nagging at him. He finally came out with it: "Branko, there's something puzzling with your list of recipients.

"Oh?" came Branko's innocent response.

"Sid showed them to me and I couldn't understand why you were having money sent to that Jewish fraternal outfit in Washington—and what the hell is anti-defamation? Eh? The Washington synagogue? Sidwell Friends School? That Negro hospital in New Orleans? And who the hell is this Shayndl fellow in Paris? Illuminate me, if you will."

"Sorry, Joe, but I will not."

That was good for a blessed moment of confused Kennedy silence.

Branko went on: "None of this is germane to our association. However, I do think it's important for you to realize what the ADL is all about—because, indirectly, you are now supporting this honorable B'nai Brith fund."

"What the hell do you mean by that?"

"As I was saying, Mr. Kennedy, sir, the ADL was established about twenty years ago to fight anti-Semitism and all other bigotry. They work to improve and promote understanding as well as better relationships between religions and creeds throughout the world—good Catholics and good Jews notwithstanding.

"You do agree that this goal is an important one, don't you, Joe? Of course, you do. The Pope, priests, bishops, ministers, rabbis, heads of state all over the world have publically endorsed this most noble undertaking. Why not you and me, eh, Joe?"

"Branko, you can do whatever the hell you want to with your share. But I just don't get it, old boy!"

"May I digress? Once your Archbishop William Henry Cardinal O'Connell of Boston hears of this—and I shall see that he does—I would think you'll become a veritable saint in his eyes. As luck would have it, Father Francis Patrick Duffy of The Fighting 69th and I broke stale bread with Cardinal O'Connell during his several visits to the battlefields of France in 1918. He and Duffy ran around the front lines, holding mass in the open as if the Germans were using pea-shooters. Frankly gutsy, but both certifiably nuts! I always had three of my platoon's best sharpshooters covering their rumps. Finally, Saint Joseph, I wouldn't be surprised if a Papal Mass in Rome someday commends your heralded generosity, in the name of The Father, The Son and The Holy Ghost."

Branko was sure he heard a loud, gulping gasp on the other end. He grinned from ear to ear as he quietly said, "Bye, Joe!"

One diabolical caper...over!

Meanwhile, another election year was bearing down on Washington. A restless and depression-beaten public was clamoring for change. The Democrats had the momentum going with them and not a pundit in the land could minimize their chances for recapturing the White House. Increasingly, it looked like Franklin Delano Roosevelt would be the front runner for the Democratic party, with the ill-fated incumbent opposing him.

May 24, 1932

For a short but satisfying weekend in Charlottesville, Branko joined Jesse's father and step-mother to attend the young man's graduation from the University of Virginia. Sarah's family was there for the big day, also. The lovebirds graduated with honors and, naturally, this pleased their guests. Jesse also announced that he was asked to try-out for a team in the Appalachian League. He promised his dad and Branko that if he made it, he would probably only give it one year just to get the experience of playing professional baseball. He was one of three teammates to have opted to try out in Bluefield, West Virginia that next week.

Edith had not thought it appropriate to attend the ceremony and so on Sunday night, back in Washington, she hosted a lovely dinner. In attendance were the two graduates as guests of honor, their families and selected friends. Branko thought it was a beautiful gesture. An evening of good fellowship was enjoyed by all.

The Bernsteins were nearly overwhelmed by being asked to dinner by the former First Lady. She was, as usual, gracious, making the evening for the Kanters and the Bernsteins one that started out as strangers and ended in friendships.

Jesse had no plans for graduate school at that moment, but he promised Branko that after a summer of minor league baseball, he would look into an internship with the State Department. Not surprisingly, Sarah had already been invited to take one there.

Fair enough, thought Branko, *if he can make the team.*

June 1, 1932

More than ever, veterans around the country were showing anger toward Congress and the President for avoiding the proposed bonus action.

For the past several years, Branko feared it would someday come down to this and now it was happening. There were countless demonstrations in cities, towns and hamlets throughout the country. So far, at least, there was not one report of violence or anything indicating the civil unrest that was most assuredly just beneath the surface. However, in this election year, with small groups of vets forming, "traveling platoons" to converge on Washington, there was certain to be an eventual confrontation. Sooner, not later.

They came from every corner of America and were likened to the four thundering horsemen of the apocalypse—an eschatological allegory in a proverbial cloud of smothering dust. Allegory? More than that! The horses of pestilence, war, famine and death? These American veterans knew death, war and hunger. And they knew of the diseases mainly afflicting the poor.

They used every conveyance available to them, including their poorly-shod feet. Upwards of 15,000 vets and their families set-up makeshift camps around Washington, wherever they could. The majority concentrated on an isolated, marshy Anacostia River strip in the southeast of the district known as the, *Flats* and soon to be known as, "Hooverville." They proceeded to use a wide variety of scrap building materials for some semblance of shelter that they had rummaged from a nearby dump, ignoring any and all codes. They were intent on sending a clear message to congress: *"We are here and we ain't giong home until you do us right!"*

General Horvitch immediately sought and received the approval of Secretary of War Patrick Hurley to open up the College to house a number of families. Those in the flats were only two miles away and Hurley arranged to bus-in mothers with their younger children as well as pregnant women. While helping to settle them in the barracks, Sergeant Winslow noted that never in his life had he seen such abject poverty. Most of their husbands and fathers had been out of work since the early days of the Great Depression. With the College year on a short hiatus until September classes, the Commandant lobbied every staff and faculty member to share the already reduced dining hall rations with the families—especially the children.

Calling from her home, at Branko's urging, Edith Wilson had already contacted every dairy in town for milk and cheese donations. Within a matter of days, overwhelming support poured in from relevant government agencies, private citizens and a number of lawmakers from both sides of the aisle. Meanwhile, Edith used her influence to appeal for help via a broadcast on radio station WKWD. In response, the phones rang for more than an hour.

The Red Cross also responded with its usual menu of milk, hot coffee and doughnuts, appearing at seven of the campsites. And then there were the citizens—the people of the district who were quick to show their unconditional support for the vets in their aggressive endeavors.

These God-sent acts of mercy did not go unnoticed by Ned McLean and his *Washington Post*. His charmingly eccentric wife Evalyn had already made herself quite well known to the Bonus

Expeditionary Force, and her captivating column appeared in the *Post* that week:

Bonus Army Invades Washington

Last weekend I saw a dusty truck roll slowly past my house. I saw the unshaven, tired faces of the men who were riding in it standing up. A few were seated at the rear with their legs dangling over the lowered tailboard. On the side was an expanse of white cloth on which, crudely lettered in black, was a legend: BONUS ARMY.

Other trucks followed in a straggling succession and on the sidewalks of Massachusetts Avenue, where stroll most of the diplomats and the other fashionables of Washington, were some ragged hikers, wearing scraps of old uniforms. The sticks with which they strode along seemed less canes than cudgels. They were not a friendly-looking lot and I learned they were hiking and riding into the capital along each of its radial avenues; that they had come from every part of the continent. It was not lost on me that those men, passing anyone of my big houses, would see in such rich shelters a kind of challenge. I was burning because I felt that crowd of men, women, and children never should have been permitted to swarm across the continent. But I could remember when those same men, with others, had been cheered as they marched down

Pennsylvania Avenue. While I recalled those wartime parades, I was reading in the newspapers that the bonus army men were going hungry in Washington.

That night I woke up before I had been asleep an hour. I got to thinking about those poor devils marching around the capital. Then I decided that it should be a part of my son Jock's education to see and try to comprehend that marching. It was one o'clock, and the Capitol was beautifully lighted. I wished then for the power to turn off the lights and use the money thereby saved to feed the hungry.

When Jock and I rode among the bivouacked men I was horrified to see plain evidence of hunger in their faces; I heard them trying to cadge cigarettes from one another. Some were lying on the sidewalks, unkempt heads pillowed on their arms. A few clusters were shuffling around. I went up to one of them, a fellow with eyes deeply sunken in his head.

"Have you eaten?" I asked.

He shook his head.

Just then I saw General Glassford, superintendent of the Washington police. He said, "I'm going to get some coffee for them."

"All right," I said. "I am going to Childs'."

It was two o'clock when I walked into that white restaurant. A man came up to take my order.

"Do you serve sandwiches?" I said. "I want a thousand. And a thousand packages of cigarettes."

"But, lady—"

"I want them right away. I haven't got a nickel with me, but you can trust me. I am Mrs. McLean."

Well, he called the manager into the conference and before long they were slicing bread with a machine; and what with Glassford's coffee also (he was spending his own money) we two fed all the hungry ones who were in sight.

The next day, Walter Waters, the so-called commander, came to my house and said: "I'm desperate. Unless these men are fed, I can't say for sure what won't happen to this town."

With him was his wife, a little 93-pounder dressed as a man, her legs and feet in shiny boots. Her yellow hair was freshly marceled. She had just gotten off a bus after an interminably long ride.

I thought a bath would be a welcome change; so I took her upstairs to that guest bedroom my father had designed for King Leopold. I sent for my maid to draw a bath, and told the young woman to lie down.

"You get undressed," I said, "and while you sleep I'll have all your things cleaned and pressed."

"Oh, no," she said, "not me. I'm not giving these clothes up. I might never see them again."

Her lip was out, and so I did not argue. She threw herself down on the bed, boots and all, and I tiptoed out.

That night I telephoned to Vice-President Charlie Curtis. I told him I was speaking for Waters, who was standing by my chair. I said: "These men are in a desperate situation and unless something is done for them, unless they are fed, there is bound to be a lot of trouble. They have neither money, nor any food."

Charlie Curtis told me that he was calling a secret meeting of senators and would send a delegation of them to the House to urge immediate action on the Howell bill, providing money to send the bonus army members back to their homes.

Evalyn Walsh McLean

June 14, 1932

During the past week, Branko personally visited all of the Bonus Army encampments and shanty villages throughout the Capital. He was warmly welcomed at every turn. There were cheers, backslapping and cries of, "Talk to us, General!, talk to us!"

That's all he needed to hear and talk he did—straight from his heavy heart. Mainly, he assured them that they were within their constitutional rights as American citizens to lawfully gather and protest. They were not breaking any laws and he implored them to not do so. Of necessity, his speech was the same at each encampment and also each time he wished them well in their noble quest. This was not a case of just telling the vets something they wanted to hear. With every sense of his being, every fiber of his soul, he believed in them and their cause.

And they all knew he believed.

At one location near the Army College, retired Marine Corp General Smedley Butler, an encouraging proponent of the march, gave Branko first billing while introducing him as, "the leading advocate of veteran's rights in America." It wasn't as if the gathering hadn't known this for more than a decade, but Butler quickly added, "You see, I read *Time* magazine, too, General."

When the laughter died down, Branko, turned serious. He advised the vets to proceed with caution for the sake of safety for their enjoined families.

"I will do everything I can," he went on, "to tone down any presidential action to use the troops now stationed all around the city. But obviously I cannot guarantee it. General Douglas MacArthur, the Chief of Staff, has arranged to amass an impressive array of infantry and cavalry, including a half dozen tanks. He has sent a directive to me to meet at my office at The War College this afternoon. I'm afraid I know what's coming. We fought together in France as officers with the Fighting 69th, but that won't amount to a hill of beans in tempering his duty-bound posture if ordered to use our army against you."

What Branko did not add was that the prevailing view of many in the military was of General Douglas MacArthur as an omnipotent and omniscient character. It was a flawed and dangerous assessment.

At the prescribed time, a fleet of command cars and two truckloads of armed infantry were admitted to the College grounds. They pulled up to the administrative buildings and MacArthur, in leather campaign jacket and high laced boots, literally marched into the building where a waiting Sergeant Winslow escorted him into the Commandant's Office. They saluted each other and Branko offered his hand to shake. He should've known better. It was summarily ignored by the spit-and-polish West Pointer.

"Well, well, Brigadier General Branko Horvitch, I've been meaning to contact you, for old time's sake, since I became Chief of Staff. Not that I haven't followed your exploits since the war—I have. You've been a busy soldier, haven't you? So have I."

"I did send you a note congratulating you on your promotion to Chief of Staff, General. And by the way, I assume you've heard that Father Duffy is deathly ill up in New York, and not expected to live much longer. I received a telegram yesterday from our former comrade, Bill Donovan."

"Damn sorry to hear that. Duffy was one in a million. A true American hero. But we are both busy so I'll make this short. I'm here to tell you that we are commandeering your college to use as my Command Post and as quarters for my Fort Howard troops, for what I believe will turn into a confrontation very soon."

Branko heard the words loud and clear, stood tall and didn't hesitate for one second. He responded, "General MacArthur, this is a place of learning and I don't intend to offer it as a place of war. That's our creed, and I stand by it."

"You are refusing my request, which I can easily turn into an order. I would advise you not to make it necessary for me to go to The Secretary of War or The Commander-in-Chief."

"Mr. Hurley has long ago given me full and incontrovertible command of The United States Army War College. In fact, we have already moved into our barracks, female and child refugees from the Bonus Marcher's largest camp in Anacostia. I will not, under any circumstances, evict even one of them."

"So, in order to continue to house their sorry asses you will flirt with a court martial, General?"

It was everything Branko could do to keep from physically escorting the martinet out the door. "Be that as it may, old comrade, I'm asking you to remove your troops, post haste. I'm also hereby warning you not to do bodily harm to any of the marchers should you be ordered to attack them. The American public will roast your balls if this happens, and I will light the God damn fire myself."

With that, the Chief of Staff did an angry about-face, sans salute. He stormed out of the office and the building. The accompanying roar of cars and trucks faded into the afternoon sun.

With his desk just outside the office door, Sergeant Winslow stood with a pained look on his rugged face. He said to Branko, "Begging your pardon, sir, but what in hell did you just do?"

"Not everything I *wanted* to do, Sergeant. Let's just say it was out of respect for Father Francis Patrick Duffy, and let it go at that."

That evening, Patrick Hurley phoned Branko to report that he was approached by the mad-as-hell Chief of Staff.

"Good show, Commandant," Hurley added. "Did you really tell him the people will roast his balls?"

"I did."

"Damn, I wish I had told him that. Within thirty seconds, he saw the futility of appealing to me and probably went off to see his ultimate boss. I can tell you that Hoover is frightened to death of a confrontation with the vets, which both you and I know would effectively end his presidency. My guess is that you'll never hear anything further from the Chief of Staff."

June 17, 1932

The unraveling, downward spiral, started in earnest. Even though the, "immediate bonus payment" bill had passed the House on the 15th, with room to spare, thousands of marchers gathered at the capitol for the Senate's vote on the bill today.

The date for total payment of the Military Service Certificates, was originally not due to mature until 1945. However, the gist of the bill out of the House was that the payment date was being moved forward substantially.

The impoverished and the unemployed veterans, all depression victims, demanded payment in full—now! At the very least, it would help them to weather the killer storm, even if only to a minor degree.

The Senate did not follow the House's lead—the bill was roundly defeated before noon by a whopping vote of sixty-two to eighteen. Walter Waters, who was recognized as the titular head of the marching groups, ordered the protesters from the Capitol steps, saying, "Sing *America* and go back to your camps."

They did, but they also began a silent "Death Watch" a few days later, marching to and fro in front of the Capitol with relevant handmade placards. By this time Branko knew full well that the time bomb was ticking.

To heavily compound this pallor of sadness, Bill Donovan phoned to announce that Father Francis Patrick Duffy had recited his last prayers on June 26th. Branko wept, awash in a stream of so many memories and had to compose himself to carry on the conversation. Bill said his own eyes had not yet dried.

The funeral was to be in three days. When Branko explained that he could not leave his embattled post, Bill understood. He had been reading and listening to news about the conditions every day.

"You're once again in the front lines, comrade," Bill remarked. The good Father would most certainly give you his blessing. By the way, they're also planning a celebration of the man's life on earth—in New York in mid-August."

"If this damned disaster can somehow be peacefully resolved by then, you can bet I'll be there to hoist a bottle of bootleg beer in his good name!"

When the phone call was over, Branko went to his photo albums, took out a beautiful photo of himself posing in a trench with Father Duffy in France—and wept again. The man among men had made an indelible mark on Branko's life.

In mid-July Congress adjourned for summer recess without the slightest concession to the vets' demands. But a recess wasn't an option for the vets and so the hordes of Bonus Marchers did not leave Washington. In their various encampments thousands lingered on disconsolately.

At the College, Branko increased temporary housing for women and children from the Anacostia Flats. He did this by opening fourteen rooms that were still under renovation.

Hoover was determined to get rid of the vets by using government funds to help pay their way back home. When the emergency funding Howell Bill passed, a downtrodden 5,000 accepted the offer.

The remainder stayed put. But it was increasingly evident that this would not end amiably.

July 28, 1932

It was hot summer's day. Tempers and tolerance were shortening as the mercury inched up.

The Attorney General of the United States of America, William D. Mitchell, issued the order for the District Police to evacuate the Bonus Army veterans, wherever they were within the district boundaries. In charge, Chief of Staff, General Douglas MacArthur, gathered a potent show of strength under his command, which had already formed-up on Pennsylvania Avenue. MacArthur was to be aided by two of General Horvitch's Army College alumni. One was the recent graduate Major George S. Patton and his cavalry of a half-dozen of the most modern tanks. The other was one of Branko's favorites, who spoke so elegantly at his induction, Major Dwight D. Eisenhower, assigned to be the liaison officer to the Washington District Police Force. To the latter fell the responsibility to prod the police into action, as distasteful as it may be to any of them.

The first contingent of marchers in front of the Capitol building resisted and the skittish police shot live ammunition into their ranks. Two veterans were killed and in the melee of rocks and glass weapons several police officers were badly injured.

Thus was the tragic beginning of one of the blackest days in American history.

The President heard of the clash from the District Commissioners who requested immediate help. Hoover ordered MacArthur and his troops to takeover and continue with the forced evacuation. To the Chief of Staff this was nothing less than all-out warfare. Weeks earlier he had prepared for this eventuality by amassing troops of infantry and positioning the cavalry, including six tanks under Patton's command. As if this wasn't enough to quell an uprising of unarmed, undernourished veterans, MacArthur had also ordered-up a lethal machine-gun squadron.

As this heavy force sweltered in battle stance on Pennsylvania Avenue, it was nearing five o'clock and thousands of civil service office workers were lining up on the sidewalks to observe. They began shouting, "Shame! For shame!" These were the most civil among the terms of derision aimed toward MacArthur and the cavalry under Patton, whose very audible voice was heard to order over the chanting, "Charge! Charge!"

This "overkill" force, equipped with protective gas masks, quickly dispersed the "enemy" by using adamsite gas. The military pursued the veterans to the river banks, where they fled to their encampment at Anacostia Flats. It was at this crucial juncture that Hoover had a firm message sent to MacArthur to stop the assault and not to enter the camp.

The Chief of Staff chose to ignore the President. He ordered the troops to "fix bayonets" and to continue into the campsite. Again using the nasty adamsite gas they over-ran, "Hooverville" setting the pitiful shacks on fire, killing two more veterans and injuring hundreds of others and their families, babes and all.

The gas in question, named after it's discovering chemist Professor Roger Adams, had been stock-piled during the recent world war and was never used; but to employ it against your own civilians was deemed acceptable by MacArthur on this day in July. Among numerous insidious symptoms were immediate vomiting, lung irritation and choking. The accompanying panic sent most of the affected to the district's hospitals. One pregnant wife suffered a miscarriage and two children died. The deaths of the children were never directly attributed to the day's events in what later passed for the so-called investigation.

Unofficial casualty figures for the one-day disaster were disputed by many of Hoover's administration officials, but nevertheless they reported 1,017 injured civilians, and sixty-nine District Police officers. Most of these required hospital attention. The four deaths, including two of the Bonus Army were never recognized by the government in any way.

When word of the one-day war reached those at the College, Branko immediately ordered the gates closed and many had to be gently restrained from leaving. He didn't want any women or kids walking back to Anacostia or walking on the streets of the capital that evening. They seemed to understand his reasoning and fearing that casualties would be high they requested to at least have their husbands visit them with news, as they had many times during the past two months.

Branko expected many of their husbands to be approaching the gates and ordered the sentries to let them in immediately. Earlier, Edith and Aretha drove onto the campus and helped one of the cooks to arrange for an ice cream, "party" with a local dairy, to be held in the dining area for all of the, "guests" and more specifically, as a distraction for the children. The poor little waifs were ecstatic and some of the mothers even smiled for the first time. Whatever the case, Branko's own childhood served as an incentive for him to do whatever he could to insulate the children against the grim news of the day. And as Edith said, "Cookies, cakes, ice cream and candy will do that every time!"

The Commandant began receiving reports in the afternoon. Pat Hurley had sent six of his office staff out on the streets to report, minute-by-minute, and every word of the information was relayed to Branko. When news came in of the adamsite gas and fixed bayonet attacks, he was heartsick and furious at the same time. Branko quietly hoped for the well-being of his veterans and their families while cursing the very ground upon which MacArthur strutted.

Pat Hurley had ordered Branko to not even think of appearing on the street or in the camps that afternoon. Branko reluctantly accepted. He knew enough of his own mind to realize that if he were to come across MacArthur amidst the carnage, he wouldn't wait for the

American public to, "roast the balls of the Chief of Staff." Knowing that he would do more than just light the fire with his own match Branko was resigned to the reality that there was absolutely not a thing he could do. He reflected that the mad truly had inherited the earth.

July 29, 1932

The *Washington Post* opined that the Chief of Staff's overt high-handedness exceeded the President's intentions and explicit instruction not to move into the encampment at Anacostia Flats.

The morning edition printed that there could not be excuses for what occurred the previous day. MacArthur had audaciously said that he was convinced of a communist-instigated plot beginning with this emboldened attack on America: The *Post* called the statement, "ludicrous."

McLean himself wrote a stinging editorial vilifying MacArthur's actions. His wife Evalyn endorsed it by characterizing the use of fixed bayonets and adamsite gas on civilians as, "appalling" and, "criminal." She also wrote that it was, "laughable, if not sophomoric, to have six tanks ready as backup. For what?"

The woman was indeed mad as hell. Most of the country's news media followed suit and took MacArthur to task with uncompromising wording. Hoover fared no better.

Meanwhile, Branko had placed a call to Henry Luce and described the mayhem. He urged Luce to write a piece about the reprehensible actions in his next issue of *Time*. Luce asked if he could cite Branko.

"Hell, yes, you can cite me," Branko came back. "By all means, Henry! If I'm going to be court-martialed or even just reprimanded, I might as well add to the charges while I can. After nearly seventeen years in this uniform, perhaps it's time for me to get back into civvies! Maybe I'll even hang that bastard MacArthur in effigy out on the College parade grounds."

Branko had basically dedicated the entire day to what he referred to as, "Massacre on the Anacostia." His phone call with the National

Commander of the American Legion resulted in an immediate nationwide proclamation condemning the action, signed by the Legion's Advisory Board members. The three local commanders were equally incensed, including that post commander who had a run-in with Branko a few years earlier. On this, however, the two men were in complete agreement.

President Hoover's Press Secretary, Jimmy Whitaker, phoned Branko to express his sorrow for yesterday's actions, where everything seemed to get out of hand. Knowing and respecting Branko's long and dedicated association with the veterans of America, the White House wanted to convey the President's disappointment in the handling of the evacuation.

"Bullshit, Jimmy!" an angry Branko fired back. "Your boss failed. He couldn't handle the likes of MacArthur—who shouldn't have been brought in on this in the first place. What happened was no damn surprise to anyone with half a brain. And you can tell *your* boss that anything less than immediate dismissal of the Chief of Staff is violin music as far as I'm concerned."

Branko slammed the phone down.

The one call that he didn't expect came from a very shaken Major Dwight Eisenhower.

"Dammit, sir, I'll never forget the looks on the faces of those vets...ragged, ill-fed and badly abused by their own government. To see everything go up in flames just broke me up. But please tell me, what the hell could I have done to stop it?"

"Dwight, I would have thought better of you. You and I know Patton has a short fuse and at times borders on the maniacal, but you are an intelligent human being and a fine soldier. You walked off with the highest grades this institution has ever seen, but only your conscience could have saved the day. You know the procedure of arresting a superior officer who is acting irrational. I thoroughly cover this in one of my, *Command and Response*, lectures every year—and you know it. The time to ask for his handgun would have been precisely when he ignored Hoover's order to 'stand down, cease and desist' just before burning down the God-damn shacks. Do you realize how many innocent people could have been killed by flames?"

"To do that would have been the end of my career, General. I couldn't."

"Your career?" Branko echoed in a hollow tone. "Well, I guess that about sums it up, doesn't it? What else is there to discuss, Major Eisenhower?"

"Begging you pardon sir, but as a Brigadier, couldn't you have arrested him with the same procedure?"

"No. Remember, the arresting officer has to have had the opportunity to observe the subject's mental state during some sort of an action, endangering the lives of his troops or innocent bystanders. That would put you square into the scene on the banks of the Anacostia, with every right to act accordingly. It was there for you, Major."

But I guess your career was more important than lives of innocent men, women and children, Branko thought, but didn't add. It was, Branko felt, a blemish on Eisenhower's otherwise stellar character. He was saddened that it was there and that the man would have to carry such a burden. But having observed Eisenhower's resilient demeanor while he attended The War College, he was sure that he would overcome this adversity. He had little doubt that Eisenhower would continue to build an exemplary career while serving his country.

August 30, 1932

It was now a month removed from MacArthur's clash with the Bonus Army and General Branko Horvitch had trouble sleeping. Between the events of that horrible day and so many other parts of a life as usual, he drifted in and out of a light sleep, on the verge of a stream of consciousness connected by the most random of threads:

The Bonus Expeditionary Force is still in town but diminishes every day. The only hope they have is Franklin Delano Roosevelt. Realistically, he will have a truckload of problems to face from his first day in the Oval Office. Where the bonus will end-up on the docket is pure guesswork. When the campaign gets rolling in a few days, maybe there'll be some sort of hint from FDR. I'll get Donovan to use his influence with him. Can't hurt! I'll enlist the help of Jack Steel if he stays on as Buildings and Grounds Superintendent, but a personal meeting with the new "boss" heads my agenda, too.

That was some enjoyable visit from Harry Truman. Too bad he wasn't in town earlier so he could have observed MacArthur, his old hard-ass nemesis in action. I kidded him about someday giving up his judgeship and running for congressman or senator. But he was damn serious about it. He seemed to think that with Roosevelt in office there would be room for a feisty Missourian somewhere in the Capitol Building. He'd sure as hell shake up this lethargic town.

I enjoyed dinner with him and swapping war stories. He was sure excited about meeting Edith when joined us for coffee and dessert. He is definitely an old, true Wilsonian. She charmed the bow-tie right off him. I'll bet he's still wondering what my friendship with her is all about—like everyone else in town. Of course, he proudly showed his pictures of Bess and eight-year-old Margaret, the apples of his eye!

Yep, the artillery captain is one old-fashioned family man through-and-through. He wore me out wanting to walk everywhere—to every historic site that appealed to the squire of Kansas City. Good thing I had Larry follow us in the Olds—walking-up the Washington Monument steps nearly did me in. Harry took two at a time! He's a veritable bundle of energy, that man!

I feel relieved that I wrote to Tante Shayndl, asking her to have Charles set-up some accounts in Switzerland—good place to which the black gold money can be sent. With his banking expertise he should have no problem. Still, I'm a little uneasy about them still in France, especially with these goodly sums of money in French banks. So many of them have gone under in the past few years. At least Charles didn't resist the idea according to the brief note from Tante yesterday. The time will soon come when they will have to make a permanent move to Switzerland. Anyone close to the pot-boiling situation predicts that Hitler is bound to be the next German Chancellor sometime next year. According to Wild Bill, all over Europe it's a "given."

The New York "celebration" of Father Duffy's noble life was certainly worth it. It was sweetly nostalgic seeing a few hundred of the Fighting 69th boys. After the first few beers and illegal "hard *stuff" it got lively. Irving Berlin at the battered old plinky-plunky piano at Hibernian Hall, "Silk-Hat Harry" O'Rourke singing twenty verses of,* Danny Boy, *couldn't help the rushing river of tears flowing down Broadway. With Irving playing the old favorites, every last tipsy man saw himself as the greatest Irish tenor who ever lived!*

And that surprise appearance by George M. Cohan—we loved it! Great duets with Irving and everyone else joining in. It's a Long Way To Tipperary, Give My Regards to Broadway, It's a Grand Old Flag, When Irish Eyes are Smiling, Rose of Tralee *and of course every verse of* Mademoiselle from Armentieres. *Even the womenfolk laughed aloud at the risqué version.*

The many toasts to the life of Father Francis Patrick Duffy... And former-Corporal Dinny McGinty, three sheets to the wind, shakily standing, to answer the guy who quoted the Old Irish saying, "I sure as hell hope old Francis got to heaven before the devil knew he was dead."

What a laugh, with Dinny saying, "My Irish arse! Father Duffy got to heaven, picked the lock of the pearly gates, and held high mass even before the friggin undertaker knew he was dead!"

Well, the wives helped soften the raucous songfest. Sister Mary Margaret, Duffy's delightful sister—another unexpected joy. That snappy Irish-dancing troop of girls and boys from her church did the wildest step-dancing Irish jigs I've ever seen. And that was quite a story that the former 69'er and Irish Republican Army General told me about some long range plans in the works for a movie about our old outfit. That would be some kick! I'll have to contact him some day to find out more, since he handed me a card, asking me to keep in touch. John Prout, that's his name.

The Roumanische Shul on Eldridge Street the following evening— that place has been around forever. That impromptu gathering, which my old fusgeyer friends, Mordecai and Mendel, arranged for the NYC contingent—surely warmed by heart. Never engulfed with so many loving hugs and kisses in my life. All those family members that they brought. Great evening of comradeship, delicious kosher food from Katz's Famous Deli around the corner, and a mountain of cherished story-telling reminiscences to go along with the cheese cakes! Boy, what a ribbing I took for that Time cover!

Can't say I'm unhappy that Jesse didn't quite make the cut for the Appalachian League. The competition was more than he expected. Takes standout years in high school or college and Jesse's college baseball career was a good one but "outstanding" wouldn't fit. Now, he can concentrate on nailing down an internship at the State Department. It's with the possibility of a new administration coming into office. I intend to make few phone calls to State. If I can be of some help, why the hell not? With Sara already there, she might be an asset, too. Earning some money by helping his dad again this summer is a positive step for him. I really respect the way he handled the baseball disappointment.

Retirement? I suppose someday I'll take the plunge. I'll have twenty years service by '36. Then we'll see about it. I've heard a lot of rumors that twenty years will soon be the mandatory maximum, depression and all. Slicing our armed forces with the world sitting on a powder keg? Bad move!

*****

Koncentration Lager, Sobibor,
General Gouvernment, Poland
September 30, 1943 (1100 hours)

General Branko Horvitch (United States Army, Rtd.) could not close his tired eyes, let alone sleep. Instead, there was a plethora of random thoughts and "what ifs" floating through his brain.

A fine mess I'm in, he thought echoing the mad-cap movies of Laurel and Hardy. It was more or less a summation of it all.

He was particularly preoccupied with one of his co-prisoners, a man named Alexander "Sasha" Pechersky. Even though Pechersky was purported to have military experience in the Soviet Army, he was a prisoner nonetheless. At Sobibor, the humiliating, striped, pajama-like prisoner uniforms were nowhere to be seen. One just wore the ragged clothing in which he or she was apprehended. And the only prisoners in military uniforms were the captured Soviet soldiers. And so Branko's "wardrobe" was completely nondescript; so too was Pechersky's.

But Branko wanted to believe that the Russian Jewish officer indeed did have the background everyone around him believed. The alternative was to be suspicious of the man, and that served no good end.

Thus Branko had went out on a limb, as it were, and with confidence in Pechersky as a competent leader shared the word "escape" several times in their whispered conversations. Perhaps this newfound reason for allegiance to Pechersky was due, in part, to the man's plan to break out *en masse.* "Everyone goes," as he had put it. There was not another hope to hang onto anywhere between the barbed wire fences.

What Branko couldn't know was that the ruddy-faced Russian was equally impressed with Branko's ability to speak Yiddish, Russian and German, as well as passable Romanian. This, however, had not prevented Pechersky from demanding that Branko drop his pants to prove that he was circumcised—and thus who, or rather what, *he* claimed to be.

Branko had been using the false name of Yuri Litno and had not dared confess to Pechersky that he was an American. He had been careful in his speech, and had refrained from lapsing into even an occasional commonplace Yank phrase. The two men had been in a metaphorical dance, of sorts, each wanting to assure the other of being reliable.

For his part, Branko was convinced that Pechersky considered him a Jewish partisan of Russian origin and not a Nazi plant. But even more importantly, according to Pechersky, was the fact he was able to pressure a *kapo* to place Branko into his work battalion—because the trim and muscular American looked fit enough to do a hard day's labor.

Were it not for that excellent physique, Pechersky informed Branko during a recent hushed conversation, he would have been facing death in the gas chambers within hours of arrival. As it was, he had been equally fortunate in not being assigned as a *sonderkommando* charged with emptying out the gas chambers of misshapen bodies, defecation, vomit and urine. Those who did the ghoulish work were usually eliminated after a few weeks and replaced by a fresh group of hapless inmates. As a death camp Sobibor was only one link in the insidious Nazi chain of *Koncentration Lagers* that ignobly stretched from Germany to Russia.

The most frightening thing Perchersky shared with Branko, had been surreptitiously delivered to him by one of the more docile office *kapos*. Confidential files reflected orders to replace the often haphazardly drunk Lithuanian and Ukrainian guards by the end of October. The new guards were coming out of the crack 30th Waffen Grenadier Division of the SS 1st Belo Russian Volunteers. This unnerved Pechersky and prompted his moving-up the escape date to within a few days. The drunks would be far easier to deal with during the planned escape.

Not weeks, but days. The two units named in the communique were known to be specially trained in erasing all traces of Sobibor as a death camp. This meant murdering the entire prisoner population before the Russian troops were within artillery range. The escape simply had to take place before the 30th Waffen Grenadiers arrived and before the usually drunk guards were replaced.

And while neither Branko nor Perchersky were privy to the information, the German *Fuhrer's* direct orders were that Herr Himmler and his henchmen were to destroy any evidence of all the *K-lagers*.

Having been in custody for more than a week, Branko had at least started on more substantial worker's rations, as sickening as they were. Actually, it was the same soup, potatoes and bread as they were now being served but Branko's rations had been only in slightly larger portions. And now he had the pleasure of his own bunk of wooden slats. Having shared bed space in the barracks with two other captives for that first week, existence was humiliating and surreal all around.

One of his bunk mates threatened to punch Branko unless he moved an extra inch away from him. Not that there was an extra inch to be had. Branko smiled at the head-shaven beanpole and with a clipped, soft but menacing tone and said, "Do that *chaver*, and you'll meet God a little sooner than you would anyway."

The sad shell of a man went speechless and quickly traded bunks with another unsuspecting prisoner. The self-evicted prisoner must have said something of a warning, as the new man was all sugar and nice as spice. The human will for survival, for even an extra day, was still evident in Sobibor.

The penetrating smell of urine and body odor began to make Branko nauseous. The ghost of a young religious man, still in the garb of a *Chassid*, lay in the bunk above. Saying that he saw Branko whispering to Pechersky that evening, the ghostly one volunteered his opinions of the Russian. Surprisingly, they were positive and full of scuttlebutt to boot. In his sing-song Yiddish he sounded like he knew something of Pechersky's plan, but in reality, did not know details. Branko, having not heard of the final plan, just nodded and thanked the young man for his input. One interesting speculation emanating from the *Chassid* was that the goal was to get most of the camp's prisoners at least as far as the forest.

Well, hell, that's not too far-fetched, thought Branko. *I think this young Yid is guessing, while peppering it with logic that's part of a Chassid's psychic mystique anyway. But how in hell did he qualify for this battalion?*

I'm just comfortable in knowing that by using an alias, and having no meaningful papers of any kind, it will continue to make it nigh impossible to tell who or what I am. Coming this far, I can only hope the Ukes didn't spill anything to the guards that I spoke English. If they did, I would think I would have been tortuously interrogated the first day here.

He correctly supposed that they went back on the road as soon as they collected their money for his body. He further figured that they were already back in the marshlands for a week, stone drunk from all the *vodka* and *slivovitz* they were able to buy, making them even more trigger happy.

It was obvious to Branko that Pechersky's latest information on the scheduled guard changes made his plan imminently crucial. He would not have the luxury of delaying it until all the pieces fell into place—even if they ever would. The prior week, Pechersky caught sight of a sadistic brute of a Uke with the affectionate name of "Ivan the Terrible" beating a skeleton of an inmate to death with a massive wooden truncheon. The reason for doing so was unimportant. The guard, Ivan Demyanyuk, had become the epitome of animalistic perpetrations of the Ukrainian guard contingent. Most of them, Red Army deserters or hardened criminals, full of hatred, had proven to be far more treacherous than their German counter-parts.

Damn, this is pointless thinking and I've got to sleep so I can perform on the fire wood battlefield tomorrow, Branko thought as his consciousness began fading. *It seems like a hundred years ago when my personal goals were to move on—places to go, things to do, experiences to feel. Sure!*

Now I have only one mission...to stay alive.

IN THE SERVICE OF HIS COUNTRY

Washington, D.C.
October 25, 1934

The first years of the Franklin Delano Roosevelt administration was akin to living in the vortex of a maelstrom; in a whirlwind for the ages, the eye of the hurricane, a roller-coaster ride to infinity. This President, who dealt out of a fresh new deck to his fellow Americans, knew not the words "can't, must not," or "it's never been done before." All the while he amassed more friends than enemies, more praise than threats and more admirers than despisers.

This is not to say that his presidency or far-reaching policies were without controversy or opposition: Indeed, much of his initial efforts, like Hoover's, were beyond his Constitutional reach. But whatever else would fall into the purview of historians, he did give a beaten-down country hope for something better.

At least this was the articulate summation of Wild Bill Donovan. For once Branko found little or no fault with the assessment. In fact, he even began to slightly succumb to Bill's broken-record insistence that he make every effort to honor the golden invitation to eventually join his budding intelligence program—and to eventually meet with the man who had no fear of anything but fear itself.

"What the hell for, Bill?" Branko said to his friend in a phone conversation. "The man is the busiest president in American history, juggles 300 balls at a time and, as you pointed out, is pissing off half of America while being worshiped by the other half. Where would I fit in?"

"Where I've been telling you for years, Commandant: With me—in the vital intelligence game, that's where! I know damn well you've been thinking of retirement at twenty years of service—that would be in '36, right? The military is looking askance at those who want to extend, so you will be strongly encouraged to say 'bye-bye.'"

"Dammit, Wild Bill, Edith has been telling me the same thing. I suspect that the two of you have conspired against me for years."

"No, Branko, Woodie's First Lady only has eyes for you, you cute little bastard. Especially after that *Time* cover, eh? Now hear this well, sir. I will be on FDR's agenda for a meeting sometime this next year and I'd like you to be with me at that time. As you might imagine, I've told him a great deal about you in the past and he seems comfortably warm to the idea of you coming aboard. Remember, he helped to swing your first War College appointment. It's been like pulling teeth, but with the extended intelligence budget we expect will be approved, this is your chance. You can take off your khakis, retire and then jump headlong into the fire! The die has been cast, so shut the hell up and wait for my alert for when we shall meet for 'awfternoon tea' with the *Hahvidd* boy!"

"I'll give your *Hahvidd* boy this kudo: I've fought for the vets bonus long enough to understand why he didn't want to drag a fight through a depression-weary Congress during these early days of his administration. And I salute him for at least trying to assuage the veteran's unemployment picture—even though it has substantially worsened since the election. His offering to put 25,000 men to work on his Civilian Conservation Corp was a master stroke of morale-building and encouragement—and all America benefits."

"Probably far too little and much too late, Branko," his friend responded. "And, by the way, I must have told you this after those bloody bonus marches of '32, but I wish I had been there with you to roast old Dougie Mac's balls!"

This elicited a healthy and mutual laugh. They agreed to talk again, soon.

That wild-ass Irishman has my number now and won't be giving up, Branko thought as he dropped the phone into its cradle. *The College has been going so smoothly and I'm still enjoying it immensely. Was I made to be a school master or a spook creep? Well, I won't give him the satisfaction of thinking he wore me down. I'll just say that I've been considering this move on my own for the past few years. Screw him!*

Without even realizing it, Branko's thoughts had shepherded him straight onto Papa Roosevelt's lap.

In the meantime, Branko's age-old habit of recounting, reassessing, and reconsidering took over. Sitting in his living-room, a cold beer at hand, he drifted back into the newsreel of his agile mind.

He visualized Jesse working toward a graduate degree in foreign affairs at Georgetown and the great career move that would be. Jesse's internship at State had earned him a scholarship along with promises for an entry position in foreign affairs when he received the degree next spring.

That wonderful kid has proven to be a winner on all fronts, Branko mused. *Sara continues to be a positive influence on him, too. I'm happy that she's decided to wait another year before going for that accelerated M.A/Ph.D. Program at Maryland. She has lately set her sights for a college teaching position aiming for an assistant professorship somewhere... Perhaps UVa., Maryland or GW. She hinted last week that their engagement may be forthcoming. I don't think she meant to, but it slipped out and the ever-wily Edith caught it right off. Meanwhile, Jesse has said absolutely nothing. There certainly hasn't been a cooling-off between those two that I can make out. Love 'em both!*

How his mind wandered from there to prohibition was through a moderate stream of consciousness related to a news item he had heard on WKDR radio, which in turn had reported nationwide crime figures appearing in the morning edition of the *Post*. He found it interesting that since the return of legalized drinking last December, crime had appreciably dipped The *dry* proponents had apparently been wrong by saying prohibition *kept* crime levels down. The improving crime statistics seemed likely to continue—even amid the ongoing depression.

Take away something people want and they'll resort to any tactics to get it, legal or illegal, Branko thought. *Give it back to them and damned if the criminal element doesn't begins to fade.*

Kennedy crossed his mind next and according to Bobby Ray, a newly formed company called *Kennedy-Slick* was going better than anticipated. Bobby Ray and Stanley had formed the venture and with only one client were having a grand time of it. They had employed six Guthrie-Stillwater area vets who had formerly been hospitalized at Oklahoma Baptist and the new V.A. Hospital.

Gotta hand it to Joe for endorsing that, Branko thought.

As for slick Joe Kennedy himself, it was widely predicted that he would once again come out on top when FDR made him his unpopular choice to head-up the new Securities Exchange Commission.

Joe Kennedy, the watch dog of Wall Street: "What a joke!" was a common reaction to this. Some in the press called it an audacious selection by Roosevelt, while others call it a blatant travesty. Meanwhile, his company had never missed a royalty payment to Bobby Ray and Stan or to Branko's "preferred list of proceed recipients" including the Anti-defamation League, Sam Du Bois and "that Shayndl fellow" in Paris. Sam had even said to Branko, "We ought to light a candle for both you and Mr. Kennedy every Sunday."

Not a bit necessary, Sam old boy, thought Branko, *but having that comfortable cushion has meant a great deal to me. Not having to count on my twice-monthly government paycheck any longer. Strange as it seems seem, Joe has not spoken with me since the good Cardinal O'Connell commended him in that Easter Morning sermon as, "the true measure of Christian humanity."*

Branko couldn't help but smile at how the Cardinal went on to say that the benevolent son of Boston was heavily supporting the honorable worldwide work of the Anti-Defamation League of B'nai Brith.

"All of you good practicing Catholics of Greater Boston can take a leaf out of Brother Kennedy's fine work-book," O'Connell said, "and begin to look for ways to actively promote such honorable endeavors regardless of the sponsoring religions—Catholic, Protestant or Jewish."

Keerist, and that's an unforgiveable pun, Branko thought. *I had no idea the Cardinal would go to such flowery lengths. Good show, Padre! Good show! Do I think this is the end of Joe's outspoken bigotry? Not by a longshot! Next question, please!*

Branko was relieved that he could help the untenable position of Tante Shayndl and Charles: Now with enough money they had seriously began looking for a lake-side home in Geneva and planned to move there in the next few years. Branko resolved to pester them until they did. Tante believed that her loving family would likely follow them there. This pleased Branko, who thought that rapidly approaching dire conditions would eventually envelop all of Europe.

Who knows what Hitler's next move will be. Not a peaceful one, that's for damn sure. No question, he has completely locked down his hold over the Third Reich and has made numerous unveiled threats to all of his neighbors over these past two years. It's just a matter of time until he sneaks an attack on someone, somewhere. Most of those in the know, like Wild Bill, are guessing Poland, though a few feel it will be Belgium and France. Bill's "on the spot" experts don't see the Reich ready with enough supporting air power for another three to four years. It all remains to be seen—and feared.

There was no denying that his friendship with Edith over the past fourteen years had been the anchor of his life. Even though at times the opportunity to pick-up and leave had presented itself, not once had he experienced the need to get-way. Through it all, she remained his first— and now—only female friend. He hesitated to call the two of them "buddies" but that was what they were. He found that her demeanor, character, humor and unconditional friendship was a way to measure the women he occasionally met after Eva died.

Edith had occasionally—and facetiously—claimed that whatever was good about her came directly from her established genealogical lineage back to Pocahontas. When she married Woodrow, the newspapers went to great lengths to highlight this regal bearing of hers, calling her "Indian Princess" from time to time.

Branko had run with it, and when it fit into taunting posture he used the phrase "little wanton" which was the accepted translation of Pocahontas. It later came to light that more than just a few other Virginians also laid the same claim to celebrity-hood, but none with the power to impress the press that Edith had.

Of course, that warm spot in Branko's heart for Rivka had resided there for more than thirty years.

Often discouragingly, he mused. *That and unrequited yesterday, unrequited today and on into the future.*

Even so, Branko had always been truly happy for her as well as for her great love, Sendehr.

Admittedly, there had been more than a few "ships passing in the night" affairs to which the dashing General was exposed. He frequently laughed that off, insisting that the women had meant as much to him as a bowl of Wheaties without the milk. None of this caused any anxiety on his part, but he questioned whether there was anybody for him out there.

I doubt it, he answered the qualm as cooly as he faced most barriers. *Hell, I'm not close-minded, but I'm certainly not on the perpetual prowl, either. Too damn much effort to expend—and for what?*

Maybe someday. Just maybe.

Edith had recently mentioned that she received a nice note from Grace Coolidge. Both she and Branko shared a little guilt at not having been in touch with the lovely lady since Calvin's funeral of the previous year. They at least felt good about being in Vermont to say goodbyes to a very special person. After the funeral in Plymouth, Branko took the occasion to tell Grace that if Heaven had a baseball team, old Cal would certainly be allowed to pitch a few. Branko often reminisced that his happiest days in the White House were those Coolidge years.

Bless both of them, he thought, thinking of the former president and his wife.

On the political front, news from Missouri claimed that Harry Truman continued to have a commanding lead in his race for Senator. He was expected to win in the November elections.

Branko loved hearing that.

That son-of-an-artillery gun is going to make it. God, I hope he does. Bright breath of fresh air for this stale city.

Speaking dates continued to pile up unchallenged. There sometimes seemed to too many. But he truly loved to speak about the College, its history and related matters. Of course, there were the veterans and their plight about which he had special insight to offer. But there were other, equally important matters, for which he was an especially effective speaker. There was the fallacy of reducing the military due to the lack of war threats; careers in the military, his life as an officer in the United States Army, the modern army's and navy's ability to respond to attacks and so on.

He tried not to be out of the campus too often during the day and in doing so, managed to schedule evening engagements more often than not. One annoying problem—the travel radius—had expanded significantly to all points of the compass. For example, in just the last two months he had appeared at the Naval War College in New London, Boston College, Duke University in Durham and The Citadel in Charleston. For August he was scheduled at Fort Bragg, Parris Island Marine Base, Quantico and Aberdeen Proving Grounds. Branko had also accepted an intriguing invitation to speak at the dedication of a new monument at the Jewish Confederate Veteran's Cemetery in Richmond. The last speaking engagement had the potential to be Dern's most controversial topic since becoming Secretary of War. Branko didn't think that Pat Hurley would even give it a second thought, but Dern of Mormon Utah was known as a bit of an old school fuddy-duddy. Meanwhile, the usual local requests kept drifting in.

Simply gotta cut 'em down, Branko thought, not for the first time. Branko promised himself that he would have to learn the difficult task of saying, *no*.

The military had always adhered to the unwritten rule that a commanding officer earnestly begin grooming his replacement long before it came to pass. The question of Branko's successor was already chiseled in stone. Everyone in any way associated with the U.S. Army War College knew that Branko's choice was Colonel Peter Underwood.

Underwood had been as loyal, hard-working and effective as anyone reporting to Branko in the past twenty years. Underwood now had six years on the faculty and two years as second-in-command. Branko was completely comfortable with him

Having him take over my twice-weekly lectures had turned him into the most popular instructor, too, Branko mused, realizing that Underwood's popularity was owed to his skill rather than the opportunity. *He deserves to be the next Commandant and I haven't any qualms whatsoever in appointing him. I just wish he would shave that silly looking William Powell pencil mustache. I'll have to talk with Sally Underwood about her dapper Colonel—soon.*

In the increasingly wide-spread "monkey business" arena, the so-called "Banksters" were coming out of the woodwork. Branko took great satisfaction in seeing the *new, boss giving 'em hell.*

In his fireside chats, he repeatedly talked about the "epidemic of deceit" spawned by the private bankers and the brokers that had precipitated the crash of '29. Although Republican pundits thought otherwise, it wasn't just more White House malarkey. Closing the banks took a great deal of insane fortitude, followed by FDR's appointment of Ferdinand Pecora. Pecora was a no-nonsense, bullmoose investigator, who was taking on the lords of finance, including the granddaddy of 'em all, J.P. Morgan's son J.P. Jr. With diligent approach to Morgan and others of his ilk, the corruption that fueled the depression stood naked for the country to see. For a worn-out society in need of morale-boosting laughter, there was plenty humor to go around when the younger Morgan verbally spared with the no-holds-barred Pecora at the Banking and Currency Committee hearings.

As the *Post* printed, Congress, of course, had always been remarkably decorous in "what went wrong" but Morgan erred in opening up with the self-serving, "I state without hesitation that I consider the private banker a national asset and not a national danger." Pecora shot back with an impeccable sense of timing, "And what is your business or profession, sir?"

Morgan's delayed and sheepish answer, "Private banker," spurred a burst of laughter. From there, it all went downhill for Junior in brutal fashion. Soon thereafter the newspapers coined the term, "the Banksters," to describe the growing list of culprits.

No doubt Branko's old "friend" Joe Kennedy, was in for a rough ride corralling this bunch. As Branko recently interjected during a phone conversation with Wild Bill, *he just might surprise the naysayers and do a respectable job. I'd bet on it—with his money.*

When General John Prout had recently called, Branko once again adjusted to his thick Celtic brogue. He was able to decipher that Prout had finally been contacted by Hal Wallis of Warner Brothers Studios in Hollywood. The prolific and popular producer had developed a long-range plan to do a film on the Fighting 69th—sometime in the next few years. He had asked Prout to be the technical military consultant. Wallis confided that the film would require being on location for only a few months of shooting the film. He also conceded that, in light of the current economy, by the time budget for an expensive war film would be fulfilled, it could be as much as four or five years down the road.

Prout had promoted Branko as someone with a better knowledge of the 69th's battles in France and that perhaps the two of them would be the best way to go. Prout, was reserved and had always been overly modest about his abilities.

Branko's initial reaction to Prout's call had been to take a wait-and-see posture and make no commitments, but he also told Prout that if he were to take on the task, it would likely be after retirement—which wasn't that very far down the road.

In truth, Branko had always wanted to see Hollywood and the West Coast. The plum movie assignment seemed the perfect opportunity to do so. He smiled broadly at the prospect, wondering what Gloria Swanson was up to these days—what with being without lover boy Joe Kennedy hanging around. As the S.E.C. Commission head, Kennedy would have hell to pay should the word of another of his Hollywood dalliances come out. And that, Branko knew, was why the starlet and the money man weren't any longer an item.

He sat back on the couch and thought, *but for an unencumbered old fool like this "retired" General here... Yeah, man! C'mon, stop the school-boy day-dreaming, Horvitch! You go to Hollywood and stars like her will be everywhere. When do I start?*

From Hollywood's fantasy world, Branko moved on to his son. Rivka hadn't written anything to him concerning Emanuel in over a year. Her last tidbit had announced that the boy received his M.D. from Western Reserve in '30. He had then went into practice as an emergency-room surgeon specializing in body-invasive traumas such as bullet and knife-wounds. Rivka hadn't known where Emanuel's practice was located and Branko could only hope that she would soon find out from Miriam. He had full confidence that Rivka would learn his, as she hadn't yet failed in getting information on the boy.

Boy, Branko thought. *He's a doctor now. A man.*

Branko did not even have a photograph of Emanuel. Naturally enough the urge to get the least amount of gossip—or better yet, to see him—was more pronounced than ever. Through his mind was stream of sobering and ensuing headlines that could read: *Estranged U.S. Army General Shows Up To See Son He Abandoned Almost Thirty Years Ago.*

With this in mind, he could only shake his head, thinking how that would go over big among the legions of DC dirt-diggers. He could count on Ned McLean and his precious Post to lick their chops over such an ugly little bombshell—not to mention every radio station and newspaper across the country.

No thanks, he convinced himself, *but who knows—maybe after retirement. Miriam most certainly did a thorough job of erasing me from Emanuel's mind—and her own.*

He finally left the lobby and returned to his room. After going to bed, his sleep was fitful with his thoughts marching on in cadence.

**March 20, 1936
The Oval Office**

After the usual handshakes, coffee and tea, they enjoyed the scones service. Then, with the social amenities behind them, the man behind the desk buried his head between his shoulders and scrunched forward. Without so much as a side glance at Branko, the President addressed his first remarks directly to Bill Donovan.

"Well, Wild Bill, I'm indeed honored that you again brought General Horvitch along. At least we'll have a gathering of modern intelligence at this modern intelligence gathering, eh?"

"Thank you for your kind and cordial statement, Mr. President," replied the nonplussed Donovan with a twinge of sarcasm in his manner and speech.

"Now, Bill, let's cut out this formal horseshit and get to our agenda."

Branko thought for a moment he was hearing an Eddie Cantor-Parkyakarkus sketch on evening radio.

But the dialog isn't meant to be humorous, Branko thought. *It's coming from the exalted President of the United States of America and his second banana William "call me 'Wild Bill'" Donovan. Heaven help this country of ours!*

As the two college *boys* put aside the frat pranks and got down to the business at hand they became decidedly more rational. As the conversation wore on, Branko was impressed with what seemed to be an honest spirit of inquiry upon the part of the President. His occasional questions to Branko were not merely window dressing but searches for relevant input. From Branko's point of view, it spoke well of the President that he knew his own limitations.

What seemed to primarily occupy the President's concern was the revised intelligence budget and by extension, future expenditures. The budget now was on its nearly unobstructed path to approval, scheduled for a vote by mid-year. The enormity of the amount slated for a universal intelligence network was shocking to Wild Bill and Branko, both of whom expected substantially less. Of course, one doesn't look a gift horse in the mouth and they wisely did not register surprise. FDR, on the other hand, was outwardly apologetic for the "meager numbers."

Over the years, Bill had been masterful at convincing Roosevelt that only a world-wide, central intelligence effort could be even minimally effective. It had worked and the New Dealer was on his way to becoming a solid intelligence booster. His posture told of his keen interest: The cigarette and its holder was firmly pointing skyward from his lips, illustrating his determination. It was a pose that the news outlets had already photographed a thousand times or more since the inauguration.

As for FDR's *meager* intelligence budget, Branko could almost hear Wild Bill's brain crunching the numbers. Without a doubt he was re-allocating based upon the unexpected windfall from FDR—a million here, $3 million there, $4 million in Europe, manpower, training, office space, secured communications, world-wide arming of agents, the necessity for exclusive commercial transportation… A network also had to be put in place before Hitler made an irretrievably aggressive move or before the Japs could advance their Greater East

Asia Co-prosperity Sphere's agenda. In the short term there was the expense of immediate arrangements to work with current, potential and expected allies.

As FDR spoke, Wild Bill tossed sideway glances toward his co-conspirator, as if to say, *See, I told you the Hahvidd man was a captive of my incessant salesmanship.*

Branko certainly couldn't argue that Wild Bill had crafted the groundwork well. And considering the volatile world in which they lived, Branko wouldn't argue the need for operations just like Wild Bill and the President were planning.

Perhaps Branko thought, *this is indeed to be my second career—and a chance to make a difference. Whoever said that my journey through life's adventure was for the faint of heart?*

He was still Commandant of The War College and had already discussed this informally with Secretary of War Dern. Diplomatically, Dern had tried to convince Branko to stay on for a few more years. It had been futile, as Branko had already cast his view on a different future.

September 30, 1936

The Commandant formally announced that he was standing down at the end of the year—ending two decades of service at nearly sixty-one years of age. Wild Bill had been wrongly informed about the military enforcing the new twenty-year maximum, and Branko was never pressured to make the announcement he made at the opening of the staff meeting. Of course, by now word of his next venture had begun to float around and had even made its way back to the President's Cabinet.

Naturally, the incoming Secretary of War—Harry Woodring—had previously met with Branko about his decision.

"Thanks to you," Woodring had remarked, "the College has never been in better shape to train America's upper-ranked officer corp."

Woodring had also agreed with Branko's proposed appointment of Colonel Peter Underwood as the next Commandant. The new

Secretary was, Branko felt, a patriot rather than merely a politician. Instead of brow-beating his predecessor, Woodring praised the restoring of the previously slashed military budget.

Woodring had been generally thought of as a dour, dyspeptic Jayhawker while serving as Undersecretary to the late George Dern—who had passed on just weeks before. But it was an undeserved image. Woodring was intending to not only praise Dern's efforts, but also champion a strong standing army while so many in Congress rallied for ongoing reductions.

And Woodring was adamant about rebuilding the armed forces to war-effective levels—sooner rather than later. He agreed that the saber rattling "heard round the world" was becoming more pronounced by the day.

Gathering all of this upon his first meeting with Woodring, Branko couldn't help but feel he was missing out on an association he would have enjoyed.

Apparently on the same page, Woodring remarked, "General Horvitch, it would have been my good fortune to have you as the War College Commandant during my tenure."

Branko smiled.

"And if it means anything more," Woodring had added, "our Boss once told me that he was proud to have supported your assignment to the College."

"Well, you know politicians," Branko had finally said, trying to mitigate the flattery.

"Yes," the Secretary agreed, "always looking for credits!"

Branko laughed aloud at the comment.

Woodring seemed to take the laugh as permission to go on—sort of like a comedian waiting anxiously for an invitation to issue a secondary punch line—and this he did: "Repeat that to FDR—or anyone, soldier—and I'll have you shot on the White House lawn at dawn... Without a blindfold or the customary last cigarette."

With ice-breakers like this, Woodring had made Branko more comfortable about announcing his leave. Well before the meeting had ended, the Jewish immigrant and the native Kansan were well on the way to becoming solid friends.

"If you wouldn't mind," Woodring said at one point, "I don't see why the both of us shouldn't spend our few remaining months together on a first name basis."

"I'd like that."

"Branko," Woodring said.

"Harry."

The two men laughed.

"I always liked the sound of your first name, Woodring admitted. "Sort of a 'Soldier of Fortune' ring to it, and I'm not the only Cabinet Member or DC'er who thinks so."

This fellowship had gone on for a good hour, with Branko briefing Harry Woodring on concise and classified plans involving the curriculum being designed by Colonel Underwood.

Branko didn't envy Woodring's future with the state of the world as it was. There was the Ethiopian incursion and Mussolini's rampant nationalism mimicking the Third Reich and Franco's revolutionary mess in Spain that was basically a case of more totalitarianism snuggling up to Hitler.

Not that the China-Nip bloodbath is a bed of roses, either, Branko had reflected.

But, of course, Americans were more likely to concern themselves with Europe and the Secretary was no exception to such thinking. And that was understandable—what with the price in lives that America had paid for the freedom of France.

Any yet it seems like today's world has long-forgotten why the hell we fought in France, Branko had mused at the time. *War to end all wars, my Fighting 69th ass!*

Edith was in her usual attentive-listener mode when Branko recounted the Woodring meeting. Her feedback was positive and she mentioned having heard from those in the know that Woodring had practically run the War department even before Dern's fatal illness.

"Not that any of this will make a difference, Branko," she added. "You'll soon be out on the street selling apples—in your uniform with all those shiny medals!"

Seeing a scowl on Branko's face she quickly regretted her feeble attempt at humor.

He proceeded to gently chastise her for her thoughtless remark. There were still millions of the unemployed selling apples—and everything just short of their souls—to feed their families. The depression era had not ended, as if by a signal, once FDR took office in '33. The structure to defeat it was in progress, but there was a long, painful way to go.

A month later, and as a not-quite-so-unexpected footnote, President Roosevelts' landslide victory over Kansas Governor Alf Landon came and went as swiftly as a summer shower. The adroit and bold campaign of the New Dealer crushed his opponent, who won only two states. The Republican party, in disarray, could begin to immediately look for a candidate with better than a chance in hell to win four years hence. There were already rumors that FDR would run for an unprecedented third term in 1940. Such momentum could prove unstoppable.

A few months previously, Edith had casually suggested an engagement announcement in January and a June wedding for Jesse and Sara. Branko, Harry Kanter and Sara's parents were all for it, as were the lovebirds. The kids had been on remarkably strong parallels in their respective careers and evidently were feeling more confident to take the knot-tying step, even in unpredictable times such as these.

Jesse, with his Masters at hand, was understudying a very experienced department head in the foreign stations office. There were some indications that he would one day be assigned to a European embassy. Branko was hoping that Jesse might finally meet Tante Shayndl.

Sara was back at the State Department after earning advanced degrees at Maryland. As one of a handful of female employees, she was assigned to the training wing. She taught European history and culture to future overseas assignees. She and Jesse decided they would work things out if and when Jesse was sent to a foreign station. And if it did come to that, Sara's plan was to have already become a valuable enough employee to warrant assignment to the same embassy.

Babies? That was something else to be "worked out."

January 2, 1937

Retired Commandant Branko Horvitch was determined to fade into the woodwork during the induction ceremony for Colonel Peter Underwood. It was his show and Branko remembered how gracious his own predecessor had been during the ceremony. So a few parting words were all the attendees would get from Mr. Horvitch. One thing he was able to accomplish during the planning prior to the induction, concerned the traditional brief speech by a recent graduate of the College. In this case, one of those on the "short list" was a Major Huntley Murgatroyd. In fact, he was the top choice of Underwood himself—until he learned from Branko that the Major was MacArthur's second-in-command in July 1932 and had led the infamous bayonet attack by the infantry into the bonus marcher's camp at Anacostia Flats.

Branko would have none of that. Not during the final moments of his watch! Underwood—who had indeed shaved off his pencil-thin panache-mustache—completely understood the problem with Murgatroyd. The replacement speaker was Lieutenant Colonel Omar Bradley, class of 1934. Both Underwood and Branko had been impressed by Bradley's calm assurance and outstanding scholastic aptitude, notably in the strategic command seminars. He could best be described as stoically brilliant with an inner strength that came through in a very positive way. He was a leader, and everyone in his presence recognized it.

The ceremony went off beautifully and Branko issued his few words of *adieu* to a standing ovation that lasted for minutes—to his embarrassment. He couldn't stave off teary eyes and a lumpy throat. The new Commandant also praised Branko in his speech, which included a reference to the War College's growing cognizance of myriad, tenuous world affairs and their effect on the posture of the institution. Commandant Underwood also had no qualms in plagiarizing a line from Branko's 1930 induction speech: "General Horvitch, it has been my pleasure entirely, to serve under your great leadership. You may expect that I will be calling you whenever I have a question or a problem—even in the middle of the night."

Before any delayed reaction came from the audience, Citizen Horvitch quickly responded, "That's if you can find me, Pete!"

The hearty laughs came roaring. Edith Wilson thought it was brilliant, of course.

The President and Mrs. Roosevelt were most cordial to both gentlemen during the reception, as were the numerous cabinet members, congressmen and the press. Among Branko's many friends present were Bill Donovan and freshman Senator Harry Truman, the Democrat from Missouri.

As was the case during Branko's induction six years prior, his family seats were reserved for Edith, Aretha and her husband, Branko's trusted driver and friend, Larry Lincoln.

It was truly an exit with grace and an entrance with style.

*****

Sobibor Koncentration Lager
General Gouvernment, Poland
October 10, 1943

Pechersky managed to get his entire work battalion assigned to the same barracks during the last week.

"Amazing what one can do with a handful of the favored currency," was his stock reply when asked how he pulled this off.

Branko could only shake his head at this simple, but vague answer. Instead of pressing the issue he said, "Sasha, I'm growing old waiting for you to go over the plan with me."

"Tomorrow night there will be six of us meeting at 8:00 in the north corner of the barracks and you will be there. I know you are sensitive about leaking your identity, but I know exactly who you are and believe me, it stays here."

"Well, comrade, that's a godamm surprise to me. Where did you get any information about me in this esteemed institution?"

"Branko Horvitch, retired American General. Gigantic prize for Berlin should you be compromised, old man."

Perchershky had again side-stepped the question. Branko said, "So my false paperless identity, name and all, fooled everyone except the person giving you the correct information?"

"*Sha! tovarisch*, your secret is safe with me. The person who shared this was killed by the beast Demjanjuk two days ago—beaten to a pulp over two heels of bread hidden under his cap. He was with one of the Jewish partisan units in Belo Russia, and came across you several times in the past few years. He recognized you the minute you came into Sobibor and reported it to me. Thence, I quickly gathered you in for my work battalion. Luckily, he swore he had only told me. Poor bastard was going to be a major cog in the plan."

"Go on, Sasha, give me some godamm details, *Commissar*."

"That's enough for now. I'll spill all tomorrow. It won't be easy, Branko, but we can do it if everyone does his job—perfectly."

Branko grunted his impatience at that.

"Stay with it—it won't be much longer. By the way, you are now the ranking officer among all of Sobibor's military prisoners. For three German cigarettes, I'd point the finger at you myself—if I didn't desperately need someone of your discipline."

So went the whispered Russian-Yiddish chat, as if the two were planning a vacation trip to the Greek islands.

October 14, 1943

The debating, re-planning, reconsidering, voting and re-voting over the most minute step-by-step segments finally came to an end. The Sobibor escape mechanism was ready to be put into action; It was a death-defying precision of choreography in the literal sense. By the next night, the dancers would be dead or free.

Some choice, thought Branko. *I'll take 'free.'*

FIRE AND THE FURY 16

Sobibor, Koncentration Lager
General Gouvernment, Occupied Poland
October 14, 1934

Fire, fury and bedlam.

There was no other way to describe the hour between 1400 and 1500. The stench of death permeated every square meter of the camp. It all began with the first series of knifings and hatchet-slayings of four S.S. who were unlucky enough to happily accept Gelbfein the Tailor's invitation to come in for final fittings of their new uniforms.

As a result of a quick instructional lecture by "Professor" Sasha Pechersky during the previous sleepless night, the killing squad expertly wielded the weapons. With Pechersky in command, the act was swift. The rapidity of the action was enough to squelch the victims' screams.

Perchersky then oversaw the handing out of three machine-pistols and three Lugers. More weapons would follow.

In the carpenter shop nearby, three S.S. Officers were having storage cabinets made for their quarters. It was perfectly timed for them to show-up for inspection of the final products. Within minutes the tailor shop guests had been sent on their merry way to hell, drenching the shop in blood.

In the kitchen the two prisoners working there had been ordered to set fires when they heard pistol shots. Pechersky's signal was for the remaining workers to dispatch the guards within the closed-off work battalion compound, using well-hidden shovels and axes. More than a dozen corpses were piled-up as a result.

Under Branko's tight command this was accomplished post-haste. All was over-and-done within ten minutes and with only minor injuries to the attacking prisoners. Aside from Sasha and his few Red Army comrades, many of them had never physically harmed other human beings. Now, however, their anger-sparked gusto was astonishing and frightening. The elements of shock and disbelief made sudden widows of ten of the Reich's S.S. *hausfrau's* at home.

As for the Ukes, their daily brutalities were paid back in spades—in some cases literally—when bludgeoning shovels had found their targets. As most of the guards and S.S. officers were un-helmeted, brain-matter had profusely spilled over the lager grounds.

Earlier in the day the *kapos* had delivered well-whetted and vital knives from the kitchens. Thus far, Pechersky, Branko and Feldhandler were satisfied with the way the six *kapos* had relished their end of the killing plan. Of course, there was no surprise there. Their fellow prisoners knew damn well that escape was the one and only chance to avoid their own inevitable gassing. The *kapo* phenomenon was just a necessary evil in the concentration camp environment. For the most part, they had always done what they were ordered to do by the sadistic guards, but ever-so-slightly restrained the punch, the whip or the truncheon as much as they could manage without detection. On the other hand, there were always the overzealous who went a few steps beyond.

Because of this the three "escape" leaders were prepared to deliver killing blows to any of the *kapos* who so much as balked. However thus far the leaders were privately relieved that they didn't have to kill any of the *kapos*—yet. Nevertheless, they were to be scrutinized every moment.

By 1440 hours, the remainder of the camp—having heard the shots—knew to run like the wind toward the west forest line. 300 of those strong and mobile enough attempted the 200 meter run over open space. It was later estimated that 150 of them were either blown apart by the closely planted mines or killed by bullets from the Ukrainian sharpshooters in guard tower. Gruesome thought it was, the field of slaughter was as noble a death as any prisoner could hope for in such tenuous circumstances.

Of those who actually reached the thick forest alive, the greater percentage expected that they had delayed death by only hours or days.

Lieutenant Pechersky had not yet told Branko or Baruch Feldhandler of the final stage of his unorthodox escape plan. He now hand-signaled to each man, motioning to the far side of the barracks. They could see that he was armed with wire-cutters and was pointing frantically toward the east.

But why east?

All surviving Nazi's and Ukes were now focused only on those running west to the forest over the landmines. "To the east" meant clandestinely crossing the nearby River Bug (*boog*), which was heavily patrolled by veteran elements of the S.S. barracks from the town of Vwodava. Forty-four men and six women, all from the work battalion, followed Pechersky and Branko while killings continued between the barrack fences, barbed wire and the tree line.

Regardless of Pechersky's plan, Feldhandler insisted on leading his group of Polish-Jews—fifteen cadaver-like stick-figures—to the northwest. His goal was to reach the German-free Parczewski region he knew as a child. Waiting until evening for the cover of darkness to mask their movement, they stayed with the others for now.

In late afternoon, the remaining guards were ordered into the forest, pursuing those who had managed to stay upright. The sheer will to live seemed, for a time, to overcome the malnourishment each one was suffering. Skeletons could only run so far and so fast before the fragile bone structure would break down in complete exhaustion. The pursuers were counting on it. The *rat-a-tat* of machine pistols, and repeated rifle fire filled the forest.

Unfortunately, many of the trees in the forest were deciduous and had begun dropping foliage a week before, making more visible targets of the escapees. Within the hour the green forest turned red as the would-be escapees fell to the enveloping enemy. There was no need to take captives. For what purpose? They would all be killed soon after they were returned.

All those who stayed behind, unable to run, would be fodder for the gas chambers within hours or days. It was common knowledge among the prisoners, *kapos* and the guard force that the unstoppable Russian troops were steadily on their way; that Himmler had issued orders to dispose of remaining prisoners and level the camp before the end of the month. There simply could be nothing left for the Red Army to discover. This was destined to eventually be the *modus operandi* at all remaining lagers in the vast Nazi Koncentration network.

Counting on dusk to arrive soon after they had cleared the

unmined, unguarded camp area north of the officer's quarters, Pechersky and Branko prodded their charges along, faster and faster. With only a few sets of cuts needed for the barbed wire, this part of the plan went quickly and smoothly. Within minutes, they were walking among the heavy brush along the banks of the Bug. In stretched-out groups of tens, the fifty selected men and women, former members of the work battalions, were holding up very well. The initial sweet taste of freedom erased whatever doubts, illnesses or aches and pains they had. Glancing backward to the glowing flames of the kitchen fires, the enormity of the impossible deed began to set in—not that it was even close to the time when they could once again breathe freely.

Loaves of fresh-baked bread taken from the kitchen stores and lugged along in sacks by three of the *kapos*, would have to wait for a few more kilometers before it would be safe to pull off small chunks to distribute. The six large canteens of water would also wait for a safe time to be meted out, along with the caution to take just a sip or two. No one could hazard a guess as to how long it might be before finding food or potable water again.

A flight to freedom certainly makes for strange bedfellows Branko thought with a forced grin. *Yesterday these unsavory kapo scum were targets of deep and continual hatred, and now they're bloody buddies of those they had helped to harass—mentally and physically—and often truncheoned and murdered. But with dangers lurking around every bend, there's no denying the bastards are precisely the type of animals we need in this forced comradeship.*

Baruch Feldhandler's smaller contingent broke-off with sad goodbyes. They were to be shepherded to a rumored safe haven of myriad lakes, hidden caves and streams Pechersky and Branko hugged Baruch. They wished him well, cautioning him to travel by night while hiding and resting by day. His group was provisioned with short supplies of water and bread. This had been provided by *kapo* Plotkin, who had treated Baruch harshly over the past few weeks. Understandably, the latter had to summon up all of his inner strength to refrain from shooting the *mumzeh in* the balls or between his beady eyes.

So it was in Eastern Poland, on this extraordinary day of hope and redemption.

October 16, 1943

There were no signs of Nazi search detachments bordering the Bug as they had feared. Not a man in uniform was seen anywhere. Two of the escapees, Poles, who had meandered up the road to forage for food, came across a family—who were also Poles—driving a few head of livestock. Considering that the ragged twosome could very well be among those rumored to be escapees from Sobibor, the Poles also volunteered that there were not any Nazis in the area on either side of the river.

Sasha allowed them to stop and talk. Perhaps there was a false sense of security involved with his decision, but they had discovered a good-sized potato plot in the process. They gathered as many as they could carry, even those that appeared to be on the way to rotting.

The sun was ready to drop when the Poles ahead of the group came back into the heavily wooded area where everyone quietly waited. The welcomed news from the locals was that up-ahead, near the town of Stavki, the Bug was at its shallowest and easily forded. Sasha and Branko agreed that there was no reason not to cross over, as all this added up to the possibility that a German retreat had, in earnest, begun again. Both Pechersky and Branko noted that perhaps the possible withdrawal was precipitated by Himmler's plan of the camp's destruction and their escape. Even more likely, they knew, was that the hunters didn't want any part of the bloody bestiality demonstrated by the desperately hunted escapees.

Before they continued on, Sasha sent a larger group of hungry foragers to grab more potatoes—as many as they could handle—using empty bread sacks into which to load them. They returned when they had more than forty. They dug a large pit and using matches that the *kapos* carried, started a small, controlled fire. This made for some tasty baked potatoes, with enough unbaked left-over for the contingent to count on some starchy sustenance in the uncertain days ahead.

That evening, the moon-less river crossing went well. Several of the waders slipped on the rocks that lined the bottom of the Bug and got themselves a good dousing.

"You need a proper bath, anyway, Moisheleh," one of them joked. Morale was high once again. The Polish family that had given them the tip about the shallow river crossing was evidently not a vindictive bunch of Jew-haters and had told the truth. Many of the parched fifty took a mouthful of cool water from the river.

"Not a good idea," warned Pechersky, who suspected that the Bug was likely polluted with raw sewage from both Sobibor and the S.S. Barracks at Vwodava.

The commander kept them walking that night, quietly avoiding any villages and farmsteads while penetrating into what would soon again be Russian soil. The thought was a most hopeful and uplifting one.

Branko began thinking again of catching up with Timoshenko, of home and his loved ones. He tried hard not to get caught up in that elusive reverie. It didn't work—his thinking wouldn't and couldn't stop. As bone-tired as he was, these thoughts propelled him smoothly along the trail. He even began softly humming an old Russian folksong from his childhood days with Tante Shayndl and her family in Odessa. Sasha immediately recognized the tune and the two little boys of yesteryear sung the words ever so quietly. Those within earshot who knew the language, wept what they hoped would soon become tears of joy.

> *vyhkhazhu odna ya na dorogu*
> *skvoz tuman kremnistyi put blestit*
> *noch tikha, pustynya vnyemlet bogu*
> *i zvyesda a zvyesdoyu govarit*
>
> *v nyebesach torzhestvenno i chudno !*
> *spit zyemlya v siyani golubum*
> *chto zhe mnye tak bolno i tak trudno*
> *zhdul chyevo? zhaleyu o chyom?*

uzh nye zhdu ot zhizhni nichevo ya
i nye zhal mnye proshlovo nichut
ya ischchu svobody i pokoya
ya khochu zabytsa i zaznut

(What more do I expect?
I've nothing to be sorry for.
I want only freedom and peace.
I seek oblivion and rest!)

October 22, 1943

Eight days passed, fraught with dangers, but few encounters.

A gaggle of honking geese, led by a young woman and two farmers hauling a cart of piglets back to the sty, were a cause of slight alarm. Sasha knew that this one-time Belo Russian territory was well-populated with Russian *partisaners*. No doubt, the woman and the two farmers mistook them for a large unit, and wanted no suspicion of being Nazi sympathizers, even if they were. Partisan revenge was something not to be tempted. Both Pechersky and Branko, looking lean and mean with machine-pistols slung over their shoulders would give pause to any thinking enemy. The hatchet-swinging clusters and savage-looking, truncheon-wielding *kapos* would scare the living hell out of the devil himself!

And then it happened. Six horsemen riding at a gallop over the hilly horizon, were swiftly bearing down upon the Sobibor alumni. While everyone else cowered for cover in a roadside ditch, the two leaders and three *kapos* stepped forward forcefully, weapons at the ready.

The lead rider bellowed forth in baritone Russian, "Identify yourselves, NOW!"

Lieutenant Pechersky did the introductory honors and then waited for the response that immediately dissolved the forthcoming onslaught.

"Captain Arkady Kolginov, Voroshilov detachment, *Partizaner* 'Force Blue,'" the lead rider identified himself and his men as he dismounted. "We heard all about your exploits, Lieutenant. We picked-up a desperate German broadcast for re-enforcements more than a week ago. Happy to see you alive and in good spirits. You'll have to tell us all when we return to our bivouac. It's only a few kilometers. I'll leave one of the men here to escort you."

Not yet willing to identify himself and still using his alias, Branko chimed in with his plausible Russian: "Will we be able to send a radio message when we get there, sir?"

"Sure. All communication restrictions have been tempered since our armies have crossed the Dnieper. I suppose you will want to contact Comrade Stalin himself, eh?"

"No—Commander Timoshenko will do!" Branko couldn't resist responding.

In a cloud of dust, a loudly laughing Kolginov and his troop rode off toward a landscape of heavily forested hillocks.

Throwing caution to the winds, the corp of ragamuffins whooped and hollered, kissed and hugged! Four even danced an impromptu *kozatski* to a chorus of hand-clapping.

Now they were truly close to taking that very deep, free breath.

*****

**Washington, D.C.
(The Oval Office)
October 24, 1943**

"Mr. President, Mr. President!" Harry Hopkins called—almost gleefully shouting. "Eureka! Hallelujah! We found him, we found him! Branko escaped from a death camp at Sobibor in Poland. He's alive and well—and safe with the Russkies!"

Wildly waving a communique from Ambassador Harriman in Moscow, Harry Hopkins had never been so animated in his life. In short order FDR was equally elated—uncommonly rising to his feet without assistance and hugging Hopkins. He then invited the outer office staff in to share in the joy of General Branko Horvitch's rebirth thousands of miles away. Old-timers in the FDR administration revered Branko from his days of sharing a White House office with Wild Bill Donovan. They were all overjoyed with the good news.

As the celebration wound down a bit, FDR proudly added: "To top it off, we have just received word that our boys have shattered the last major Nazi resistance on our road to Rome. I just knew that once we got past that damned Monte Cassino, things would open up fast. Thank God! At the same time, our naval efforts in the Pacific are paying off more and more every day. And now this news of a man who gallantly fought in France during the last war, went on to show his mettle with Russian partisan forces and escaped from one of the death camps? He's a veritable one-man-gang, I tell you!"

Bill Donovan was in London, but he was at the top of the list for Harry to call. The relief in Donovan's voice clearly came through. He asked Harry to phone Edith Wilson and Jesse and have either of them call Tante Shayndl in Switzerland.

Knowing that Senator Truman would want to know the good news, Hopkins next phoned him at the Senate Office Building.

Meanwhile, FDR ordered Hopkins to bring Branko back to the USA as soon as possible. Not a simple task, but certainly with the number of Military Air Transport (MATS) planes in Europe, it would be done.

*****

Washington, D.C.
October 11, 1938

Branko was surprised to receive a letter from Hal Wallis, the Warner Brothers Executive Producer for the proposed movie, *The Fighting 69th*. The letter included a "firm" shooting schedule for the movie. Branko phoned John Prout to learn that he also had gotten a copy of the letter.

Branko next had to petition Bill Donovan for a three-month leave of absence, beginning the following March. He had warned Bill that this was likely to happen.

Even though he had amicably arranged for the leave, Branko couldn't help but feel he was abandoning people who had gone out their way to be accommodating. Wild Bill had arranged for them both to have office space in the White House rather than in the Senate Office Building as the budget had called for. It was true that the arrangement wasn't for Branko's sake, but rather because Donovan wanted to be within easy reach of Harry Hopkins and FDR. Intelligence decisions were made quickly and these logistics suited that purpose well. More importantly, FDR insisted on these arrangements.

Truths all—none of which assuaged Branko's nagging sense of duty. Since officially joining Bill's "unofficial intelligence operations" he had learned volumes concerning the inner-workings of a worldwide spy network; Planning, building, implementing and safeguarding. During a hectic fifteen months, regular, lengthy phone conversations and communications had exposed Branko to clandestine contacts that Bill had developed since his days with Roosevelt's Naval Intelligence hacks in the 20s.

Donovan had set up an almost impossible route toward excellence in the intelligence capabilities of the United States—and he had done it almost single-handedly, at that. During the first half of the year, he had spent two weeks as a guest of London's British Intelligence and made forays into Portugal, Spain, France and Turkey. These were preparatory visits requiring follow-ups in the near future. This is where Branko would come in and why Bill connected him with "local friends" in each of those countries.

This was all being done under deadlines imposed by Donovan, who firmly believed that a war with Germany was inevitable. And he wasn't the only one thinking this. It was agreed upon in every county that he visited. Every country, that is, excluding Spain where the fascistic Generalissimo Franco proved to be immovable in his allegiance to the Fuhrer.

Franco had his hands full and was planning an all-out attack on the Nationalist forces before the year end. The Germans and Italians continued to pour in all varieties of equipment to defeat the rebels and the odds were piling up on their side. Russia seemed to pull back from spending good money after bad in the dying cause. At this advanced stage Stalin and his advisors no longer saw any sense in it.

During Donovan's flitting around Europe, the American Ambassador in Berlin arranged a private meeting with Adolf Hitler. The uncharacteristically cordial Chancellor made no attempt to hide his plans for additional *lebensraum*. The *Anschluss* in March, giving him Austria outright, was not near enough to satisfy his lust for conquest.

The Oxford-educated linguist provided by the Ambassador was able to present a smooth translation to both parties, immeasurably enhancing the sensitive conversation.

"Of course, the United States is always welcome to become my ally," Adolf Hitler remarked during the meeting. "The insular English have no true love for your country or mine and fickle France is merely a poor lost schoolboy chewing on leftover *foie de gras*. You must know that the English gassed me in the war—damn them to hell! Many of my comrades did not survive the hideous attacks or have since led wretched lives. There are still occasions where my breathing is severely labored. I do not forget nor forgive."

"You neglect to mention the Soviets, Herr Chancellor."

"I have no place in my future for communist world domination goals, Herr Donovan. They are the very real threats to all of us, you understand. My council is pleading with me to enter into a non-aggression pact with Stalin. But that pipe-smoking ass wants to sign only to forestall an invasion by my storm troopers that would gobble-up the entire Soviet Union. Will we do that? Yes, we shall, even after signing such a document—and Stalin knows that all too well. Don't strike first and you will be defeated. That is a proven Teutonic principle of war that I vow to adhere to as long as I am Chancellor of The Third Reich. The Thousand Year Reich, mind you, dear sir."

If Wild Bill had any doubts of Hitler's bent, they were now buried forever.

Branko was not sure of it a few years back, but facts were persuasive and now Wild Bill had made a staunch believer out of him. President Roosevelt had been solidly in this camp since avidly reading a translation of *Mein Kampf* during his recent vacation in Warm Springs. Eleanor roundly chastised him for reading such self-serving propaganda, but after he lectured her on some of the tome's salient points, she, too, had wavered and read it.

Aside from the more vocal isolationists in congress, a slim majority of America's citizens saw Hitler's Germany as the main threat to continued world peace. Widening pools of blood spilt in the mountains, cities and plains of Spain, as well as China, testified that a frightening world war would once again be waged. The urgency imparted by Bill Donovan and the intelligence community, could not be ignored. But there was also a determined, growing opposition that was difficult to overcome. One such voice was Colonel Lindbergh, he of the solo Atlantic flight and an isolationist hero to all "America First" advocates. He branded Donovan, Roosevelt and their ilk as, "naive rabble-rousers who were driving their ill-prepared nation into an unwinnable world war."

On the evening of the day in which the Hal Wallis letter arrived, Branko attended a dinner at the Wilson house.

"One rule before Aretha sets the table for a scrumptious dinner," Edith remarked. "General, or should I say *ex-General* Horvitch, no further discussions on the sneaky-peaky game you and your Wild Bill are playing. Hear?"

"Edith, you know there's nothing much I can discuss, anyway. You're beginning to sound like our illustrious, peripatetic Senator from Missouri who periodically calls and takes me to lunch—mainly to ask what we're up to. He's quick to say that the intelligence phenomenon is one of Congresses great unknowns. Can you imagine?"

"Surely, you're joking."

"No, it's incredibly true. And whatever I do tell you will probably be a bald-faced lie anyway. So there! But there is one exciting, totally unclassified thing I can share with you that came today from the far-away land of make-believe and palm trees."

"Oh please, do tell me!"

Branko went over the Hal Wallis/Warner Brothers' letter in detail. He was to be in Hollywood around March 15th, all expenses paid and serve as associate military consultant along with John Prout. The actual filming was scheduled for mid-summer. The entire production of *The Fighting 69th* would be in and around Southern California; He and Prout anticipated to be "on set" for less than three months. This was for the part of filming that covered the 69th training camp and the horrific battle scenes—all to be shot in the trenches of Hollywood.

"My God, do you realize that David Selznick is planning to film, *Gone with the Wind* at about the same time?" Edith responded. "His studio is in contract talks with both Vivian Leigh, a British actress, for the lead role of Scarlett, and none other than Clark Gable, a handsome Rhett Butler, indeed."

"Edith Wilson, the inveterate movie fan, knows all and tells all about the latest Hollywood gossip. Tune in your radio at 9:00 p.m. for the full details!"

"Oh, Branko, you know that I am a fan. A big fan! I've read the book twice since it hit the shops in '37. How in the world are they going to be able to film such a vast expanse of a story, I'll never know. I cast the film while I was reading the book. I wanted Ronald Colman and Katherine Hepburn. It's sort of a game that has been played for the last year. Newspapers, radio shows and magazines have all had 'cast the movie' contests. I would have lost!"

"Maybe we of the heroic *Fighting 69th* could trade Pat O'Brien and Jimmy Cagney for Cluck Gobble and what's her name—Leigh!"

"It won't happen, Branko! Personally, I think Cagney is much too short to play Scarlett O'Hara, even with high heels and a wig."

"I wonder if Margaret Mitchell will also be coming out to Hollywood in the spring?" pondered the ever-ready, old but worldly, soldier. "Hell, I'll even take her to dinner at some fancy Hollywood nightclub, like, uh, the Coconut Grove."

"Branko, I tell you, she is nothing less than the world's best novelist, bar none. The poor, sweet thing has been deluged by her massive readership wherever she has appeared for book signings. I wonder how much she'll have to say about the actual filming? Probably little or nothing, I hear. Damn, I would love to be out there at the time."

"Why not? Maybe we can arrange something," said Branko, half in jest and the other half with a sense of possibility.

"Well, Mister, work on it and we'll see."

Branko smiled at that.

"Meanwhile, I hear from Jesse that they will be soon moving into a new apartment," Edith then said, abruptly shifting topics. "Just blocks from your place, near DuPont Circle."

Jesse and Sara weren't the only ones who had moved. While the Kennedy oil dollars were significantly shrinking, Branko had still been able to swing for himself the purchase of a handsome 1890's Queen Anne cottage on *P Street*. He had managed the purchase, in part, by extending the lease of his apartment to a young military couple.

"True," Branko said to Edith. "A brand new, elegant apartment building on Kalorama Street and they're moving in about two weeks. Jess and Sara came over last night to show me some of the long-lost additional wedding pictures that had been misplaced by the photographer. Can you believe such a haphazard operation? They and the Bernsteins are now working on printing these separate selected pictures to place in albums for Harry Kanter, and for you and me to have."

"How nice of them. By the way, even though it was over a year ago, I keep getting comments from friends who were there. Everyone gushes about how beautiful and meaningful it was. And this is from the likes of Betsey Peabody and Ann Castleman—both of whom had never been to a synagogue wedding before. The emotionally meaningful act of holding the service in the Eva Horvitch Hall broke everyone up, including yours truly. They all especially loved meeting Tante Shayndl and Charles."

"And I got to dance with my lovely auntie after all these years!"

"Getting them to come was a coup on your part, Branko. They were the hits of the event. I so thoroughly enjoyed touring them around town in the Rolls. They sure turned a lot of heads whenever I drove up to the Willard entrance to fetch them with my Fed-boy in tow. Booking them there was a perfect gesture."

"Tante never stops writing about the trans-Atlantic crossing and the great American adventure. They're getting a lot closer to the Swiss move, she recently informed me. I can't wait for that to happen—the sooner the better!"

"Not having seen them since the war really bowled you over, didn't it?"

Branko conceded that with a nod.

"Hopefully, you'll get to Europe on a Donovan assignment when you return from Hollywood. You could then visit them at their new home in Switzerland."

"Well, there's been talk about a 'grand tour' to meet with our contacts in Portugal, Spain and Turkey," Branko admitted. "That might provide the chance. Even if Hitler makes another move soon, that shouldn't affect the plan. No one expects either of those countries to be anything but neutral. But first things first. Maybe it'll be 'California here we come!'"

"Reminds me," Edith added, "I could ask Betsey to come with me. She's widowed for nearly two years now and probably would love to go along. I think she's never been west of her native Ohio."

"That would sure as hell solve the possible problems from the Hollywood gossip brigade. I hear they're much more visibly active than the dirt-digging crews here."

"Branko, you know that at last I finally got approval to reduce my security watch. Now it's only put in place when there's an official state dinner or public affair or anything like that.

"Don't count on it, Edith. Even FDR's snoop contingent has been cut in half for all domestic operations. He'll still have a full crew for anything involving foreign travel. Even the unfunny Harry Hopkins jokes that one can now bring a flock of hookers into the White House without detection!"

Branko liked the idea of Edith going west with him. The two of them, and yes, Betsey dear, would have a grand time discovering the dens of tinsel town. General Prout did not appear to him to be a "night-on-the-town" kind of guy, anyway. Decisions would have to be made soon in order to reserve Pullman accommodations. Branko had considered flying, but it was such a hassle these days, with multi-cross-country stops and uncomfortably crowded planes. Relaxing on Santa Fe's Super Chief out of Chicago would be more of a vacation and a chance to see a good bit of the countryside.

So be it, he thought.

HOLLYWOOD: TAKE ONE 17

Washington, D.C.
February 7, 1939

Plans were taking shape for the journey to the West Coast. Santa Fe Super Chief reservations were in order and lodgings booked while anticipation ruled the day.

Edith and Betsey opted for a two-bedroom suite at the posh Hollywood Roosevelt, while reservations for Branko and John Prout were handled by the Warner people. Hal Wallis, the popular Production Chief, had suggested single suites at the Roosevelt also, even though one of the owners was the arch rival and constant nemesis, Louis B. Mayer ("don't ever call me 'Louie'") of MGM.

The arrangement likely rankled the hell out of the cantankerous Jack Warner, but if so Wallis handled him like no one else could—as he had every day of the week and twice on Sundays. And as Wallis was quick to say, "That's no picnic at the beach!"

Meanwhile, Edith had decided to "pull rank" and on her official Wilson House stationery wrote to David Selznick, asking for a visit to his studios during filming of *Gone With The Wind*. To her surprise he phoned her on the day he received her letter.

"I would be delighted and honored if you would visit the Selznick Studios in Culver City," were his exact words. He asked where she would be staying and for how long. As she was to be in town for a month beginning March 14th, he promised to send a studio limousine for her on a day or two when the filming would be most interesting.

She mentioned her dear friend, Betsey, would also be coming along, of course.

"About time you played that card, dear madam," Branko remarked when hearing of the phone call. "Why the hell you've always been so reluctant, I'll never understand."

"You know very well that I've never condoned anyone in Washington using their position to gain favors, even though so few actually do!" she said with a broad grin.

"Edith, come off the goody-two-shoes pedestal."

She affected a, *whatever do you mean by that,* posture.

"What you've done is natural and I doubt that Selznick looks at it in any other way," Citizen Horvitch responded with unabated sincerity. "Are you sure you don't also want to spend a day or two watching the troops wallow in the mud in a make-believe trench in Burbank? I can make it happen."

Mutual laughter ended this "scene" with a bang. The resulting film could very well become the Fighting 69th battling General Sherman's Yankee troops over where the former First Lady would spend her Hollywood tour. The competition would undoubtedly include shopping at the elegant Bullock's, a night or two on the town and night-clubbing at Trocadero or Earl Carroll's. Of course there would also be dining at any number of headlining establishments: The Brown Derby, Musso and Frank's, Perino's and the Coconut Grove. Naturally enough, the famous Dave Chasen's red-hot chili could not be ignored—for as much as three days following ingestion, some devotee's would add."

Shortly before the trip to Hollywood Branko old friend, Henry Luce of *Time* Magazine, phoned. The call had been triggered by a tip from New York's venomous gossip, Walter Winchell, otherwise known as "the mouth that roared."

"Branko," came Luce's cheery voice, "I know for a fact that you are heading for Hollywood to be the Military Advisor for the *Fighting 69th* film. Tell me about it, man!"

"Not much beyond that to tell. I'll be spending about three months on the set, along with Retired General John Prout, also of the 69th."

"Well, my favorite cover-guy, you can bet that I'll have one of my staffers in Movieland on this tidbit with scratching claws.

"You don't say?" Branko came back, smiling

"Sure enough. And I hope *Gone With The Wind* doesn't completely overshadow your production."

"Well, I doubt—"

"It'll be a damn blockbuster, Branko!" Luce went on

"I'm sure that—"

"Where are you staying and when do you expect to be there?"

Branko waited a beat before answering—just to make sure Luce wasn't asking another rhetorical question.

The phone conversation was unusually long for the hectic peripatetic, but he finally closed by saying that a Dariel Sidney from *Time's* L.A. office would be in touch with him when he arrived at the Roosevelt. He also intimated that Prout would not be even the slightest story fodder and asked Branko not to say anything about it to the Irish General.

There was not much Branko could do or say after this conversation with Luce. He would certainly try to keep the *Time* interview confidential insofar as he could. The word would have been out with or without *Time*. He was sure that those who made the stars twinkle would be on this and anything else to do with the film-to-be. He did not understand just how the rumor-mill worked.

What he did not know was that the Warner people had been tossing little daily bits and pieces to the gossip-feeding frenzy for months. There had been numerous interviews with James Cagney and Pat O'Brien, the popular lead actors, on network and local radio. *Variety*, *The Hollywood Reporter* and the *Los Angeles Times*—midwestern and eastern newspapers—had all spilled "ink" about the Fighting 69th unit and the film. But even with the media primed well before the cameras began to roll, the potent competition of *Gone with the Wind* had severely disadvantaged Jack Warner and his brothers in firing up pre-distribution interest. Additionally, the growing overseas market—especially Ireland, England, France and Italy—was not to be ignored. Germany was still a question mark at this time.

Obviously, *Gone with the Wind*—or *GWTW*, as the media shortened it—was far-ahead by virtue of a best-selling masterpiece. So even without the Warners greasing the skids of gossip *GWTW* came with all the attendant publicity of a bestseller for the past two years.

But Jack Warner was certainly not one to cower. He was candid, embarrassingly so at times, and more than ready to take on the Selznick crowd as well as Margaret Mitchell herself—should the occasion arise.

And then there were the dark clouds of yet another all-encompassing war with which to contend. The Hollywood shakers and breakers at home and abroad were wondering whether the depression-affected movie-goers were ready for a Civil War epic *and* a World War battlefield film. The smart money had decided that Warner and Selznick would each benefit by filming these projects a year apart. In the meantime, a feel-good film like MGM's, *Wizard of Oz,* could end-up the current big winner in the battle at the box office.

But Branko was not about to lose two seconds of sleep over any of it. He had a job to do and would do it well. Let the profit chips fall where they may!

Los Angeles, California
March 14, 1939

Throughout the mid-west gray clouds had deposited a blanket of snow along with temperatures in the forties at station stops in La Junta, Colorado and Santa Fe, New Mexico.

But now, de-training at Union Station had all the elements of a Chamber of Commerce booster film in which the motion picture foliage crew had changed the set. A deliciously exotic aroma of orange blossoms wafted through the Sunday morning air and the front doors of the magnificent terminal led out into a small park laden with majestic Birds of Paradise—California's state flower.

With a brass cart, a Redcap managed their luggage and the most industrious of the waiting taxi drivers leapt out, asking, "Where to?"

It was a long ride to the Roosevelt, but sans the traffic of a weekday they arrived within a half-hour, filled with the cabbie's running spiel of Hollywood's wonders. If nothing else, the self-appointed tour guide garnered a sizeable tip from Branko. While the cabbie may have thought that his passengers were three mid-western yahoos about to fall for Tinsel Town, the five-dollar bill was a decidedly welcomed windfall.

At the hotel desk, a message awaited Branko. Prout had telegraphed that two of his flights were delayed due to snow storms west of Chicago. He didn't expect to arrive until late the next day. Branko, who thoroughly enjoyed the train journey, even with less than good weather, was quite relieved that he decided to travel by rail. He firmly believed that there was still a good bit of tweaking necessary to make air transportation convenient and statistics showed that the majority of Americans agreed with that assessment. Whether that would change very much in the foreseeable future was still anybody's guess. In a recent radio interview, Charles Lindbergh had said that huge airliners carrying up to two-hundred passengers across the country in ten hours was solidly fixed in America's future. Some call-in reactions favored Lindy's statements, agreeing that if anyone could offer an educated prognosis, it would be the famed cross-Atlantic soloist. Still, most Americans classified it as pure fantasy. An airplane carrying two-hundred people, plus crew and crossing the USA in ten hours was beyond the realm of sensible thinking.

Exhausted from three days on the train, Edith phoned Branko and suggested they all freshen-up before meeting in the lobby for dinner.

When they finally met, it was nearing 6:00 p.m. and the concierge recommended that they sample the hearty food at the unusual Pig 'n Whistle, which was a few blocks walk in the pleasant spring evening.

After a less than elegant but quite tasty meal all three were eager to return to the hotel for turning-in early. However, as the tourists they were, they first stopped at Grauman's Chinese Theater across the street from the hotel and enjoyed seeing the famous footprints. The feature showing was Darryl Zanuck's, *Tail Spin*, starring Alice Faye, Constance Bennett, Jane Wyman and Charles Farrell. Also showing was a Republic Studios cowboy "B" picture with sure-shootin' Hoot Gibson, one of Branko's "oater" favorites. Evening movie-goers were lining up for good seats in the theater which looked like the entrance to a Ming Dynasty Pagoda in mysterious Shanghai.

The three were agog by the many celebrity foot and hand-prints cast in cement at the entrance and stood gawking along with dozens of tourists standing nearby. Branko's shoes dwarfed Clark Gable's foot-print while his hand also smothered the actor's hand-print. Edith and Betsey both quietly applauded as off they went with no one daring to suggest a nightcap at the Roosevelt cocktail lounge.

In the elevator, Edith asked if either of them knew the story of Sid Grauman, the rather eccentric, wild-haired theater magnate who built both the Chinese and the Egyptian-themed theater down the boulevard. Neither knew anything about the man.

Edith coyly whispered, "He's a homosexual. Not only that, but he was the first Hollywoodian to come out in the open and proudly proclaim it."

As a long-time fan, Edith knew her Hollywood history well, as told in a growing number of the sensationalist fan magazines she received. According to what she read on the Grauman matter, the community's reaction had been barely tepid with blasé statements ranging from Jack Warner's gruff, "So what the hell has that got to do with exhibiting my films?" to Samuel Goldwyn's, "Fairy, shmairy—I should care? As long as he fills his seats to capacity whenever showing any Goldwyn films!"

To a man, each of the major moguls, including Mayer, William Fox, Carl Laemmle, and Adolph Zukor—all of whom experienced being "different" in European and American societies, responded similarly: *Ho-hum.* To them it was about as shocking as the occasional alcoholic star showing up for a "shoot" hung over. Throughout Southern California, frankly, no one seemed to give a damn!

Warner Brothers Studio
Burbank, California
March 15, 1939

Wallis sent a Packard limousine to pick up Branko at noon. Prout had not yet arrived, but Jack Warner wished to meet for lunch at his office. Branko wore his uniform, as Hal Wallis had suggested. As Branko realized, there were no restrictions at the time for a retired officer to wear the uniform with his last highest rank. The hotel had done a perfect job of pressing, up to and including razor sharp pleats. The dress blues, so much in vogue in the small standing army of the 1930's, were Edith's favorites, but Branko had rarely worn them during his War College days.

"So this is our famous Brigadier General Branko Horvitch, eh," Warner greeted upon the first meeting with Branko and Wallis.

"So good to meet you, sir."

"Well, we'll see what you have to say after working with us a few days or weeks. Right, Wallis? This is one helluva tough business and nice guys don't even finish last. They're drummed out before the godamm race even starts. But, we certainly appreciate the time and effort you'll be contributing to the success of our noble film project.

"Branko, Warner Brothers Studios is nothing more or less than a factory and we build nothing other than dreams for America and Americans. *The Fighting 69th* has all the potential of being a fine piece of filmmaking and you are going to help make it so."

"I'm ready to do anything I can, Mr. Warner."

"Aw, come off that formal bullshit, Branko. Just plain old *Jack* to you. I'll soon tell you what we expect from you and what's his name —Prout? We're prepared to pay you the handsome sum as noted in the contract and treat you as we would any executive. I believe Hal will be singularly responsible for that, or I'll fire his chubby ass."

Wallis was not the least bit annoyed by his irascible chief's statement, even knowing that on a recent day, he axed fifteen employees for a wide variety of what he believed to be good reasons. Mr. Warner was not exactly Mr. Loveable.

Lunch was an opulent affair in the studio's private executive dining room off the main commissary. The mustachioed Warner, nattily dressed in a $200 blue serge double-breasted jacket and white yachting pants, waxed forth with personal stories that even Hal had never heard.

"Branko, I wanted the most experienced military advisors we could find and I had my secretary compile a dossier on you. I must say it's impressive, even to a curmudgeonly skeptic like myself. We did a war movie back in 1919, and without any advice on authenticity we made a helluva lot of inexcusable mistakes. They probably weren't that evident to the film-goer, but I knew and I was embarrassed by them—even though it was widely acclaimed. In '30, we made *Dawn Patrol* which was a few notches better than the aforementioned *My Four Years in Germany*. I've been very reluctant to do any war pictures until *The Fighting 69th* came along and this time out, we're demanding authenticity. Without Cagney, I doubt if we would have undertaken it. The little bastard is a hard-ass to work with. Can you imagine what he says about me?"

Branko, laughing at the last remark, was warming up to the man.

Of course confession and self-deprecation was something he admired and was known to practice on occasion. He was also not naive enough to think that the relationship couldn't change in a split-second. Compared to his military roots and espionage experience, he felt he was playing in a different league.

"I was a punk kid when my older brothers and I stumbled onto this whacky business," Warner was now saying. "We got a kick out of watching a few of the nickelodeon shows in Pittsburgh. We agreed then and there that this business had possibilities. Going ahead with our plans, we found some adequate store-front space in New Castle, Pennsylvania—very close to our home in Youngstown, Ohio. All we lacked was money to lease that sizeable of a store—and the projecting equipment, film and chairs for the audience. Our father was a butcher who had a pitiful, rag-peddling business on the side and a healthy horse that we pawned for $200. I told the old man it was stolen."

An incredulous Branko, shaking his head, jumped in with, "I'd say that took a helluva lot of *chutzpah!*"

"You ain't heard nuthin' yet, Branko. I was the horse thief, but it had to be done, old boy. We had just enough to pay a month's rent and lease the film, *The Great Train Robbery.*

"With nothing much left, I spotted a funeral home a few doors down the street and made my first successful business deal...with an undertaker! We could use as many of his 'mourning' chairs we wanted, as long as they were back in the home by early the next day. He insisted on deposit money and a sum for the actual use of the chairs. Instead, I told him he and his family could have free tickets for the shows anytime they wanted, but they had to leave the 'stiffs' behind. Deal done."

"I'm not surprised that you closed a very good deal, Jack," interjected an entertained Branko.

"Of course it was, with us Warner boys behind it. And, hell, I was only sixteen! We soon had six 'nicks' strung around eastern Ohio and western Pennsylvania. By Chanukah time, we bought back the horse and our father was delighted that we 'found it!'"

Wallis had heard these stories so often that he continued without missing a beat: "That was a long time ago, beginning of the century,

Branko. But after that Jack, saw the normal progression before him. Exhibiting films was fun and profitable but the next giant step was to produce the product."

"Damn you, Mother Wallis' boy, you make it sound like it was easy! It sure as hell wasn't. Among other things, we fought and sued the Tom Edison Patent Trust—a damned power cabal, if ever there was one. The *mumseh* was monopolizing the business, based on his tinker-toy inventions. After the Supreme Court 'robes' decided in our favor, we were on equal footing and it was no holds barred. Before that, Edison's goons busted up our productions in Ft. Lee, New Jersey. That was really the first 'Hollywood.' And that whole filthy Edison scene was why the Laemmles, Mayers, Goldwyns, Zukors, Foxes and my brothers and I headed west. It took a continent to get away from that corrupt East Coast thinking. And little did any of us realize that we were creating a constellation as brilliant as any other in the skies. Here we were free to innovate—to manufacture the films that make up the American dream.

"So that's all you have to know, soldier, and I'll bet you never realized any of this while attending Hollywood's movies. Now you do. I think it's important as you are now a member of the inner circle —well not quite—but you know what I mean, *boychick*!"

"I'm more than just fascinated," Branko responded. "For years I've read about some of these things, but hearing it from you in person—that's something else entirely."

Branko's comment brought an expression of satisfaction from Jack Warner.

"Thank you, Jack," Branko added. Diplomacy was one of his most valuable assets.

After some good-natured story-swapping as well as a round of cognac and cigars, Wallis announced that there was a short staff meeting at 3:00 in the Board Room. It would be an initial opportunity for Branko to meet the screenwriters, a few cast members, and get his feet wet, so to speak.

"I'm sure you understand how important your advisory function is to this film," Warner said to Branko. "Our proposed weaponry has largely been guesswork and that has to change. The panoplies for the extras and cast members have to be in line with what you remember. We have a good supply of khaki uniforms and more being made by our costume department. And of course, the choreography of the battle scenes has to be precise and totally realistic within a miniscule margin of error."

"Jack, I'm confident that General Prout and I can deliver what you're looking for," responded Branko, as he stood up to shake Jack's outstretched hand.

"I don't doubt it," Warner said. "In the meantime, have a good time while you're here. I arranged a car from our motor pool for you and Prout to have starting tomorrow. And as you saw from your ride this morning it should take no more than thirty minutes to get to the studio from the Roosevelt. Providencia Ranch, where the battle scenes will take place, is only another fifteen minutes further east. Traffic seems to be light wherever you'll be driving, and that's a Godsend here in boom town."

Wallis pulled out a few sheets of paper and briefed Branko on what to expect for the next few weeks.

"These mimeographed sheets," Wallis explained, "will change almost daily. It's the very nature of making a movie—especially a Warner Brothers film with Jack at the helm.

"Got it," Branko said, bobbing his head.

"This is the very latest schedule," Wallis indicated, handing one of the mimeographed pages to Branko. The ink was a bold, almost runny-looking dark blue. The distinct aroma from the mimeographing process latched onto Branko as if symbolic for the newness of what he was now doing.

March 16th Meet in my office at 7:00 a.m. Director Bill Keighley, major cast and the writers will be present and the newest script changes will be read aloud for the first time.

March 20th   At 8:00 a.m. we will all travel to the ranch for a lay of the land before trenches, dugouts and breastworks are finalized. After lunch, there will be a meeting of the writers and the advisors in my office.

March 28th   Noon, full dress rehearsal for the Camp Mills scenes with a speech-less run-through at Providencia Ranch. (All extras present.)

April 1st   Providencia Ranch at 8:00 a.m. The entire Camp Mills scene. Back lot scenes will be shot on that Saturday, the 5th, at the studios, the French village, etc.

Reading the schedule, Branko felt like this was sort of a baptism of fire.

So this is the chaos that goes into making a movie, thought Branko. *We'd have straightened them out willy-nilly at the War College!*

The following day, the meeting with Wallis was a cacophonous mélange of clashing egos. Right off the bat, Cagney and O'Brien were a half-hour late. Wallis called them on it.

Cagney told him to go straight to hell.

O'Brien chastised Cagney for talking that way in front of a Catholic chaplain.

Everyone laughed uproariously.

Wallis told Father Pat to stick the backward collar up his keester and seasoned Director Bill Keighley shut them all up with nothing but an upraised hand.

When introduced to Branko, Cagney immediately showed-off his language skills, saying, *"Nu, Horvitch, du hast gevenn in der groisseh milchomer?"*

Branko was stunned by the star's perfect Yiddsh.

"Ich hat geboren veren und vachsen in Manhattan, east side," Cagney went on to explain while striking the epitome of Cagney stances— hands on hips and feet planted firmly apart. *"Ich hat gelernt a gitn Yiddish foon die kinder und der machers und der mamas und tatehs. Irish ich bin, aber Yiddish ich vais. Ich ken redn a zay vi deiner bubbe!"*

Wallis lost control from the start, but Keighley attempted to salvage it by shooting-from-the-hip: "Okay, Mr. Smart Ass, so you know Yiddish. Are you going to learn your lines with it?"

There would be no pampering with Keighley at the helm.

Restrained laughter prompted Keighley on: "That would be a sight to see and a voice to hear. In the heat of battle in, *No Man's Land*, you'll be on one knee—ala Al Jolson—singing a tearful rendition of *Yiddishe Mama*, I suppose. Hell, I'll get Mister Sinister George Raft and Sophie Tucker to do a Jewish-Italian duet of *O Sole Mio!*"

This time the laughter wasn't restrained.

Wooly-haired actor Alan Hale was close to convulsions and the pensive, poker-faced George Brent was egging Keighly on. Brent was an altogether different personality than the Wild Bill Donovan that he was portraying in the film.

Branko couldn't wait to tell Bill that Brent was a helluva lot better looking.

On the other hand O'Brien was meant to play the role of Father Duffy—the same feisty Irishman in every way. Cagney, as the fictitious Jerry Plunkett, didn't have to look or act like anyone else. From beginning to end Cagney would be playing Cagney, even though Plunkett was to start out as a coward who endangers his comrades in battle.

James Cagney, he of a dozen tough guy movies, usually knew when to stop, but his daggered glare toward the director could have just as easily killed him on the spot. Of course, Keighley knew enough to never give Cagney a loaded gun—even blanks from point-blank range could be disastrous.

Thus began the first day of Branko's tour of duty. He stayed a short while to chat with Norman Reilly Raine and Fred Niblo, the veteran screenwriters. Of course, Cagney lingered for a minute to further befriend Branko and was nothing but pleasant. He explained, once again—and in English—his knowledge of Yiddish.

Branko felt that the session with Cagney and O'Brien had gone well. Both beloved actors were widely-known for being edgy to the point of non-cooperation, including an occasional walk off the set. Branko didn't think they would disappoint from what he had just experienced.

In just one day he found out more about Hollywood than he ever wanted to know. It was a world light-years away from his life with in-the-flesh Wild Bill Donovan or even the War College. This much he knew; he would earn every last dollar received in the next three months.

Dinner at the heralded Musso and Frank's a few blocks east on the boulevard included the appearance of the A.W.O.L. John Prout. He had survived that long and exhausting trip by air, but the wear and tear showed all over his craggy, aging, chalk-white face.

"Never again!" he proclaimed with a pained gaze.

Edith and Betsey eagerly asked Branko to recount his day at "school" and Prout joined in.

"I'd sure like to hear what I missed. But I suppose I'll find out tomorrow. Do we have any homework for tonight, Branko?"

"You bet we do, John. I have a copy of the 122-page script for you to peruse. Sort of a familiarization briefing for you, General. There may be a true-and-false exam tomorrow. Failing could mean twenty lashes from His Excellency, Sir 'Yankel, call me Jack' Warner."

Fortunately, somewhere along the way, Prout had been clued-in on the Yiddish name that the press and friends sometimes used for Jack Warner.

At Edith's prodding, Branko did a fast and thorough job of reviewing the day at Warner Brothers. He elicited a few guffaws from his dinner partners, especially with regard to Cagney's Yiddish exercise. At this, the worldly General Prout responded in a guttural County Mayo brogue, "*Oy vay and begorrah!* Cagney speaking Yiddish, Saints preserve us all! What has Hollywood done to that fine Celtic lad? Has Father Fame captured the poor boy? I've seen most of his movies, and now this adds an unforeseen dimension, I'll say!"

Branko was relieved to see Prout jump right into the conversation, seemingly very much at ease with the former First Lady present. Obviously, he had heard and read some of the trysting rumors around Washington while attached to the Irish Embassy.

For his part, Branko had never outwardly even acknowledged the rumors. He and Edith had long ago agreed to treat their relationship in this manner and without deviation Branko honored that pact.

While Branko was undergoing his studio orientation, a telephone call from the Los Angeles FBI office altered the bus tour booking that Edith and Betsey planned. Agent William Keeler was arriving at 10:00 a.m. and he would take them on a tour of the city. The arrangement, Edith was told, arose from the FBI temporarily taking over duties of the local Secret Service office that had closed. She also learned from the conversation that Harry Hopkins had made the arrangements per FDR, who had given the FBI her contact information. This was beyond the fiscal austerity policy concerning government-funded protection. As former First Ladies of deceased Presidents no longer qualified for Secret Service protection, Edith had been under private security since Wilson's passing. But what with old habits dying hard, she still referred to private security as *Fed Boys*.

Keeler turned out to be a strapping young man. When he arrived and confirmed his credentials the women were delighted to be chauffeured around town by such a handsome young G-man.

They first window-shopped some of the Beverly Hills commercial streets and then drove down Wilshire Boulevard for the stunning Pacific Ocean views from the Palisades in Santa Monica. The clear skies even allowed a glimpse of Catalina Island thirty miles to the west.

The two social butterflies of Washington thoroughly enjoyed the drive in the government-issue, black Chevy sedan. Edith suggested lunch at Chasen's—she had done her homework in preparation for the visit and ordered the famous chili dish. Across the room she spotted

Mary Pickford and Buddy Rogers and a few others who looked vaguely familiar. She knew enough not to gawk and hoped Betsey would follow her lead.

Lunch was followed by a quick look-see at the two-year old Farmer's Market for a bit of browsing among the fruit, vegetable stalls and cafes. They had never seen such an array of healthy produce anywhere in the east. Keeler pointed out the adjacent Gilmore Field where the Pacific Coast League Hollywood Stars played in the AAA league. Being somewhat of a baseball fan, this pleased Edith.

Before returning to the hotel Edith politely asked Keeler to take them through the residential areas of Beverly Hills. Agent Keeler, or *Willy*, as he insisted on being called, had similarly escorted a number of high-level government officials. Consequently, he knew where the most of the celebrities lived.

Edith was beside herself, the rabid movie fan that she was. Betsey started off somewhat blasé, but perked-up gushing and giddy before long. In rapid succession, the agent pointed out the residences of the plush and lush silver screen stars: Jack Benny, Joan Crawford, Robert Taylor, Lilian Gish, Bette Davis, Ava Gardner, Buster Keaton, James Cagney, Pat O'Brien, Stan Laurel, Groucho Marx, Jimmy Stewart, Spencer Tracy, Charles Laughton, John Wayne and several others.

Keeler pointing out Mae West's penthouse floor in the elegant Ravenswood Apartment building on Rossmore usually brought a rash of "Come up and see me sometime" imitations and antics from the Washingtonians to whom he had given tours such as this. Even though he had experienced it many times, he was still slightly embarrassed by it Fortunately, Edith and Betsy elected to stay with "ooh-ing" and "ahh-ing."

The classy El Royale apartments next door housed George Raft, Ronald Reagan other young thespians reluctant to invest in real estate until their careers blossomed. A conservative lot, they were.

Knowing Keeler was assigned to her protection for the length of her stay, Edith nonetheless expressed a twinge of guilt for taking so much of the agent's time. When she said this, he responded that he was pleased to chauffeur her anywhere she wished and would be close behind wherever she planned to go, day or night. A rookie agent would be taking the second shift and there would be no one on duty after 11:00 p.m.

That was acceptable to Edith even though she had a history of ditching her security watchdogs while being First Lady. And if she did decide to lose Keeler, she figured that being without her own car would make it an easier task.

Branko received a call from Donovan the moment he walked into the Roosevelt lobby. The Concierge insisted that he take the call from his desk in the hotel manager's office. Out of a sense of loyalty, brotherly love and comradeship, Branko had planned weekly phone calls to Bill but the spymaster beat him to it.

"Hey, partner," Donovan's voice came through the receiver, "have they signed you to a ten-year acting contract, yet? If not, why not?"

"Good to hear from you, boss! This place is way beyond what I thought Hollywood was all about. It's a loony bin twenty-four hours a day!"

"How about the job itself?"

"More difficult than Prout or I expected. They sure as hell need our help and this was only my first full day!

"Look here, General, if you need a real expert, call—I'll bail you out in no time!"

"Okay, wise-ass. How's the thrilling spooky-spy game going?"

"Well I—"

"Because if you need a real expert, call—I'll take over and bail *you* out."

That got a laugh from the other end of the phone.

The banter between the two veteran friends went on for a few more repartees and finally settled into a serious exchange. Wild Bill brought-up the baby-step status of his clandestine operation that was under blistering fire from Senate and House watchdogs—Senator Norris, especially.

A criminal waste of time and taxpayer money, Norris had recently told political reporter, Eli Cohn at WNDC. Branko couldn't help feeling that Norris was exacting revenge to get back at big, bad Branko Horvitch. The Nebraskan never got over their heated exchange of years ago.

"When you finish your stint in tinsel-town, I have some quick trips planned for you," Donovan was now saying. "We have to enlarge the network—providing we don't run out of moolah. The boss assured me that this won't happen. He said that after the elections next year, he will find a way to justify a more overt profile for us. He hasn't failed us yet, so it may very well come to fruition. I'm more concerned with what's going on in the USSR."

"I thought we were certain of an eventual non-aggression pact between the frat boys," Branko responded, referring to Hitler and Stalin. "Didn't you say your guy in Berlin was certain that von Ribbentrop and Molotov are already drafting the pact details?"

"Sure," Donovan answered, "but it only signals that Hitler is planning to invade Russia in the next few years—treaty or no treaty. Maybe the other way around, but I doubt it!"

"Are you saying that there's no stopping another godamm war?"

"Yeah. Each and every last one of our contacts predict it within months, not years."

"So, here we go again, Wild One, without thee and me in the front lines to win it by a K.O," Branko responded without the glib connotation his words would have otherwise conveyed.

"This war will be won or lost by the intelligence mustered-up by the combatants. Those with the least number of leaky holes will be the victors."

Branko grunted non-committedly.

"I swear, it'll make the Argonne woods look like a Central Park Sunday picnic! We've gotta firm-up and polish our network fast. The sooner the hell you are home the better I'll feel. Our country is going to need you again, for Chrissakes.

Branko could hear the concern in Wild Bill's tone and the retired General couldn't help but feel the heat of guilt for his otherwise well-deserved Hollywood trip.

*****

Hollywood, California
April 1, 1939

Excluding military service, Branko had never put in a more rigorous day. And even then, the re-enactment of war in the wilds of Providencia Ranch was nearly as exhausting as had been the real thing.

Maybe I just ain't getting any younger, the former soldier wearily admitted to himself.

After several tightly choreographed dress rehearsals, the first day of actual "shooting" lasted from 7:00 a.m. until 7:00 p.m.

The scene: A brawl between the Fighting 69th troops and the Alabama 4th National Guard as it had really happened at Camp Mills in the early summer of 1917. The 69th had been in camp for about a week when in marched the Alabama 4th, to be part of the 42nd Rainbow Division alongside the 69th.

But they had made a colossal mistake marching from the Long Island Railroad train station a mile away. Their brass band had led the way, striking-up a spirited version of *Dixie*. The entire troop had joined-in, singing at the top of their homesick lungs.

The provocation came as if on cue.

"You godamm sons-a-bitches, go back to your mammy in Alabamy," was the first shout from the ranks of the 69th, followed by exchanges along the lines of: "We'll shove them trombones up yer keesters… Damyankees…we'll whup the sheet out of your sissy asses…Give me my rifle and we'll make this a godamm turkey shoot, you Yankee girlies!"

This went on *ad nauseam*, until the first frenzied Irish punch was thrown. Then all hell broke loose.

Harking back twenty-two long years, Branko remembered it as if it were yesterday. Now it was to be replayed, punch for punch, insult for insult, animosity for animosity, bigotry for bigotry.

James Cagney portrayed his unlikeable character *Jerry Plunkett*, street-fighter, ne'er-do-well, to extremes but took Keighley's direction well. He had already shown his good sportsmanship by agreeably depicting the only man scripted to faint from his first inoculation. After the successful take he did a little *Yankee-doodle-dandy* Cohan jig for humor but was all business following the laughter.

Now, at the start of the Alabama-Yankee brawl, he wildly threw that first punch, followed by Alan Hale bear-hugging one of the "rebels" with a little too much gusto. Pat O'Brien's *Father Duffy* and George Brent's *Colonel Donovan* repeated their intensely rehearsed parts trying to break up the melee. A group of the Warner stable's bit actors who portrayed the officer corps of both sides, performed with the professionalism of the seasoned actors they were. One of them was Jack Warner's wife's cousin Herbie who, at forty-nine, was hoping to be "discovered" before washing-up on the shoals of celebrity.

Keighley wanted to get the fight right without too many takes, so he rode herd on his battery of production assistants, *best boys*, and *gofers*. Nonetheless, he failed to keep the takes to a reasonable number. Not that it was entirely his fault. There were just too many extras and scene elements to perfectly capture: Someone would cough, sneeze, step wrong, bust-out laughing or just out-right throw-up their arms at a blunder before the director could yell "cut" at that very thing. And with so many actors in such a demanding scene it was inevitable that they became uncontrollably rambunctious. For the few dollars a day they were being paid, they seemed to pay no attention to the director's bull-horn and it was a wonder so few were hurt and that none were hospitalized.

Finally, by 1:30 p.m., after the entire extra-cast gobbled down their sizeable lunches from the buffet tables, Hal Wallis told Keighley that he would handle the problem. He addressed the entire cast, but the extras hired from Central Casting knew that they specifically were getting a dressing-down.

"The next time any of you ignore me or Mr. Keighley," Wallis said over the bull-horn, "you'll be removed from the set by security and have to find your own way home. And don't bother coming back —ever. We don't pay for hooliganism around here."

With the horseplay now eliminated Keighley asked Branko to once more verify the way the brawl took place. Prout hadn't been at Camp Mills and for this scene contributed only generalities based upon his career in the 69th and the Irish Republican Army.

*****

For each day of filming there was a salient *modus operandi*. Nothing was to be sacrificed for authenticity; Branko and Prout had to approve everything from each morning's call for "action" through the evening's wrap-up. Wallis and Keighley called on them for each portion of every scene. If either of the veterans objected to something the producer and director acquiesced to the objection once they understood the rationale.

All of this followed the previous two weeks of concentrated sessions with screen writers and pouring over the final script with a magnifying glass, word-by-word, and line-by-line. Throughout the process—from script review though filming—a mountain of errors and broader discrepancies were easily mended. Although it was labor intensive, the entire ensemble of filmmakers and military consultants were amiable.

One of the on-going and primary concerns revolved around the front-line soldier's language. How did they talk in training camps and in the trenches? The wounded and dead stacking up like logs was easy to visually depict, but Hollywood had little insight into the dialog of soldiers amidst bombs, grenades and endless withering enemy fire.

Branko, made it especially clear that the American soldier knew no bounds when it came to language. Every four-letter word in the English language found its way into the fabric of everyday war. This was the way it had been in every war, by every country, by every army in the world since time began he explained, basing the conviction upon his near-global military background. This was the one matter of authenticity about which the screenwriters could do nothing: Since the arrival of "talkies" Hollywood was still strictly censored by the puritanical Will Hays Office. In fact, the language printed on the screens of the silent era, did not have to meet very strict guidelines. But with the advent of the Hays Office, sexual scenes and even the hint of love-making were major targets. In the case of the *Fighting 69th* the bawdiness of the village scenes in France would require constant due diligence.

Censorship was certainly not new to Jack Warner and he was carefully monitoring the censor's reaction to Selznick's *Gone With the Wind*.

After the the Hays people had objected to the final line of the *GWTW* script, Selznick was fighting them tooth and nail.

"Leave it in, Mr. Selznick," the Hays office had warned, "and you'll be fined $1,500."

Selznick's battery of legal beagles were already pulling out all the stops and expected a see-saw battle until the picture would be released. It was not the amount of money, but the basic principle that had far-reaching consequences, Jack Warner knew. And the consequences weren't just general, but specifically for the *Fighting 69th*.

The word that had the Hays office up-in-arms was in the script line that the *Hollywood Reporter* had leaked to affiliate media around the country: *Frankly, my dear, I don't give a damn!*

If the sentiments of the Hays office were to be believed, that last word in the last line of the movie would spark protests everywhere—especially in the conservative southern and mid-western states. But Warner didn't for a second believe the consensus that, *damn*, spoken on the silver screen would incite Church leaders to an apocalypse or drive people from theaters in droves.

Gambling that Selznick would succeed in his fight, the Warner brothers agreed with Wallis to leave in their own script any occurrence of *hell* and *damn*. Since *The Fighting 69th* was not scheduled for release until early next year, they were comfortable enough to proceed —even if they couldn't approach the absolute realism of dialog that Branko attributed to military men at war.

In private they occasionally joked about how that year's other potential blockbuster might play with more seasoned dialog. Squeaky clean as a baby in the bathtub, *The Wizard of Oz* would be something else with a Tin Man telling the Cowardly Lion that he was "a damn disgrace to fellow predators" or Auntie Em warning, "Take cover Dorothy—there's a damn tornado coming our way."

Hollywood, California
April 9, 1939

If Edith had ever wondered what it would be like to be in an earthly heaven of some sort, three days of watching the filming of *Gone with The Wind* was her answer.

As promised, David Selznick had phoned the hotel with a scene schedule. Edith and Betsey's departure on the Super Chief was for April 14th and so they picked the 8th, 9th and 10th to visit the *GWTW* set.

The filming was nothing short of awesome to the ladies. With Confederate soldiers lying about in wounded distress the treating surgeons and nurses seemed real. Then there were the Gray-uniformed officers on horseback that scurried around the hastily made outdoor dispensary and field hospital. The reenactment was virtually indistinguishable from the real thing.

Clark Gable was not scheduled for the scenes being filmed on the days when Edith visited the set. But, knowing of her plans he showed-up to meet the former First Lady on her last day of visits to the set. Edith was not one to swoon, but very nearly did when Gable kissed her hand. When he took Betsey's gloved hand, she did indeed experience a moment of near-fainting brought about by elevated excitement.

As he wasn't scheduled for some days yet, Gable was not dressed in the circa 1864 costume of his movie character. Rather, he was stylishly outfitted in a short-sleeved maroon sport shirt, light gray pants, white sneakers and all arriving in a silver Pontiac sports coupe. He had made quite a dashing impression when driving-up up to where they were standing. Meeting Clark Gable was a major highlight of the entire trip. Meeting Margaret Mitchell was a close second with very British Vivian Leigh and Leslie Howard in the mix for third.

Just when Edith and Betsy thought the day couldn't get any better, Selznick graciously invited them to lunch. Also joining them was Selznick's current heartthrob, gorgeous studio actress Jennifer Jones, and the rest of the GWTW cast.

When their studio limousine returned at the appointed time Edith and Betsey profusely thanked Selznick while saying *goodbyes*. All the way back to the Roosevelt they chatted up a storm. The driver caught an earful and asked Edith for an autograph to show his wife and children. Flattered, she complied with a smile and thanked him for carting them around for the previous few days. She tipped him generously.

April 13, 1939

Hank Luce had alerted Branko to expect the 9:00 a.m. visit from Dariel Sidney of *Time* Magazine. They met after breakfast in the Roosevelt lobby for the interview.

The chic young lady was well-prepared. Her assignment was to get the lowdown from Branko on *The Fighting 69th*—from the point of view of the military consultant. Her boss made it clear that Branko was the man upon whom to rely in this matter and she wasn't to talk with anyone else

Miss Sidney explained that she was to also meet with *Gone With the Wind's* David Selznick and Margaret Mitchell. Branko's interview was coming after a piece she had penned about the "little-people extras" in *The Wizard of Oz*, and for which Louis B. Mayer and star Judy Garland had been interviewed. Branko felt honored at being in such company, but recognized that his one-time magazine cover was the motivating factor for Luce.

And perhaps the unique kinship ignited by that occasion, Branko reflected.

The interview went off smoothly and the vivacious reporter promised to forward a draft to Branko before publishing. Just as she was about to take leave, Edith came into the lobby and was introduced. Meeting Edith Wilson was a rare opportunity for the reporter. Branko didn't mind the possibility of being inadvertently relegated to the role of *also-ran with the former First Lady*.

After Dariel Sidney departed and while waiting for Betsey to come down for breakfast, Edith chatted with Branko.

"Okay, Romeo," she said at one point, "tell me more about that production assistant. You know—the one who has made overtures to you. In my day, we called that flirting."

"That's all it is. Emily Laemmle is a niece to Universal Studios Carl Laemmle and now works at Warner Brothers. She's well-respected by the production fraternity and has been one of the few Hollywood females to get experience and a measure of success behind the camera. Yeah, she's a honey of a lady, all right. Has sort of a Garbo look, at that."

"Well, all I'm telling you is not to miss the opportunity, soldier. Do not ignore her gazes and just see where it goes. How old?"

"Well, let's see... She worked for Uncle Carl starting in the 20's, stolen-away by Hal about three years ago. Carl was okay about it, or so I heard. Just wanted the best opportunity for his niece. Age? I figure she's on the shady side of forty—or should I say the sunny side of fifty? I've been planning to steal second base with the next fluttering eye lashes I get."

"Good, good," Edith clucked. "No sense being alone in this palm tree zoo. You've only got a few months left in paradise, so go after it, kiddo!"

"With your blessing, my dear, how can I lose, eh?"

"That's no blessing. I'm just filling in for Tante Shayndl. Have you heard from her since we left Washington?"

"Indirectly, I guess you could say," Branko replied. "I hadn't heard from her since February but Jesse called this morning and he received a letter yesterday. She's well-entrenched in her new home in Cologny—"

"Cologny?"

"It's a lakeside suburb of Geneva."

"Her entire family there?"

"Not yet," Branko said. "In February I told Tante that if she had to she should plead with her daughters to hurry up. Guess it worked—her daughters and their families are supposed to be there by June and finally out of harm's way—thank heavens. They'll all be living five to six kilo-meters from Cologny, so Shayndl will have her grandchildren close again."

Jesse had also reported that Tante Shandyl's sons-in-law had put down earnest money toward purchasing an established gentlemen's emporium in Geneva. They had arranged this through Charles' banking contacts and introductions.

"Now here's some more big news," Branko went on. "Sometime next year, Jesse expects a transfer to Lisbon to serve as assistant protocol chief on the Ambassador's staff. As Portugal will remain neutral should war come, Sarah will join him. The Foreign Services office has already asked her to fill the new Cultural Liaison position opening-up over there there. They're both studying Portuguese in night classes at Georgetown."

"That indeed is exciting news, Branko. I'll have them over for dinner next week and get all the little details."

"Well, it's all a bit tentative," Branko admitted. "There's a lot going on in the world and anything could happen between now and then."

Edith agreed to that with a nod.

"The sabers of war are rattling through France these days, nervously awaiting Hitler's next step. My guess is still a Panzer charge into Poland, followed by a western invasion of Holland and Belgium—with France next."

April 21, 1939

The pace increased ten-fold. Jack Warner wanted a final cut as scheduled by end of summer. In addition, he wanted all battle scenes to completed by no later than June 30th. This included a series of night shooting at Providencia.

Branko and Prout had their work cut out for them and the pressure was on. Discrepancies were more than Wallis and Warner could accept. So the two military consultants became hard taskmasters—not usually within the realms of their aging personalities.

Now that deadlines ruled the roost Jack Warner's hard edged personality made daily appearances. His single-minded focus exhibited one divergence from the movie: At the end of June he asked Branko to tell the *Fusgeyer* story at his synagogue's annual brotherhood luncheon. Warner had cultivated a closeness with the illustrious "Rabbi to the Stars" Edgar Magnin of the Wilshire Boulevard Temple. The relationship was in no small way connected to a grandiose gift from Warner to the temple in 1927: A behemoth of sculpted art depicting various biblical scenes.

Warner had also asked Branko to consider a consultant's role for the following year and the studio's production of Sergeant Alvin York. Branko declined.

Not taking *no* for an answer, Warner enlisted Gary Cooper—who was slated for the title role—to influence Branko's reconsideration. While Branko found Cooper pleasant and persuasive, his loyalty to

Wild Bill and the critical intelligence project carried top priority. When Cooper was unable to dislodge Branko's priorities, he took one last, major shot. Cooper had Alvin York himself phone Branko the very next day and literally pleaded with him . York explained that he couldn't take on the project himself due to being physically under par. That much time in Hollywood, away from his-long time physician, was not a viable option for him, he said.

From the time that they met at Edith's dinner party back in the 20s, Branko had a fondness for the heroic, fellow-veteran. In fact, he respected the man enough to explain the necessity for returning to his duty in Washington. The Tennessean understood and backed off.

When the *Time* article by Miss Sidney appeared in the *Los Angeles Times* and *The Hollywood Reporter* during the same week, Warner Studios was deluged with phone calls. A wide variety of people and organizations were requesting speaking engagements from Branko. By virtue of proximity those in and around the Southern California area received priority: Within a week Branko was booked for almost the entire month of May.

He did not accept luncheon engagements unless they were on weekends and even then *The Fighting 69th* shooting schedule came first. He agreed to a few evening appearances that didn't interfere with scheduled battle scenes at Providencia Ranch.

Branko knew that once the American Legion and other veteran organizations got wind of the articles everyone would want a piece of him. He didn't believe that it was really *him* that attracted the interest: Rather, the public's attraction was to the topics on which he was asked to speak—and those were the extemporaneous aspects of his appearances he most enjoyed. His "portfolio" included veteran's affairs—past and future—the *Fusgeyers*, White House and Army War College retrospectives and his exploits with the NYPD as well as the Austro-Hungarian army.

He was a veritable one-man show of substantive history—and in Hollywood, that was something unusual. Over the years Edith had occasionally suggested that he write a book or two about what she called "his exploits." His usual answer was, *Maybe someday.*

Even though Branko had a full plate, there was still enough of the rake in him that he made time for himself. Or more specifically, for evenings and weekend-time to energize the growing romance with Emily Laemmle. On one Sunday evening, she invited Branko to a birthday dinner for her Uncle Carl. The large Laemmle Family attended and this meant a sizable portion of the Universal Studios' employees, facetiously rhymed as "The Laemmle Faemmle."

Branko found Carl to be a pleasantly authentic personality. This was quite unlike a few of the titans he had met in passing, including Columbia's bombastic Harry Cohn and the royal pretender, Louis B. Mayer. Of the entire bunch Adolph Zukor was the most serious business man and Goldwyn the most comedic. Of course, fast-talking Mr. Warner would dispute the appraisals—as if no other opinions mattered.

The party notwithstanding, Branko began to spend "off" time with Emily in her cozy, bungalow. The place offered a view just off Sunset Plaza Drive. With his extra uniform, shirts and accessories in one of her closets, Branko had taken to picking-up Prout at the Roosevelt for the drive to Burbank and Providencia each morning.

Until now—and Emily—he hadn't been comfortable with female company: At least, not since his all-too-brief marriage to Eva. There had been, of course, occasional liaisons during the late 20s and 30s. But all of those paled in comparison to this *thing* with Emily.

She was exceptionally worldly, bright as a sunbeam, wore clothing smartly and had never been involved with a man quite like soldier Branko. She had even admitted as much. Her younger days included two whirlwind flings that became unhappy marriages ending in divorces; but no children.

While it was too soon for either of them to entertain a more significant relationship, Branko was a man who wasted little time when realizing "a good thing." And in that sense, he was already planning to sway her into returning with him to Washington Not that he expected to be successful. He doubted that she would drop her career to stay with him. She had built a solid reputation and was good at what she did. Leaving Hollywood meant the loss of all that. There were not similar opportunities anywhere near D.C. or even in New York where two small movies studios had sprung up.

The dilemma was compounded by Branko's allegiance to Wild Bill Donovan. He never even remotely considered breaking his long-standing loyalty to Wild Bill's intelligence projects by staying with Emily in Hollywood. Logically, then, at best, only a long distance romance was possible.

Branko hadn't shared the depth of these ruminations with Edith since she had returned home. Instead, when they spoke over the phone every few days, Branko delighted her with the general gossip that he and Emily were an item.

As for Edith, she had kept company with Jesse and Sarah and the happy couple was anxiously anticipating the Lisbon assignment regardless of the state of unrest in Europe. Betsey, meanwhile, had been busily entertaining the intimate social circles of the city with her Hollywood exploits.

"No doubt, embellishment is her byline," Edith noted.

Warner Brothers Studios
Burbank, California
June 22, 1939

After a full week of filming the final San Mihel battle scenes, Hal Wallis announced to Branko and Prout that their duties would be over within the next two to three weeks. By then, the last of the battle scenes would be finished and post-production would be in full swing, including editing and scoring. Cagney's highly emotional death scene was being saved for last.

The ever-onstage Jack Warner was quick to remark, "Let's make it ultra-realistic—shoot the sonofabitch!"

Truthfully, Cagney had been one of the more docile cast members during the entire production. There were only a few scenes in which he demanded another take and in each case it was warranted. If nothing else, Cagney really cared for authenticity and a good script.

He realized that the callous gangster film character for which he was well-known, had no place in this movie.

All in all, peace eventually reigned upon the sets. Branko appreciated this while playing no small role in promoting a daily congenial atmosphere. General Prout was quick to follow his lead. Meanwhile, Wallis was somewhat successful in keeping Jack Warner as far from Providencia Ranch as possible.

Samuel Goldwyn Residence
Beverly Hills, California
June 29, 1939

Branko had been invited to dinner parties and beach barbecues at the sprawling homes of Hollywood's elite, but this one was different.

Given by Sam Goldwyn and his wife Frances Howard, the soiree was to welcome China's Madame Chiang Kai Shek during her worldwide fund-raising mission. Attempting to hold-off the powerful Japanese armies for more than five years had seriously breached China's coffers. With the front steadily moving to complete capitulation, the Generalissimo could trust no one better than the Madame to touch the heart and purse strings of America. Presumably, the rest of the free world would follow suit. What better way to start the ball roll-ing than picking the pockets of Hollywood moguls and its denizens.

Sam and Frances had went all-out to help even though many dubbed it a "lost cause." Not the most popular of archetypes in the breed of which Sam was a part, he had nonetheless fought as hard as any of them to build a life in Hollywood. That struggle for recognition was as likely as anything in prompting his standing-up for China as the underdog.

In this respect, Warner had told Branko up-front, "It's a brutal world and only the brutes survive."

With China, Branko privately thought, *Sam Goldwyn was supporting the survival of more than just the brutes of the world.*

Branko admired that.

Most of the attendees made their entrances dressed to the nines.

The photo-army caught wind of the occasion and were out in full force, nearly completely blocking the circular drive on Laurel Lane. For a mile cars and limousines were parked all around Coldwater Canyon. The evening could well be a veritable Chinese bonanza. As was the style in depression-era Hollywood, catered gourmet *hors d'ouevres* and a full bar flowing constant liquid refreshment replaced a traditional sit-down dinner to insure space for a larger attendance.

Jack Warner, known for his flippant *faux pas,* did not disappoint. Leaving his wife at the entry hall, he entered the scene and made a beeline to the Madame and the charming Mrs. Frances Goldwyn. After Mrs. Goldwyn made the introduction, Warner gallantly kissed the Madame's outstretched hand, saying, "My dear Madame, if I knew you'd be here, I would'a brought my laundry."

Frances made a grotesquely twisted face and rolled her eyes while nearby Branko and Emily blanched in unison.

The elegant wife of China's leader was refined enough to laugh it off, which allowed Warner the perception of legitimacy for what was otherwise a little boy's aside.

After pledge cards were distributed to guests, Sam Goldwyn, *nee* Shmuel Gelbfish—with his Yiddish accent in good working condition —officially introduced the honored guest as only the master of the malapropos could. The pugnacious self-made man was typically mercurial in action, excepting any semblance of eloquence.

"Friends, tonight we can do great things for the Chinese armies. I will let Madame Chiang Kai Shek tell you what they're up against in just a few words. Nobody needs a history lesson. You're not in school now. Ladies and gentlemen, Madame Chiang Kai Shek."

Not wishing to disrespect Goldwyn's remarks, she spoke briefly and then reminded them that legibility on the pledge cards was important.

The little tabs on the cards were from $500 up to $10,000. Even in these shaky economic times, the Wellesley grad knew with whom she was dealing.

Most paid then and there with checks made out to the China Relief Association at a San Francisco address. Those who gave their pledges to Sam would be hounded by him until they wrote their checks. Louis B. Mayer, never a friend to any of his fellow studio heads, haughtily refused to play this game and told the Madame that he would send a company check the next day. This kind of arrogance was ever-present in the land of the stars and the *wannabees*.

Branko excused himself from a conversation with Emily, Hal Wallis and Jack Warner. He strode over to the cushioned window bench where the Madame was besieged by several guests.

She immediately arose to greet him, saying, "Sir, it's a pleasure to have an officer of the American armed forces here, and a General at that."

Branko was just a little taken aback that she knew him and she facetiously explained, "My new friend, Mr. Warner, told me all."

"The pleasure is mine, Madame," Branko just managed to *not* stammer. "The courage your husband's armies are showing against such heavy odds is to be admired and saluted the world over."

Honored, she graciously nodded to the remark

Branko then handed to her a $500 check that he had filled out before even arriving at the party.

Without hesitation—and quite unexpectedly—she responded by throwing her arms over Branko's shoulders and planting a kiss on his cheek.

Driving back to Sunset Plaza, Emily and Branko enjoyed chatting-up the party, postmortem. Just as they turned into the garage she shocked Branko by saying that she would soon be moving to New York. She explained that months earlier Hal Wallis had confided that the studio planned to establish a New York production facility after releasing *The Fighting 69th*. And while Madame Chiang Kai Shek was clutching Branko, Wallis had verified the Studio's New York expansion.

Branko was ecstatic but didn't display any visible emotion. Instead he responded with a nonplused, "Sounds great—can't wait!!"

But as Emily entered the house ahead of Branko, he was just coming down after having silently—and joyously—jumped a foot into the air.

Washington, DC,
September 30, 1939

Back at work since mid-July, Branko did not miss Hollywood one bit. It was one of its citizens for which he achingly pined.

He and Emily wrote and talked on the phone, but she was increasingly vague about the transfer to New York. He wanted to write it off to her hard work preparing *The Fighting 69th* for a January release. But he wasn't so sure.

It was true enough that distributors were clamoring for a date before they could deliver commitments to exhibitors: Emily had reported as much while assisting Wallis in riding herd on the squadron of editors working overtime on the film. And the music department was widely missing their deadlines amidst a nervous atmosphere permeating the entire studio. Jack Warner was once again wearing his tyrant hat.

Legitimate reasons all, and yet Branko wasn't convinced that any of them were the reasons for Emily's apparent subterfuge.

But bothersome though all that was, as Donovan's right-hand man, Branko had other concerns. The advent of Germany's September 1st invasion of Poland had caused a heavy work load. Another critical item was the company's travel budget: They were still in official limbo and so the travel expenses had to quietly come from the White House private "slush fund."

Branko's schedule after the first of the year was to include fast-moving stops in Portugal, Spain, France and Turkey. Provided, of course, the Nazi's hadn't by then invaded any of those countries. France was busily shoring up its vaunted Maginot Line against the expected onslaught of German armor. Donovan's covert people in Paris felt strongly that Germany would not move westward until it solidified an occupation of hapless Poland. The best guesses for that pointed toward late spring. But no one in the world of foreign or domestic intelligence believed that the Maginot Line would hold off the Panzer Divisions or the lethal Stuka dive bombers.

Since the Polish border had been crushed, Scotland Yard had been exchanging information with Donovan.

"You need to know this, *pardner*," Donovan had remarked about one tidbit he passed on to Branko. It was a four-sentence communiqué reading:

HIS MAJESTY IS INCREASINGLY LEERY OF THE ACTIONS OF YOUR AMBASSADOR TO ST. JAMES COURT. SOME OF HIS MORE PERNICIOUS STATEMENTS REPORTED IN THE PRESS THROUGHOUT GREAT BRITAIN. YOUR STATE DEPARTMENT INFORMED OF KENNEDY'S LATEST INFLAMMATORY REMARKS. DISMISSAL SHOULD BE CONSIDERED.

Branko read the communiqué in disgust. Ol' Joe was at it again. Since the Nuremburg Laws went into effect Joe Kennedy's bigotry regarding Germany's treatment of its Jewish population was out-and-out psychotic. Kennedy literally saw no harm being done and went so far as to say that the victims may have had it coming.

Branko intended to read the riot act to Mr. Ambassador while he still had the title. Given the present conservative makeup of the State Department he doubted dismissal from Washington's end would happen any time soon. According to Donovan, Kennedy was likely to stay in London for at least another year—or until the Brits lost patience and wouldn't stand for more embarrassment from the Court of St. James. With motor-mouth Joe Kennedy, one never knew what kind of *faux pas* to next expect.

In mid-January, Branko and Wild Bill attended *The Fighting 69th* premiere at Radio City Music Hall in New York City. On hand were John Prout, Jack Warner, Hal Wallis, Bill Keighley, Sister Mary Margaret Duffy, the entire main cast, hundreds of regiment veterans and the noisiest of Fighting Irish band. Klieg lights spiced-up the night.

The audience enthusiastically applauded the film and Jack Warner smiled a lot! With the reunion of so many comrades stories were told and retold while the after-premiere parties flowed with seemingly never-ending food and drinks.

The premiere was an evening Branko cherished.

**Washington, DC,
February 22, 1940**

Commiserating with Branko, Edith agreed that even before the change of heart implied by her letter, had Emily truly wanted to come east—like she could have for the January premiere—she would have found a way.

But, of course, her letter made this all irrelevant. It had arrived earlier in the morning:

> *February 17, 1940*
> *Dear Branko:*
> *It looks like Uncle Carl will be my new boss. I'm signing on with Universal tomorrow and have already been assigned to direct an upcoming feature! I finally realized that there would be unconquerable barriers at WB and I would go no further than an assistant director. When I tried to press Hal Wallis, a good friend, he couldn't assure me of anything remotely positive in that respect. No female director has ever broken through at any of the eight major studios, and Hal saw no way for that to happen in the future. I should have seen it when they decided not to send me east to the premiere after the studios planned expansion to NY had been permanently tabled.*
> *What this means to our beautiful relationship, only you can answer. The futility of it all devastates me no end. But Hollywood is*

where I belong and I'm determined to make the most of my life with Universal. It fires me up, Branko, just like your clandestine intelligence work with Bill Donovan. I've cried over it, I'm sick about it. I feel like a zombie going through the motions each day. Wallis encouraged me to take the leap to Universal and I must admit that I feel good about it.

Whatt'sthe right thing to do? How will we ever know? Please respond as soon as you can. Don't phone—it's better that we write for now. I'm sure you don't want to listen to long-distance weeping. I love you with every fiber of my being, and my heart beats for you, just as it did last summer. Not one iota less.

Emily

The letter had been almost more than Branko could bear. He had gasped and choked-up. He felt a breath-taking and deep sense of loss. He never read the letter again. The only words that came forth were those from his old cantatory recital: *Places to go, things to do, experiences to feel!*

EXEUNT: ACT ONE 18

Washington, D.C.
September 14, 1940

Due to the Senate budget committee, Branko's European mission once again faced insufficient funding. It was not difficult for Wild Bill to have Harry Hopkins augment the meager dollars out of the President's emergency stash—commonly referred to as "Fala's fund."

This came after Hopkins had dilly-dallied for the first six months of the year and Donovan cajoling FDR into rigidly instructing Hopkins to meet any reasonable requests. Consequently, having *carte blanche* with the final decision on what was reasonable turned Hopkins into *Happy Harry*. The confidential $21,500 budget for a three-month journey to Portugal, Spain and Turkey was finally agreed upon by Hopkins and Donovan. However, with the Nazis half-occupying France, the Brits suffering a devastating blitzkrieg of daily bombings dubbed the "Battle of Britain" mundane transportation, lodgings and sustenance was as much a logistical labyrinth as a budgeting issue.

To reach Portugal, Branko was to fly Transworld Airways from New York to the Azores and on to Madeira. He was then to board an ancient steamer that ran once-a-week to Tangiers in French Morocco, followed by taking an overnight ferry to Lisbon. A month later, he was to travel by infrequent bus and train service to Madrid and on to Barcelona. Turkey posed a somewhat more convoluted challenge in the face of lightly-veiled Nazi threats to "holiday in the Greek Islands" by springtime. Dr. Goebbels had become the brilliant puppeteer for this insidious propaganda that was constantly fueled with similar unsettling remarks.

Their Italian allies were knocking on the Grecian door from the Albanian border. The Germans were under no illusions that the peripatetic Italians could ever advance very far without the equally maligned Greek forces counterattacking to send them scurrying. Respected strategists throughout the world agreed.

Branko's assignment within each country was straightforward: There was to be a rendezvous of individuals with whom he and

Donovan had cultivated three-year relationships. This was to classify them as, *friends, agents, operatives,* or *moles.* Categorized or not, these were people about whom they could never be sure. On Donovan's frequent travels throughout Europe prior to the previous year's Nazi invasion of Poland he had accomplished more than he ever thought possible. And now, Branko had to "seal the deal" with a select few. Avoiding the potentially dangerous umbrage of the less favored would be like walking on eggshells. Loyalties were tentative at best. Extreme care had to be taken at every step of the way.

Branko was set to leave from New York the following week.

Having dinner at the Wilson house a few days before taking the train to New York, Branko was a little too nonchalant about the travel plans. Sensing this, Edith knew he was disguising his apprehension. Without success, she tried to penetrate his cavalier posture and vague answers. Also voicing their fears were the ever-faithful Aretha and Larry Lincoln, who had joined in for dessert. Their talk of the inherent European travel dangers and the news on every broadcast of a broader war had the opposite of the intended effect on Branko. Instead of opening-up with seriousness, his atypical, smiling response was that he promised to be extra-paranoiac every inch of the way.

It was good act but no one believed the façade—least of all Edith, who knew him better than most.

Lisbon (Lisboa), Portugal
October 3, 1940

Embracing Jesse and Sara in his arms brought tears of joy to all three. After delays, missed connections and a passport dispute in Tangiers, Branko was in Lisbon and determined to hold-off meetings until he could visit the kids.

They were living in a handsomely furnished *fin-de-siecle* apartment building in the pleasant Pombal district. Branko had checked into the elegant Avenida Palace, near the train station, between Praca dos Restauradores and Rossio. He planned to divide his time between Lisbon's Avenida Palace and the luxurious Palacio Hotel in nearby

Estoril. Both were known as dens of intelligence activity. When Jesse heard where Branko would be staying whenever visiting Estoril, he was quick to respond: "Ah, Estoril—the new capital of notorious international espionage!"

"Really?" Branko had responded.

"Not to say that the Avenida doesn't have the very same reputation. To get a telephone in Estoril or Lisbon these days, it is imperative to show proof of your name and then you're included in the next issue of the semi-annual phone book—whether you like it or not."

"Why is that?"

"Mistrust of all the foreigners," Jesse answered, knowing that many of those were political refugees trickling in from every corner of the continent. "Half the listed names are German, Polish, French, Italian and English. Nearly everyone is a spy or is suspected of being one. They keep us busy at the Embassy and we had our hands full already. Of course there are the legitimate political refugees seeking entry into the United States."

"I'm not at all surprised at that."

"Which part?" Jesse asked for the sake of clarification. "All the spies or the refugees?"

"Well, all of it," Branko replied. "Right now things are pretty volatile all over. A degree of confusion would be expected."

"You got that part right. Our Marine guards spend their full days just maintaining decorum in the lobby. Thank goodness, no one has yet approached us for asylum—not yet, anyway."

"I suppose your safe enough from that as long as as Portugal remains tacitly neutral," Branko supplied, "I suppose the Canadians are undergoing the same chaos?"

Jesse answered with a nod. He then said, "I guess we should be thankful we don't have it as easy of the English."

Branko's expression showed the he didn't follow Jesse.

"Since the blitz began last month, we've heard that the clamor for papers and passage into England has significantly subsided."

"Ah," Branko grunted understanding. "Kind of makes us the flavor of the month."

"More like the best game left in town," Jesse retorted. "Process of elimination."

Branko was impressed with how far Jesse had come since first joining the State Department. And his lovely Sara was considered to be one of their brightest young cultural affairs experts. Seeing them grow into veritable polymaths seemingly overnight wasn't so surprising. They were talented young people. But Branko hadn't expected their talents would be so quickly recognized and fostered. In that regard, he was developing a new respect for what the much-harassed department was accomplishing in trying times. If nothing else, the training apparatus seemed to be very effective.

**Estoril, Portugal
October 18, 1940**

The month was racing ahead and Branko had not accomplished even half of his plan.

Equally uninspiring were his meetings, which had not yielded agent material. One couple—a dapper Sergio Francesco and his charming wife Estella—was the exception and the closest thing to what Branko was seeking. In his occasional trans-Atlantic phone conversations with Sergio over the past year, Branko detected a sincerity and eagerness that could add-up to an *agent extraordinaire* —or the greatest *flop extraordinaire*. The exotic-appearing Estella was the other side of the equation and could probably be trusted to do the right and proper thing while keeping her *bon vivant* husband in check.

They had been recommended by one of Donovan's British contacts. The Francesco couple offered a potential of securing the keystone operatives that Donovan wanted in Lisbon/Estoril, Madrid, Barcelona and Istanbul. "Courting" them for two years had resulted in Branko's communication with Sergio and meeting in person.

There was a, catch, of course. They wanted, demanded actually, a guaranteed annual $20,000 U.S. dollars placed in a Swiss bank account they had already opened. In return they would agree to be the

Portuguese conduit for all intelligence purposes, starting with a Bulgarian and two Swiss citizens as informants. They had selected these three individuals by renting a palatial apartment in Cascais and making a daily point of innocuously chatting with Palacio guests. Their efforts had produced dossiers on the two Swiss and one Bulgarian who could be of value just by keeping their ears to the ground and their eyes open.

The couple was, if anything, tenacious.

Branko insisted that they pay the informants on a *piece-work* basis and for only verifiable information. Some of the details still needed ironing-out, but the eventual funds would be issued in six equal deposits to their Swiss accounts. The ongoing Intel being purchased would be cabled to Donovan via Lisbon's U.S. Embassy.

Branko was quite certain that a high percentage of data gathered by this crew would be useless. But if even five percent was meaningful and eventually useful, then the price was worth it. This very same model of operation was the goal for Spain and Turkey.

Donovan's entire network was to be incorporated into the Office of Strategic Services (OSS) by the following year and they were on schedule—despite Branko's concerns to the contrary. The ultimate operation was expected to grow a thousand-fold by the end of 1941.

Under grudging duress, FDR pledged to pay for it—out in the open, if possible. As FDR's *duress* was responsive to the escalating cost, it fell to Donovan to goad the President into the financial distance necessary for success. In this, the ol' *Wild Bill* Donovan demonstrated the risibility inherent to manipulating a President to do what he wanted when he wouldn't pay for it otherwise. Donovan overcame the contraction by underscoring the expected budget windfall that was presumed to be coming with Democrats winning the November elections. Like the serpent in the Garden of Eden, Donovan assured FDR that an unprecedented third term would be the mandate for Roosevelt to successfully douse a world on fire.

Appearing at the Embassy, Branko collected his personal mail from the weekly diplomatic pouch. Herbert Claiborne Pell, the Envoy and

Minister Plenipotentiary, had said he would be pleased to collect mail while Branko was in Portugal.

Branko could not understand why Portugal did not warrant a full, representing ambassador, especially with the war engulfing European real estate. Pell explained that the situation was purely political and that he expected a change within weeks. His assurance had been accorded by a recent communiqué from Secretary of State, the venerable Cordell Hull.

They chatted about the recent uneasy presence of the Duke of Windsor and his star-crossed lover, American society woman Wallis, otherwise known as, *Wally*. And then there were the reports arising out of the Duke's growing association with Hitler and the Third Reich. Whispers of treason were not uncommon.

"My colleague at the British Embassy tells me that Scotland Yard has kept a wary eye on this royal bombshell since the abdication," Claiborne Pell went on to said. "When they entered Portugal in June, they were guests of Ricardo de Espirito Santo. He's a local investment banker—a wily snake—with extensive and influential German contacts. In fact he was even able to arrange for the German occupying forces to station guards at the Duke's Paris home to fend off looting. Can you believe it? But no matter, the Duke and the Simpson woman were gone."

"Right," Branko responded. "I remember hearing about Churchill ordering their *exile* last summer—aboard a Brit warship. Now we've got him lurking off *our* east coast as Governor of the Bahamas."

Pell bobbed his head at the information.

"The joke in Washington has him setting up a secret U-boat refueling depot in the islands."

Pell chuckled, prompting Branko to add, "Imagine that: The Duke, with a pump in hand, asking a U-Boat Commander ''fill 'er up, *mein Kapitan?*'"

Larry Lincoln was responsible for checking Branko's home mail. Anything beyond the commonplace was hand-delivered to Donovan's secretary at the White House. She in turn added the delivery to the diplomatic pouch bound for the State Department and Branko overseas.

A letter postmarked, *Hollywood,* and with a return address of one Emily Laemmle, made the cut after Edith Wilson okayed it. Be it good or bad, Edith knew that Emily's correspondence was beyond the commonplace.

> *Hollywood, California*
> *October 12, 1940*
> *Dear Branko:*
> *I hope this letter reaches you. I'm sending it to your "P" Street address, not knowing if you've moved or are out of town on business. I hope this note, whenever you receive it, finds you hale and hearty. I've dedicated myself to my new position and it looks like I'll have my first directing job in hand very soon. There are those who wink at this, feeling I'm one of the Laemmle's receiving nepotistm. I don't care.*
> *I've missed you, dearest Branko, but neither of us has ever had an answer for our dilemma.*
> *Honestly, I've been seeing a fellow director who has worked with Uncle Carl for the past ten years. I guess these things happen even if you can't ever imagine or feel that they will. But, I wanted to let you know. Please don't hate me. You're part of my life and always will be. I can only hope that your future goes well in every sense. Whenever in Hollywood please call and we'll do lunch.*
> *Love,*
> *Emily*

When the letter reached Branko, he grimaced and squinted. He was hurt, of course, but he had long-expected it.

Good luck, Emily, he thought. *I wish it could have worked out. Sure we'll do lunch. Hollywood bulllll-shit!*

His piercing thought, followed by the wryest smile, spoke volumes. What could have been a lachrymose moment, quickly passed.

Barcelona, Spain
November 14, 1940

The cable received from Donovan had been short and not-sweet. Severe shortages of food, fuel, clean water and jobs had finally come to an ugly confrontation:

```
SKIP MADRID. FRANCO DISPERSING CITY-
WIDE RIOTING BY MARTIAL LAW. EMBASSY
SAYS EXPLOSIVE. GO ON TO BARCELONA. OK
THERE AS FAR AS WE CAN TELL. BE
CAREFUL, PAL.
```

Branko had booked the Lisbon to Madrid train. With only an hour wait, he remained at the station, conversing with a newspaper vendor who spoke an understandable English to go along with Branko's fractured Spanish.

According to the vendor, Nazi plain-clothes goons were all over the city to show support for Franco. He joked that they were quite obvious in their leather coats even while the thermometer was hitting the seasonal twenty-five to thirty degrees Celsius. But the presence of Hitler's SS or Gestapo was no laughing matter and the two men sympathetically smiled at one another. Now that the civil war had ended the prevailing fear among the people of Spain was that Franco's German friends planned to make their country a puppet state. Franco's October meeting with Mussolini in Rome had added fuel to the wildfire of spreading rumors. That alliance between Il Duce and Hitler undoubtedly placed Spain in an uncomfortable and potentially lethal situation—and the public knew it.

The ride to Barcelona was noisy, dirty, sooty, uncomfortably crowded and without a working toilet. And the city itself was one of which Franco had the greatest suspicion in his newly established, shaky regime.

The taxi ride to the Gran Via Hotel proved that Spain was battling a severe petrol shortage. There were no long lines of traffic and vehicles were scarce. Branko's room was large and faced the wide concourse, also named, *Gran Via*.

He kept the switchboard busy for the next few hours and made contact with each of the people he had hoped to reach. Individual meetings a half-hour apart were set for the next day. Branko arranged for a sitting room with coffee, tea and cold beverages.

And on the next day, no one showed-up. The fear factor kept them away, Branko was sure. His long-term work in communicating with these candidates became one more casualty in Franco's drive to consolidate his regime and his victories in the civil war.

Frankly, Branko was relieved. He just did not relish having to meet with Spaniards who were caught up in their own domestic problems. Public rioting in Madrid and pockets of anti-Franco unrest throughout the country outweighed the implications of global war for more parochial people—or at least that was his conclusion about the no-show candidates that should have known better. The six people who had eschewed their meetings had been slated to be the nucleus of a Spanish agent force in Catalonian Spain. Now, in the span of two days, the futility of it all sank-in deep.

On his third day, after an exchange of cables with Wild Bill, Branko's began to concentrate on Istanbul.

But first, how the hell do I get there? he wondered.

Donovan's next cable insisted that all arrangements would be made in a matter of twenty-four to forty-eight hours.

Istanbul, Turkey (Constantinople, Stamboul)
November 27, 1940

The previous week began with an exhausting two-day vintage train journey from Barcelona to Malaga, followed by a ride in an old rickety, smoke-spewing bus to British Gibraltar. After an evening at the historic old Rock Hotel, he boarded an RAF DeHavilland ten-passenger military transport plane to Cairo. All orchestrated by Bill Donovan, the plane had been arranged though British intelligence and included two Spitfire escorts from an offshore aircraft carrier to as far as Malta.

After refueling, the DeHavilland went on to Cairo, and Branko was given a lift by a British army vehicle to the port at Alexandria. Branko was beginning to think that there wasn't anything Donovan could not pull out of his battered fedora. The thought was only re-enforced by an itinerary that included another three days on a neutral Turk tramp steamer, of all things.

The steamer was scheduled for a two-day cargo layover en route to Izmir—which would take another three days to reach. Wild Bill's hat tricks notwithstanding, Branko had quite enough and made an abrupt departure from travel plans.

With the help of a female Irish school teacher on sabbatical, whom he met at the bus station, Branko arranged the journey's last leg to Istanbul. It was an overnight trip on a surprisingly comfortable 1933 Mercedes *autobus.*

Looking to the adjacent seat on the autobus, Branko had found himself admiring the attractive colleen with flaming red hair.

Don't you even think it, old man, he admonished himself. *Don't get involved—You've got work to do; She's much too young anyway. Well, maybe a cup of Turkish coffee some day in Istanbul... Nah! But, the other hand General, it couldn't hurt to find out where she's staying anyway!*

And so he asked.

"The Pera Palace." she told him.

The Pera Palace, a relic of a hotel serving passengers of the fabled Orient Express, was like Estoril's Palacio minus the palm trees. It's wire-caged, hand-levered elevator placed it back into the 19th century but the restaurant/bar was alive with the seeds of eastern intrigue.

Branko expected to potentially score heavily with agents herein. Unlike the eerie atmosphere in Barcelona, everything would be out in the open—even if playing the incognito game of cat-and-mouse.

But even as he arrived and settled into the job at hand, Branko was already looking forward to heading home. He thought back to his departure from Donovan's travel arrangements, musing about how well the Germans built long-lasting transportation that was a sight more comfortable and faster than a tramp steamer. He figured he might just have to do the same for his return trip.

Because after my 'Turkey dinner,' he thought, *I'm heading home as fast as I can, boss. Like it or not.*

En route to the United States of America
December 20, 1940

Aside from the very pleasant company of Miss Kathy Kelly of County Mayo the intrigue of Istanbul had made Lisbon's spy activity seem as tame as a Sunday school picnic. Branko had not the least challenge in meeting with the contacts. Within days of arrival, he had met with three outstanding, experienced candidates who had not demanded money "up front" for their efforts. Furthermore, they understood that results produced timely payments by a United States government that backed them all the way or forever marked them as *persona non grata* if they screwed-up.

No one balked.

Branko had left a little "pocket money" for each of the three—funds slated for just that purpose. Donovan had noted in one of his cables that FDR's crushing November defeat of Republican Wendell Wilkie was expected to further loosen-up the expense accounts, as it were.

One of the contacts was Fritz Waldemar, the *nouveau* anti-Nazi, ex-SS officer who had deserted while in Spain. His depth of knowledge and grasp of global issues impressed Branko. During a "bon voyage" coffee at the Pierre Loti Cafe overlooking the Golden Horn, he had even asked the Teutonic to ride herd on the other two. Politics and war made for strange bedfellows!

Skirting the ever-expanding war zones to return to Washington, Branko had to backtrack the same basic route that had brought him to

Istanbul. Again, cable correspondence with Wild Bill had set arrangements into motion. This allowed Branko to spend a day in Lisbon with Jesse and Sara.

He was scheduled to finally arrive home on New Year's Day. His beloved country would still be at peace while the rest of the world spun crazily, engulfed by an out-of-control inferno.

Washington, D.C.
July 2, 1941

With Bill Donovan finally closing in on culminating an official Office of Strategic Services, the worldwide network was full-steam ahead with FDR's blessing and increased funding. The launching of the OSS was scheduled for some time in the next six months. Across the network in Washington, New York, Europe and North Africa, there were daily increases to the number of employees. Hoover's FBI still functioned unencumbered throughout South America while deep animosity between J. Edgar and Wild Bill went on unabashed. FDR trusted the former less and less and planned to take away his foreign spy activities when Congress officially passed blessings on the OSS.

The favoritism granted the OSS had a lot to do with Wild Bill, who unlike Hoover, was neither a headline-grabbing man nor an armchair commander. It did not go unnoticed that Donovan wasn't one to take credit for the work of others and that he still did a goodly amount of "business" travel. While Branko solidified the agency in Lisbon and Istanbul, Donovan had been in Frankfurt, Budapest and Rome. And where Branko was suspicious of surveillance that did not exist, Donovan was giving the slip to surveillance that did exist. He was at the very least as successful as Branko in shoring up the network in Europe.

There remained a critical assignment for which Branko was the man to handle: The USSR. His association with Soviet commanders, fluency with languages and his stature as a renowned American, gave him the singular credentials necessary for the mission to Moscow. It had been just a few weeks since the long-expected Nazi invasion ended a non-aggression pact that never was. Donovan and the Chief of Staff had pondered the possible outcome of a hard-fought German victory over its Communist enemy. Their fear—shared by others reaching the same conclusions—was that this would mire the United States in an inescapable quandary, as it would England, as well. On the other hand, a rallying Russian counter-attack sending the Wehrmacht scurrying back to the Fatherland could as easily pose a massive problem. The grim choice: a Soviet Europe or a Fascist Europe.

With his multilayered cover story Branko was Donovan's plausible answer of the day: The perfect stopgap observer. He would have to get a handle on the relative strengths of combatants, report on unusual or new weaponry, defensive and offensive strategies and handle a laundry list of ancillary assignments. By end of September he would exit the country via the strategic Arctic supply port of Murmansk, sail to Keflavik's U.S. Air Force Base in Iceland, whence a Military Air Transport craft would fly him to Andrews AFB in Maryland. It was a simple, functional itinerary, created by Donovan and Hopkins and supervised personally by FDR. With his unprecedented third term underway the President didn't want to give the other side any ammunition

After a pleasant Wilson house dinner, Branko was once again saying his *goodbyes* to Edith. He showed his usual cavalier mettle by minimizing the inherent dangers of the Moscow mission. Also as usual, Edith didn't believe his assessment one bit and told him during their parting embrace. She said, "Your teen-age superman attitude scares me, soldier-boy!"

He gave her his best rakish smile, convincingly conveying an iron certitude he didn't feel. Driving back to *P* Street, he was struck by how much her concern had come to mean to him.

For over twenty years I've shared my dreams, schemes, troubles and joys with Edith, he mused, lapsing into the unexplored regions of his feelings about Edith Wilson. *Maybe it's time for both of us to go forward—with each other. Yeah, there's a certain love between us. Brotherly love? Sisterly love? Platonic love? What does it matter? It's* not the hearts and flowers sort of relationship, but it has certainly survived every one of those I've had. And I do feel for her. She's the first person I call when there's a problem or some kind of dilemma. She's the first person I talk to when something joyful takes place. Our close friends joke about our being joined at the hip and the rumor-hungry press has followed their lead... Maybe that's what they see—something we are refusing to admit is there for all to see. Maybe they're right. Perhaps a few months or so in Russia will allow me time to sort this out. Or will it?

Moscow, USSR
The Kremlin
Timoshenko's Headquarters
September 8, 1941

Commander Timoshenko had let nothing stand in the way of Branko getting the information he needed. He realized that in all probability Branko wasn't writing a book but in a spirit of transparency went along with the deception. The wizened old Red surmised the true goal of the mission: The Americans also expected a showdown. When Branko politely asked to be driven somewhere closer to the front lines, Timoshenko called it foolhardy and explained that the Huns were successfully pressing toward Moscow and Leningrad.

"Semyon," Branko came back, "I have to get a closer look at the defensive posture of your troops. It has to be included in the book just as the Nazi attack tactics must be. My request is only for the sake of believable authenticity. I'm a stickler for that, as you know."

Timoshenko knew that Branko had meticulously maintained his cover story by interviewing the staff and personnel regarding Moscow's defense. Branko had also taken advantage of Timoshenko's offer of inspections. Timoshenko smiled broadly and finally agreed.

"Okay, Citizen Hero," Timoshenko said, "I'll have a staff car and driver on hand for tomorrow morning. He'll take you only as far as my Bryansk Command Post—which is still classified rear echelon—and he'll have you back within three days.

"That's fair."

"It will have to be. That's the best I can do at this moment, *tovarisch*. It could change for the worse tomorrow or the next day or next week. We're in the fight of our lives!"

They were parting with the handshake clasp of close friends when Timoshenko said, *"Bog skoroast, droog moi!"*

Branko was surprised at this. *God speed* was uncharacteristic for an atheistic Stalinist and Branko pondered it as he walked away.

Standing in the theater wings, Fate of the Ill-Fated—in the guise of a vodka-swilling Red Army staff car driver—was about to ponderously intervene.

EXEUNT: ACT TWO

Leningrad, USSR
Timoshenko's Headquarters
January 15, 1944

Semyon Timoshenko had taken command of a beleaguered Leningrad in June. That was while the city was still under a three-year siege, wherein half the population had already met an ignominious death from starvation and disease.

And it was in this Leningrad—near the end of the German siege seven months later—where Branko now found himself. From the moment he was handed-over to the Soviet High Command in Moscow he had been treated as a conquering hero.

Still fearing a German counter-attack on Moscow, a glum and stoic Stalin actually kissed the American on both cheeks and hugged him during his visit to the Kremlin with Ambassador Harriman. *TASS*, the renowned Telegraphic News Agency of the Soviet Union, hailed him as "a George Washington" and "America's best foot forward… Our comrade… Our hero!" Censored radio broadcasts gave brief histories of Branko's life that were inaccurate, but nevertheless complimentary. The fact that he was Russian-born was heavily propagandized, even though the prevailing *pogrom* mentality at the time was ignored.

Branko hadn't felt a bit like a hero and certainly never put on the required posture with a straight face.

Hero my ass, he internalized, remembering his failings rather the successes in the lives of his rescuing Maccabees. *I made the inexcusable move to request—no, demand—a visit to the weakening front and paid dearly for it. Captured, rescued by the Maccabees, captured again. Then the death camp, breaking-out and being rescued—again. In the unadulterated sense of the word, there isn't even the whisper of heroism in any of what I did. As my Tennessee buddy Sergeant Alvin York would say…aw, shucks!*

There was good reason for Timoshenko to schedule a homeward bound Branko to stop over in Leningrad. They had spoken briefly on the phone as soon as Branko was delivered to the U.S. Embassy in October. This was quickly followed by exhausting, repetitive debriefings covering his partisan duty and his legendary escape from Sobibor. Many of the interrogations were conducted by the head of the NKGB, People's Committee for State Security, Vsevolod Merkulov, in a most respectful manner.

As they reunited in Leningrad, under Timoshenko's command since the prior June, Branko's first question to Timoshenko concerned the welfare of his Maccabee commander and friend, Simcha Greenberg.

"Where is he, Semyon?"

"Branko, I don't know, but I will—"

"Did he safely reach the Soviet lines? Where can I find him?"

"Hold on! I'll get to work on it—"

"Now! *Pazhalusta,* please, Semyon!"

These were not simple questions in these frantic times. But Timoshenko made some high-level calls. Within the hour, he found that Simcha was now a Soviet Army Colonel, commanding a full brigade of four independent units numbering 200 partisans beyond the Western Front.

This brigade, in the vicinity of newly re-taken Smolensk, was called a "chase party" due to its pursuit of the enemy now in full retreat. Partisan supplementary forces had been deployed to insure retreaters weren't allowed the respite of "digging in." With elements of several Soviet counterattacking divisions moving forward at an ever-faster pace, the partisan assignment was to capture stragglers— and there were thousands. Their specific orders were to shoot-on-sight anyone resisting. This allowed the divisions to plow full-speed ahead to the former Polish borders, without having to fear rear sneak attacks from bypassed Nazi units.

Timoshenko ordered a three day pass for Simcha, requiring him to report to Leningrad immediately. With the sensitive communication curtain pulled-over partisan actions, it troubled Simcha that he had not yet heard word about Branko. The granting of an unsolicited pass did little to alleviate his concerns. Likewise, Timoshenko did not let on that Branko would also be in Leningrad by the 15th, coinciding with Simcha's arrival. Timoshenko was enjoying this happy ruse!

The wide-eyed look on each man's face, the jumping for joy, the hugs, the kisses, the tears—this told the story of their reunion. That old, hard rock of the Soviet Armed Forces stood by watching, smiling broadly, unable to hide his rapidly blinking eyes.

Knowing Branko would want to know, Simcha was quick to recite the fate of every Maccabee. Simcha proudly announced that most had made it safely to the advanced Russian lines.

Captain Raisel Ehrenburg was reassigned as commanding psychological rehabilitation officer at the military hospital in Magnitogorsk. Airman Sasha Cohen was again flying missions over the Western Ukraine and Belo-Russia. Kostya, the boxer, had been welcomed by his old outfit as they were quickly moving westward. Alyosha, the sailor, had reported to the nearest naval torpedo-boat unit in the Dnieper basin.

The civilian Maccabees had returned as close to their homes as the military would allow, while former military personnel reported to the first Red army units they encountered. There were no casualties as far as Simcha could determine but he had not received further word of the revered marksman, citizen Lev Soloveitchik. Several Maccabes had last seen Lev boarding a Soviet truck convoy that was heading to liberated Kharkov—where his wife had family. The city of Rovno, with Nazis still in partial control, had turned out to be too "hot" for Lev. The farm that he had managed had become headquarters for a Waffen SS Platoon. One could only hope that Lev was already, or soon would be, reunited with his loved ones.

For all intents and purposes the devastating blockade and siege of Leningrad, was to be officially lifted within days. Foreshadowing the end of the siege, the last of the German divisions near the northwestern entrances to the city abandoned their ammunition dumps and artillery emplacements: They left practically everything, guns and all. This was undoubtedly owed to the dwindling supply lines forcing the Nazi invaders to beat a slow and steady retreat. Obviously, Leningrad district Commander Timoshenko was pleased with this positive event taking place on his watch. Along with other Soviet Generals, he had been unfairly chastised on two occasions during the critical days of steady Nazi successes. The Nazi withdrawal, then, had been a welcome source of vindication for the old veteran.

On their first walk-through in the central and eastern sectors of the city, neither Branko nor Simcha was in any way prepared to actually see the bowels of hell with his own eyes. Here in Leningrad there were still hundreds of dead, frozen and rotting bodies littering the streets. The lingering effects of starvation were still of prime concern while cannibalism was thankfully over and done with. Much of the turn-around in conditions was a direct result of the no-nonsense, iron-fisted Timoshenko rule. It was working well as the delivery of food and medical supplies rapidly increased. The thousands of siege survivors who were still physically productive rallied to the cause under Timoshenko's blunt directives demanding the cleaning up processes. Although his main force was occupied in giving chase to the back-pedaling Huns who were last seen anywhere from ten-100 kilometers west of Central Leningrad, the critical Soviet rear echelon division within the city was basically a police and restoration force. Heavy snows had not made the formidable task any easier.

Within three days, Branko received word that the port of Murmansk, was once again ice-free. Though badly damaged by three years of Nazi dive-bombing attacks out of the German base in Tromso to the north. it was now open to the supply and relief convoys. The newly arrived convoy of ships in Murmansk's Kola Inlet included an American destroyer that would provide Branko a stormy passage on both the Barents and North Seas. After a refueling stop at Loch Ewe in Scotland's northwest, the destroyer was to join with fourteen U.S. based ships in a mini-convoy that would refuel in Keflavik, Iceland. Once there, Branko was scheduled to meet a MATS plane for a flight to Washington.

Ready and anxious to leave Leningrad, Branko and Simcha stood alongside the transport vehicle that would deliver Branko over the famed life-saving "ice road" crossing Lake Ladoga to the oft-bombed train line at Petrozavodsk. From there he was to take the night train to "tropical" Murmansk and his waiting U.S. Navy destroyer.

When the sergeant/driver of the Yakutsk troop-carrier urgently signaled for Branko to get on board, the two "brothers-in-arms" fresh from their emotional reunion and reminiscences, embraced in tears. By the next day Simcha would be off to his latest nomadic "headquarters" somewhere west of Smolensk. They both knew that only a miracle would ever bring them together again.

Observing these somber partings, Timoshenko employed the out-of-character phrase he had used more than two years ago: "God Speed, comrades!"

EXEUNT: ACT THREE   20

Washington, DC
March 1, 1944

In the previous month of February, every major newspaper and small daily across America heralded the return of Brigadier General Branko Horvitch (USA-Retired).

With the reality of his sudden reappearance, Donovan and the FDR administration had breathed a long sigh of relief: Branko was once again safe at home plate.

As soon as he had returned to Washington, Branko was able to reach both Jesse and Tante Shayndl by phone. During their emotional conversation, Jesse told Branko that in '42 he had asked for a release from his high level staff job in order to enlist for Naval flight training. From his immediate superior to the Ambassador, the request was refused. There was a mandatory freeze on any combat-eligible male hiring at State: In short, Jesse's position was essential to the diplomatic war effort. He could have resigned with the loss of the benefits associated with seniority, but that was clearly an unacceptable option. But beyond all of this, he had correctly deduced that Branko would have counseled him to stay where his future with a high ceiling was assured to some definitive degree.

Tante Shayndl was beside herself with joy at hearing Branko's voice—her little Bracheleh, that is, once she calmed-down from sobbing. She gave him the sad news that Charles passed on from congestive heart failure during the summer. She seemed to be coping well and at eighty two her doctor had pronounced her in relatively good health. For Branko, this was good news, as was the status of the rest of her family. She promised to write very soon. To no great surprise the dear matriarchal classic letter writer did just that

Branko had missed having that anchor of correspondence.

*****

March 3, 1944

It took a toll on Branko: The welcome-home greetings, dinner parties, stacks of well-wishing letters, telegrams from all over the country, the State and War Departments debriefings and just catching his breath. He was ready to forget it all and get on with work and life.

In this regard, Edith was supportive as usual, even though reeling from Margaret Wilson's sudden death in India. Even as a step-mother, she had always favored the more vulnerable, unmarried Margaret. Taking her along to Europe in '31 had solidified their relationship. They had regularly corresponded and Edith missed her immensely.

Some few weeks, after the death of Margaret and the hubbub of Branko's homecoming, Edith conveyed the details of what she considered "blockbuster" news: It was the plan for a movie about Woodroow Wilson.

"Branko, can you imagine how excited and pleased his family and I are?" she exclaimed. "That a movie of Woodrow's life is finally in the works?"

"They could really mess that up," Branko worried.

"Oh, no they can't," she came back. "We'll be routinely consulted."

"I'm flabbergasted, Miss Edith. Those people don't take that lightly—how did you pull it off, pray tell?"

"It wasn't easy. In November, after I learned you were safe in Uncle Joe Stalin's hands, Eleanor and I were invited out to the coast. We had a series of meetings with the 20th Century Fox Producer Darryl Zanuck and Henry King—the director."

Branko expression reflected that he was impressed and that prompted Edith on.

"They couldn't have cast better people. Geraldine Fitzgerald—"

"She's an Irish actress, isn't she?" Branko interrupted, pleasantly surprising Edith.

"That's right, soldier boy. She's very charming and could pass for my younger—much younger—sister. Alexander Knox will portray Woodrow. His profile is the image of Woodrow's."

"My," Branko managed to say. He knew this was important to Edith and was happy to see her so pleased.

"What's more they are both masters of their craft. And Vincent Price will play Eleanor's ex-husband, Bill McAdoo. Also signed on are Sir Cedric Hardwicke, Thomas Mitchell and Charles Coburn."

"So you'll have some script control?" Branko asked, more concerned about *how* they portrayed Woodrow than *who* portrayed him.

"Are you daft from associating with all those commies? Sure, I will be consulted from time-to-time, particularly on my life as a first lady. But Eleanor's book, *The Woodrow Wilsons,* is forming the basis for the script. She'll be the main family contact and may well spend some time in Hollywood during the shooting—which is already underway. You can bet that feisty little tootsie will insure that her father's dignity and charm will be well-protected. I can only trust she will treat my role in his life kindly and with respect."

Branko sensed a bit of doubt in that last remark, and said as much. Edith smirked.

**The White House
Washington, DC
June 8, 1944**

Two days after *D-Day*. Since returning to work, Branko's main OSS function was as liaison to FDR. In the two years of Branko's absence, Donovan had trained a wide-reaching cadre that took over Branko's one-man daily communication network of agents all over the world. Donvovan cultivated the network from the NY office, making frequent trips to U.S. bases in the UK and North Africa. These circumstances allowed him the luxury of unreported movement within the ranks of authority that now brought shocking news. Neither Branko nor the White House expected it.

Not one person among the power elite had even the remotest knowledge of Wild Bill's whereabouts on D-Day. Now, two days hence, word of his whereabouts came in the footnote of a morning Eisenhower communiqué to the White House. A sixty-year-old wild man, the communiqué indicated, had wangled passage on a command craft in the second Omaha beach wave of the D-Day invasion.

Perhaps not a grandstand play, but the sixty-year-old wild man had also arranged for six key French and German-speaking OSS personnel to parachute in behind the German lines, with him—all without approval from Eisenhower's Supreme Command.

FDR, glowing with pride over the Normandy beach-head successes, bloody as they were, was fit to be tied. His response was full of patented rancor: "The mad man is obviously trying his godamm hand at becoming an allied power in-and-of himself. He's gone a mile too far this time!"

Branko offered no reply and sensed that this act did not bode well for the future of the OSS as America's elite spy entity.

He wasn't far from wrong.

July 21, 1944

"Harry did it! I'll be damned, the Missouri curmudgeon did it'"

Branko was ebullient with the news and showed it. His good friend and fellow warrior was finally getting the party's recognition he had earned the hard way; the nomination for Vice President on the Roosevelt ticket. Furthermore, Branko did not balk at making his sentiments known to the boss who smiled, lit the cigarette in its holder, cocked his head and devilishly winked.

The morning newspapers and radio reports from the Democratic Convention in Chicago all spoke of the dark horse, last minute ballots that catapulted Senator Harry Truman (D-Mo.) into the vice presidential nomination. FDR's tacit 11th hour endorsement in the smoke-filled indoor stadium didn't hurt and the incumbent, Vice-President Henry Wallace could only take a thankless second place. There was likely to be an unprecedented fourth war-time term for FDR and his feisty running mate was determined to be a most enthusiastic campaigner wherever the Democratic National Committee sent him. Thomas Dewey of New York was expected to be a formidable foe, but as some of his fellow Republicans would lament, "If Tom would only shave off that damn Hitler mustache!"

Washington, D.C.

**The Oval Office
May 12, 1945**

Within a month after FDR departed this war torn planet, and with a final victory in Europe, President Truman summoned Branko to a meeting. This President had inherited a ton of responsibility and Branko was just the man he needed to alleviate some of the pressure. Unbeknownst to Branko, Truman had phoned Donovan in New York, asking to steal Branko for a special assignment. As if the President of the United States of American actually had to ask.

Sadly, Donovan was already watching his OSS fade before his eyes. He knew that the President was under heavy congressional pressure to discontinue the OSS—at least in its present form. And so the spy master could do nothing but reluctantly hand Branko over.

Now, sitting in front of the new president who had beckoned him, Branko waited without one clue as to what was about to be asked of him.

"Branko, I wanted to do this since you came back from your Russian vacation," Truman said. "But the time wasn't right and I didn't have the power to do it. Now I do."

There was a beat of momentary silence of which Branko felt no compulsion to fill.

"You are undoubtedly the most revered champion of veterans' rights this country has ever seen," Truman went on. "You know that, I know that, congress knows that. And I'm very uneasy with the way the GI Bill is being monitored. It is so damn far-reaching that... Well, we can't afford any hiccups or scandals regarding college tuition, housing or any of the rights that our returning vets deserve a-hundred-fold. There will be millions of troops coming home during the next year, all ready to claim their government's assistance in recouping their lives. The VA is understaffed and will be overwhelmed. Congressional oversight has been spotty at best."

The President paused again and Branko thought, *Uh-oh, whatever it is, here it comes.*

"I want you to apply the full measure of your advocacy that you displayed in the 20s and 30s."

"Mr. President, sir," Branko began, but got no further.

"Hold it right there," Truman interrupted. "That's *Harry* to you, soldier! I've already paved the way with Wild Bill—"

"Whoa," Branko cut right back. "Headlines are gonna' read 'Truman and Donovan guilty of conspiracy to sabotage America.'"

That earned a loud guffaw from Truman, joined by an understanding chuckle from his longtime buddy. After the harrowing past few months, the President enjoyed any opportunity for a good laugh.

In the lengthy discussion that followed, Truman said he would issue an Executive Order on the following day, announcing the appointment of Branko as GI Bill Liaison to the President. Beginning immediately, Branko would have unrestricted access to all government files and facilities pertaining to any segment of the GI Bill. Branko's portoflio would be ministerial and the Veterans Administration was to assign to him clerical staff post haste. Among other duties, Branko would appear before any congressional oversight committees whenever the Chief Administrator of the VA was required to be present. Since Branko had forged a good working relationship with the VA in the past, he foresaw no inherent problems.

In a series of phone calls Branko and Donovan reluctantly admitted it was inevitable.

While Donovan's OSS liaison efforts weren't needed within the Truman administration, the biggest blow for him was in not being considered to lead the surviving entity. He wasn't even up for a role in the transition to the new rumored central espionage agency. Truman had enough trouble gaining cooperation on the hill, so fighting Congress for one man—Donovan—simply wasn't in the cards.

It was hard for Wild Bill to let go

*****

Washington, D.C.
The Oval Office
September 10, 1945

When Harry Truman assumed the mantel of presidency, the one most surprising thing of which he learned was the atomic bomb. And, in fact, about this he was more than just a little surprised. It angered him that a weapon of such massive destruction had been developed without his knowledge.

Even knowing it was important to the war's ending, the decision to horribly kill so many with only two bombs was not an easy choice to make. Beyond those responsible for the bomb there was one person in whom Truman confided the decision that effectively ended the war in the Pacific. Branko Horvitch.

Now that the surrender had been signed, Truman had an urge to talk with someone about the decision responsible for that surrender and Branko was again the man to whom he turned.

"You know how much of a backlash I've been getting," the President remarked to Branko. The two men were sitting in the Oval Office and a radio off to the side droned on about General MacArthur, being named Supreme Commander over the forthcoming occupation of Japan. A nearby serving cart sported pastries and a coffee pot from which each man had poured his own cup.

Truman went on to add, "Even from those who at first cheered the move. My Bess and Margaret have lately asked me 'why?' But the buck stops here!"

"Harry, you don't have to justify anything to me or anyone else."

Truman shrugged his shoulders as if to say, *maybe*.

"History will be your judge and I feel strongly that it will be just. All I know, having seen war up close as you also did, is that the Japanese were preparing for a long suicidal defense of the home islands. At worst, your decision saved millions of lives, including Japanese. And at best—well, we may not know that until history has made its judgment. But this country and its allies grew tired of this war long ago.

Truman agreed with a nod, adding, "True."

"You chose to end the war by sacrificing—what, two-hundred-thousand lives in order to save another several million? Frankly, this is a postmortem exercise in futility. It's foolish to try and second-guess everything you prevented and it's time to move on, Captain."

"That's a pretty good point."

"Uh-huh. You did what any other president would have done and I again commend you for your courage to do so. Now get back to work. I'm paying your salary!"

After an absence of five years, Jesse and a pregnant Sara were reassigned to Washington in October. Late as it may have seemed they were now more than ready to start a family. For the happy occasion, Edith hosted a welcome home dinner for the parents-to-be and their families. Branko only hoped that she wouldn't drag out her 16mm. copy of the *Wilson* movie at some time during the evening. Edith and the Wilsons were right to be very pleased with the final cut, but he had already sat through it three times.

At thirty-five Jesse's return included a leap to a promotion as top assistant to the Undersecretary. Obviously his two climbs up the ladder while in Portugal caught the eye of said Undersecretary. It didn't hurt that his performance was embellished by glowing recommendations from all three Ambassadors to Portugal under whom he had served so well. Jesse now had over ten years with the department and was on track to even greater heights. The reports on Sara's accomplishments as Cultural Attaché' were equally impressive. She took pride in having been the only women on staff during her entire tenure. She had also quietly confirmed that she was offered a solid pay increase whenever she decided to return to State. Her parents winced at the thought.

Washington, D.C.
April 28, 1946

At one month old, Eva Sharon Kanter was the apple of Branko's eye, a great joy to the Bernstein and Kanter grandparents and the center of her proud parents' universe.

Branko had been at her side almost every day that first month. He needed that little daily respite, as he had been working long, tense hours to marshal the GI Bill on a smooth path. More than a million of the nation's veterans had already begun receiving GI housing and college or trade-school tuition.

Of course there had been problems—millions of them if you had asked a harried Branko—but praise was far outweighing criticism. Against all odds the badly-strapped Veterans Administration was performing admirably through it all. Meanwhile Branko's offices were manned by a small, but very efficient staff of recent veteran's and a more than adequate clerical section of former servicewomen from the WAVES as well as the WACS.

From the very beginning, Branko had insisted that this hiring procedure be practiced, at least in his corner of Washington. And this type of productive umbrella organization had worked so well that Branko managed occasional speaking engagements. He was once again on the usual circuit of veteran's groups, realtors, builders, business associations, civic organizations and college administrators. But at the same time this was the new territory of the post-war world for all the aforementioned.

Of course, the educational institutions, the home builders and realtors had profit-axes to grind but each was feeling the pinch in frustrating ways. For on-campus housing, temporary Quonset huts were more likely to be built. Across the spectrum there was a rapidly increasing need for classroom space, faculty, books and supplies. All of this boosted the number of starts for low-cost GI housing. Arising from scratch it was a monumental headache in America.

In and around post-war Washington these and similar pandemic issues typically merited blown stacks and ruined careers. It wasn't that government was staffed with lesser personalities, but rather that the stress cut that deeply. But through it all, Branko kept relatively calm and cool. This was not, after all, the horrors of war and he was comfortably satisfied at being part of a major effort to embrace the GI Bill—while cutting off problems before they occurred.

By mid-1947 nearly six-million ex-GI's were benefitting from one GI Bill program or another while the post war economy was growing by leaps and bounds. The Bill was difficult to administer, but would not have worked in any other environment

Even in its battle-a-day mode, the Truman administration liked what was happening. The Democratic National Committee was bordering on giddy. They were daring to think that the Missourian might possibly pull-off a term of his own in '48.

*****

Washington, D.C.
September 23, 1947

A letter from Tante Shandyl never failed to please Branko and every few months he had taken to phoning her. Since the end of the war the overseas circuitry had improved remarkably and it was worth every penny to hear her cheerful voice.

> *22 Rue de Lac Leman*
> *Cologny, Switzerland*
> *14 September, 1947*
>
> *Dearest #1 nephew:*
> *I hope you receive this before the holidays. I want to wish you a most wonderful year. Please give my best regards to Jesse and Sara, little Eva and Edith, of course. With Rosh Hashonah coming next week, I'm so fortunate to be surrounded by my entire family including Charles' children living nearby. We all miss Charles so very much. He gave me such a beautiful life. God bless his memory!*
> *Dovid came in for the holidays with his*

lovely wife. Their two married children are staying in Jerusalem for the holidays with family, but Dovid and Nina will be here until after Yom Kippur. Can you believe to get here it took two days? First, they flew to Athens, stayed overnight, and then flew on to Vienna. From there they had to take a train to Geneva. He says the talk all over the country is "Independence." He's still a Reserve Captain in the Palmach, having joined them a few years ago when he was managing the kibbutz. He doesn't talk any details, and is very quiet about most everything dealing with the Arab threats. I can see it troubles him deeply. I overheard his conversation with son-in-law Pierre and he said he has to carry his automatic weapon wherever he goes. To shul, driving, shopping, at a restaurant. Oy, gott, I can only pray for peace!

Your work with Mr. Truman is so important and I know it's something you've so strongly believed in all these years. What you've done for the former soldiers of your America is a mitzvah among mitzvahs. A baruchah auf dein keppeleh, mein seeza Bracheleh! You make me so proud to be your tante!

Please try to telephone me again after the holidays. It's so good hearing your voice.

Much love to all,
Tante Shayndl.

*****

Washington, D.C.
January 15, 1948

With the new Central Intelligence Agency well-underway, the days of the OSS quickly became old news. When Wild Bill came to Washington on legal business, dinner with Branko at the Willard became little more than a griping session. Branko had never seen Bill in such a state. In short order, Donovan damned nemesis Hoover, the FBI, Truman and the Truman administration. While damning several senators and congressman he described them as, "gutless as the entire cabinet of puppets." After a few more drinks at the Willard lounge, his second wind was an alcoholic haze through which he blasted most everyone he knew in Washington.

Branko remained luckily unscathed. When Donovan tearfully hugged Branko before shakily sauntering up to his room, it was almost as if he was bidding a final goodbye to his fellow 69th hero. On the positive side, Branko felt certain that once Donovan got his New York law offices on firm footing again, he would once more become the man-eating tiger he always had been.

The Oval Office
March 16, 1948

"Branko, I know for a fact that you have a lot of confidence in Jack Steel," the President said, leaning back in his chair. The expansive Oval Office desk separated the two men. "I think selecting him as your second in command, so to speak, was a solid move. The guy has served his country well and has certainly shown a noble interest in veteran's affairs since his retirement. I suppose most of that was your doing, General."

"Well, retiring at such an early age, he contributes a lot to our mission. He's tenacious and fits right in. And the VA folks love him. Whenever I leave town, I don't give it a second thought. Jack and I have been friends since he served under me right here at the White House."

"So I've heard. I also understand he saw a little South Pacific action," the president commented, thinking of the walking cane that Steel used.

"Guadalcanal," Branko confirmed. "But's he's fully recovered from his wounds. The ol' war-horse hasn't slowed down one iota."

Truman smiled and Branko caught it.

"Hey, wait a damn minute," Branko said. "Do I dare ask why you bring Jack into the conversation, Harry?"

Truman smirked momentarily. He had wanted to speak with Branko privately for just over a week—even going so far as to consider a discussion over a White House dinner that the General had attended with Edith.

"That's why I asked you here today."

"Because of Steel?"

"Well, no," Truman admitted, "It's a lot more important than that."

"I'm all ears, Captain Truman. Or should I be? Give it your best artillery barrage!"

The President leaned across the desk, almost whispering. "Branko, I've got a dilemma to end all dilemmas in the Middle East. I know damn well that Israel is getting closer to declaring independence. I've already been approached by the DNC, the President of the Jewish Agency, six Jewish congressmen and Justice Frankfurter."

"To do what—make *aliyah?*" Branko couldn't resist.

"I know what that means, soldier. Remember, I had a Jewish partner at one time. Which reminds me, Eddie Jacobson can be a good sounding board for me on this one. I just don't want to be pressured by him or anyone else."

"So what's the dilemma, chief?"

President Truman went on to talk about Israel's battles yet to come. He anticipated that Independence would not be taken lightly by the millions of well-armed Arabs surrounding a new Israeli state. Truman was certain that the Arabs would vow to push the Israelis into the Mediterranean.

It wasn't a hard call to make. In the previous year they had got off to an ugly start with saber rattling and violence. Just in the time that Truman had been trying to work Branko into this meeting, the Arabs had burned a Jewish settlement to the ground. Nearly thirty Israelis had died. The President knew it would get even bloodier and said as much. The odds simply were not in Israel's favor. For a country made up of so many Holocaust survivors, Truman realized that the situation posed a psychological, economic and military problem.

Of course, none of this was news to Branko. For decades he had followed the Jewish struggle to exist. With his family living there and Tante Shayndl coming so close to making *aliyah* when her husband Berel was still alive, Branko warily watched from afar.

With a grim look, Truman went on. "The question of recognition has been lurking around Washington since our war ended. Regardless of what I do, I'm the good guy—or bad guy. I'm sure some fully expect me to be the first to salute the Mogen Dovid. That might be a bit much, but I *will* be penning my conclusive document of recognition. And I'm under no veil of ignorant illusions about it, either. This has far reaching significance. Aside from total animosity and deep hatred from our Arab friends, up-to-and-including retaliation, many of our Western friends will no doubt look askance at our sticking our proverbial necks out."

Truman paused and yet again Branko found himself thinking, *Uh-oh, here it comes...*

"I need your help and guidance, Branko," the President of the United States said. "I need a personal emissary and you're it, buddy."

Branko was not at all surprised. He had seen it coming and was too frozen to duck. Now the only question left in his mind was, *What the hell does he mean by help? Do I go around collecting blue pushkies? Have tea with the local Hadassah ladies? Or what?*

Naturally, Truman knew what Branko was wondering. His answer, momentarily suspended in mid-air, was now rocketed toward home plate. The President said, "Go east, Branko."

"Go East?" Branko echoed, not even sure the words made sense coming out of his mouth.

"That's right," Truman responded. "I want you to go to Palestine, soon to officially become Israel. Meet with their brain trust. Hold hands with wild-haired Ben Gurion and Chaim Weiszmann. Interview their military leaders. Find out where they stand with supplies, weapons, planes and know-how. Most of all determine if they have the will to fight—and die—for their independence and right to exist, as we did a hundred and seventy five years ago."

"Hey, boss, that's some gigantic mission you're asking a seventy-three-year-old ex-General to perform."

"You know damn well I wouldn't be asking if I thought for one moment you would or could turn me down, Branko."

"Damned if you're not stuck with a broken record: *Only you can do this Branko, the country is counting on you Branko, you're the man, Branko.*"

The President had remained seated longer than he could tolerate. Standing, he began pacing the room. Without missing a beat, the savvy man from Kansas City was in full, presidential mode.

"I've arranged a formal top secret briefing for you Wednesday, next week, at 9:00 a.m.," he said to Branko. "All travel details, papers and contact coordinates will be disclosed soon thereafter. I could name you a *Minister without Portfolio*, but instead you'll only be presented as my personal emissary. We'll want you there by late April, and home after the declaration is announced to the world. I don't have to tell you this, but no heroics, just information gathering will do."

Stunned might have been a slight exaggeration for what Branko was feeling. *Mesmerized* fit nicely. He figured that Harry's strategy for this sensitive matter had been in gear for weeks, if not months.

No matter, Branko thought. He was already thinking ahead to what he was going to say to Edith, Jesse and Sara. At the same time he was considering a visit with Tante Shayndl in Switzerland on the way back home.

EXEUNT: ACT FOUR

Jerusalem
King David Hotel
April 30, 1948

Being enclosed by sandbags and barbed wire was nothing new to Branko. Being within shelling distance of an enemy's artillery was also something he had experienced.

And that is where they put him up. Meetings had also been scheduled to occur in the hotel, as well as at undisclosed locations elsewhere in the city. The British were to officially abandon the hotel and lower their flag in five days. As the place was close to empty there seemed to be no problem with Branko—an American citizen—staying at the King David.

On the day of Branko's arrival, Ben Gurion and Chaim Weizmann were cordial and open in their preliminary discussions over dinner at Weizmann's home. Both Israeli representatives wanted him to know that they expected President Truman's recognition the moment independence was declared. The date they talked about was in two weeks.

Damn, was Branko's first thought, *these guys must have gone to the same school that Harry did. They rant in the same cocky manner and I doubt that either of them has ever taken "no" for an answer. They don't ask—they just tell. Why do I feel that I'm a long-awaited pawn in this international chess game? Chess game? Hell, it's a downright pissing contest!*

Naturally, Branko had a few expectations of his own and those would require full cooperation. This was settled quickly as they named the people who would meet with Branko over the next few days. These individuals included officers in the Palmach and Haganah, as well as the notorious Irgun.

Branko was to visit some of the defensive positions the troops occupied and receive a detailed briefing of enemy fortifications as well as their expected plans of attack. There was no room for deep philosophical discussions on Zionism—these people meant business and hard-assed decisions were being made on the spot. At stake was nothing less than the precious longevity of a precarious new State.

Branko's credentials were familiar to every Israeli he met; his impressive WW I record, War College experience, his two years with the partisans in the Russian forests, the OSS, and his *fusgeyer* role leading Jewish immigrants from Romania to the United States. Of course, for the latter achievement, the ultra-chauvinistic Israelis were no doubt thinking, *nu, nu, why did they not come to Eretz Yisroel?*

Branko briefly visited for a meal at Dovid's kibbutz near Lydda. It was emotional, with memories going back to Odessa and much of the conversation revolving around Shayndl. Dovid had spent the day with a team shoring up the defensive perimeter of the kibbutz one more time.

"It's never enough, Branko," he said, "never enough."

But falter or waiver they do not, Branko observed. He had a mountain of pride in what he had seen of these Jews.

May 12, 1948

Two weeks went in a veritable blur and Branko wrote his first lengthy, all-encompassing report to his commander-in-chief. It had been sent by a trusted clandestine Reuters courier service. They promised six days delivery to Washington, via boat from Haifa to Cyprus and chartered plane from Nicosia. The cost was stratospheric, but Branko wanted it in Harry's hands as soon as possible.

As expected, President Truman was the first to issue recognition, followed by Josef Stalin.

It was May 14th, Independence Day.

Jerusalem, Tel Aviv and every kibbutz and settlement in the country wildly celebrated the Day of Independence. It was no surprise that Lebanon, Jordan, Syria, Iraq and Egypt officially declared war on the little thorn in their sides. The various Arab armies were expected to strike immediately, often and everywhere.

And they did.

**Road to Yad Mordechai
via Ad Halom and Majdal
May 21, 1948**

The massacre had occurred on the Tel Aviv-Jerusalem road. Striking just one day after Israel's Independence, the Arabs had destroyed all medical supplies in a convoy ambush that took the lives of seventy-nine doctors and nurses. This seriously jeopardized Israel's developing defensive logistics. Hadassah Hospital on Mount Scopus had shut down immediately, cutting the new nation's already inadequate medical facilities to levels dangerously unacceptable for a country expecting war. Throughout the Tel Aviv and Jerusalem areas the scarce field hospitals were left ill-prepared for an influx of wounded they all knew would be coming.

Now, six days, hence, the Israeli intelligence spy network reported to all defense units that Egyptian armored infantry and artillery battalions were forming at the Sinai coastal town of Al 'Arish. Estimates anticipated an attack within a week. The first incursion would be the communal town and kibbutz Yad Mordechai, a sparsely armed Jewish outpost overlooking the sea.

Having developed a friendship with Colonel Yitzkhak Rabin of Jerusalem, Branko requested a ride-along to Yad Mordechai in a small reinforcement convoy of Palmachniks. It was a good opportunity to see how the country's kibbutz structure would defend against a greater Arab force. Rabin conveyed Banko's request up to Haganah command which was consolidating loosely affiliated military elements into an Israeli Defense Force. The Haganah chief agreed but stipulated that Branko must return on the same day, with the convoy vehicles and immediately after viewing the kibbutz defensive alignments.

The trip down the coast was uneventful. From the heavily armed convoy, Branko was able to glimpse Yad Mordechai's trench spiderworks. As an old veteran of trench warfare, he offered constructive comments to pass along to the kibbutz command staff. Everyone to whom he spoke was confident of holding off superior numbers. Admittedly, they all saw their role as a delaying action give the Haganah more time to prepare coastal road defenses. They were determined to stop the enemy battalions before they would be able to proceed beyond Ad Halom. In any case, it was plainly obvious that the Israelis were prepared to fight to the death and Branko had already anticipated that very conclusion in his report to Truman.

These Jews are more than tough enough to have fought shoulder-to-shoulder with the Fighting Irish in France! he had written in the report to the President.

At exactly 4:00 p.m. (1600 hours), they were returning to Jerusalem. Caches of stolen British arms were known to be secreted at Arab villages along the highway and as a deterrent to potential trouble the convoy's three American Jeeps sported mounted machine weapons.

Riding in back of the lead vehicle, next to the gunner and his machine gun emplacement, Branko was startled to see three Arabs scurrying along the ridge separating the highway from a small village. He tapped the gunner on the shoulder and pointed.

The Palmachnik wasted no time in squeezing the trigger but it is no easy matter to hit moving targets from a moving vehicle—even when using a machine gun.

Unscathed, the three young kaftan wearers stopped in their tracks, and pulled out British automatic Sten weapons. In a flash they sprayed the vehicles while the Palmach machine gunners returned deadly covering fire.

Two of the ambushing boys were killed and the third escaped.

The convoy sped on, never stopping. There was a burst of radio traffic to the lead vehicle, reporting that in the rear jeep of the convoy one of the gunners had been hit.

The gunner in the lead vehicle overheard the report. He turned to convey the news and also congratulate the American General on his eagle-eyed sighting of the ambush: It had saved lives.

Branko was slumped over, bleeding from the nose and from his back.

"He's hit, dammit," the gunner cried out in Hebrew. "He's hit! Our American is hit!"

The lead jeep driver slowed only long enough to dislodge the vehicle's first-aid kit and hand-it-over to the gunner.

As the convoy sped northward, the gunner attended to Branko.

"How is it?" the driver called back to the gunner.

"Not good, Avram," answered the gunner amidst his efforts. "Not good at all."

"Then I'm heading to Rehovot," the driver shouted back. "It's the only field hospital in these parts!"

"He's lost consciousness," the Gunner said after a moment more. His voice was one of pure panic. "And I can't stop the bleeding—I poured a sulfa pack over the wounds but it isn't enough!"

After what seemed an eternity, the convoy roared-up to the tented field hospital between the small towns of Rehovot and Lydda. Doctors, nurses and aides rushed to the wounded, placing the two men on stretchers and taking them into the tent. The wounded gunner from the rear of the convoy was Russian and alert. He was talking up a blue streak in English, Yiddish and Russian. He was only alive, he said, because the first salvo of weapon fire had startled him into action less detrimental than that of being a sitting duck.

The American remained unconscious. He was bleeding profusely from at least three wounds.

"He's still alive," one of the frowning doctors noted "but just barely."

Three American volunteer doctors feverishly worked over Branko Horvitch. Two nurses assisted and one of the doctors, a trauma specialist, was overseeing details to insure nothing was missed or left to chance.

Branko's breathing became more labored and he was losing blood at too fast a pace. One or more of the bullets had pierced his left lung and transfusions weren't keeping up. As his vital signs dangerously waned, oxygen was of diminishing value. As a matter of policy sulfa drugs and penicillin were sparingly used—the massacre of the previous week had resulted in rationing.

Doctor Heshy Kellerman of New Orleans finally looked up from the patient on the table and at the other two doctors.

"Any ideas?" he asked his colleagues, both of whom were from different cities in Ohio. Chuck Greenblatt, the doctor from Youngstown, was in his early 50s and merely shook his head *no*. The trauma specialist out of Cleveland, a younger man of forty years of age, was completely unreadable.

"Alright then," Kellerman said after receiving no response. "We might as well close 'em up."

Once they had done all they could, Kellerman looked to the nurses and ordered them to make Branko as comfortable as possible. It was a useless gesture, they all knew.

Kellerman and Doctor Chuck Greenblatt, emerged from the critical patient tent.

Kellerman lit a cigarette, inhaled deeply and exhaled a blue cloud. Like Greenblatt he was in his early 50s and the last two hours had physically drained him. He said, "According to his papers, the poor guy is nothing less than a personal representative of President Truman. Damn, with the chronic lack of supplies and nursing help since the massacre. The poor bastard is going to have a struggle—"

"Struggle?" Greenblatt interrupted incredulously. He was a skilled surgeon and like the others had worked up a drenching sweat while trying to save Branko's life. "Let's be honest. Mr. Horvitch has no appreciable chance of making it through the night."

The two exhausted doctors stood in silence, both with deeply drawn expressions on their faces. Both excellent surgeons in their own right, they had labored against the odds in vain—and they each knew it. In fact, every doctor in attendance was an American veteran of battlefield horror—both in Europe and the Pacific.

"He's sure taking it hard," Greenblatt said after a time, tilting his head back to the tent and meaning the trauma doctor. Greenblatt had noticed the younger doctor repeatedly drawn back to the face of their critically wounded patient. For a time he had even held one of Branko's cold, limp hands.

Kellerman, billowing out another cloud of smoke, grunted and then added, "He's young, I guess."

"I happen to know he's seen this sort of thing a lot," Greenblatt responded, not adding that he thought forty years of age wasn't that young.

Kellerman shrugged and under his shoe snubbed out the butt of his cigarette on the ground. He said, "I'm going over to supplies and try to scare-up some more morphine. Make sure those nurses keep our General under—I don't expect he'll last that long, anyway."

Greenblatt nodded and watched Kellerman head-off to another tent in the camp. The Ohio Doctor turned and went back inside. He found his Cleveland colleague pretty much where they had left him. The other Ohioan had moved a chair over to Branko's side and was somberly sitting, staring at Branko.

"Hey," Greenblatt said.

The seated doctor looked up, his eyes glassy.

"For God sake, the man is a goner," Greenblatt said. "You've seen this at your Cleveland Clinic many times and know damn-well there is nothing you can possibly do."

The younger doctor nodded that he knew.

"Then why are you taking this so hard, Emanuel?"

"Branko Horvitch is my father."

2:00 a.m. (0200 hours)

The theater was now open and the newsreel of Branko's mind was in motion.

It was Movietone News, Paramount News and the British Pathe' News neatly spliced together. His ebbing life was attuned to the silver screen, narrating in a frantic stream of consciousness:

I know them all I see their faces. Edith, Tante Shayndl Jesse Sara little Eva, my dear late Eva. There is Mama and Tateh Rachel and Malka Captain Rudoff and his ship the crew, Boris the blacksmith, valiant Azriel and all Birlad my Fusgeyers on the march. Mendel, Mordechai, Sendehr, Rivka lovely Rivka, Avi, the Golub boys, Simcha Greenberg and the Maccabees, Alex Perchersky, Comrade Timoshenko: There's Jack Steel, Peter Underwood, Samuel DuBois, Bobby Ray and Stanley in the black gold fields. There's Wilson, Harding, Coolidge, FDR, Harry dear Harry. They're all waving at me with such big smiles—such love, such endearment, such memories.

Wild Bill, Father Duffy—my comrades. I can't stay with you all—I'm crying—why am I crying? I'm going home, I'm going home—they're calling me but I must go now I must go now I must...

There are places to go...things to do...experiences to feel...
Exeunt.

EPILOGUE

Washington, D.C.
June 21, 1948

The array of humanity vying for standing-room only in the Washington Hebrew Congregation covered all walks of the capital's life.

The red, white and blue for which Branko Horvitch served valiantly for so many years draped a simple, pine box coffin. Nearby there stood an eagle-headed standard—the new official flag of the nascent state of Israel: **A** large blue *Mogen Dovid* on a field of white with blue above and below. For this, Branko served above and beyond the call of duty.

Among those in attendance were President and Mrs. Harry Truman; the Truman Cabinet; the Supreme Court Justices; Eleanor Roosevelt; Congressman and Senators of both parties, including Massachusetts second-term Congressman John F. Kennedy and his father Joe Kennedy. A contingent of former OSS officers were seated with Wild Bill Donovan, while the Ambassador from the USSR was nearly elbow-to-elbow with the former spymaster. General Peter Underwood, the U.S. Army War College Commandant was also present, having driven in from the new location at Carlisle Gap, Pennsylvania. Of course there were *Fusgeyer* families from New York, Boston and across the country. A broken-hearted Tante Shayndl was unable to attend; at eighty-six and frail she had been forbidden to travel to the funeral by her doctors and daughters.

The newspapers, radio and fledgling TV stations were all heavily represented but the over-eager photographers lay-in-wait on the front steps. And then there was the unusual attendance of a Hollywood entourage led by Jack Warner and the cast of *The Fighting 69th* that sat right alongside a contingent of 69th vets.

As for the rest of those attending the funeral, Branko would have most certainly been embarrassed by the outpouring of homage. Nonetheless, the genuine expression of loss and love would have moved him to tears.

At precisely 11:00 a.m., Rabbi Aaronson, who also officiated at the funeral of Eva Horvitch, began his eulogy. Edith Wilson, citing numerous examples of Branko's appreciation of brevity, had counseled the Rabbi to keep the service short, but meaningful. Whether it was from advice or a heavy heart no one could tell, but the veteran clergyman complied. There followed a brief and poignant eulogy by Bill Donovan. Appearing drawn and shrunken his famous bravado was now lost to history. He saluted the coffin, momentarily breaking and tearing-up.

There were others who spoke and to a man, they too, yielded to brevity and emotion: Mordecai Anieloff, Mendel Buchman, Sendehr Efraim and Albie White (Avi Semelweiss) of the Birlad *Fusgeyers*, old friend Dr. Samuel DuBois of New Orleans, WW I hero and friend Sergeant Alvin York; Oklahoma "black gold," seekers and veterans, Bobby Ray Summers and Stanley Hagenworth, Harry Hopkins and Larry Lincoln.

Near the end of the ceremony, Jack Steel came up to the dais alongside Jesse Kanter and they both spoke in heart-rending tones. Jesse then stood for a brief moment with his hand on the coffin. He was a mask of stone, withering on the inside while whispering a farewell to the man who had shaped his life by love and example.

That the body of Branko was here at all was remarkable in and of itself. The few who had learned of the circumstances surrounding his death had been astounded at how quickly the body had been returned for burial. Absolutely no one in the synagogue knew what the President had done to ensure this. And the Man from Missouri, burdened with having sent Branko to his death, never spoke of it. There were rumors, of course. The kernel of truth was that he gambled on a bluff that wasn't a bluff at all, threatening to revoke Israel's official recognition. Both Provisional Council Leaders David Ben Gurion and Chaim Weizmann, who had planned to have Branko permanently interred in Jerusalem, were not amused. That was fine by Harry S. Truman; he had not intended to amuse them. In the end, Truman's firm demand was wisely met. An international incident of biblical proportions was avoided and Branko came home.

It was fitting that this was the man to last speak. He approached the dais and momentarily stood, gripping the podium with both hands. Peering out over a sea of grieving faces, he was heavy with the solemnity of the task at hand and the admiration for the man lying in state before them. After a long moment of silence, the President of the United States of America began.

"On the battlefields of France, Captain Horvitch of The Fighting 69th once stood between Captain Harry Truman of the 129th Field Artillery and a court martial of a third party's making. His cool head prevailed over my hot head. The third party—still in uniform—now works for me."

The president offered the customary subdued clearing of the throat and chuckles rippled through the throng.

"Today and for many tomorrows, we celebrate the life of this true American hero. Branko Horvitch stood for and practiced lifelong the very things that this great land of ours means to us all.

"Had Branko been there in the 1700s, our Founding Fathers could very well have used this noble life as a template for a model of America. And it is certainly true that this man epitomized everything that our founders idealized. I use the phrase neither often nor lightly, but *a legend in our time* is appropriate. Branko is one of the few Americans I've known who rose to the heights in everything he accomplished. He lived at that lofty level to his very last breath. Of all the souls I have met, no better man have I known. He was as good a friend as he was a soldier—and he was the *very* best soldier. It is my sacred honor to thank you and salute you, General Branko Horvitch."

The ceremony ended at exactly 12:00 noon. The pallbearers and honorary pallbearers escorted the coffin to a waiting hearse, followed by everyone leaving the synagogue. Automobiles were parked for a half-mile in every direction and people began making their way to the hallowed grave site at Arlington National Cemetery.

The President, followed by his Secret Service detail, walked over to the family limousine awaiting Edith, Aretha and Larry Lincoln, Sara, Jesse and two year-old Eva. He embraced each of them and patted the little one on her curly head. He then assured Jesse that he would receive the flag after the Arlington ceremonies.

"Harry, my wish for this country of ours is simply a Branko Horvitch every few decades," a subdued Edith softly offered. No formalities between these two.

"Let's make that a full regiment of Brankos, Edith."

*****

Branko's gravesite was among the regiments now visited by those who silently wandered the tree-shaded paths of Arlington National Cemetery. It was a hallowed ground of valor, in a country that chooses to remember.

And it was a most beautiful June day. There were green trees, full blooming flowers, birds singing, bees buzzing and seasonal scents filling the air.

Fare thee well, good soldier. Farewell!

Acknowledgments

I honestly don't know who started the custom of acknowledging the many people responsible for producing a book. I do know, that it's a difficult thing for any author to write the acknowledgments in an appropriate fashion. There are no rules or guidelines and in my case, there is a menacing-looking editor with a stopwatch lurking over me! And that's a good thing

For my previous historical novel, *The Wayfarers*, also published by The Lighthouse Press, I commenced to write the acknowledgments and literally (pardon the pun) did not stop for ten pages. The editor whittled it to six pages and there it stood. Perhaps not a world record, but certainly a Guinness nominee for "wordiness."

Once again faced with the formidable assignment, I was determined to keep it short. Just one look at the guy with the stopwatch ensured that!

Unfortunately for the first time in five books, I have been without valuable spousal support in my efforts. My dearest Roz, to whom I gave well-earned credit for seeing me through the highways and byways of Europe, is incapacitated with a serious ailment. I feel that she senses that another novel is on the way.

On prior offerings my late first wife, Judy, was always in the wings ready to comment favorably or otherwise. And she did, adding solace whenever an idea or character didn't pan out.

But through it all I've been blessed with a crew of well-credentialed previewers from around the world (all of whom are still on speaking terms with me). Their comments can be found inside the first few pages of *Branko* or on the back cover. Without going into detail, their myriad ideas have all been somewhat incorporated within these pages. If not, I'll get phone calls and nasty e-mail.

In the constantly shifting background stand my prodigious number of characters. After five years of tedious research and writing with each character in mind, I have an intimate knowledge of what makes each one live and breathe. Yes, I know that I may be slightly warped in this regard.

"After all, they're mere literary characters," some would say, "fictional and a few factual—you're only the ventriloquist."

But if you've read at least as much as the foreword, then you know that Branko Horvitch is a man who has been part of my every waking moment for five years. I've tried mightily to show him reasons and respect for every move he makes. We've become a two-man Band of Brothers. So it's Branko Horvitch and all for which he stands that I need to acknowledge without reservation.

It's no secret that every publisher makes the final decision for the life of each book. But Ron Richard of The Lighthouse Press is a little different in this respect. After listening to the author and editor, he leaves a lot of a manuscript's direction in their hands. Ron and his Lighthouse Press (also the publisher of my *Wayfarers* as an Amazon.com e-book after ten years in circulation) deserves a salute in every sense for the way he is diligently planning the future of The Lighthouse Press. I'm on board all the way.

As for DL Tolleson, who shepherded *Branko* through the rapidly changing vagaries of the publishing world... I would need an additional chapter to shower enough praise for his mountainous contributions to the end-product in your hands. His sensibilities, knowledge, willingness to compromise and dedication to perfection are exactly what every writer must have in his arsenal. Without such a person, I can't see a project as meaningful as *Branko* ever seeing the light of day. I can't thank you enough, Tolleson, but I'll keep trying.

On a terribly sad note, one of my long-time best fans and an insatiable reader, daughter Gayle Tower Brinkenhoff, recently lost her final battle in a twenty-three-year war on cancer. Gayle would have loved the saga of such a heroic, literary paragon as Branko. I will close with the very words I said for my late wife that happen to fit Gayle's character perfectly:

> All that is sweet...multiplied.
> All that is beautiful....magnified.
> All that is good....personified.

Stuart F. Tower
Los Angeles, California
2013

About The Author

Like real world adventurers, the resourceful Stuart F. Tower went straight out of high school to enlist in the Army during historic times —specifically, during the U.S. Occupation of Japan. He returned to academics and graduated from Emerson College, cum laude, in History/Social Science with a minor in Educational Psychology. He also garnered a Masters in Education from Boston University with Psychology-History as a minor and attended a UCLA Doctoral Studies program with emphasis on Educational Psychology.

He has since taught and counseled at all levels of the professional and academic worlds. His experience ranges from The Rand Corporation, Honeywell and the Arthur Young Company to establishing management programs for many international clients. More recently, he has taught several history classes for the Elderhostel organization in California.

Throughout his career he has extensively researched and traveled throughout the United States, Eastern Europe and many other parts of the world. Among his published work are two nonfiction titles, *Withered Roots: The Remnants of Eastern European Jewry* and *Hear O Israel: Poetica Judica*. His most recent books are the two historical fiction titles, *The Wayfarers* and *Branko*, both available from The Lighthouse Press, LLC.

Stuart Tower resides in Southern California, with his loving family nearby.

CPSIA information can be obtained at www.ICGtesting.com
Printed in the USA
LVOW12*1241300913

354646LV00001B/1/P